S^{THE}ultan's SNARE

DAVID SAGE

For information about this title or to order other books and/or electronic media, contact the publisher:
David Sage
davesageinstory@gmail.com

ISBNs:
978-1-7336402-3-7 (print)
978-1-7336402-4-4 (eBook)

Printed in the United States of America

With Thanks

To our granddaughter, Annie: you are wonderful!

To our son Tyler for inspiring me to write historical fiction for the Christian market. I think these stories actually embrace several markets with their truths of honor and dignity.

To our daughter Tierney who has spent countless hours collaborating with me on scenes and dialogue, in addition to designing the cover. The book was vastly improved through your contributions.

To son Dave and his wife Beth, who have stood by in quiet encouragement.

To my wife Marcia, who sourced the idea about a story of the Barbary Coast Pirates, what a brainstorm you had!

And finally to the readers who reviewed *Sold into Shackles* and gave it such a high rating, it pleases me beyond measure that you enjoyed the book. I apologize for making you wait on *The Sultan's Snare*; I honestly thought I would have had it out long before this.

TABLE OF CONTENTS

FOREWORD

M URAD IV WAS BORN IN 1612 and, after a series of revolts and
political intrigue in the corrupt government, became Sultan of
the Ottoman Empire in 1623 at age 11. The early years of his rule were
directed by his mother, Kosem. In 1631 a number of high officials were
killed in yet another revolt by the Sipahis (cavalry with a status like that
of an English Knight) and the Janissaries (slave soldiers), and Murad
was forced to accept a Vizier (high civilian official) that he didn't like.

In 1632 Murad took control of the government and began a
career that characterized him as both an able administrator and a
man of immense cruelty: he ordered 500 leaders of the 1631 revolt to
be killed. In another incident he had 20,000 men executed. However,
he brought corruption under control in both the government and the
army. He took on the long-running Safavid War (1623-1639) against
Persia and captured Baghdad after a 40-day siege in 1638. There was
no question about his bravery: he was the last Ottoman Sultan to
personally lead his men into battle.

A huge and powerful man, Murad loved wrestling and jousting;
unfortunately, his temper matched his size and when his brother Bayezid
unseated him in a 1635 joust, the Sultan ordered him murdered. Fearful
of political plots against him arising in public meeting places, Murad
banned alcohol, smoking, and coffee houses from the Empire. He was
fond of taking to the streets in disguise at night and beheading anyone

he suspected of violating his restrictions. The limitations did not apply to him, however, and in 1640 Murad IV died from alcoholism.

Coincidentally, particularly in Portugal and England, equestrian events in Europe had begun to take on popularity, setting a trend that continues to this day. Although performance horses were primarily owned by the rich, there was a burgeoning interest among common-ers in the results of such activities. Viewed in the past as primarily a work animal by the citizenry, the horse was beginning to take on a sporting role previously not contemplated. The narrative of this book is equally inspired by those developments and by the Sultan's personality and reign.

Prologue

In June of 1631 Barbary Coast pirates attacked the fishing village of Baltimore, Ireland and captured 108 men, women, and children. They were taken to North Africa and sold into slavery. Included among the captives were the three O'Shea siblings: Cormac, 16; Finn, 14, and Bran, 8, whose father was killed trying to save them.

Sold into Shackles chronicles six years in the lives of the three: auctioned separately at the market, each endured unimaginable hardships at the hands of their owners, but strange and unforeseen events combined to finally reunite them despite impossible odds.

Following a desperate battle to regain their freedom, the O'Sheas set sail for Ireland accompanied by scores of former slaves they liberated. On the journey home, they were intrigued by an astounding business proposal made as they departed from the harbor in Tunis.

Storm

1

THUNDER ROARED, BRILLIANT FLASHES of lightning streaked through the heavy overcast, and blinding sheets of rain slashed the deck. The laboring ship, sluggish with a hold full of whale oil and stricken by a damaged rudder, was being driven inexorably towards cliffs, spotted dangerously close in the final light of dusk, but now terrifyingly invisible.

The helmsman, roped in place to prevent being swept across the deck, struggled mightily to swing the bow into the wind to give the captain a chance to order sails lowered enough to tack away from land, but the rudder wouldn't turn the bow more than a few degrees into the wind—nowhere near enough to execute the maneuver. In addition to the wind, mountainous waves, rolling against the craft from starboard, were tipping it perilously close to overturning. Only the tons of oil stored below gave enough stability to stay upright; however, stability meant nothing if they were forced onto the jagged rocks at the base of the cliffs.

The two-masted English ship had been in the North Atlantic for three months hunting whales and was returning with a full cargo of oil, highly valued for a variety of uses in Europe. The Captain had set a course south along the western coast of Ireland to the Celtic Sea, intending to sail eastward from there to the English Channel and London. Just hours short of clearing the southwest corner of Ireland, a monster storm had struck from the west. The rudder had inexplicably failed when Captain Haversmith gave orders to bring the ship into the wind, so he had the men set a small storm sail in hopes they could clear the coastline and let the tempest drive them east in the Celtic Sea where they could ultimately fix the rudder. But the last light of day showed they had not quite cleared the coast.

Now, standing beside the wheel with one arm locked in the rigging, Haversmith leaned forward and bellowed in the ear of a sailor who was lending his strength to the helmsman.

"Jonathan, make your way to the bowsprit with a sounding rope and check the depth. I spotted cliffs in a flash of lightning. We're very close but I think we're almost past the rocks!"

The words were intended to inspire hope, but the Captain didn't really believe them: the ship's forward progress was just too slow.

Jonathan Strong, 17, was ruggedly handsome with a firm jaw, wide-set gray eyes and shoulder-length black hair now plastered to his head in the driving rain. Slender but muscular, he had stowed away on Haversmith's ship four years before, wanting to become a harpooner like his father. The crew, who hated stowaways because they usually proved worthless, had tested him relentlessly. Over many months the boy had gradually earned their respect and became a valued sailor. At 15, he had ensured his future as a harpooner. A massive whale had destroyed two longboats with its flukes, stranding a dozen men in freezing water far from the ship. Trailing behind in a small support dinghy, Jonathan had dispatched the whale at very close quarters, saving the men.

He cautiously made his way forward to the bow with the sounding device: a line with knots attached to a heavy weight. The number of knots that had passed through his fingers when the weight hit bottom told him the depth. Two men went with him to relay the information back to the Captain.

The bowsprit was a long spar, or length of wood, extending out over the water from the bow. Lines from it stretched up to the front mast, both to secure the mast and to use for small triangular sails when needed. The lines were wrapped around the bowsprit about every six feet, thus Jonathan had to squirm his way around at least two of them to be well clear of the bow for measuring the water depth. In a calm sea he would have sat and straddled the spar, now he lay full length, ankles locked around the line behind him, one hand holding the line in front. The ship was rolling and pitching, wind screaming in the rigging, and the driving rain stung his skin like needles. Tying the end of the line around his right wrist, Jonathan began feeding the weight down with his left hand, counting the knots as they passed through his fingers.

"Eight fathoms*," he yelled at the top of his voice to the man standing behind him on the bow. Since the ship cleared four fathoms they were safe.

"Seven fathoms!" Ten minutes later.

"Six fathoms!" Five minutes later.

"Five fathoms!"

As the messages were relayed to him, Captain Haversmith gritted his teeth. The hull was six feet above the bottom. If they struck, the ship could be stuck or split asunder by rocks on the ocean floor.

"Four and a half fathoms," came the relayed report. Then silence except for the howling wind and vibrating rigging shrieking from the force of the gale passing through it. They had three feet of clearance...

---

* A fathom is six feet.

Haversmith wondered whether they could lower the whaling boats in time to save the men if the ship foundered.

By now the depths were being passed to the crew below decks as well. Minutes dragged by as every man on board waited for the grinding noise that would spell disaster.

"Five fathoms!"

Then immediately: "Six fathoms!"

"Seven fathoms!"

The ragged cheer from the men topside was blown away by the wind. They had cleared the tip of Ireland and were in the Celtic Sea. Below deck, sailors pounded one another on the shoulder.

When one more sounding showed eight fathoms, Jonathan began retrieving the line. The helmsman had gained a degree or two to port and the wind was noticeably starting to come from the stern; the ship swinging crossways to the waves instead of broadside. As he scrambled back onto the bow, the harpooner knew that the Captain would order sea anchors into the water to slow and stabilize them even more. They were safe. He and the nearest sailor grinned and clapped each other on the back.

At that moment there was a deafening crash of thunder and a bolt of lightning hissed and crackled like a living creature as it flashed down, enveloping the main mast and splintering a gaping hole in the deck.

2

JONATHAN AND HIS COMPANION had only a second to glance up before the mast split and fell, carrying spars and rigging with it to the deck in a tangle of ropes and timber that crushed everyone beneath. As the screams of injured and dying sailors rose above the roaring wind with piercing clarity, Jonathan saw the Captain and helmsman swept overboard by a swinging timber that hit them like a scythe.

A spar from the main mast swung wildly through the rigging of the foremast and struck it with a tremendous "crack." With horror, Jonathan saw, almost in slow motion, a great fracture appear in the wood of the mast and the upper half start to fall toward the two of them on the bow.

"Jump," he shrieked, leaping onto the railing to jump overboard. The other man didn't move fast enough and was crushed by the debris. Just as Jonathan propelled himself off the railing he felt a numbing blow to his left leg and realized that he'd been hit by some part of the rubble. The frigid shock of the icy water paralyzed the sailor for an instant, but he immediately began to swim away from the stricken ship. Unlike many of the men, he was a strong swimmer although his left leg was now completely useless. Letting it drag, he stroked powerfully with his arms, kicking strongly with the right leg until he was many yards away from the foundering vessel.

Turning around, he witnessed the onset of the worst nightmare for any wooden ship. From the area around the base of the main mast, flames began to rise despite the driving rain. He realized that the lightning strike had ignited kegs of oil stored beneath the deck. As he watched, men began to emerge from hatchways, some covered with flames, and fling themselves overboard. The ship only carried 26 crew and many had been crushed under the debris; moments later there was no further movement on board.

All at once hatch covers started flying up into the air, blown skyward by intense pressure from the burning oil below. Jonathan watched in awe as the heavy wooden pieces erupted into the night, to be swept away downwind by the gale. As the last one hurtled skyward, however, it unexpectedly veered at right angles to the direction of the wind, blowing to his right, and came toward him. When it was nearly overhead, the wind ceased for a few seconds, replaced by an eerie quiet, and the hatch cover splashed onto the sea only 40 yards away. The tempest immediately resumed, but the harpooner was already swimming desperately toward the floating square of wood. The useless left leg slowed him, but desperation lent an almost inhuman energy: if the hatch cover drifted away he would die. He never saw the burning ship behind him vanish into the sea in a spasm of steam, plunging the area back into darkness.

After 30 minutes of swimming he had overcome waves and wind to bring himself within 10 feet of the cover, but he was barely able to move. His arms felt like lead weights, his right leg unable to kick.

"I'm not going to make it," he thought and felt himself start to sink.

Suddenly, memories flooded his mind's eye: he was balanced in the dory, harpoon in hand, the body of the great whale a few feet away. He drew his arm back and then it flashed forward with the deadly lance… but instead of seeing the blade enter the whale, he felt his hand touch the edge of the hatch cover.

3

"HE NEEDS YOU," the little girl in the blue dress said, pointing out to sea, "he really needs you."

She was about five, with curly blond hair and blue eyes, sitting cross legged beside Bran on the flower-covered hillside above Baltimore. Her small fingers were holding a bouquet of gardenias as she spoke. Bran was leaning against a smooth boulder, enjoying the soft breeze and watching the sun's sparkling reflection on the ocean and harbor below.

"Who needs me?" she asked absently.

"The boy floating on the ocean."

The green-eyed girl with long black hair shot up in bed, the smell of gardenias in the air and the vivid dream crystal-clear in her mind. She rose quickly and quietly, careful not to wake the young woman sleeping on the other side of the room. Instinctively slipping a bow and quiver of arrows onto her back, she donned a specially designed cape that gave quick access to the weapon and rushed silently into the front room of the little stone house.

"Seamus, get up!" She hissed to the snoring figure lying on a bed of hay along one wall. "Someone's in danger on the ocean! Run to the docks and ready the boat. I'll get Cormac and Finn. Hurry!"

A tousled head and a freckled face stared up at her, one hand rubbing blue eyes, as the 12-year-old struggled to come awake.

"It's still dark," he said. "Too early for fishing."

"We're not going fishing," she said over her shoulder as she went out the front door and headed across the cobblestone street.

Muttering to himself about the peculiarities of 16-year-old girls lately returned from North Africa, Shamus nevertheless hurried down to the docks, impressed by her urgent tone.

The house she headed toward was almost identical to the one Bran slept in. Vacant for six years since North African pirates had raided the village for slaves, it was now occupied by the girl's two brothers and her sister-in-law. There were many such vacant houses in Baltimore: their previous occupants either deceased or enslaved in Tunis. Only Bran and her brothers had been able to escape. Easing into the front room, she hurried to the door of one of the two sleeping rooms in back. Her soft knock brought Cormac from his bed.

Now 22, her brother had a heavily muscled body from his years of slavery in a stone quarry and as an oarsman on a pirate galley. Long, flaming red hair and piercing blue eyes were offset by a great white scar extending from above his right eye across his forehead to his left hairline. No stranger to sleep interruptions, he was fully alert as he met her glance.

"She came back," said Bran.

"Who came back?"

"The little girl with the gardenias. She told me there's someone at sea who needs my help, someone floating."

"I'll get Finn," he said instantly, noting the gardenia smell clinging to his sister.

Silently opening the couple's door, Cormac breathed, "Finn," into the dark, the word almost inaudible. Habits borne from years of slavery are not easily lost and there was an immediate stir in the bed.

"It's all right, love, Cormac needs me," said his brother softly in Arabic.

"Come back soon," was the sleepy reply.

Finn stepped into the front room, shaking back a shock of long blond hair. He was slender and strikingly handsome with a slightly hooked nose, straight in his youth but since broken by the butt of a slaver's whip, and brown eyes highlighted by little gold flecks. At 20, he was an inch taller than his brother and moved with fluid grace.

One whiff of the lingering gardenia fragrance and he was fully focused. He had experienced that scent before and knew what it meant. A few whispered words from Bran had both men dressed in seconds and following her rapidly down the street.

4

"A T LEAST THE STORM stopped," said Cormac, as broken strips of clouds showed above them in the predawn gray, "but still a few weeks until winter weather stops the fishing."

"The fishermen haven't been able to go out for four days," said Finn. "I'll wager some are already at the dock."

He was right. As they approached the low buildings and stone wharf that marked the edge of the harbor, dark figures were moving about, loading nets and gear into the small fishing boats they would embark on to catch sardines.

They passed two men talking as they carried buckets of water to their moorings.

"What was that you said, Rogan?" asked Cormac, pausing beside them.

"I was telling Niall here that I saw the strangest sight last night," said a husky man a few years older than the redhead. "The rain had stopped and I came to the dock to make sure the boats were secure after that wild wind."

"Aye," said Cormac, "we were worried about the thatch on the roof."

"Well, I satisfied myself that no one's boat had been damaged and was about to leave when I saw the oddest golden light just at the edge of the western horizon. I watched for a minute and suddenly it vanished. I didn't know what to make of it."

"What direction exactly?" asked Bran.

Rogan paused to contemplate the question. An experienced man of the sea, he wanted to give an accurate answer.

"I'd estimate almost due west," he finally said. "Why?"

But the three had already sped away toward their late father's boat.

Donegan O'Shea had been killed years ago during the raid on Baltimore after cutting down the pirate carrying little Seamus to the dock. The terrified six year old, heeding the fisherman's shouted instructions, had fled like a rabbit between houses and thrown himself into a thick patch of brambles on the hillside above the village.

When Fiona O'Shea returned to Baltimore from her sister's farm the day after the attack, she found her husband dead and their three children gone. A few days later someone found Seamus wandering in the hills, too terrified to come back to the village. He was the lone survivor from a family of ten and was brought to Fiona, a now child-less mother. She took the boy in and raised him as her own, staying in the little house and selling eggs and vegetables to the few people remaining in Baltimore.

Gradually more fishermen moved to the port, but Fiona resisted all offers to buy Donegan's boat. It remained pulled well up on the beach, keel resting on sturdy pieces of lumber, propped upright and covered with sail cloth. Seamus was charged with checking it regularly to make sure it remained in good condition.

When Seamus was 10, the boat had been launched and he began to learn the business of sardine fishing under the guidance of an old fisherman who had no boat of his own. Currently, the boy and his newly returned adopted brothers kept it tied to the dock, the single mast wrapped with its sail, in preparation for setting out on the daily search for sardines. Two oars were on hand for moving out into the harbor where they could catch the breeze. Cormac noted with approval that the boy had already loaded a bucket of drinking water.

"See if you can find some bread for us," he said to Seamus, "it may be a long day."

The lad dashed off, returning in five minutes with a basket full of bread and apples.

"I asked the other boats if they could contribute some food to our trip, telling them it was so urgent we had no time to prepare," he reported, "Each offered apples or bread."

"Well done," said Finn, touched by the willing generosity of those who had so little already. "We'll repay them in kind when we return."

In minutes they were on their way, Finn at the oars, Cormac handling the rudder, Seamus and Bran ready to unfurl the sail.

There were several ships at anchor in the harbor and Cormac glanced longingly at them. A ship would be much faster on the open ocean than their little fishing vessel. In addition, a lookout on the crow's nest could cover a vast area of water that they would never see. His own ship was traveling around Europe delivering to their homes the many ex-slaves and children he'd rescued from North Africa. Some of them had been gone for so long, however, that finding their families would be difficult and he didn't anticipate that the ship would return until spring.

He expected his captain, Gael, to return to Baltimore with nearly a full crew. Some months earlier, elevated to a position of pirate leader but still technically a slave, Cormac had freed 280 oarsmen thralls from his galley to help wage a brutal battle to rescue his brother and sister from the Pasha of Tunis, and then to man the ship he sailed to freedom. Most of these men had originally been sailors and many had no families to go home to. On the trip to Ireland a majority of them, well acquainted with his leadership and code of honor, had expressed their desire to sail with the redhead in his future endeavors.

So, at the moment, the O'Sheas had no choice but to use their father's boat. Having spent years helping Donegan, setting out in the craft was like slipping on a familiar old glove to Cormac and Finn. Seamus had kept it in excellent condition and the brothers were familiar with every nuance of getting maximum performance under sail. Cormac found his father's compass wrapped securely in oilskin under the stern seat; mounted on the little stand Donegan had built on the gunwale, it read due west as they cleared the harbor.

Despite the enormity of finding a single person out in the ocean, Cormac was not concerned. All three siblings had experienced wonderful and inexplicable guidance during their time of slavery; the little girl of Bran's dream had spoken to her more than once.

"What are we doing?" whispered Seamus to Finn as they sat portside to balance the wind's thrust.

"What do you mean?"

"Bran told me about her dream. First, it was just a dream. Second, it's impossible to find one person out on the vast ocean using any craft, much less a sardine boat!"

Finn put his arm around the boy and grinned at him.

"Seamus, what you say is absolutely correct. However, lad, if I'm not mistaken you might witness the impossible today."

5

Dawn roused Jonathan from his stupor. His first conscious thought was of being cold, then agonizing pain from his left leg brought everything back. He had no memory of dragging himself onto the hatch-cover before passing out, but he was lying on his back, legs and feet still in the water. Rising to his elbows he stared around.

The rain had stopped and there was a gentle swell to the ocean. Broken clouds aloft indicated that the storm was over and fair weather was in store. Of the ship there was no sign, however, a large expanse of the water was littered with bits of wood and rigging. He scanned the surface for survivors, but could see no one.

Lying back, he contemplated his situation. He was somewhere off the southern coast of Ireland in the Celtic Sea. The good thing was that the area was a common route for ships headed to England, or ships bound for America from England or Ireland. On the other hand, he had a broken leg, no food or water, and no means of signaling a passing ship. A man lying on a small piece of debris would be almost impossible to see unless a ship was within a few yards of him.

He thought back to the night he had crept down the dock, sneaked up the gangplank to Captain Haversmith's ship and slipped through an open hatch into the hold. He had watched the whaling vessel being loaded and heard that it would sail in the morning. His father had crewed for years as the Captain's harpooner, until he was killed in a freak accident at sea. When Jonathan's mother died the previous winter, he had been taken in by a kindly aunt, but the 13-year-old had determined to stow away on Haversmith's ship as soon as he had the chance. If he was discovered before the ship weighed anchor, the sailors would hustle him down the gangplank to the dock and warn him never to try it again. If he was discovered after they were at sea, his father had explained what would happen to him many times, lecturing him not to stow away under any circumstances. He had done it anyway because there was nothing left for him on shore.

Prone on the hatch cover and staring at the sky, the harpooner smiled as he remembered the testing. His first trials took place in the galley: he was forced to clean it constantly all day long as the cook deliberately made much more of a mess than he needed to. When the boy became adept at keeping ahead of the cook, he was put to work swabbing the deck in his spare moments. Then the work expanded to cleaning the galley, swabbing the deck, AND polishing the brass brightwork. He completed every task, never complained, and maintained a cheerful attitude toward even the most abusive crew member. He worked the same schedule as the men: four hours on and four hours off, sleeping in a hammock in the front compartment of the vessel. Gradually, seeds of respect began to grow in the crew for this orphan who had sought them out.

Many weeks later he was roused from the hammock by a gruff sailor and told to follow him up the rigging. (Rigging is like a rope ladder allowing the men to get to the spars--cross pieces of timber across the masts from which the sails are suspended--to either tie up or let down sails.) One uses only bare feet: there is too much danger of slipping with shoes. The man went up the rigging like a monkey, with Jonathan close behind. The boy had constantly peeked at the men climbing up and down the rigging while he was working on the deck. He knew not to use it like a ladder, but to keep hands on the side ropes and feet on cross ropes. The latter got worn by constant use and broke all the time. If one used it like a ladder and both hand and footholds broke, the fall to deck or ocean could be fatal. Climbing properly, with hands on the upright ropes, prevented the possibility of such a fall.

Up and up they went past the sails until they reached the crows nest, 90 feet above the deck. The sailor didn't step onto the tiny platform but locked one elbow in the rigging and let one leg swing free.

"Nice view, ain't it?" he said innocently, stealing a glance at the youth.

Jonathan opted to copy the man, only he didn't dare let one leg free because the ship was rolling slightly side to side as it sailed along. That high above the deck, the motion was greatly magnified: one minute the mast would be 90 feet above the open water to starboard and the next minute it had swung to be 90 feet above the ocean to port. The deck below looked tiny and appeared to be swinging beneath them like a pendulum with a motion that made the stomach churn for first-timers. What the sailor saw, however, was far from what he had expected: yes, the boy had a good lock on the rigging and both feet were firmly in place, but there was a smile on his face and a glint of pride in his eyes!

Back on the deck, the man told Jonathan he could go back to rest. As they entered the forward compartment and Jonathan climbed into the hammock, all the men were watching as the sailor nodded his approval.

The same test was later conducted in a howling winter storm, with ice on the rigging and ropes actually whistling in the wind. Heavy clothing was used, but bare feet were still necessary, even more so because of the need for gripping with the toes. When the nod of approval was shown again in the front compartment, Jonathan became fully accepted as a member of the crew.

Lost in these memories, and warmed by the sun, the exhausted harpooner drifted off to sleep. Some hours later, a jarring blow to the bottom of the hatch cover brought him wide awake. The sun was high in the sky and he had to squint as he raised his head to study the ocean. Wreckage was still strewn around but there was movement in the water: a score of gray, triangular fins were knifing through the debris. As one passed within five yards of the hatch cover, he realized that he was not entirely clear of the water and tried to jerk his feet onto the wood. The right leg came up but searing pain flashed from his left leg and he saw that it was bent at an odd angle below the knee. Using both hands under his thigh, he pulled the damaged limb completely onto the wood just as the fin swung by again after a short circle.

No sooner were his feet clear than there was another strong blow to the underside of the hatch cover. This time, an audible "crack" accompanied the impact and, to his horror, Jonathan saw the start of a split across the middle of the cover.

The hatch opening in the deck for this particular cover had been four feet by four feet, with a raised wooden lip 10 inches high extending up from the deck on all four sides. The cover was made slightly larger, with wooden boards 10 inches wide extending down from all four edges to fit snugly over the outside of the lip, thus preventing water from pouring into the compartment below. Normally quite strong, the cover must have been weakened by the tremendous heat and pressure of the explosion which blew it off the ship.

For the moment there was nothing to worry about, but 30 minutes later another shark rammed the wood and this time the crack opened enough to let water through. The crack was in the center of the cover, extending almost edge to edge, so Jonathan shifted his body to one side to avoid direct downward pressure on it. He fervently hoped the 10-inch boards extending down on all sides of the cover would hold it rigid despite the crack.

An hour later, the fourth blow caused the crack to separate by several inches in the area where his head rested. Water came up and began spreading to either side. The harpooner couldn't understand how this was possible because the 10 inch 'lips' extending down on all four sides should have kept the cover rigid; however, when he explored with one arm the edge of the cover, his fingers encountered only water: the 'lip' was gone. Further investigation revealed that three of the four 10 inch 'lips' were gone: torn off when the hatch-cover was blown into the air.

There was no time to think because the split in the wood was rapidly widening and beginning to create a V down into the water, which would result in the cover breaking apart in minutes. Turning on his stomach, despite the tremendous pain it caused in his left leg, Jonathan reached both arms to the sides and pulled the cover back together, his body spread-eagled across the crack. But water was pouring in and the whole apparatus began to sink. Even with all his strength the youth could barely hold the cover together.

Then another shark rammed the wood from beneath. The cover split open, floating to either side, Jonathan's fingers were pulled away from the edges, and his body slid into the water.

6

THEY HAD BEEN SAILING due west for four hours, the green bulk of Ireland two miles away to their right, or starboard, side.

"I've never been this far from Baltimore, nor this far from land," said Seamus, staring about wide eyed.

"Ahhh, the memory of this scene is exactly what kept me going on the caravans. After I escaped, it's what I would describe to the kids far, far out in the desert at the oasis," said Finn. "I would talk about the blue ocean, exactly as we see it, with the great green hills beyond. Every once in a while I'd add in a whale or a huge fish because they never seemed to get tired of it. They would ask me to tell it over and over because they had only a small lake to look at and no great green hills."

"Aye, it's what kept me going in the early months at the quarry," said Cormac from behind them. "Else I might have given up."

"The little girl would let me see the Baltimore harbor and ocean beyond to keep my spirits up," said Bran from her spot on the bow, eyes ceaselessly searching the ocean.

"I can't imagine what it was like to be torn away from this," said the youth.

There was a moment of silence as each of the siblings was lost in memories of their early months of slavery. A grunt from Cormac rent the air.

"What?" said Finn, looking back at his brother.

"The rudder handle just swung to starboard and we're off course," replied Cormac, straining with his right arm to pull the handle back toward him and straighten their direction. "We're a degree southwest of west," he said, glancing at the compass. "That's not the direction Rogan told us."

Years of quarry work and rowing had made the redhead incredibly strong yet, after minutes of struggling, he couldn't change the angle of the rudder. Fearful of actually breaking the handle, he sat back and stared at Finn.

"Perhaps you are meant to leave it alone," said the blond quietly. Bran, looking back at them from her station up front, nodded in agreement.

Insight flooded through Cormac and he relaxed.

Half an hour later, Bran stood up in the bow.

"I see things in the water," she exclaimed excitedly, stepping up onto the gunwale and steadying herself by gripping the shroud that ran to the top of the mast, "straight ahead!" Suddenly her voice rose to a shout, "There's sharks everywhere!"

Another minute or two passed as the little boat moved steadily forward under the thrust of the wind.

"That way," Bran suddenly yelled, pointing to her left. "There's a body on a piece of wreckage! Hurry, it's starting to sink!"

"Seamus, the oars," said Finn urgently. In an instant both oars were in the oarlocks and extended over the water. Finn, facing backward, began pulling with long powerful strokes which sped up the little boat until the water hissed past the hull. At the exact same moment, the handle of the rudder came free and Cormac was able to point the craft in the direction Bran was indicating.

Seamus, crouched just behind Bran, was horrified by the sight of the body stretched out on the sinking piece of wood among so many sharks cruising the area. They were still fifty yards away when he saw the hatch cover rise up in a V, split apart and separate into two pieces. The body dropped down into the water.

"Faster," screamed Bran above him.

Finn doubled the rhythm of the oars, but Seamus could see that they weren't going to make it in time: a gray fin was surging through the ocean toward the figure barely floating on the surface. What followed was seared forever into the boy's memory.

A few yards from the cover, the shark rolled on its right side and opened a fearsome mouth to take the body. Simultaneously, there was a flutter of movement above the youth and he glanced up to see Bran's cloak split open and a bow with four arrows appear miraculously in her left hand. In a blur that his eyes couldn't follow, two arrows were released. He snapped his head back toward the shark just in time to see one shaft, immediately followed by the other, drive deep into the shark's exposed eye. With a flip of its tail, the shark dove into the depths, and Seamus could see blood on the water.

Suddenly fins were heading toward the spot where the shark disappeared, some descending under the surface well before they reached it. The water around the sinking cover erupted with bubbles and froth as the arriving sharks viciously attacked the bleeding animal. In the frenzy, some were bitten and began to bleed themselves, creating yet another melee.

As the boat arrived on the scene, Cormac spilled the air out of the sail and Finn stopped rowing.

"He's sinking!" shrieked Bran

Finn spun around on the rowing bench, took one step forward and dove into the water. As he went under he glimpsed the gray swirl of fighting sharks to his right. A plume of black hair stretched up from the sinking youth below him and he grabbed it with one hand. Kicking to the surface, he grasped the gunwale and lifted the head clear of the water. Cormac was already kneeling at the bow, both arms extended. In one motion he grabbed the body under the armpits and pulled it onboard.

Cormac turned to help his brother, but Finn, using both hands on the gunwale, had already hoisted himself up by the side of the boat and had swung one leg in. Suddenly a wide open mouth full of deadly teeth lunged up from the water at the other leg. Seamus, anticipating something like that might happen, had armed himself with the heavy wooden mallet they kept on board. He swung it with all his strength down on the shark's nose, giving Finn a fraction of a second to get fully aboard. The beast sank down and disappeared.

"Well done," said the redhead. "That was close. Let's get away from this feeding frenzy."

As Cormac swung the boom to catch the wind and get the boat moving again, Finn bent over the body and began rhythmically pressing down on the chest.

"Watch his leg," gasped Bran, "it's broken."

They all stared at the oddly bent limb below the left knee.

"We'll let that go for the moment," said Finn without changing his motion. "If we can revive him, old Conner will take care of the leg. I'll warrant he's seen worse. Come on lad, take air into your lungs."

After a few more compressions, all of a sudden the eyes fluttered open, water shot out of the mouth and the lungs began taking great gasps.

"Good, good," murmured Finn, rolling the body on its right side. "We got to you before the sharks did. That hatch cover lasted just long enough."

"I'm thirsty," croaked the sailor.

"We've just the thing," said Finn, propping him up gently against his chest as Seamus scrambled to the bucket and handed him a cup of water. "Sip it for the moment," advised the blond, "you've taken in a lot of sea water."

There was much coughing and retching as the cup was emptied, but the young man asked for more and this time it went down smoothly.

"Do you think you can eat a bit of bread?" asked Finn. At a nod, Seamus tore a hunk of bread from one of the loaves given them by the fishermen. The survivor ate two bites before his head slumped against Finn's chest in a dead faint.

"Did I not tell you that you might see the impossible today?" Finn whispered to the awestruck boy.

7

WHEN JONATHAN OPENED his eyes, a beautiful woman with long black hair was staring down at him. For an instant he thought it was his mother, but the blue-green eyes and smile were those of a stranger. All at once, the memory of the shipwreck flooded back and he stared about in confusion. He was in a stone room with one good sized window through which streamed rays of sunlight. He lay on a soft bed of what he guessed from the smell were sweet grasses, and a warm blanket covered him. His last memory was of the hatch cover splitting wide apart, sliding into the water, and sinking beneath the surface. One part of him assumed he was dead.

"Where am I?" he ventured, not even sure if he had a voice.

"Baltimore, on the southern coast of Ireland," said the woman gently.

"How did I get here?"

"My four children brought you in last night," she said. "I mean, my three children and my adopted son."

"They rescued me? How's that possible, no one knew where we went down."

"You'll have to ask them," she said mysteriously. "Ahhh, here's one of them now. It's my daughter Bran." She turned toward the door. "He's awake," she said.

A lovely girl walked up to the bed and peered at him. She also had long black hair, but pure green eyes. Immediately he saw a resemblance to the older woman.

"How are you feeling?" asked the girl in a soft, gentle voice.

"Fine," was all he could get out, distracted by her beauty.

"We were all worried about you," she said with a smile. "It was a close thing."

"I remember sharks ramming the hatch cover," he said finally. "I held it together for as long as I could, but the last blow split it wide apart and I went down."

"We arrived just as you sank," she said. "My brother Finn dove in and grabbed you by your hair before you were out of reach."

"He jumped in the water *with* the sharks?" he exclaimed.

"Yes, they were momentarily distracted, but one lunged right out of the ocean for him after Cormac lifted you into the boat. But for Seamus he might have lost a leg."

"Seamus?"

"My adopted brother Seamus was an orphan my mother took in when the rest of us were captured by Barbary pirates six years ago. We are only just home after escaping from North Africa."

"Our crew often talked about the Barbary Coast pirates capturing people off ships for slavery," said Jonathan. "But they said no one ever escaped."

"Well, we did," she said flatly, "Cormac from a quarry, then a galley, Finn from the caravans, and I from the harem, along with more than 300 people we freed and brought back with us."

"How could you rescue yourselves, much less 300 others?" he asked in amazement.

"I didn't," she said, "though I helped a bit. It was my brothers who were responsible. They're down at the dock right now fetching old Conner to take care of your leg."

At that reminder, the dull pain of his left leg forced all other questions out of his mind and Jonathan could only stare at Bran until voices at the door caused her to turn away. Three men and a boy walked into the room and clustered around the bed.

"Now, let's take a look at that leg," said Conner. His weathered face was covered with a gray beard and he wore a gray wool cap and the rough clothes of a fisherman. Kneeling down, he pulled the blanket away. "Aye, sure 'tis broke below the knee. What happened, lad?"

"I'm not sure, but I think a spar hit me when the foremast fell," said Jonathan.

"Hmm," grunted Conner, feeling about the break with stubby but gentle fingers. "It feels like a clean break, which would follow a sharp blow from a spar. Gave you some trouble in the water, no doubt?"

"It was useless," said the harpooner, "almost cost me reaching the hatch cover, in which case I'd have drowned. If the sharks didn't get me first," he added.

"Seamus, fetch a stout piece of kindling for me," said the old sailor.

The boy, with blue eyes and a shock of brown hair poking out from under a woolen cap, hurried out of the room.

"Been sailing long?" asked Conner.

"Four years on Captain Haversmith's whaling ship," said Jonathan. "I'm a harpooner."

At this, the old man's eyebrows raised. "And a young one at that," he said. " Well, you'll have all winter to recover. Anyway, I'm sure you've seen injuries during your time at sea."

"Yes."

"So you know what I'm going to ask you to do."

"Yes."

"Then let's get on with it," said the old man as Seamus handed him a sturdy round piece of kindling. Jonathan opened his mouth and Conner placed the kindling between his teeth. "Bite hard," the fisherman instructed, as he grabbed the leg. With one strong hand gripping below the knee and the other well below the odd angle of the break, he slowly but firmly pulled and twisted it until the bones were set straight and the leg resumed a normal outline.

"Done," the old man announced with satisfaction. Everyone watching sighed with relief except the harpooner, who had passed out at the first manipulation of his leg.

8

THIS TIME THERE WERE three sets of eyes staring down at him when Jonathan woke up. They belonged to three of the most beautiful young women he had ever seen. He recognized Bran's face, but the other two were new: one with curly blond hair and striking blue eyes, the other with dusky skin and black eyes set in a perfectly shaped oval face, a black scarf over her hair. When they began speaking in an unintelligible language, he briefly wondered again whether he had died and these were angels speaking a heavenly dialect.

"Tiziri doesn't speak English," said Bran. "We were explaining to her in Arabic about your accident and broken leg."

"You speak Arabic?" asked Jonathan, simultaneously realizing that the pain in his left leg had vastly diminished. "How do you know it?"

"A slave learns very quickly when whipping follows any misunderstanding of orders," explained Bran.

"You were all slaves?" he asked.

"No, only Abigail and I," she said. "Tiziri has always been free. She is Finn's wife and the daughter of a great Tuareg warrior."

"Tuareg?"

"People from the vast sands of North Africa," said Bran. "There are places in the desert, uhh...which is made up of miles and miles of scorching hot sand...with water and grass, called 'oases.' That's where the Tuareg live with their camels and horses. Finn was a slave at one such place and saved Tiziri's father from being killed by a lion. Her father is a great Tuareg leader and he freed Finn in return. In time, my brother became a Tuareg warrior and married Tiziri. In Arabic, Finn's name is 'Amnay' which means 'rider,' because he has special skills in training camels."

"The only thing I've ever heard about camels is that they don't have to drink," said Jonathan.

"That's not exactly true," said Bran, after she had translated for Tiziri, "but they can go for a long time without water. Now, how are you feeling?"

"My leg feels much better," he said, "but my jaw is sore."

"That's from biting on the stick," she said. "When we pried it out of your mouth, there were deep tooth marks in the wood. You must have a strong jaw."

When he didn't answer, they realized he had already drifted back to sleep.

9

CONNER FOUND TWO OLD CRUTCHES made from tree limbs and before long Jonathan was hobbling around the little house, his left leg bound securely between two boards. When the three girls left to visit Fiona's sister for a couple of days, he sat on a bench Fiona had moved into the garden and talked with her while she weeded and tended vegetables.

They laughed as Fiona recalled Bran being terrified of the geese kept in an enclosure beside the garden and how she would scream for Finn to help her as they chased her around the pen at feeding time.

In more sober moments, she described returning from the farm to find the village ravaged, its inhabitants missing or dead, and having to bury Donegan; how she had prayed everyday for the return of her children, never giving up hope that she would see them again. Six years later her prayers had been answered.

While gardening one afternoon she had noticed a ship come into the harbor below, but gave it no thought because it was a regular occurance in Baltimore. An hour later, the sound of a squeaky hinge had caused her to turn and glance behind her. She saw two grown men and three women grinning at her from the garden gate. Rising to her feet, she wondered who they might be. Then Cormac's red hair, blue eyes, and Bran's headlong dash into her arms gave her the answer and she burst into sobs, falling to her knees as she was overcome with emotion. For many minutes all four of them clung together, tears coursing down their faces. Finally, Finn stepped back and gathered close to him a beautiful young woman in a blue robe with a black scarf covering her hair.

"Mother, I want you to meet my wife Tiziri," he had said in Arabic first, repeating it in English.

Fiona burst into tears all over again and embraced the two of them.

"My son is married!?! And to one so beautiful!!" she'd exclaimed, with Finn translating, "Welcome to my home."

Tiziri blushed and dropped her eyes, only to raise them and smile at Fiona amid a stream of Arabic.

"And you are as beautiful as my mother Kella. Someday we will take you to meet her and my family. Your son, Amnay, is revered among the people of my father's band. I loved him from the moment I first saw him as a slave. He is now free and a mighty Tuareg warrior."

When these words were translated, Fiona had stared in shock at Finn. Her son a warrior?

"And this is Abigail," Bran had said, pulling the blond girl close. "She helped train me to be the personal slave to the Pasha's daughter. When Cormac and Finn freed me I knew I had to bring her along. She has no family, but I told her she could stay with us in Baltimore."

"And so she will," said Fiona, hugging both girls to her.

Jonathan asked Fiona to repeat the reunion story several times.

"I'm an orphan like Seamus," he explained, "and it makes me happy. I wonder what it would be like to see my mother or father again."

As the days passed, Fiona began to learn about the harpooner's background. He described stowing away, his testing, lancing the whale to save the men, and the storm. Time after time he asked her how the siblings and Seamus had not only known that he had survived the shipwreck, but had been able to find him at the exact moment he was starting to drown.

"I don't know exactly," she said. "I do know that each of them had amazing things happen while they were slaves. In your case, Bran apparently had a dream in which a little girl told her that you were in trouble and needed help. This same little girl appeared to her at times during her six years of slavery and the scent of gardenias always accompanies her."

"But, how could they find me out there?" he said.

"I don't know."

When Bran returned and he asked her about it, she was strangely non-committal, saying that she just had a dream.

When he questioned Seamus, however, it was another matter entirely.

"I don't know too much about the dream," the boy said, "but I'm positive about two things. That morning she was urgent about getting down to the boat quickly and there was a strong smell of flowers all around her. When I asked Finn in the boat how we were ever going to find a single person out in the middle of the ocean, he told me he thought I would see the impossible that day. And so I did. But there's even more!" He added excitedly.

"There's more?"

"Yes! First, we were heading due west, just as Rogan had told us to."

"He told you to sail due west?"

"That's right, he had seen a glow on the horizon the night before, due west."

"The ship burning," mused Jonathan.

"Probably. But, about half an hour before we found you, the rudder suddenly turned and sent us about one degree south of west."

"The rudder turned…by itself?" asked the harpooner.

"Yes, and Cormac couldn't straighten it. You've seen his muscles. He stopped trying because he thought he would break the handle. Finally, Finn just said he should leave it alone…and Bran agreed!"

"What happened then?"

"We sailed right up to you!"

"You sailed right to me?" asked the incredulous sailor.

"Yes, and that's not even the end of it. A shark was swimming at you, rolled up on its side with its mouth wide, just a yard or two away. Bran is standing on bow, the boat is rolling in the swell: she flings aside her cape, a bow and arrows appear in her hands and she shoots two arrows so fast I can't see them leave the bow. Both hit the shark's exposed eye and it dives from sight, trailing blood. Almost instantly other sharks attack it, and in the frenzy Finn dives right in and pulls you out."

"Two arrows?"

"Two arrows. From a pitching boat at a moving target perhaps 1½ inches wide."

10

WHEN THE FALL WEATHER PERMITTED, Jonathan continued to sit in the sun and watch Fiona tend her garden. She was usually accompanied by Tiziri and either Bran or Abigail, or both, to help translate. He never got tired of listening to them chatter because the mixing of languages was so fast between them that it created a soft dissonance, interspersed with giggles, that was quite appealing. Sailor talk was usually loud and gruff and often accompanied by brusque gesturing. These conversations were quite the opposite: musical and quiet, with the rapid change of languages back and forth adding an air of mystery.

With this pleasant background, he would stare over the harbor to the ocean beyond and think about the events that landed him in Baltimore. As the days went by, and he reviewed the shipwreck, he became more and more convinced that the chances of him surviving and being rescued were nearly impossible. Seamus had mentioned Bran's dream, but Fiona had continued to be vague and Bran non-committal. Then there were the matters of the rudder and the timing of their arrival. From what Fiona had said about strange occurrences during their time in North Africa, Jonathan decided that sometime he needed to learn more about the siblings' experiences as slaves.

As winter rolled in, the ocean often became too rough for fishing. Frequent heavy rains forced everyone inside to the long table in Fionna's house for tea, meals, and conversation. It was a relaxed and pleasant setting, with a peat-moss fire always glowing on the hearth and shortly after Christmas, Cormac gathered the family together after dinner one evening.

"It's time to discuss plans for the coming year," he began. "For those of you who were not on the dock at Tunis the night we escaped last summer: we were preparing to set sail when the pirate captain, Suleyman Reis, whose galley I had been commanding, appeared at the wharf. This was immediately following the battle to rescue Bran…and Abigail," he added, blushing as his gaze caught her beautiful face. "And of course there were many others," he stammered, completely disarmed by the look in her eyes. Clearing his throat, and oblivious to the looks that passed among the others, he went on.

"During my years on the galley I saved the Reis' life twice. After the second time, he freed me from the oars to direct the galley and to stand by him during raids to protect him on the left because that arm had been rendered useless from a sword blow. In return, he promised me a percentage of our plunder and full freedom after two years. At the time of our escape, my two years were nearly up and he was holding a substantial amount of gold for me, more than enough to pay for the ship I was taking. He wanted to know why I was leaving, because he had offered me my own ship if I would continue sailing for him.

"I introduced him to Finn and Bran, described what they had done to honor their owners while still slaves and how they had come to be free. I told him we had to go home to our widowed mother. The Reis stared at us for many minutes without speaking. We were astounded when he finally offered all three of us the opportunity to join him in future enterprises after we had been reunited with our mother."

"Surely not in the practice of enslaving people?" Fiona interrupted.

"Of course not," Cormac affirmed. "During those last two years, we took no slaves from the ships we raided, we fought almost no battles, and the merchant ship Captains readily turned over their valuables to us because of it."

"How was that possible?" she asked.

"Because MacLir Reis was known as a pirate not interested in taking prisoners as long as the goods were handed over, and he had a weapon no mercenary on the Mediterranean dared challenge," said Finn, momentarily interrupting his translation for Tiziri. By now she understood a great deal of English, but when the language was spoken quickly, with technical words thrown in, her husband was ready with an explanation in Arabic.

"MacLir Reis?" said his mother.

"Your son Cormac," said Finn, gesturing toward the redhead and bowing. "It's a name of high honor; he's widely respected throughout the Mediterranean."

Fiona stared at her boys in wonder.

"A Tuareg warrior and a respected pirate," she murmured. "Who would have suspected it from the boys who always complained that their father worked them too hard."

This brought a chorus of laughter from around the table.

"A weapon?" asked Jonathan, fascinated about what it could have been.

"That's for another time," said Cormac. "On the trip home to Ireland, the three of us discussed it and decided to accept the Reis' offer. The people of Tunis love European goods. Gael has a letter from me to the Reis saying we will deliver a shipload of merchandise to Tunis this coming summer. The letter will be carried by a merchant ship bound for Tunis from London. Our plan is to stop in Marseille, France, to acquire the goods then proceed across the Mediterranean. But first Finn and I are going to make a short trip in search of fast horses."

"Horses?" asked Seamus, who shared Finn's love of animals.

"Yes. You may not know it yet, but your sister Bran is an excellent horsewoman. And, Finn's name in Arabic is 'Amnay,' which means 'Rider.' He has an amazing gift with animals."

Seamus stared wide eyed, it was the first time he had heard these things.

"Horse racing is part of the culture in North Africa and Tiziri's father, Jugurtha, loves it," explained Finn. "The battle at the harem concluded with him and the Pasha of Tunis, who is actually his brother-in-law, ending hostilities that had existed between them for years. Honor bound, Jugurtha can no longer attack the Pasha's caravans for riches.

"However, when we met with him later to say goodbye, Jugurtha had come up with another plan to take the Pasha's riches: betting! He gave us a sack of gold and told us that if we can find European horses to compete with the Pasha's Arabians, to pay any price. Furthermore, he will give us a percentage of his winnings if we're successful. It just so happens that the Reis and the Pasha are good friends, so the bets against the Tuareg could be quite large. Thus, our business dealings in North Africa now have a two-fold focus."

There was dead silence in the room as the others contemplated these developments.

"When Gael returns in the spring, we'll make some modifications to the ship for transporting horses," Cormac said into the silence. "Afterwards, Finn and I will make a short trip in hopes of acquiring some animals I've heard about. Then we'll be off to France for merchandise and on to Tunis."

"Not without us!!" chorused Fiona, Seamus, Jonathan, and Abigail.

11

ONE PARTICULARLY STORMY DAY in February, Jonathan positioned himself across the table from Cormac, left leg stretched in front of him.

"How's the recovery?" asked the Irishman.

"It's still awkward and stiff since Conner took the splints off, but my flexibility is improving every day."

"Good," the redhead smiled.

"I've been wanting to ask you," said Jonathan. "How did you manage to escape from slavery?"

"We fought our way out," said Cormac.

"Yes, but how did you get free to fight? Bran said you were in a quarry and then enslaved on a pirate galley. Surely the pirates didn't just let you go?" asked the sailor.

"No, they didn't," said Cormac. "I earned my freedom from the quarry and then from the galley."

"How?"

"First, by becoming the best stone worker in the quarry, later by convincing the oarsmen on the galley to excel at performance, and finally by saving the Reis' life" replied the Irishman.

"But wouldn't those acts make you much more valuable to your owner, and much less likely to be freed? And how could Finn escape a caravan out in the middle of the desert? And how could Bran escape from a harem? I don't know anything about North Africa, but the talk on my ship was that no one escapes slavery," said Jonathan, staring straight into the blue eyes.

By now, everyone at the table was quiet except for Finn's occasional murmur to his wife. She actually understood everything that was said; however, she sometimes asked Finn to translate anyway because she loved the touch of his lips against her ear and the caress of his breath on her cheek.

"What brought this up?" asked Cormac.

"I've been thinking about surviving the shipwreck and being rescued. That was about as impossible as all three of you, let alone more than 300 others, escaping from slavery."

The silence dragged on for almost a minute. Then the redhead nodded.

"Tell me about the shipwreck."

"We were in a raging storm with a partially disabled rudder. I was lending my strength to the helmsman to try to keep the ship turned as much as possible into the wind, but we were being driven toward cliffs and the captain decided to take soundings to see how close we were to being driven aground. He picked me for the job, even though there were other men close by.

"I made my way to the bow and crawled out the bowsprit because the seas were too rough to stand on it. The water became shallower and shallower until we had just a little over three feet of clearance. It looked like the hull was going to be ground to pieces against the rocks when suddenly the depth increased slightly, then more until it became obvious we had passed the cliffs. After making sure that we were in the clear, I pulled in the sounding weight and returned to the bow.

"No sooner was I back on the deck than a great bolt of lightning struck the mainmast, splitting it and causing some of it to crash into the foremast, which also split. The foremast and rigging pitched forward; if I had still been on the bowsprit I would have been crushed. I jumped overboard to avoid the falling debris, but I wasn't fast enough and a piece of wreckage hit my leg.

"All of that could be described as dumb luck, until I think about what happened next."

"What happened next?" said Cormac.

Jonathan leaned both arms on the table, his gray eyes fixed on the redhead's blue ones.

"When I got clear of the ship, it started to burn. It was filled with barrels of whale oil. As the fire blazed, hatch covers began to get blown into the air, probably from the heat underneath. Up they went, to be carried away in the gale. All except the last one. It flew up, but the wind suddenly changed and instead of blowing over the bow of the ship like all the others, the hatch cover was blown directly toward me. Then the wind completely died for an instant and the cover fell to the water 40–50 yards away. As soon as it hit the water, the gale started again."

Everyone in the room was focused on the harpooner.

"I immediately swam as hard as I could toward it because I knew it was my only chance for survival. But it was drifting away on the waves, my left leg was useless, and my arms rapidly lost strength. I don't know how long I swam, it seemed like an eternity, but when I got to within six yards, I could barely lift my arms and my right leg was so weak that it was as useless as the left. I remember putting my face in the water and willing my arms to keep moving, but I couldn't lift them."

He paused and glanced around as though almost afraid to go on. No one moved, and after taking a breath he continued.

"Suddenly, like a vivid dream, I was seeing myself back in a dinghy with two oarsmen, more than a year ago. We were supporting a pair of longboats on a whale hunt. But a harpooned whale had breached twice, each time smashing one of the longboats with its fluke. There were now 12 men in the water and we were heading to assist them when the whale rolled up again, right beside the dinghy, flukes high above us. I yelled at the oarsmen to pull ahead along the whale's side before we were struck. I scrambled forward and grabbed the spare lance stored at the bow. I watched my right arm drive forward and hurl the lance into the whale. In the dream my arm was extended from the throw. In the ocean, my outstretched hand touched the hatch cover…that had been too far away to reach a moment before."

12

T HE ROOM WAS silent.

"Seamus told me about Bran's dream and the stuck rudder," said Jonathan. "And you arrived precisely as I was going under."

Cormac glanced at his brother and sister, fingering the great scar on his forehead.

"Go ahead, tell him," said Finn. Bran nodded in agreement.

"We were captured on a Monday, before dawn," the redhead began. "Aboard the pirate ship every morning a group of women met with Mrs. Doyle, who was seized along with her five-year-old twin girls. The twins, in spite of the circumstances, were happy, lively, and energetic. They became great favorites with the pirates. Their mother was amazingly calm and peaceful; a comfort to the other women, all of whom were terrified.

"We had just lost our father and Mrs. Doyle stood a good chance of losing her daughters once we reached Africa. How could she be so calm? One day I stopped close to the group to listen. She was telling them about what the priest had read on Sunday, the day before the attack. I've never forgotten it.

> 'For He will command His angels concerning you,
> To guard you in all your ways...'

At the time, I was so angry, all I could think of was, 'Where were the angels when our father was hacked down on the street outside our house?'

"None of us had paid attention to the priest that Sunday, we were only there because Mother made us go every week."

He smiled at Fiona, who grinned back at him.

"She prayed for our return every day for six years...and one day we came back," he said. "During those six years, each of us had experiences we couldn't explain."

Cormac looked at Bran.

"I was mysteriously comforted by a little girl with flowers on my first day in the harem," she said. "She appeared again and again to give me important guidance, always leaving behind the smell of gardenias. It was she who told me in the dream about you needing help out on the ocean."

"How could she know..." Jonathan began, but Cormac held up his hand and looked at Finn.

"I was dying on my first week with the caravans in the unbelievable desert heat," said the blond. "A man suddenly appeared beside me with water and saved my life, yet no one else saw him. Years later, he appeared again when my camel and I were close to death from lack of water on our escape from the caravan. He led us to a spring and guided us across the desert to the Tuareg oasis."

"I was guided several times by an audible voice in the quarry, although we were subject to absolute silence throughout the day," said Cormac. He touched his forehead. "There was also a man who appeared from nowhere and saved my life in the accident that gave me this scar. He was seen by two of my fellow workers for an instant, placing a massive log over me for protection, before he just disappeared."

"The way that we all came back together again involved events one would have to call miraculous," added Bran.

Jonathan looked back and forth at all three of them.

"Have you been to see a priest since your return?" he asked.

"Yes, of course," said Cormac.

"What did he say?"

"He was non-committal, said that he didn't know anything about angels. 'It isn't for us to concern ourselves with these kinds of things,' he announced."

13

IT WAS EMBARRASSING, Cormac thought. Whenever he was around the women he couldn't help stealing glances at Abigail. She was just as beautiful as Tiziri although her skin was fair, her hair blond and curly, and her eyes as strikingly blue as his own. She had been picked as a personal slave by the Pasha's First Wife, who named her Abraj: 'beautiful eyes.' Her training had developed in her the tendency to be quiet and attentive; however, she was completely comfortable laughing and joking with his sister and sister-in-law whenever the occasion arose. He was oblivious to the fact that those two were well aware of his staring.

As Bran had predicted, Fiona welcomed the English girl as though she was one of her own children. Abigail's parents were dead and she had no brothers or sisters. Fiona O'Shea's family, at one time reduced from five to one by the raid, now numbered seven total, plus one shipwreck survivor.

Meals were a happy affair at the long table and in the hubbub Cormac was blissfully unaware that Bran and Tiziri seemed to be occupied with others when food was passed out. It was Abigail who always delivered a plate to him, then somehow found the seat directly across the table. As time went by, others began to notice what was going on and a plot was hatched as spring came on and fishing began again.

One morning, when all signs pointed to a sunny and beautiful day, Cormac, Finn, and Seamus were at the wharf making preparations to go out when Bran came running up.

"Tiziri's not feeling well," she said to Finn. "It might be a good idea for you to spend the day with her."

"I'll go up to the house immediately," he said.

"Wait," said Cormac, "we need three people to handle the boat and the nets. Bran, you'll have to come with us."

"I can't," she said. "Mother needs me to go into the hills with my bow and bring back some partridge for supper."

"We'll have to get Jonathan," said the redhead reluctantly.

"No, he's helping Conner work on a boat today," said Seamus. "I've got an idea." With that he raced away across the wharf and up the street.

"We'd better go," said Bran and she took off with Finn for the house.

Cormac found himself alone at the edge of the dock staring at the boat and wondering how they were going to fish. All at once he heard a shout and turned to see Seamus approaching with another fisherman wearing the ubiquitous wool cap, long sleeved cotton shirt and calf-length cotton pants.

"I found someone to help," called the boy as they approached.

When they stopped in front of him, Cormac was astonished to see that it was Abigail, blond curls tucked under the cap! He flushed bright red before finding his voice.

"What are you doing here?"

"Well," she said, looking him straight in the eye. "Seamus told me you needed another hand on the fishing boat today, so I came to help."

"But, I need someone who knows how to handle the sail or the rudder while we're busy with the nets," he stammered.

""Have I never told you that my father was a fisherman and I grew up helping him on his boat?" she asked innocently. "One day while I was in school he capsized and got badly chilled. He caught the influenza, passed it on to my mother and it killed both of them. That was seven years ago, when I was 13."

Cormac could only stare, mouth agape.

"I'll loose the sail and get the oars ready," said Seamus, jumping into the boat.

"Don't you think we should get under way?" teased Abigail, as the Irishman stood rooted in place. "The other boats are already leaving the harbor."

"Uhh, of course," he said, tearing his gaze away from her beautiful eyes. "Let me help you into the boat." He held out his hand.

"No need," said the girl, stepping down into the bobbing craft with perfect balance. "Would you like me to row?"

"No, no," exclaimed Cormac, dropping into the boat and squeezing past her. "I'll row and you can handle the rudder. Seamus will raise the sail when we catch the wind."

"You should have seen it," said Seamus to Jonathan that evening when they slipped outside. "He was so flustered staring back at her as he rowed that we barely made it out of the harbor afloat! We would have hit the jetty if she hadn't warned him how close it was."

"How did she do during the day?" asked the sailor.

"She's really a good fisherman. She knew exactly what to do; he almost fell overboard watching her when she helped us pull in the nets. If I hadn't grabbed his sleeve, he would have."

"What's going to happen now?"

"I think we're going to have a new crew member on the boat," said the boy.

Horses

·····························

1

G AEL RETURNED THREE WEEKS LATER and, as predicted, brought back a full crew of ex-slaves who wanted to sail with the O'Sheas. Cormac reluctantly left the sardine boat and turned his attention to the ship for the modifications he'd been thinking about. First, he designed hinged covers to hide the single row of 12 gun ports on each side of the vessel, transforming its appearance from a fighting ship to that of a merchant ship in keeping with their planned activities. Next, He had the men convert the large captain's quarters into three smaller, but comfortable, cabins, all sharing the large windows that stretched across the stern.

"Until we get another ship, I need a cabin for Finn and Tiziri," he explained to Gael as the work began. "I also need a cabin for my mother Fiona, Bran, and Abigail. All three have said they want to join us, at least on the initial trips to Tunis. You, as captain, need the third cabin."

"Initial trips to Tunis?" asked Gael with a shocked expression. "We just escaped from Tunis."

"Remember the letter I had you send from London? That was to accept a proposal." Cormac then explained his conversation with Suleyman Reis at the wharf.

"What's your plan? Surely not to become Barbary Coast pirates."

"No," Cormac said, "not after what my family and every man on this ship experienced as slaves. Piracy for treasure and slaves is not the only way to do business in the Mediterranean. The entire population of Tunis, from the Pasha's court to the least of the merchants, desires more European goods. Piracy brings in treasure and slaves, but very little else for legitimate business people. If we supply silks and other fine merchandise from Europe to the Reis for brokering to shop owners, as well as to the Pasha, there will be profit for all of us, including the crew."

"Your reputation as MacLir Reis might prevent us from being attacked on the Mediterranean," mused Gael.

"Should a pirate captain make that unfortunate mistake," said the redhead, "he'll face the fury of our hidden cannons, as well as the chance for revenge from every man on board enslaved by pirates."

"You take the third cabin, you own the ship," said Gael after absorbing this information.

"I do, but I'll stay with the men, just as it was on the galley," replied Cormac. "You've captained this ship and I'll not compromise that. The men need to know you're in charge. If we run into trouble I'll help of course, but otherwise I'll direct our business operations."

The conversation turned to reinforcing the deck amidships to accommodate the weight of several horses. On a true merchant ship, stalls would have been built below decks, but on the converted pirate ship that level held cannons, so they had to improvise. Cormac's plan fascinated the captain.

"I've heard that Arabian horses are very fast," said Gael. "Can you find horses in Europe to compete with them?"

"I don't know, but an old Portuguese quarry slave named Armando used to tell me that there is a breed of horse used in Portugal to fight bulls. He said the animals are extremely fast and agile. When we finish with these modifications, we will sail there to let Finn explore the possibilities."

"Finn knows about horses?" asked the captain.

"Finn has an uncanny knack with animals," said the Irishman. "He'll know when we find the right horses."

While the modifications were being made, Finn replaced Cormac on the sardine boat. Although Jonathan was almost completely healed, Bran quietly suggested that he help Fiona, so that Abigail could continue as part of the crew. Seamus and Finn learned to leave the house a few minutes early each day because no matter how early they planned to sail, the redhead was always up and waiting to accompany Abigail to the wharf. Once there, he would bustle around making suggestions about this or that with tasks she was perfectly capable of doing by herself.

Gradually it dawned on Finn that his brother, who knew from crewing with the girl that she needed no help, was deliberately creating the opportunity to be near her until they left to fish. On her part, Abigail clearly encouraged it.

"Do you think this buoy is properly attached to the net?" she would ask innocently, handing him the piece of cork in such a way that their hands lightly brushed together.

"Let me take a look," the redhead would say, his hand lingering a moment longer than necessary against hers.

"Would you look at this weight?" It looks like it's bent and might fall off the bottom of the net," she'd say, knowing perfectly well that it was securely fastened.

"I think it'll hold at least for today," he'd say, knowing that it wouldn't need tightening for at least a month, but leaning close to inspect it allowed him to almost brush her rosy cheek with his.

Finn watched with amusement the ritual the pair went through when preparations were complete and it was time to leave. The boat would be parallel to the dock, Seamus in the bow, ready to push it away toward the harbor, and Finn seated on the bench facing the stern, poised to row as soon as both oars were clear. When Cormac was part of the crew, the English girl would step nimbly down onto the stern bench, sit, and grab the rudder handle. Not so now.

"Would you like my hand?" the redhead would say, kneeling on the dock above the bench and rudder, reaching out one hand even though Seamus was holding the craft perfectly steady.

"Oh, yes. Thank you," Abigail would answer, as though this was a new maneuver instead of something she had done hundreds of times in the past. Holding his hand, she would slowly step down, not releasing him until she was actually sitting on the bench and reaching to take the rudder. At that point Seamus, who had been observing the whole thing from the bow, would give a mighty push away from the wharf and duck his head so no one could see him laughing.

No matter how late they returned in the evening, the ship's dory was always tied at the dock and the redhead waiting as Finn rowed in the last few yards. The oarsman knew that his brother could spot them entering the harbor from the high deck of the ship and row the little dory to the wharf in plenty of time to be on hand to meet them.

The morning ritual was repeated between Cormac and Abigail as they all dealt with the catch, the nets, and the little details of wrapping up the day. In spite of the couple's obvious infatuation with each other, Cormac's extra set of hands did help to speed things up and free Seamus and Finn to head up the hill, giving the pair time to amble slowly home. And slowly it was…the whole family was well into supper by the time the couple arrived, so engrossed with each other that they hardly realized the meal was almost over.

2

As soon as the crew had completed the ship modifications, Cormac and Finn made preparations to go in search of horses. Jonathan replaced Finn on the sardine boat while Bran and Tiziri took his place in the garden with Fiona as soon as they returned from their morning hunts to provide wild game for the market.

Leaving the house at the same time as the sardine crew, the two dark heads would have disappeared in the morning mist covering the slopes well before the others reached the foot of the street. From the beginning, Bran had discovered that Tiziri had sharp eyes and often spotted game before she did. Slipping noiselessly through the grass and foliage of the hills, the orange sky of dawn above them, they would freeze in place at Tiziri's touch on Bran's arm. A little nod from the Tuareg, in one direction or another, would tell the Irish girl where to look.

"When we were little, our father would take us on hunting trips in the hills close to the oasis," the Tuareg girl explained. "Rabbits, partridge, and even desert sheep blend in perfectly with dirt, rocks, and the sparse vegetation. Jugurtha always said that if we were ever stranded out there, spotting game could spell the difference between life and death. We took him seriously."

If they were really close, the rabbit might bolt, or the pheasant fly, but the speed and accuracy of Bran's shooting was such that the prey was always brought down. At other times, if the quarry froze it might take some time for Bran to see what Tiziri had spotted; however, the end result was no different.

"I've never seen anything like it," Tiziri had said to Finn, Jonathan, and Seamus one day. "She holds extra arrows against the handle of the bow to be ready for multiple targets, but her hands move so fast I can't make them out, and I've never seen her miss!"

"You should see her in battle," Finn said. "Without question she saved our lives on the night of the fight at the harem. Our backs were literally to the wall, the soldiers threatening to overrun us, when she started shooting through a small speaking hole in the door. It was dark, with just a little light from the soldier's torches, but she never missed and the arrows were coming so fast the enemy couldn't close with us."

"Seamus told me about her putting an arrow into a shark's eye to save me," said the sailor.

"It was impossible," said the boy. "The distance, unsteady boat, speed of the shark, size of the target, but she did it."

"That's because you've never seen the thousands of shots I've tried and missed," laughed Bran, as she joined them. "Over months and years of daily training," she added.

"But how could you practice in the harem?" asked Jonathan.

"The oldest daughter of the First Wife, about my age, is named Pinar and she loves archery. Somehow I was able to convince her that a personal slave who could learn to shoot, and was dedicated to her safety, would be helpful. She managed to persuade her father, the Pasha, to let me be her personal slave."

"One of the eunuchs garding the harem was a famous archer named Bako, from south of the desert. He trained us daily for years, not only on stationary targets, but on smaller and smaller moving objects. He also taught us how to shoot rapidly like a warrior in battle. It came in handy when four men on horses tried to kidnap Pinar, her sister, and the First Wife in the marketplace.

Bako also taught us to shoot from the back of a running horse with the same accuracy."

"Cormac mentioned that you're a rider, but you can shoot an arrow off a running horse?" asked Jonathan in astonishment.

"Not just one arrow, but many if necessary," she said.

"I'd like to learn," said the sailor, "all I know how to do is throw a harpoon or lance."

"Me too," said Seamus.

"Shoot an arrow, or ride a horse?" asked Bran.

"Both!" they exclaimed.

"We don't have much here in the way of horses to ride," she said, "so we might as well start with the bow."

The next day was Sunday and Bran led Jonathan and Seamus a short distance up the hill above the house to her practice area. It consisted of a flat expanse at the base of a steep grassy hillside. At the far end of the level ground she had set up a heavy plank, three feet wide and four feet high, on which she had painted in red an assortment of images, most of them quite small: circles, stars, rabbits, and birds.

Striding off 15 feet, she strung her bow, notched an arrow, and handed it to Seamus after showing him how to hold it and sight the target he wanted to hit.

"They're all so small," he said.

"Just try to hit the board anywhere," she said.

Seamus tried to pull the bowstring back the way Bran had shown him, but it was so stiff he could only stretch it a few inches until his arm began to shake with the strain. Finally he released the shaft.

"Where'd it go?" said Jonathan.

"I don't know," the boy said, "I just couldn't hold it any longer."

"It's over here," said Bran walking to the hillside 20 feet to the right of the plank and retrieving the arrow from the dirt.

"How'd it get way over there?" asked Seamus.

The girl returned and took the bow.

"I wasn't thinking," she said. "As Pinar and I got better and better, Bako would have the armourer make us stronger bows. The ones we started with had a very light pull because he wanted us to focus on accuracy. As we progressed, each new bow was slightly stiffer. The length of this one is sized to me but the stiffness is for a man. One of the local fishermen is also a cooper and trained in making bows and arrows: I'll have him build each of you the proper bow to start with."

"Let me pull it," said Jonathan, not believing his ears.

She handed him the bow. The sailor was strong from years of work on the ship, but the best he could do was a 70% draw, even then the hand holding the bowstring was shaking.

"Part of it is technique," she said, taking the bow back. "After a while, you'll learn to pull the bowstring quickly and release the arrow, not try to hold it and aim. Don't worry though, before long both of you will be putting arrows in the smallest target on the board."

"Show us," said Jonathan.

She pulled three more arrows from her quiver, gripped all four in the hand holding the bow and stepped back until she was more than 50 feet from the plank. Suddenly her hands became a blur and the four arrows were released with blinding speed, to wind up dead center in four of the smallest targets on the plank.

Jonathan and Seamus looked at each other and shook their heads.

3

GAEL DROPPED ANCHOR IN THE harbor of Lisbon and soon the dory was headed toward the wharf. On board with Cormac and Finn was Bonifacio, a former slave from Lisbon who had elected to stay on and sail with MacLir Reis. After spending a few minutes among the workers at the dock, Bonifacio returned with a smile on his face.

"We're in luck," he said in Arabic, the common language for all three, "there is a Corridas de Touros being held in the city tomorrow."

"What's that?" asked Cormac.

"It's a spectacle where a highly trained horse is used to challenge a deadly bull in a ring around which spectators sit behind a high fence," he said.

"A highly trained horse is one thing," said Finn, "but are they fast?"

"Very fast and agile," said the sailor. "They have to be or the bull would kill them. They are Lusitanos, the finest horses in all of Portugal and specially trained for this work."

Cormac stared at Finn, raising an eyebrow.

"These must be the horses Armando told me about in the quarry," he said.

"Then these are the horses we've come to see," said his brother.

The next afternoon, Bonifacio escorted them to a large, high, circular enclosure near the center of the city. They were admitted through a gate and shown to seats on the top level of the structure. Below them, the floor of the arena was covered with sand and enclosed by an eight-foot high wooden wall with several narrow openings in its perimeter. Between the wall and the foundation of the stadium itself was a space of about ten feet, also covered with sand. In that space they could see a few men standing near the openings. More people arrived, filling the benches until there were more than 300 spectators present, all talking animatedly.

At length, a man in colorful dress entered the ring through one of the openings in the wall and blew a loud blast on a trumpet. Instantly, the crowd went completely silent. The trumpeter stepped back behind the wall. There was a moment of silence before two large doors, directly across from the O'Sheas, opened and a black bull charged into the ring, turning its head this way and that as though searching for an object to attack. A low murmur of awe passed through the crowd.

Cormac had never seen an animal so menacing. Massive shoulders and neck supported a head from which emerged a deadly-looking pair of horns pointing straight forward. It was about the size of a dairy bull, but most similarities ended there. Its torso tapered to powerful hindquarters bulging with muscles; the general appearance was that of an animal with great strength, totally unafraid of anything and capable of extreme aggression. It trotted majestically into the center of the sand, head raised defiantly.

"How can a horse stand up to that beast?" he whispered to Finn.

"I don't know, but it has to be special."

All at once a horse and rider appeared below them on the sand, apparently having entered from a door beneath their seats. The horse was striking in appearance: cream colored, with a black mane and tail, and black on all four legs from the knees down to the polished hoofs. The rider, sitting on a small saddle, wore white pants tucked into knee-high black leather boots, a white blouse, red vest, and a strange looking small dark hat.

The bull immediately charged. To the astonishment of the brothers, the horse accelerated into a run directly at the oncoming bull and with no visible guidance from the rider neatly sidestepped the charge and passed the enraged animal at full speed. Moving to the center of the ring, the horse pivoted on its back legs to face another charge. Launching forward, the horse passed so close that the bull's shoulder brushed the rider's left boot as it hurtled by.

"Do you see how quickly that horse reaches a full run?" asked Finn, eyes gleaming. "That's the kind of animal we're looking for."

The pattern was repeated twice more, now accompanied by a roar from the crowd each time the two animals passed. After the last charge, the horse moved to the side of the ring where, from the top of the wall, the rider was handed a pair of sticks two feet long, wrapped in colorful cloth.

"Wait a minute," said Cormac as the rider turned to receive the sticks, revealing a long ponytail that had slipped out from under the hat. "Is that a *woman*?"

"Yes," said Bonifacio with a wide grin. "That's a 'cavaleira,' a woman bullfighter. Some of the best riders are women. Watch what she does now. The sticks have sharp metal points on one end."

The horse trotted around the edge of the ring; the bull in the center slowly turning to face it. All of a sudden the bull charged. The horse spun away from the wall and raced headlong at the oncoming black menace. The rider held one stick in each hand, shoulder high, having dropped the single rein across the horse's neck. At the last second, with no guidance from the cavaleira, the horse swerved and the woman leaned far out to jab both sticks into the top of the bull's shoulder muscles.

"What's that for?" asked Cormac.

"I'm guessing to weaken the bull's neck," said Finn. "But I don't know why."

"Ahhh, you're right," Bonifacio said, with an admiring look at the blond, "but how did you know? Placing the bandarilhas has to do with the second part of the spectacle, the Pega."

"Do the riders ever fall?" asked Finn, as horse and rider repeated the process, placing two more sticks into the bull's shoulders.

"Occasionally," said the sailor. "Or the bull might gore a less-skilled horse. Either way it is exceedingly dangerous because if the horse goes down, the bull will attack the rider instantly. Workers run out to distract it, but sometimes not in time to save the cavaleira."

The horse and rider left the ring, to be replaced by eight men on foot. Each wore what looked like black slippers, white stockings to their knees, topped by tight black pants, and long-sleeved shirts. One of the men wore a bright green cap.

"Those men are called 'forcados'" whispered the sailor, "watch."

The men lined up, one behind the other, with the forcado in the green hat at the front. He advanced a few steps toward the bull, stamping his feet and waving his arms. The bull, pawing the ground with one front hoof then the other, charged. As it reached the man, he made a diving leap high in the air, landing between the horns and wrapping his arms around its neck. Instantly the other seven men threw themselves on the bull and a wild melee ensued as the bull whirled this way and that trying to gore anyone that it could. But its vision was partially blocked by the lead man's body and legs slamming up and down on its forehead, while the others stayed well behind it if they were thrown off.

After about ten minutes the bull was lying exhausted on the ground, all eight men on top of it. One by one the men got off and trotted over to the gate. The bull got wearily to its feet and was herded out of the ring, accompanied by loud cheers from the crowd.

4

J OANA MATIAS WAS MOUNTED ON the Lusitano outside the arena, surrounded by a crowd of well-wishers, when she spotted the approaching strangers. Both sported knee-high leather boots into which were tucked pants secured by wide belts. Each wore a loose white shirt with long sleeves and had a light cape thrown back over their shoulders. Soft felt hats with wide brims completed their attire.

One was slightly taller and slender, the other more muscular; both moved with a grace that spoke of confidence. But it was the eyes and hair that captured her attention. Shoulder-length red hair and startling blue eyes marked the one on the left, while long blond hair and piercing brown eyes flecked with gold marked the taller one on the right.

Edging their way through the throng, they arrived a few feet from the horse's right shoulder. It was then that she noticed the sailor accompanying them.

"The horse is even more beautiful close up," said the blond.

"Señora," said the sailor in Portuguese, "these men are most impressed with your horse."

"Oh, I'm very pleased to hear that," she said in English, noting the startled expression on both faces.

The two, having been preoccupied with staring at the Lusitano, raised their eyes to see a beautiful young woman, perhaps a few years older than they, gazing at them in amusement.

"Some of us from Lisbon speak English, though not many." she said. "But your accent is not exactly English."

"No, we're Irish," said the redhead. "My name is Cormac and this is my brother Finn."

"I am Joana Matias, cavaleira and horse owner."

"Yes, we just watched you in the arena," said Finn. "We have come to your country to find horses that are quick and fast. This animal appears to excel in both traits."

"As do all my horses," she replied.

"All your horses?"

"Yes, why don't you come out tomorrow and see them?" she said. "Alphonso will give you directions." She pointed to a mounted man at the edge of the crowd, thanked her well wishers, and disappeared up the street.

The next morning a carriage delivered the O'Sheas up a long tree-lined drive, covered in white gravel, to a magnificent mansion on the outskirts of Lisbon. Surrounded by large pastures, the two-story building was 75 yards long, made from pale colored rock. Large windows were spaced along both levels and a massive entrance featured a pair of huge mahogany doors.

The pair was shown through the residence to a beautiful courtyard, filled with potted trees and flowers. Joana, along with an older couple, was waiting for them at a marble table beside a small pool filled with flowering lily pads. After introducing them to her mother and father, the cavaleira asked why they were looking for horses.

"We are interested in finding animals fast enough for racing," Finn explained.

"Surely not at Newmarket?" said Joana. "I could never let a horse go to race there."

"Newmarket?' asked Cormac.

"Yes. It's in England, north of London, and a great center for horse racing. I compete there frequently and I wouldn't want to do so against one of my own animals," she said with a laugh.

"We didn't know about Newmarket," said Finn, "but we wouldn't be in competition with you anyway. We want to take horses to North Africa to race against Arabians. We need quickness and speed, but also endurance. Desert racing can cover several miles."

"Arabians," she mused. "I've heard that they're very fast, although smaller than the Lusitanos."

""They are smaller, but exquisitely proportioned, and built for speed," said Finn. "That's why I liked the agility and muscle structure of your horse yesterday. I noticed that it's a mare."

"Yes, the mares are better for bullfighting because they learn quickly and are less headstrong. There's actually a three-year-old sister to my horse that likes to run more than dodge. Perhaps you should look at her. She's in the large pasture just outside the courtyard."

Finn quickly agreed and the three of them walked from the house a few yards to a gate in the fence bordering the pasture. Joana grabbed a few apples from a nearby basket and whistled to the grazing horses. At least 10 animals immediately approached, including her mount from the day before and cream colored mare with exactly the same markings.

"Would you like to ride her?" asked the girl, "I can have one of the men bring a saddle and bridle."

"That won't be necessary," said Finn, glancing at her for permission before opening the gate and walking into the pasture. He slowly approached the second mare, talking softly. She immediately responded by walking up to him and giving a gentle bump with her forehead. Joana raised her eyebrows.

"She only did that with me after I'd worked with her for a week," she said quietly to Cormac.

"I suspect that Finn will surprise you," was all he would say.

Walking back to the gate, the blond handed his hat and cape to Cormac and returned to the horse. She had never taken her eyes off him. Talking continuously, he rubbed her neck, back and head for another few minutes, and ran his hands down each leg, and examined each hoof. Then he moved to the front and put one hand on either side of her jaw and looked straight at her, murmuring softly. What happened next caused Joana to gasp, hand over her mouth.

The Irishman walked to the mare's side and in one smooth motion vaulted lightly aboard. She turned to look back for a moment then, with no apparent guidance, made her way out of the group of horses and broke into a full speed run across the pasture. Two hundred yards away she stopped, spun, and raced back. Joana observed that Finn's body moved in complete harmony with the horse as comfortably as though he were on a saddle, his hands lightly on either side of her neck. The horse came to a sliding stop and the blond slipped off. He repeated the process of looking straight into the horse's eyes for a minute and talking, all the while gently stroking her velvety nose, before returning to the gate.

"We'd like to buy her," he said.

5

A MONTH LATER CORMAC AND FINN topped a small hill in the English countryside, the blond riding the cream-colored mare and the redhead on a beautiful gray Lusitano mare they had also purchased from Joana. Below them was the small village of Newmarket, surrounded by a broad, grassy plain. Off to the left, at the edge of the town, stood a magnificent palace surrounded by an acre of manicured grounds and trees. Nearby was a beautiful three-story lodge with its own gardens and landscaping.

"That must be the palace they told us about in London, built nearly 30 years ago by King James I," said Finn.

"Yes, and there's the lodge built 10 years later for the Prince of Wales," said Cormac. "Apparently the aristocrats loved horse racing as much then as they do now. Three years ago they even created a race called the Gold Cup. Sounds almost like the Arabs. I wonder if the English bet as heavily?"

"I've no doubt, after talking with Joana."

The lane they were following, flanked by low stone fences and trees, descended the hill and entered the village. After the horses were put up at a stable the brothers found rooms at a nearby inn. That evening, after a dinner of shepherd's pie in a large room downstairs with a great fireplace along one wall, the brothers began asking the locals about horse owners in the area. Although courteous, most were evasive in their answers, other than stating the obvious: the palace and the lodge both had full stables of horses. Finally, they encountered a talkative farmer seated by himself with a tall flagon of ale on the table in front of him.

"Alfred's the name," he said by way of introduction. "And what would the likes of you two be doing here, asking about horses?"

"We're looking to buy a fast horse to race," said Cormac.

"And for certain, no one is going to sell you a horse fast enough to beat themselves in Newmarket," Alfred observed.

"True, and well noted," the redhead laughed. "But we've no interest in Newmarket racing. If we can find the right horse, we'll take it across the sea to race in another land."

"I'll wager France, Germany, or Spain," said the farmer, with keen insight.

"You've more than a farmer's knowledge of racing," observed Finn with a grin.

"Aye. From time to time I work in the stables at both the palace and the lodge. They appreciate me because I keep my mouth shut on what I hear about their animals."

"It's to North Africa we're going and Arabian horses we want to challenge," explained Finn.

"So, it's Arabians you want to go after. We haven't seen any here yet, but talk is that they're fast," said Alfred.

"Are there any unusually fast horses in either stable?" Cormac asked.

"Aye, there's fast horses in both," said the farmer. "But if you're looking to buy one, forget it! They're groomed and trained for King Charles and the Prince of Wales. Neither will give up an animal that might beat the other's horses."

"Hmm...what about the local farmers?" asked Finn. "Do any of them have race horses?"

"A few of the larger ones do," said Alfred. "But if they have a promising one, they either keep it or sell it to the King or Prince. Those two will outbid each other grandly for a good animal."

"No farmer would sell a fast horse to us if he had one?" asked Cormac.

"Not unless he was soft-headed, like farmer Thumburton, and had a wild horse like that stallion."

"Thumburton? Who's that?" said Cormac.

"Aye, he's a farmer who got taken by a huckster claiming to be a traveling horse salesman a year ago," said Alfred. "He thought he was gonna get rich and beat both the King and the Prince, but he never has been able to race the animal because the blighter turns barmy and attacks him every time he goes near it!"

A slow smile spread on Finn's face.

6

SEVERAL MILES NORTH OF TOWN the next morning, guided by instructions from Alfred, the brothers approached a small farm in the hills. A cozy stone house with a thatched roof, flanked by several outbuildings, fronted an enormous but slightly barren vegetable garden.

"Finest peas, beans, cabbages, and cucumbers in the whole region," the innkeeper had told them. "We buy all the produce we can from Thumburtons. But they're not growing as much this year because of all the time he spends on that crazy horse. Thinks it'll make him richer than the farm will, but it'll more likely kill him first!"

As they rode into the yard, a barefoot young girl with red hair and a cloth sack strung around her neck was throwing handfuls of feed from the sack to a flock of chickens scratching in the dirt. Following her was a shoeless younger brother with a shock of blond hair, outfitted with a smaller sack, doing the same. Both stopped to stare at the visitors.

A boy about 12 emerged from the pigpen off to one side and politely asked if he could take their horses.

"Thank you lad," said Cormac, doffing his hat as the men swung down. "I see that your sister and I have something in common." He smiled gently at the girl as he shook out his red hair.

The girl blushed and dropped her eyes before tearing around the side of the house calling for Mum and Dad.

"Are you knights?" asked the youngest, staring at the strangers.

"No, son," said Finn, going down on one knee to be at his level, "but we've sailed the seas to faraway lands and seen many strange sights."

"Ohhh, what kind of sights?" asked the boy, eyes wide.

Before the Irishman could answer, a man limped around the corner of the house in tall gardening boots. His left arm was supported by a sling and white cloth encased his head. He was clean shaven and appeared to be about 10 years older than the brothers. Behind him came a slender, pretty woman with blond hair covered by a blue kerchief. She also wore gardening boots. Finn and Cormac swept off their hats.

"Farmer Thumburton?" said Cormac, "Mrs. Thumburton?"

The man nodded, but his eyes were taken with the two Lusitano mares. His wife stepped forward.

"I see you've met Liam," she said as Finn rose, "I hope he hasn't been a bother."

"Mother," interrupted the boy, pointing at Cormac, "he has the same color hair as Emma!"

"Yes, I see that he does," said the woman, with a smile at Cormac. "My bairn has a habit of speaking his mind. And I see Oliver has taken charge of your horses."

"And fine horses they are, Anna," said the farmer, turning his gaze to the brothers for the first time. "Lusitanos?"

"Why, yes," said Cormac with a startled look, "how did you know?"

"I've seen their likes at the Newmarket races. From time to time a girl from Portugal brings them to run."

"Joana," said Finn. "In fact she sold these horses to us on the condition that we wouldn't race them at Newmarket."

Now it was time for the farmer to be startled.

"You know her? Then why did you bring the mares here?" he said.

"For riding purposes only. To come and see you," Finn replied. "We heard that you own what might be a fast horse."

"Hard to say, because he won't let me get near him," said the farmer, with a scowl.

"Took a piece of James' scalp only last week," said Anna, "and ran him into the fence a fortnight ago. Hurt his leg and nearly broke his arm getting through the crossbars. That animal's a menace and now I'm having to do all the gardening."

"Somehow I know he's fast," said Thumburton, "but I'm at my wits' end to control him."

"Can we see him?" asked Finn.

James waved at a fence to their left which extended over a small hill and out of sight. It was a typical stone fence, waist high, made from rocks pulled out of the fields, but heavy wood posts had been set into it, with crossbars between them, increasing the height to six feet.

"Yes, as long as you stay on this side of that fence," said the farmer. "We don't want anyone to get hurt."

7

ANNA AND THE KIDS RETURNED to work while James led the way to the top of the hill. Below them, the fence enclosed several acres of grassland with a small stream flowing through the lower end. In the middle of the pasture grazed a black horse, which lifted its head to stare at them as soon as they appeared. They watched it for several minutes.

"Seems normal enough to me," said Finn.

"Yes," said Thumburton," but go to the fance and climb up on a crossbar. Do not climb over."

The blond strode to the fence, hopped up on the stone wall and stepped onto the lowest crossbar, which put the top rail at his waist. He placed both hands on it and waited to see what would happen.

The horse immediately spun on its hind legs and raced up the slope, tail streaming behind. A few feet from the fence it stopped and reared, striking out with both front legs, ears flat back on its head and unearthly screams coming from its throat. Cormac stifled a gasp and stared at Thumburton. He was watching impassively, apparently used to such behavior. Finn never moved, though the hooves were coming dangerously close. After a while, he stepped to the ground.

"Can we go back to the farmhouse?" he asked.

The three retraced their steps; only when they passed from sight did the horse cease its screams. Back in the barnyard, Finn asked James how he had come to buy the stallion.

"A man came through the district a year ago with a high-sided wagon and this horse," he said. "He would fasten a rope around its neck before letting it out of the wagon and always had a long whip in hand. By tightening the rope on its neck and striking it with the whip he could make the horse stand for inspection, but no one dared approach it because the ears would go flat back and its eyes would become wild. Even the King's grooms and those of the Prince of Wales wanted no part of it."

"Why did you buy it then?" said Cormac.

"It's a big, strong animal," Thumburton answered, "I thought I could tame it and win money at the races."

"Where did the horse come from?" asked Finn.

"The man said it came from the Turkoman Desert," said the farmer, "far to the east of the European countries and bordered by a sea. He said the people there prize their horses for speed and quickness."

"Speed and quickness we can see," said Anna, who had reappeared, "when he's loose in the pasture. Sanity is what's lacking."

"I've seen enough to know that your instincts are correct," said Finn, "but I don't think Newmarket is the place for him." He gave a slight nod to Cormac. "If you're willing, we'd like to buy him. Would you accept a gold sovereign?"

Cormac reached into a pocket and pulled out a shining coin.

James and Anna stared at each other in shock.

"That's far more than I paid," the farmer stammered. "If you're willing, of course we'll take it. I've been wasting time with that animal

for a year, it's time I got back to doing what I know best: growing vegetables. But where will you take him?"

"The desert in North Africa, to race against Arabians," answered
Cormac.

"Africa? Arabians? What about the Lusitanos?" asked the farmer.
"Are you taking them also?"

"Sir, you do have a natural eye for good horses. The mares will be
going to Africa with us as well."

"I'm curious," said Anna. "You've no wagon and I see no sign of
whips. Do you plan on taking the horse with you?"

"Yes," said Finn.

"How?" she asked

"By making a friend," said Finn.

8

THE ERSTWHILE TUAREG WARRIOR started back up the hill, followed by his brother and the entire Thumburton family. The horse was still there, now grazing; however, at the first sight of people it resumed its previous behavior: rearing, screaming, and striking out with its hooves. The Irishman stood across the fence for a few minutes watching the enraged animal. All at once, to the horror of the others, he quickly moved a few yards back along the barrier, stepped up on the rock wall, vaulted over the top rail and immediately sat cross legged on the ground.

The reaction of the stallion was instantaneous. It charged at the man, ears flat, emitting a scream, reared high above him and plunged both front feet down with all its strength. Whoomph! The hooves landed inches from Finn's legs. The man stared into the infuriated animal's eyes and began murmuring in a soft voice. Whoomph! The hooves plunged down again, narrowly missing Finn. Again and again the horse reared high and slammed its hooves into the ground until there wasn't a blade of grass left on the ground in front of the Irishman.

Finn never flinched, or moved, his eyes steady on those of the stallion. His soft voice continued uninterrupted with strange words.

"What language is that?" whispered Anna to Cormac.

"He's speaking Arabic," said the redhead.

"Arabic?" echoed the farmer with wide eyes.

"Yes. It may be a language the horse is familiar with."

"How does your brother know Arabic?" asked Thumburton.

"We both do. We were captured by Barbary Coast pirates almost seven years ago and enslaved in North Africa."

Husband and wife stared at him, wide eyed.

"We've heard of the Barbary Coast pirates and their slavery," murmured James, "but we've been told that no one escapes."

"Almost no one," Cormac corrected. "We had special help."

"It must have come from a powerful source."

The redhead turned to stare at Thumburton for a long minute.

"Yes," he said, "I'm beginning to understand that it did."

All at once the action across the fence changed. The black horse spun around so that its hindquarters were toward Finn. Over and over it tipped onto its front legs and unleashed wicked kicks with its back legs, the hooves reaching to within two feet of the man's face. The blond never flinched and continued the stream of words.

Suddenly the animal stopped its kicks and without a backward look trotted away over the hill and out of sight. Finn rose to his feet.

"He's probably thirsty," he said, "after all his screaming and antics. This is going to take a while, perhaps until the morning. Could we spend the night at your farm?"

"Of course," said Anna, "I'll make soft beds for you on fresh hay in the sheep fold."

"We're happy to pay," said Cormac.

"Not after what you've given us for the horse," she said, "and I'll have a nice supper of mutton and greens for all of us."

Finn walked rapidly over the brow of the hill, the others hurrying to keep up on their side of the fence. Sure enough, the black was down at the little stream drinking. When it caught sight of Finn walking towards it, the stallion again charged, but slowed as the man immediately sat down in the grass. The horse approached within 15 yards of the man and stopped. Ears flat, it screamed and made a few false charges, then stood watching as Finn raised his voice a bit and continued speaking in Arabic.

"What's he saying?" asked Thumburton.

"Most of it is simple soothing," said Cormac. "He's repeating over and over that there's no need to be afraid, that the stallion's not going to be harmed, and that he's going to be well taken care of. Every once in a while he tells the animal that he's going to love running fast with other horses and beating them in races."

"He's telling the horse that?" asked James. "As if the horse understands him?"

"Well, don't you talk to your sheep, chickens, or pigs like they understand you?" asked Cormac with a chuckle.

"Of course. You should hear him go on with the animals," said Anna, giggling. "You'd think they were all going down to the pub together in the evening for a flagon of ale!"

9

Supper was served on a long table with benches to either side. While eating, James questioned Finn about how he had decided to buy the stallion so quickly. The Irishman explained that he had been sold to a caravan operator and spent years working with camels.

"I almost died during my first week in the desert. The sun was blinding and the heat was terrible. The only thing that saved me from falling, and being whipped almost to death, was to cling to my lead camel's neck both for support and to help me keep moving forward. I would talk to it all day long about Ireland, the ocean, fishing, anything I could think of to distract me from fainting away. In time I found that the animal responded to my voice and even developed affection for me.

"After I became hardened to desert travel, I began talking to each of the five animals in my care. They all seemed to like it and would crowd around me in the evenings for more attention. From there it was easy to begin showing them what I wanted them to do, like kneeling quietly after they were loaded until I gave the command to stand, and rewarding them with praise and affection."

"So you never got whipped?" asked the farmer.

"Oh no," Finn laughed grimly. "Make no mistake, we would get whipped for the smallest mistake and sometimes for no reason at all. If you were to look at our backs," gesturing toward Cormac, "and the backs of our legs, you would see many scars - mine from the caravans, his from the quarry."

"You poor men," Anna looked aghast and the children stared with wide eyes. "I don't know how you survived."

"Many slaves didn't. Some lasted for years until they were just too old for the work and were killed because they couldn't keep up anymore. After four years, I managed to escape and fled with a camel across the desert. Both of us were nearly dead…actually we should have been dead twice over…when the camel smelled water and stumbled into an oasis occupied by a band of desert people."

"After recovering, I became a slave of those people and was put in charge of their camels. I began training the animals for hunting and warfare, using the same techniques I'd developed in the caravans. The few Arabian horses they had responded to the same methods."

"What's a camel?" Liam interrupted, despite a mouthful of food.

"I'm going to tell you all about them after supper," said Finn with a smile before continuing. "The stallion's behavior doesn't bother me because I know we can become friends; it was his physical attributes that attracted me."

"What attributes?" asked Thumburton.

"He has small hooves, smaller than an Arabian. If he came from a desert, it means the surface is probably hard and gravelly: small hooves are more suited to that. Arabians have larger hooves because of the sand they live in. However, races are usually held in the low places between the sand dunes where the surface is firm and packed, so the black will be at no disadvantage. Being from the desert, he will also be able to endure intense heat better than a horse from a cooler climate."

"He has a longer back than the Arabian. This means his stride will be somewhat longer: he has to take fewer strides to cover the same distance. In a long race that advantage could be important."

"He's taller than an Arabian and his size creates big and powerful muscles. The Arabian has strong muscles, but a bigger horse might have a bit more power.

"The stallion has a narrower body than the Arabian. This may not be an advantage in racing, however, it definitely would make for quicker turns in warfare. Both breeds have wide foreheads and large eyes, traits I believe indicate intelligence."

The farmer and his wife were silent for a few minutes, reflecting on the details Finn had picked up so quickly.

"But, at Newmarket he could…" Thumburton began.

"Hush," said his wife. "These gentlemen have their plans. Besides, that Portuguese girl probably doesn't want to see them at Newmarket."

All four of them laughed at her outburst.

"Farmer Thumburton," said Finn with a twinkle in his eye, "as I mentioned before, you do have an eye for good horses. But those bandages suggest it's time to reclaim you and your wife's prestige as the best produce growers in the district."

Later, Finn sat in a chair before the hearth. A smoldering fire of peat moss gave off a pleasant breath of heat to the room. Liam sat on his lap, Emma and Oliver on the floor before him, and the adults on the benches to the side.

"Now about those camels," he began, and for the next hour he regaled them with stories about the old jamal who had saved his life, fierce sandstorms, desert lions and sheep, blazing heat and freezing nights. There was not a sound from the listeners. Anna finally slipped over beside him and gently lifted the now sleeping youngster from his lap.

"Time for bed," she whispered to the others, putting a finger to her lips as they started to protest. "Perhaps he can tell one more story at breakfast."

And so he did.

10

THE SUN WAS STILL BELOW the treetops when Finn walked back up the hill, armed with a few apples from Mrs. Thumburton and a length of rope from her husband. The family and Cormac, who was grooming the Lusitanos, heard screams from the stallion as soon as the Irishman disappeared from sight. But the noise stopped almost as suddenly as it had begun and, save for the clucking of chickens and grunts from the pigs, nothing disturbed the silence of a beautiful morning.

Several hours later, the redhead was dozing in the sun on a bench beside the farmhouse when Anna's voice roused him.

"Mercy sakes, will you look at that. I never thought I'd see the day."

Cormac got up and peered around the corner of the house. Coming down the hill was his brother; beside him walked the black with a loose halter fashioned around its head. The two walked into the farmyard and stopped. The stallion looked around in a curious way, ears straight up. Finn's hand rested on its neck, a continuous stream of soft words in Arabic coming from his mouth. The gathered family stood stock still, wondering what to do, but ready to scatter if the horse went rogue.

"It's all right," said Finn. "Just don't move too suddenly or raise your voice. We need to give him a few minutes to get used to his surroundings." He turned to Cormac. "You can saddle the Lusitanos, although I'll probably walk for the first mile or two."

When the mares emerged from the barn the Turkoman snorted and raised its head, ears up, eyes studying them, but made no other move. Cormac, standing between the two holding their bridles, didn't know what to expect. The Portuguese horses studied the stallion for a minute, then swung their heads toward the redhead to have their jaws rubbed.

"Just as I thought," said Finn, switching to English. "These animals all know that we care for them, and they won't worry about anything else." After saying his farewells, with a wave of his hand he started out of the barnyard with the black walking quietly at his side.

"Goodbye," called Liam, "please come back and tell us more stories about lions."

"He might just do that," said Cormac from atop his horse. "After all," he grinned at James, "as your father knows, there's always a race to be won at Newmarket."

The two men and three horses disappeared up the lane.

"I've never seen the likes of that," muttered the farmer to his wife. "You could knock me over with a feather."

"Not yet, dear, we have work to do in the garden."

The Sultan's Court

1

The huge man stood just outside the sand circle in the Janissary*
compound. He was stripped to the waist, chest and arms chiseled with muscle. His black hair was hidden under a yellow silk scarf. Intense brown eyes, radiating cruelty, topped a heavy black beard ending in a point below his chin A wide belt and loose white silk pants above bare feet completed his attire. He grinned at the crowd of soldiers surrounding the ring.

"I'm only 24. What chance do I have against these three hardened and experienced soldiers?" He gestured at the men already waiting in the ring. "This is the third challenge I've faced this month. Maybe they think they can wear me out."

---

* Professional soldier, originally a slave.

A loud wave of laughter rippled through the watching crowd, who knew that the challenges were designed to stroke the ego of the young Sultan and could potentially provide additional rations for all of them.

"Do you really think you can defeat me?" He addressed the three.

"This is the day, Excellency," the oldest lied. "No more victories for you in the wrestling ring."

"See their confidence," Murad IV roared to the crowd arrogantly. "They forget that I was leading the army when we breached the wall and entered Baghdad six weeks ago."

The gathered men shouted their approval. Every one of them knew this statement to be true. The Sultan had indeed been in the front lines of that war. He had shared their hardships during the entire campaign and had swung his great mace and sword with devastating effect in the thick of every battle. They also knew that their three comrades would tussle and struggle with him hard enough to be convincing, but not hard enough to win. Winning meant death.

The young Sultan stepped into the ring. He was a full head taller than his opponents, all of whom had equally chiseled physiques. He moved to the center and they spread out around him. The soldier in front immediately dove for one of Murad's feet and received a kick in the chest that catapulted him backwards on the sand. One of the men in back timed his dive with the kick and, grabbing the Sultan's other ankle, upended him on the sand. The third man leaped on the giant's chest and managed to get him in a headlock just as the first man dashed back and wrapped both arms around the Sultan's ankles. The man who had tripped up the giant sat on the sand behind the Sultan's head, both feet pushing against Murad's shoulders, and with both hands pulled his left arm straight back.

The observers watched carefully, but it was almost impossible to see the deception that occurred as the tide turned. A close-up view would have revealed the soldier's arm around the young leader's neck loosen ever so slightly, so that when the Sultan's free arm grabbed at him the headlock was broken. Still on his back, Murad, with his enormous strength, literally threw the man out of the ring with his right arm. The crowd roared. Once out, the wrestler could not re-enter the ring.

Now the giant turned his attention to the soldier braced against his shoulders. The man eased his pressure just a fraction so the Sultan could roll on his side and reach up with his right arm to grab the soldier's wrist. The man exerted just enough pull on Murad's left arm to make his grip appear to be solid, but as the Sultan yanked on the wrist the fingers appeared to lose their grip and Murad's arm came free. Struggling to his knees, the young giant threw this man out of the ring. From there it was an easy matter to pull the last man from around his legs and heave him into the crowd.

Sweating profusely the Sultan stood, victorious arm high in the air, and slowly turned in a circle to the cheering janissaries. His three opponents stepped into the ring and went down on one knee, heads bowed.

"So, 'this is the day,' huh?" said Murad with a sneer.

"We really thought we had you," said the leader, "but once again you proved yourself the best wrestler in the Empire."

Ego soothed, the Sultan became gracious. "You put up a good fight," he said, gesturing to a page. "See that all the men get extra portions tonight at the kitchens."

After the Sultan had departed for the palace, soldiers crowded around the three.

"Well done, Arif," one said to the leader. "I could barely tell."

"He's incredibly strong," said Arif. "He could probably have broken the headlock anyway."

"No sense in taking a chance," said the other. "You know what happened to Bayezid."

In fact, they all knew and that was why they subtly rigged the matches. Bayezid was one of Murad's brothers. He was a skilled jouster who had competed successfully throughout the Ottoman Empire and beyond. Three years earlier, the Sultan had challenged him to a joust. Murad was unhorsed by his brother. A few days later he ordered

Bayezid's murder. Recently, for obscure reasons, he had ordered the death of yet another brother.

Athletic and given to competition, Murad was also immensely cruel. The janissaries had no misunderstanding about what would happen to anyone beating him in a contest.

2

THE NEXT MORNING THE YOUNG Sultan attended to the affairs of his Empire in the magnificent courtroom of his palace. The room, huge and circular, featured a great golden dome overhead and continuous arches around its perimeter, each supported by 15-foot marble pillars. The floor was a mosaic pattern of colorful tile in which were set the images of wild animals: lions, leopards, oryx, desert sheep, and even a crocodile.

In the very center of the room was a large, three level, circular dais. The top level was made from rare orange marble and held an enormous throne covered in gold leaf. On the level below were two oversized red chairs, 15 feet apart, one to each side of the throne above and behind them. These chairs were for two Viziers. The lowest level contained eight black normal-size chairs, separated into two groups of four divided by the same 15 foot gap. They were occupied by the eight highest ranking Janissary officers. At floor level, ornate mahogany tables stretched almost entirely around the dais, but with a 15-foot separation below the throne. Thus, anyone approaching the dais faced a wide aisle, flanked by the tables, then by eight men, then two, ascending directly to the Sultan himself. It was an imposing setting.

On this day Murad was dressed in a yellow silk shirt, purple silk pants, gold slippers and a magnificent orange turban with ostrich feathers rising from the front. Over all of this he wore a padded silk overcoat with shining buttons that was stiff with embroidery, the cost of which would have fed a small village for a month. To his right and below sat Grand Vizier Kemankes Mustafa, an ex-Janissary captain whom he had appointed to the highest civil position in the land. To his left sat Vizier Hadim Ali, also ex-Janissary, who assisted Kemankes. Both Viziers were dressed in white silk robes and white turbans.

The eight captains were dressed in purple robes and white turbans. Below them, the mahogany tables were covered with documents and attended to by a large number of pages, who took turns announcing the issues to be decided on

"A dispute concerning crowding of merchant ships on the docks," a page might call out from the bottom of the dais. Vizier Hadim Ali would signal him up and read in a loud voice the contents of the document the page delivered. The Grand Vizier would quickly issue a decision.

"A matter concerning a dispute between villages in Bolyadin over well rights."

If it was a routine civil matter, Kemankes would make an instant decision. If it was a military matter, such as an uprising of bandits in some area of the Empire, the Grand Vizier would ask for a recommendation from the janissaries. Before issuing a decision, however, he would turn and look at Murad. A flick of the hand, or a quick downturned thumb, would render the verdict.

"What does his Eminence think?" Kemankes would ask, with uncanny perception, on any other matter for which he felt Murad wanted to decide.

Although it usually appeared that the young Sultan was daydreaming, the Grand Vizier knew differently. Despite his cruel disposition, Murad was an able administrator who had greatly strengthened the Empire. A Janissary revolt resulting in the death of his uncle, Sultan Mad Mustafa, had made Murad the Sultan at age 11. In the early years, his mother Kosem, as Custodian of the Sultanate, directed the affairs of the Empire through the Grand Vizier appointed by the Janissaries. However, under this arrangement corruption vastly increased and finally the young Murad stepped in. He had the Grand Vizier killed, along with the original Janissary leaders who had murdered his uncle. He appointed a new Grand Vizier loyal to him and set about cleaning up the drain on Empire funds from multiple disloyal sources. He also banned alcohol, coffee, and tobacco in Constantinople, believing the substances distorted men's thinking.

Although he was powerful in his own right, Kemankes knew that human life meant absolutely nothing to the young Sultan and that he was as subject to death as anyone else. He had survived for years by deferring almost all decisions, except the most rudimentary civil matters, to the Sultan. If Murad was disinterested in a matter, the worst Kemankes suffered was an irritated wave of the hand.

"A matter concerning the disappearance of the redheaded pirate MacLir Reis from the Mediterranean," announced the next page.

3

Silence filled the court as everyone stared at each other in confusion.

Hadim looked at Kemankes. Kemankes glanced up at the Sultan, who was staring at the page with narrowed eyes as though trying to remember something. The Grand Vizier gestured for his assistant to signal the boy up.

"Our spies report that the pirate galley captained by the renegade Dutchman, Suleyman Reis has not been seen on the sea for months," read the Vizier.

"What does that have to do with MacLir Reis?" interrupted the Sultan from above. "And who is he? I can't place it, but I remember something about a red-haired pirate."

Suddenly Kemankes remembered.

"Your Eminence," he said, "the incident you may be recollecting happened just before you left three years ago on the campaign against the Safavid at Yerevan."

"What incident?" prompted Murad.

"Merchants in Europe promised the Empire a huge reward if you would rid the sea of the pirate Suleyman Reis. His galley had been plundering their ships for years.You directed the Janissary Captain, Zehab, to fill a cattle ship with some of his men, plus a large number of mercenaries and ambush the pirates. We put out a rumor that the cattle ship was carrying a shipment of gold."

"Yes, I remember now," said the Sultan. "Wasn't there a message, just before we attacked Eruzurum, that the ambush had failed."

"There was," said the Grand Vizier. "The galley fell for the ruse and attacked as we planned and Zehab nearly captured it, but a blue eyed, red-headed slave led the oarsmen in a counter attack and defeated the mercenaries. The galley's ram had pierced the cattle ship, nearly causing it to sink, but the men managed to make repairs and limp into Malta."

"Are you telling me that half-dead galley slaves defeated our Janissaries and the mercenaries?" Murad's voice took on a dangerous tone as he pictured the emaciated condition of his own galley oarsmen.

Having seen what the Sultan was capable of when he used that tone of voice, Kemankes began to sweat under his robe.

"Not exactly," he said, thinking quickly and concentrating on keeping his voice steady. "Zehab said a demon rose up out of the galley and attacked our men."

"A demon?" Murad's voice now had a touch of confusion.

"Yes, Eminence. The men all said that the redhead conjured a terrible demon out of nowhere. He was huge and black as night, the size of two men. He gnashed his teeth and roared awful noises. His arms were like whirlwinds, and whenever they touched a man, his head would fly off or explode."

"Their heads would fly off?" The Sultan was all ears and the menacing tone disappeared. In his years of battle, he had never heard of such a thing.

"Yes, and arms and legs too when he touched them," Kemankes played to Murad's fascination. "Why, they reported that the demon commanded sharks to jump out of the water and snatch men right off the galley deck." He paused to let this revelation take effect.

"Even so, our brave men managed to lift a small cannon up to the rail of the cattle ship to blow a hole in the galley, but when the demon saw what they were doing he reached out one of his arms and sliced the head right off one of the men carrying it. The cannon fell from the railing and exploded, killing all the men next to it."

"What did the demon do next?" The Sultan couldn't help thinking what an asset such an ally would have been in his recent siege of Baghdad.

"He disappeared. But the surviving mercenaries said the galley pulled alongside the cattle boat and the redhead told them never to attack Suleyman Reis again or he would bring the demon back to kill them all."

Silence again filled the court. Even the most hardened warrior present had heard stories of supernatural occurrences: voices and crazed laughter at night, people mysteriously disappearing leaving no trace behind, blood stains suddenly showing up on walls and floors. Kemankes, though only attempting to deflect the ruler's anger, had succeeded in introducing uneasiness and even fear into everyone in the room.

"What about the redhead?" Murad finally said.

"It was reported that Suleyman Reis was badly wounded in the battle," said Kemankes, desperately trying to remember everything that had been told to him. "When he recovered, it seems his left arm was useless and from that time on the redhead stood at his side when they attacked merchant ships. It's said that no one resisted them for fear that MacLir Reis, as he came to be known, would conjure up the demon. Apparently he has disappeared; perhaps he was a demon as well."

"And Zehab?" said Murad.

"He fled to Europe with his remaining men in shame at his failure and disappeared. Sometime later, our spies found him in

Italy and brought him back. I sent him to the dungeon to await your return from Yerevan. Unfortunately, when the Safavids immediately recaptured Yerevan and we began planning the Baghdad campaign, I forgot all about him.

"An oversight I hope you won't regret. Bring him here tomorrow," ordered the Sultan in an icy voice.

4

"I'LL GET HIM MYSELF," said the Grand Vizier that afternoon, as a guard prepared to collect Zehab from the prison.

"As you wish, Vizier." The man bowed his head and stepped back in deference to the most powerful civilian leader in the Empire.

With two pages accompanying him, Kemankes hurried through the streets to the huge, circular, three-story prison in the Yedikule fortress. The structure had been incorporated two centuries earlier into the great wall along the Marmara Sea which protected the city from a naval attack. Constructed of gray granite, the only openings were occasional small grated windows along the circular stairs that spiraled up inside the walls. All cells, except those on the highest level, were windowless and located in the middle of the structure.

Two guards hurriedly opened the massive wooden door at the Grand Vizier's approach. Inside, torches in iron sconces on the walls gave dim light to the table and chair of the jail keeper. As Kemankes swept into the entry, the man leapt to his feet and bowed.

"To what do we owe the honor of this visit, Excellency?" The man was a Janissary completing the temporary assignment to the prison required of every soldier. His tone was courteous but not obsequious. Fighting men recognized the importance of civilian administrators but did not buckle under to them.

"At the Sultan's directive, I've come for the prisoner Zehab," said the Grand Vizier.

"Ahh, let me check," said the man, consulting a large book on the table. After several minutes he said, "Yes, lowest level, if he's still alive. I'll send for him."

He rang a small bell on the table and another Janissary appeared from the shadows.

"Cell 3, lower level, prisoner Zehab. Bring him up."

The soldier disappeared down descending stairs to the left and the others waited in silence until the sound of shuffling steps announced the prisoner's approach. Emerging into the light was the pitiful, thin, stooped figure of a man who had once been above average in height. A black beard shot through with gray extended below his waist, matched by equally long black and gray hair matted down his back. He wore the filthy remains of what once had been a robe and his feet were bare. Even in the dim light of the torches he had to close eyes that had seen nothing but darkness for years. The stench that accompanied him was nauseating.

"Blindfold," said the Vizier and one of the pages stepped forward and wrapped a wide piece of cloth around the prisoner's head. Uncertain of the Sultan's plans, Kemankes did not want Zehab to be literally blinded by the daylight. "Put a hand on his shoulder," he ordered the prisoner, gesturing for the other page to step close and guide the man's hand to his shoulder. Nodding to the jail keeper, Kemankes led the way out of the dungeon.

When they were well out of sight of the dungeon, the Grand Vizier sent the two pages ahead to prepare a bath, fetch a barber, and obtain clothes for the former Janissary captain.

"We might all lose our lives if we presented him like this to the Sultan, the odor alone might drive him into a rage," he explained. "I'll guide him myself." Glad to be free of the sight and smell, the two young men hurried off.

"Zehab," Kemankes hissed to the prisoner as soon as the pages disappeared.

"Yes?" rasped a hoarse voice that hadn't spoken for years.

"You are alive only because the Sultan was taken up with the Safavid wars when we imprisoned you for the cattle boat disaster. The matter came up yesterday when dealing with the affairs of the Empire."

"How?" croaked Zehab.

"Information from our spies indicates that the red-haired pirate and his black friend have disappeared from the Mediterranean. The Sultan had completely forgotten the report of your unfortunate disaster. He was so enraged yesterday that galley slaves had defeated both janissaries and mercenaries that I was sure he would feed you to the dogs, so I explained that the redhead conjured up a demon to subdue your men."

He went on to explain the details of what he'd described.

"You organized the expedition," said Zehab in a hoarse whisper, "I suspect you were also seeking to protect *yourself* from being fed to the dogs."

"Since he didn't issue an immediate order," said Kemankes, ignoring the accusation, "I think he may have something else in mind."

"Maybe he'll feed both of us to the dogs in front of the Janissary corps to demonstrate the price of failure."

"Maybe," said the Vizier in candor, "but you are to stand before the Sultan tomorrow morning and I suggest that you echo my story. It might just give both of us a chance to prolong our lives."

5

THE MAN ESCORTED INTO THE Sultan's court by two janissaries the next day bore no resemblance to the apparition that had appeared from the bottom of the dungeon. Dressed in a simple white cotton shirt and trousers, and wearing plain sandals, his hair and beard had been trimmed short. He still had a slight stoop and one could tell he was extremely thin, but his gray eyes, having been allowed to gradually adjust to light, were clear. The three stopped at the bottom of the dais.

"The prisoner Zehab," announced one of the pages.

"Accused of fleeing to Europe to escape the Sultan's judgement, after failing to destroy the pirate galley commanded by Suleyman Reis of Tunis," said the Vizier.

Silence descended on the room as the young giant seated on his throne dais toyed with an enormous mace.* He stared down at the prisoner with cold eyes.

"You failed miserably at destroying a mere pirate galley, although you were supplied with trained janissaries and mercenary soldiers," he finally growled.

The prisoner bowed his head and remained silent.

"You may speak," said the Grand Vizier

"Excellency," said Zehab in a raspy voice. "It was not a normal galley."

"Ohhh," said Murad in a menacing voice. "Just why not?"

Again the prisoner remained silent until given permission to speak by Kemankes.

"Excellency. We were defeating the pirates and one of my men was about to kill Suleyman Reis when the redhead drummer conjured up a fierce and powerful demon who rescued the Reis and attacked my men."

He went on to describe essentially the same story the Grand Vizier had related the day before, emphasizing the flying heads and the sharks. In fact, his story was so convincing that the Janissary captains glanced at each other in unspoken relief that it hadn't been one of them leading the expedition. When he finished, silence reigned except for the slap of the mace handle as the Sultan tossed it from hand to hand.

"I've struck many men in battle with this mace," he mused finally, "but I've never been able to make a head fly off a body."

He gestured to Kamenkes. "Who is this Suleyman Reis?"

"A renegade Dutchman," said the Grand Vizier, "who defected to Tunis many years ago for the purpose of engaging in piracy. Our informants say he has prospered greatly and operates ships in the Atlantic, as well as galleys in the Mediterranean. They say he prefers to lead his personal galley in the Mediterranean because of proximity to his home and other business interests."

"What is his relationship with our Pasha in Tunis?"

---

* Alleged by historians to weigh 135 pounds, which he could wield one handed. A staggering feat.

"All the pirates operating out of the harbor pay tribute to the Pasha."

"Does he forward it to us?"

"We do receive monthly payments from the Pasha," Kemankes answered carefully.

"**All** of the tribute from harbor operations?" Murad's tone brooked no nonsense.

"We receive gold, however we get no accounting," the Grand Vizier answered truthfully. "It is the same amount every month, and not insignificant."

"How does it compare with our other ports in North Africa?"

"Slightly more."

"And you say this Dutchman has ships operating in the Atlantic as well?"

"Yes Excellency, as do other pirates." Kemankes' instincts were screaming at him to divert this line of questioning away from his area of responsibility. "However, our spies have reported that the Pasha and the Dutchman are close friends," he added.

"It is the day of your good fortune Zehab, you are only going to lose your left hand and not your life," said the Sultan, making an instant decision. "When you recover, the Grand Vizier will supply you with ships and men. Sail to Tunis and teach that city a lesson about loyalty to the Ottoman Empire. Bring the Pasha and Suleyman Reis to me. Unharmed."

He gave a resounding slap of the mace head to one palm.

"Fail, and the janissaries will observe whether I can emulate the demon and make your head fly off your body with this mace."

He directed a cold look at Kemankes. "Cut off his left hand. If he does not return this time, I will feed you alive to the dogs."

Silk Merchants

1

"WILL YOU LOOK AT THAT!" said Seamus from the bow, as the sardine boat rounded the passage into the harbor at Baltimore.

"What?" asked Jonathan who was facing the stern and about to start rowing.

"I don't believe it," said Abigail sitting in the stern handling the rudder and facing forward like Seamus.

Out in the harbor, heading towards the beach, was the black head of a swimming horse. Next to it was the unmistakable head of a man with long blond blond hair.

"It's Finn," yelled Seamus, jumping to his feet. "He's swimming with a horse! And there's two more already on shore." Indeed, two horses with strikingly colored markings were grazing at the edge of the narrow beach.

"They're back," said Jonathan who had swung around to see the sight and immediately spotted the anchored ship belonging to Cormac. From one side, a great boom attached to the main mast stretched out over the water with a large block and tackle attached to its end. Suspended from the apparatus were thick ropes attached to a wide band of canvas. Even as he watched, men on the ship were pulling the boom back and securing it to the front of the mast.

"Amazing," said the sailor, recognizing the purpose of the rig immediately. "He lowered the horses into the water so they could swim ashore. The water at the wharf here isn't deep enough to take a ship alongside."

Simultaneously Seamus and Jonathan turned to face Abigail.

"He's home," said Jonathan, keeping a straight face.

The English girl blushed a deep red.

"Tend to your duties," she said gruffly. "The two of you are liable to run us into the rocks if you don't watch where we're going."

She dropped her eyes but not before both of them saw the happy light filling them.

"Please steer us past the shore on the way to the wharf," requested Seamus, "they're just getting out of the water."

Abigail complied and a few minutes later, with Jonathan pulling hard on the oars, they drew parallel to the shore. Finn, his powerful build showing through soaked clothes, stood facing a large black horse and two slightly smaller ones. All the animals, coats glistening with water in the late afternoon sun, were pressing their heads toward him; he appeared to be talking to them while rubbing their cheeks.

To Seamus' shout of greeting Finn raised one hand in salute, then their attention was caught by movement to the right. Streaking along along the wharf came a figure, blue robe gathered above her knees, black hair flying behind. She gave a mighty leap off the dock and, without missing a step, flew across the sand and into Finn's arms. With her head buried against his neck she was swung round and round, while all three horses watched curiously, ears up and pointed forward.

Jonathan didn't stop rowing because he could see that after a quick glance his companion on the rudder was paying no attention to the scene on the beach: her eyes were on the ship at anchor 200 yards away.

"The dory's coming," Seamus yelled.

"Hush," said Abigail, blushing again, "you don't have to tell the world!"

A quick glance showed Jonathan that they'd reach the wharf ahead of the dory and he imperceptibly eased the power of his strokes: although the cadence remained the same, the fishing boat moved more slowly through the water. Sure enough, from the corner of his eye he saw the little craft from the ship reach the dock just ahead of them and a redheaded figure leap up to secure it.

As the sardine boat slid alongside the wharf, Seamus secured the bow; Jonathan shipped the oars and pulled the craft tight to the dock with his hands. Abigail stood up, stepped onto the stern bench and was about take the short jump onto the dock when Cormac appeared slightly above her.

"Would you like a hand up?" he asked, as though he hadn't been away for weeks.

"Why, yes," she said, holding out her hand and stepping lightly up to the wharf.

What happened next startled the two watchers, used to the formal little ritual of leaving and arriving in the sardine boat.

Cormac suddenly pulled the girl into his arms in a great hug. For an instant her body was stiff, then both arms went around his neck and she clung to him. Oblivious to Jonathan, Seamus, and others returning from a day of fishing, the two stood and held on to each other for many minutes while the Irishman murmured things to the blond head nestled on his chest. Gradually a small crowd of fishermen gathered around them. Bran, who had come down to the dock with Tiziri, was in the front row.

In the months since fishing had begun again, the lovely Abigail had won the respect and affection of every man who went to sea to fish.

No matter what the conditions, she was at the dock with the earliest of them, a smile and a kind word for everyone, helping to make sure everything was in order for the day's work. No matter how late the O'Shea boat returned, she set to work energetically with the crew to take care of the day's catch and ready nets for the following day. Many a fisherman privately wished she was part of his crew.

"Looks like Baltimore's best fisherwoman has made a catch," Rogan said.

"Don't know who'll handle the rudder now," said Niall.

"Probably have to be Bran," said Rogan. "She's the only other one who can deal with these boys." There was a loud guffaw from the assembled men, but Cormac and Abigail paid absolutely no attention.

"No, not her," said Alistair, "my family has gotten too fond of the game the cailin* brings from the hills." A number of shouts underscored his statement.

Finally Cormac broke the embrace and faced the group, left arm holding Abigail tightly against him. Both of them looked at the assembly with happy faces.

"Sorry to disappoint you lads, but the O'Shea family, including fishers and its hunter, are going to be gone for a while."

'Where?" said Niall.

"See those horses Finn swam ashore?" said the redhead. "We're taking them to North Africa, within three weeks."

Stunned silence.

"But you just escaped from there last summer," said Rogan finally.

"True," said Abigail, gazing up into the intense blue eyes so close to hers. "But they and the cailin left as free, highly regarded warriors with whom the pirates want to do legal, and hopefully profitable, business."

---

* 'Girl' in Gaelic

2

S UPPER THAT NIGHT WAS A lively affair as everyone shared experiences that had occurred while the brothers were gone. Jonathan had been knocked overboard one day when not paying attention to the boom while Abigail was tacking into the wind, resulting in unmerciful teasing about the experienced sailor ending up in the ocean. Seamus, on the other hand, had slipped on sardine slime on the wharf one afternoon and wound up in the harbor, putting an end to some of his jabs.

Only Abigail appeared to have escaped disaster, and was left out of the ribbing until the two boys began talking to each other as though no one else was present.

"It's hard enough to do all that work every day on the boat," said Jonathan, "but it's doubly hard when you're starving."

"Yes," said Seamus somberly, "especially when the nets are full of fish time after time. Why, the strength just flees from one's arms."

"Now boys," Abigail began, in an intimidating tone.

"No, no," said Cormac, "please go on, I was near to starving most of the time in the quarry so I know exactly what you're talking about." He put on an innocent, inquiring expression and didn't look at Abigail, even though she was sitting right beside him glaring up at his face.

"Well," began the sailor, "you know that we ALWAYS bring a bucket of food to get through the day."

"Always," echoed the redhead.

Tiziri ducked her head; she knew what was coming.

"You know how the swell can get rough off that point a mile west of the harbor," said Jonathan.

"We know it well," said Cormac, "Finn and I usually had to stabilize the boat with the oars when our father ventured up there. But there's always been good fishing off that point."

"About three weeks ago, we thought to give it a try," said Jonathan.

"Sardines had been scarce for a few days," added Seamus.

"Yes, well the swell was particularly heavy that day with a strong wind blowing," said Jonathan. "The boat was rocking side-to-side pretty strong."

"I know exactly what you describe," said Cormac with a deadpan face, sensing what was coming.

"I couldn't even stand up in the bow," added Seamus.

"Before I could get the oars extended, the top of a swell broke on the starboard side and we took on quite a bit of water…Seamus, you'll have to go on, it's just too upsetting what happened next," Jonathan said, covering his face with both hands in a tragic fashion.

The two brothers' eyes locked on Seamus, who paused to build the suspense.

"We weren't going to sink," he said, "but we needed to bail the water out quickly. Our steersman quickly grabbed a bucket, scooped up some water and hurled it over the side…"

"And…?" said the redhead.

"It was the food bucket and all our provisions for the day were flung to the depths," the boy replied woefully.

The table dissolved in laughter.

As Cormac bent over in mirth, Abigail doused him with a pitcher of water.

"That'll teach you to lead those boys into horrible revelations" she said.

Still cackling, he caught her arm and pulling her to him, stole a kiss.

3

WHEN THINGS FINALLY SETTLED down they all, Bran in particular, wanted to know more about the horses. She had walked with Finn and Tiziri up to a farm on the hilltop where the animals had been turned loose in a pasture. It was occupied by a small herd of sheep and two huge old plow horses who greeted the new arrivals with loud snorts and swishing of tails.

"They're beautiful," she said after studying the Lusitanos. "And the black looks like he's built for speed."

"He is," said her brother, "but don't underestimate the mares. Both are very fast."

Now, Cormac did most of the talking, allowing Finn to translate for Tiziri, when she didn't recognize a word or phrase.

"When we were kids," he began for the benefit of the newer family members, "and Mother took us to her sister's farm, we were forbidden to go anywhere near the pasture with the big dairy bull."

Finn and Bran nodded in agreement.

"He was normally grazing and pretty calm, unless someone came into the pasture. Then he would immediately become enraged and charge with no warning. Several times our uncle barely escaped serious injury."

"I had to warn you kids morning, noon, and night about that bull when we visited," said Fiona. "Particularly Finn."

"The fighting bulls in Portugal are black, heavily muscled, and so dangerous looking that no one, under any circumstance, would even *think* of going near them. They make that old ornery dairy bull seem like a kitten!" Cormac said. "When one of these bulls entered the arena, I was glad to be high in the stands and out of reach, but was shocked to see that the bullfighter was a woman."

He then went on to describe the bullfight in detail. When he got to the part about the men wrestling the bull to the ground the only sound in the room was the occasional whisper of Finn's voice in his wife's ear.

"It was dangerous for the men," the redhead conceded, "but even more so for the woman and her horse. The Lusitano and bull were charging full speed at each other, the rider guiding the horse only with her knees in order to have both hands free. The two animals passed within inches of each other; the horse had to be so agile that if the bull hooked with its horn she could dodge before it gored her. If the horse went down, the bull would have instantly gone after the rider. Women have been killed in such circumstances."

"When I saw the speed and agility of that horse," said Finn, "I was convinced that we needed at least one. As you know, we managed to buy two from the horsewoman."

"Based on promising not to race them at Newmarket in England," added Cormac. "Despite the distance from her home, Joana loves to take her horses to race there."

He then went on to describe how they left Gael to supervise some alterations to the ship in a London shipyard and set out on the two mares for Newmarket.

"I didn't do any riding in North Africa," he said, "but the Lusitanos are incredible horses, and their strength and grace reminds me of the Arabians I saw there. They seem to instinctively know what you want them to do. Of course, they love Finn."

He then went on to describe their visit to Thumburton farm and the miraculous conversion of the black stallion. When it came time to offload the three animals in the Baltimore harbor, the redhead explained that Finn had descended the block and tackle rig with each horse and swam to shore with them.

"With him close, talking to them all the time, the horses were completely calm while experiencing a situation that could have really frightened them," he explained. "Most of the harbors in Europe are deep enough to offload animals directly onto the docks."

"I can't believe the black attacked that farmer," Bran exclaimed. "He stayed close to Finn on the way up the hill, but certainly didn't mind me rubbing his cheek."

"It wasn't the farmer's fault," said her blond brother. "I suspect it was whoever first owned him. Apparently he could only control him with a whip. And we know well enough what a whip can do."

"Aye," said Cormac, "one never forgets."

Bran, who had been spared the scars her brothers carried but had endured her share of physical and mental abuse, nodded in agreement.

"The hardest part of our shopping is done now, but there is one more promise to keep before we leave Ireland," said Cormac. "Within a day or so, Finn and Tiziri will make a short trip with Gael to Lochinver on the west coast of Scotland. He promised to find the family of a slave who helped him survive the first terrible weeks of caravan life, and became a dear friend and mentor. Years later the man perished in an accident during the terrible sandstorm that allowed Finn to escape."

"Thaddeus was a fisherman who was captured one morning with his crew," explained Finn. "He took me under his wing and treated me like a son. As he was dying, he asked me to find his family and tell them what happened. I gave him my word and I will keep it."

4

G AEL EASED THE VESSEL INTO THE harbor at Marseille under
minimum sail. A short time later the ship was securely tied to
the wide cobblestone quay which surrounded the U-shaped harbor
on all sides. Although it was late afternoon, the whole O'Shea group
descended the gangplank to the dock, hardly able to believe their eyes.
Three and four-story buildings bordered the quay along its entire
length. With the exception of Jonathan, Bran, and the brothers, none
of them had ever seen structures of such size. On the bottom level of
each building were businesses of all kinds: shops, taverns, inns, a coffee house with outdoor seats, a large fish market, bakeries, and even
a vegetable market.

"I'm going to take the girls for a look around," said Fiona.

"Be back at the ship before dusk," said Cormac, "no telling who
will emerge from the shadows at nightfall."

"We will be," promised his mother.

"Aye," muttered Jonathan. "The women should be on board well before evening begins."

"Bran has her bow under that cloak," said Finn, "but we should never take their safety for granted

"If they're not back before the sun goes down we'll go looking for them," said the redhead. "Now, let's see if we can find out where Chinese merchandise is sold."

On the journey from Ireland, Bran and Abigail had detailed what the women in the harem, and particularly the First Wife, liked in the way of material. The most desirable material was silk, and valued above everything was the beautifully patterned Chinese product brought across the Silk Road from the Orient. Several cultures had been able to reproduce silk, and it was made locally from Constantanople to Italy, but the quality and beauty still did not compare to the fabric produced in the far eastern regions of China. The demand in Europe was so great that little silk made its way to North Africa, making it highly prized among the wealthy in Tunis.

"This will be good merchandise for Suleyman Reis to sell in the city," Cormac had said. "Plus a generous gift to the First Wife."

"Yes," said Abigail, former slave to the First Wife. "She always dresses her two daughters in the finest material available."

"Kelebeck is the youngest and loves to dress up; she drives her nurse crazy by changing clothes four or five times a day," said Bran. "Her older sister Pinar, who owned me but finally became more of a sister, cared about archery and riding more than clothing until she noticed a certain young man who appeared at the court whenever she was there. I advised her to hide her abilities with horse and bow and try to appear more lady-like. A few robes of Chinese silk will serve her well."

"But, what about her riding and shooting?" Seamus had asked.

"Plenty of time for that, I'm guessing," Fiona said wisely, "but matters of the heart often take precedence."

The brothers and Jonathan had asked Jacques, a Frenchman from the galley who had elected to sail with Cormac, to interpret for them.

After conversing for a few minutes with a group of men on the quay, he returned.

"Years have passed since I was here," he said, "but things haven't changed. The place to start is Rue de la Casserie. It was originally laid out by Greek settlers almost 2,000 years ago, and has always been a street of commerce. It's not far from here."

"We'll go in the morning," said Cormac. "Abigail, Bran, and the ladies will know what to buy, but we'll need you to guide and translate."

"In the meantime," said Finn, "we should find a stable and arrange feed for the horses."

A short time later, Jacques' inquiries led them to an establishment close to the quay and Finn negotiated for a supply of hay and grain sufficient for the Mediterranean crossing. As they made their way back to the ship in the gathering dusk, they noted with satisfaction that Fiona and the girls were walking up the gangplank. What they did not notice was a small group of men near one of the buildings staring intently at them.

"Even with the hat, you can see the scar," said the large man with a black beard. The others nodded in agreement.

"The red hair too," said a thin figure with a drooping mustache and cruel eyes. "There's only one man on the sea with red hair and a great white scar."

5

For the next week the O'Shea group frequented the shopping areas near the harbor. In addition to the Rue de la Casserie, Jacques found other streets with shops offering merchandise from the Orient. Before long, bales of silk, beautiful pieces of carved jade, porcelain and lacquered furniture were being delivered to Gael for careful storage on the ship. Almost every day one of the women would find something unusual to be marketed in Tunis.

Tiziri in particular was entranced by the sheer array of goods available. Wealth in the desert was determined by camels, horses, and gold. Her father was very wealthy by those standards, but she decided her family needed a few things to show that it was worldly as well. She loved the green jade and picked out a small carved lion for Jugurtha; a carved duck for her mother Kella and tiny jade hummingbirds for her sisters, Tinitran and Tamenzut. A small, low, black lacquered table with red designs completed her purchases. She and Finn agreed that it would be perfect to serve meals on.

Finn found a Chinese sword in a beautiful scabbard for Jugurtha. It had a dragon etched on either side of the razor sharp, double-edged blade and could be wielded with either one hand or two. He also bought bolts of beautiful black silk, with small colorful designs, for Tiziri, her mother, and sisters to make robes for wearing inside the tents since straight black was worn outside.

Despite the success of the shopping, the blond warrior had a strange feeling as they walked the streets each day that they were being watched. He mentioned it to Cormac and to his surprise the redhead concurred. Not wanting to alarm the others, they took to studying the people around them, but the neighborhoods were crowded and neither of them could spot anything unusual. Nevertheless, the feeling persisted and they both added swords to their daily attire.

Abigail, Bran, and Fiona had Gael pack bolts of silk, small carved jade figures, and items like silver combs and clasps, in separate chests to be opened upon return to Ireland. Fiona also bought lengths of white, blue, and red cloth that she had delivered to her cabin on the ship. When asked about them, she just shook her head mysteriously.

Jonathan found a beautiful lance blade. It was made of shining steel, 30 inches long, and extremely sharp on both sides.

"That's Toledo steel," the merchant said through Jacques. "Made in Spain. The metal is very hard, the finest in the world."

"Fit for a harpooner, or a fighting man," said Finn. "We'll get a hardwood shaft for you in Tunis."

Seamus stayed on the ship. At 13, he was more interested in climbing the rigging than in shopping. Gael had promised him a position as lookout on the tiny crow's nest atop of the highest mast, if he could demonstrate his ability to travel up and down the rigging like the seasoned sailors. On the way from Ireland, some of the men had worked with him on it. He wasn't daunted by the motion of the ship, having been in plenty of rough water on the tiny sardine boat, but the sheer height of the mast made him cautious.

'Don't look down," counseled the sailors, "it will fill you with fear because of the height. Keep your eyes on the ropes directly in front of you, or the rigging just above, until you reach the crows nest. It takes a long time to get used to how far you are above the deck."

Sure enough, upon reaching the relative safety of the little platform, the youth would be amazed at how far up he had come. His companion, casually balanced with one hand and one foot on the ropes would grin.

"Good job, laddie, you're getting the hang of it."

Seamus couldn't help but return the smile, bursting inside with pride. Now in port, on a stationary vessel, he was improving his speed daily. One day Jonathan found a perfect gift for the boy: a small brass telescope.

"It's not the size of the ones Gael and Cormac use, but it will give you a huge advantage up there," he said to the delighted lad, "all you have to do is earn the right to be a lookout."

To the joy of the crew, Cormac bought new white cotton shirts and loose blue pants for every man on board. This was just one of many kind gestures he made for them and the sailors revered him for it. These men, headed for nothing but a certain death when captured and enslaved, had a fierce loyalty and love (though none would ever use that word) for the man who had given them back their lives. Every single one of them would have given their life for the blue-eyed Irishman. They had a ready audience in Jonathan and Seamus and the stories of his feats of piracy on the high seas would issue forth whenever the two were present with crew members off duty.

"Aye, lads," said one sailor, with arms like stout oak branches, after Cormac had gone below with Gael one day. "When those blue eyes turn gray, I pity the man he's staring at. Why, I'll never forget the time we were ambushed by a disguised cattle boat filled with armed men sent to destroy us. I was on the starboard side, looking straight up into the faces of a hundred screaming mercenaries…" And off he went, with only a bit of exaggeration for effect, recounting the disaster when Suleyman Reis was nearly killed. The two boys stared at him in rapt attention as other sailors gathered around and added graphic details.

6

"Tomorrow's the final day for shopping," said Cormac during supper. "We'll sail at first light the next morning."

"Well," said Fiona. "I don't think it would hurt to take a quick last turn through the streets with Jacques." The girls all nodded in agreement although they were well satisfied with their purchases.

"Cormac and I will join you of course," said Finn.

"I'll stay with Seamus and help him on the rigging," said Jonathan. "I heard he slipped a bit the other day." Indeed, trying to impress the watching sailors with his speed, the boy had put both hands on the horizontal lines of the rigging and they broke, pitching him forward against the webbing. A firm hand on the seat of his pants from the sailor climbing with him kept him from falling.

"That's why we always have hands on the vertical lines, feet on the horizontal," the man had said. "If the ship was rocking, you would have been thrown out into the wind."

"Yes, sir," the shaken boy had replied. He looked forward to one more day with Jonathan at his side before heading out to sea.

The next morning the family set out into the town, accompanied by the French sailor. By now they all knew the way to the best markets and Jacques was there only to translate their negotiations. As usual, when the women ducked into a store, Cormac and Finn sauntered about casually inspecting nearby goods, or sat on an available bench in the sun to discuss matters of the upcoming trip. Under wide hat brims, however, their eyes were constantly studying the busy street.

"The feeling of being watched is gone today," said Cormac.

"I noticed the same thing," said Finn. "Perhaps we've been deemed harmless and not worthy of spying on."

"Maybe," said the redhead, but somehow he didn't quite believe it.

It was mid-afternoon when they headed back to the ship. As they neared the quai on Rue de l'Eveche, heavily armed men suddenly sprang from the alleys and surrounded the family. Nearby shoppers scattered to seek refuge in stores and in seconds the O'Sheas were alone, circled by 25 murderous-looking ruffians. Cormac and Finn were quickly disarmed, Fiona and the girls grabbed roughly, their arms quickly tied behind them and a knife put to each throat.

A tall burly man, black beard covering his chest, strode up to Cormac and snatched off his hat to reveal flaming red hair.

"MacLir Reis, if I'm not mistaken," he growled with an exaggerated bow. "Captain Drucker at your service. How is it that you're *buying* plunder now, instead of stealing it from the rest of us at sea?" A chorus of angry voices rang out in agreement.

"And who might 'the rest of us' be. I don't recall stealing any treasure from you," said Cormac calmly, although his blue eyes had turned gray at the sight of knives pressed against the necks of the women he loved.

"After the renegade Dutchman was wounded and you took charge of his galley with that black henchman of yours, you stopped taking slaves, and concentrated on plunder. Every merchant captain knew that if they didn't resist no one would be hurt and no one taken. They simply hove to and gave up. You covered so much territory that the rest of us often attacked ships that had already been robbed by you," spat the man. "You took all the rich targets and forced me and others to raid along the coastlines, where there's little profit and the constant threat of patrolling warships."

"Dumaka and I were galley slaves owned by the Reis, subject to the will of our master." said Cormac, "I have the scars on my back to prove it. Last summer we fought our way to freedom and left the world of piracy."

"And you just walked on to that fine ship tied yonder to the quai and sailed away?" sneered the captain. "However you managed it, I think the vessel will be fine compensation for the losses you caused us."

"There's a crew of ex-slaves on board who risked their lives for that ship," the Irishman said. "They'll not take kindly to being ordered off."

"Oh, I think they will," said Drucker with a crooked smile. "When they see me cut the throats of these lovely ladies…one by one."

7

"Shall we walk on down to the quai to your ship?" asked the pirate, gesturing with his arm toward the harbor in a gracious manner. He led the way, with the brothers and Jacques close behind, followed by the women, from whom knives had been withdrawn for the moment.

Bran gradually moved over until she was walking beside Tiziri.

"I'm not securely tied," she whispered in Arabic. "When possible, move behind me back-to-back and untie the knot."

A tiny bob of her head indicated the Tuareg girl's understanding.

People on the wharf took one look at the leader, well known as a pirate captain, and quickly hurried away. In minutes the whole dock was empty for 100 yards in either direction from Gael's gangplank. Sailors, including Jonathan and Seamus, crowded to the ship's railing to see what was going on. Angry voices sounded as they watched the women herded to one side: a little group surrounded by three sneering men.

"We've come for the ship," shouted Drucker when Gael appeared at the top of the gangplank.

"I've got 200 men up here," said the captain. "We've no quarrel with you."

"I don't care if you have 500 men on board," yelled the leader. "You're going to turn the ship over to me."

"Gael," Cormac started to say, but a man behind him delivered a savage blow with the butt of a sword to the side of his head, dropping the redhead unconscious to the dock.

A roar went up from the sailors on deck and several started down the gangplank, but stopped when Abigail was dragged forward by one of the pirates who put a knife to her throat.

"Give up the ship or she dies," said the leader. "Her blood will be on your hands." He pulled out a large brass pendant watch from his vest. "Every minute you delay, I'll kill another one."

Abigail was being held just to the right of Drucker. The men on board were stunned to see her suddenly spit right in his face.

"That's for my man," she yelled, nodding at Cormac sprawled on the dock. "He's got more honor and courage than all of you combined!"

"Quiet," roared the captain, wiping his face with one sleeve and striking her in the face with a cruel backhand blow. "I've a mind to cut your throat myself."

Bran, standing off to the side with the others, shuddered with anger as Abigail slumped forward. Only the pirate's hold on her tied arms prevented her from falling to the dock. The man grabbed a handful of blond hair with his left hand and pulled her back upright, right hand holding the knife to her throat.

Tiziri was beside Bran, staring at her with a helpless look: one of the remaining two men guarding them was staring at the girls intently. There was no chance for them to get back to back.

All of a sudden there was a commotion at the top of the gangplank. A slender young man with black hair, loose cotton shirt, blue cotton pants and bare feet forced his way past Gael.

"NO. NO," he shouted. "That's my sister, you can't kill her. She's all I have!" He rubbed his eyes with both hands to wipe tears away and took two steps down the walkway.

"Stop," yelled Drucker. "Tell the Captain to give up and I won't kill your sister."

Everyone standing below was transfixed by the dramatic scene. Bran gave a quick glance at the pirate guarding them, but he hadn't allowed the disturbance to distract him. In spite of her desperate desire to get free, Bran's eyes were drawn back to the gangplank. Jonathan had taken two more stumbling steps down and was holding his hands out to the pirate captain in a piteous gesture, pleading for the girl's life.

"Please, please," he begged, "our parents were killed by the plague and she's all I've got in the world. She raised me herself when I was a baby." He staggered forward another two steps.

"Stop right there," ordered the pirate in a voice that brooked no argument. "It's your own captain that will cause the death of your sister. All he has to do is surrender the ship and everyone will go free."

As Bran stared at Jonathan, she suddenly felt the unmistakable touch of fingers on her wrists. She wondered how Tiziri had managed it, but when she glanced to the right Finn's wife was still beside her watching the gangplank. Nevertheless, the rope tying her wrists together was being loosened.

At Drucker's command, Jonathan turned to stare back up at Gael. The man made no move, staring stonily back.

"Oh, no," wailed Jonathan, turning and shuffling down three more steps towards the quai. "You've killed my sister!"

All at once he seemed to trip, his left hand going up in the air and the right one appearing to reach down to the gangplank for balance, but it never touched the wood. Instead, his hand flashed backward and forward faster than the eye could follow. The pirate holding Abigail gave a gurgle and fell to the ground, the leather-wrapped handle of a knife protruding from his throat. Almost simultaneously Drucker grunted and stared down at a knife handle dividing the beard covering his own throat. He slumped to the wharf. The man standing to Drucker's left turned to look at his captain and grunted softly as a third knife pierced his heart.

In the stunned silence that followed, Bran's hands were suddenly free. The two pirates guarding them stared at the foot of the gangplank, wondering what had happened. In an instant she flipped open the special flap on her cloak, freed bow and arrows and put a shaft through the chest of each man before they could react.

"Run!" she said in a low voice to Tiziri and Fiona. "Up the quai to people, I'll take care of Abigail."

The two raced away and Bran turned toward the remaining pirates. No more than 15 seconds had elapsed since Jonathan had thrown the first knife. All that the men around Drucker knew was that their leader and two others were down; it had happened so fast they really didn't comprehend the cause. Then more men started dropping, as a deadly hail of arrows erupted from Bran's bow.

Simultaneously, Jonathan, screaming like a banshee, charged down the gangplank and took a stance over Abigail, armed with the knife pulled from the neck of her would-be assassin. He was followed by Gael and a horde of sailors carrying chains, hatchets, and whatever else they could lay their hands on.

The captain went down on his knees beside Cormac and cradled his head; the rest of the men raced past and into Drucker's crew. It was over in five minutes. Not one of the pirates survived.

8

Blue eyes fluttered open. Close above him a beautiful face with a deep bruise on its left side stared at him with a worried expression. Beneath him he could feel the hard surface of the quai and then memory of the attack came to him. The redhead shut his eyes and lay quiet, mentally checking his body. Everything felt normal but his ears were ringing and the right side of his head throbbed angrily. A probing hand encountered stickiness in his thick hair and opening his eyes he saw his fingers red with blood.

"What happened?" he croaked.

"Jonathan saved us my love," said Abigail. "With knives. And Bran with her arrows."

"Aye, the boy's quite an actor," came Gael's deep voice and Cormac raised his eyes to see above him a ring of worried sailors' faces, among them Jonathan, Finn, Tiziri, Bran and Fiona. "Why, he had those barbarians believing that Abigail was his sister and that I was indifferent to them cutting her throat."

"I just needed to get a little closer," said Jonathan, "didn't have much margin for error since he was holding Abigail's head close to his face."

Cormac struggled to his feet, supported by Abigail under his right arm and Finn's strong grip on his left. A wave of dizziness came over him and he almost fell, but the girl stepped in close and put one arm around his waist, stretching his right arm across her shoulders.

"She'll hardly let any of us help," whispered his brother from the left. "Told Drucker you were 'her man' when they knocked you out and spit in his face. She got the bruise when he backhanded her for it."

They made their way slowly up the gangplank, men in front and behind ready to step in if Abigail faltered in any way. But she didn't and they reached the deck just as the last cart from the pauper's cemetery rolled away with the final pirate bodies.

On the deck Seamus' eyes went wide when he saw Cormac's dazed condition and the spreading bruise on Abigail's face up close.

"Are they going to be alright?" he asked Jonathan.

"He'll probably recover faster than she; that's a mean bruise. But there's more to the story."

"What?" said the younger boy.

"Well, you heard her call Cormac 'her man' but then she called him 'my love' when he woke up, though he probably won't remember that."

The two exchanged happy looks and went to join the men in the forward compartment.

Gael gave up his cabin and Cormac was tucked into the bunk by Abigail and Fiona. He went to sleep immediately. Abigail sat on a stool beside him, bathing his head with cool cloths when it appeared he was getting feverish.

After supper, with the sun still above the horizon on the warm spring evening, everyone gathered with the crew on the main deck to hear what had happened on Rue de l'Eveche and the march to the ship.

"I guess the reason I didn't feel that we were being spied on anymore was because we weren't," Finn said. "They had studied our patterns and knew we normally returned to the quai down Rue de l'Eveche. It was just a matter of setting the ambush."

"In a real sense, Drucker was right about us taking his business," said the captain. "During the last two years on the galley, when Cormac was acting as the Reis' lieutenant, we were enormously successful. Part of it was the fact that your brother didn't take slaves. After a few incidents, the merchant vessels simply came about and let our pirates board with no resistance. The whole process was much quicker than in the past, so we were able to raid more ships. No pirates wounded, no damage to the galley, and excellent food supplies kept all of us strong and fit.

"Suleyman prospered, Cormac was earning his freedom, and we were well fed. And how could we know that freedom was waiting for all of us when Bran became trapped in the harem?"

"Which brings me to another question, how did you get free to use your bow?" asked Finn.

"On the way down the quai, I whispered to Tiziri," Bran said. "I told her that the knot on my wrists was loose enough that I thought she could undo it if we stood back to back. Ever since I was a guardian slave to the Pasha's daughter I have worn a special cloak in public which has a quick release to access my bow and arrows. The quiver is designed to lie along my back, revealing nothing. I practiced with it for countless hours until it became second nature to flip it open and pull out the bow and arrows. Once, the disguise of the weapon saved the lives of the Pasha's First Wife and two daughters from a kidnap attempt."

"How did Tiziri untie the knot?" asked Seamus, returning to the subject at hand.

"She didn't, the guards were watching too closely," Bran said.

"Then you must have." said the boy.

"I didn't, Bran said. "I felt fingers on my wrist and thought Tiziri had somehow fooled the guards, but she was still standing beside me, not daring to move. All of a sudden my hands were free; I grabbed the bow and started shooting, right after Jonathan pulled off his great act."

Everyone stared at her in confusion.

"I was standing behind Bran and I saw the rope just fall off her wrists," said Fiona. "She told us to run and as I turned to go there was the smell of gardenias in the air."

9

AFTER A LONG PAUSE Finn finally turned to Jonathan, seated among the sailors. "It would seem you've been hiding something from us...let me take a look at one of those knives, how many do you have?"

"Just three," said the sailor, he reached behind him, under the loose shirt, pulled out a knife and handed it to Cormac. It was made of a single piece of steel eight inches long and a bit more than an inch wide. The blade was four inches long, razor sharp on both edges, tapering to a narrow point. The handle was squared steel wrapped tightly with leather.

Finn whistled softly. "That's not a working knife. You have two more, how do you carry them?"

Jonathan pulled a leather sheath off his belt and handed it to Amnay. It was specially designed to carry the three knives parallel to each other across the small of his back, tilted sideways in such a way that his hand could pull them out quickly for throwing.

Finn held the sheath and knives up for all to see. "Who designed this?" he asked."And why would a sailor have not one, but three knives like this? These men and I have been around enough weapons in the past years to know that these blades are designed for fighting."

"The design was created by my father, but the throwing didn't start precisely for fighting," said Jonathan. "When I was nine, he began showing me how to throw a knife. He said the coordination between hand and eye was the key to becoming a successful harpooner. "'Most men don't have it, or aren't interested in taking the time to develop it,' he said. 'Harpooning is dangerous because one has to get close to the whale; lancing is even more dangerous because the harpooner is very close to the whale and has to throw the lance with great accuracy.'"

"But you throw a lance overhand and it looked to me like you threw these knives underhand," said Gael.

"True, but in the beginning he taught me to throw overhand to train my arm to follow the direction of my eye. For two years I practiced for hours every day with a standard work knife and a small version of a lance. I threw at a heavy piece of wood my father set up on the inside of our garden wall. My mother had to warn me constantly not to step on the vegetables."

Fiona nodded in understanding.

"By the time I was eleven, I was hitting the target on the wood every time, with both lance and knife, from more than thirty paces," said Jonathan.

"Impressive," said Finn, who knew that a lance thrown from the back of a camel was usually released from a shorter distance.

"Then one day things changed," said Jonathan. "My father had returned home late in the night because some men attacked Captain Haversmith's ship at the dock. They saw extra barrels of oil on deck and thought to steal some for their own profit. They waited until most of the crew had gone home, except my father, the Captain, and a few others. There was a short battle. All my father said was, 'those men will never bother anyone again.'"

"The next morning we went to the garden and I threw the lance and knife for him. 'Well done,' he said, 'but now it's time to learn something new.' With that, he suddenly reached back under his shirt and threw not one but three knives underhand in succession so quickly I could barely see his hand move. All three hit the middle of the small circular target painted on the wood; separated by no more than a quarter of an inch from each other."

There was not a sound on the deck.

"And you can do this?" asked Finn.

"Yes, now I can. My father explained that the docks can be rough," said the sailor. "He told me that men often look to steal, kidnap for ransom, or even kill others if they think there's profit in it. 'I want you to know how to defend yourself,' he said. He had knives made for me like the ones he carried. It took two more years of daily practice to perfect the throws, but the last time he was home, I was able to match his skill. After the accident that killed my father, Captain Haversmith put his knives away, meaning to find me and pass them on when I grew up. I saved him the trouble when I stowed away, but both my father's weapons and mine were lost in the shipwreck.

"While I was recovering in Baltimore, I checked in with old Conner down at the dock and found out he had a forge. I started helping him with it whenever I could and in return he made these knives and a lance head for me. Rogan made the sheath to my specifications. After that it was just a matter of practicing on Bran's targets until I had the feel of the new sheath and blades."

"We know what you did at the gangplank, but can you do it again?" said Gael, trying hard to grasp the accuracy of hitting a very small target with knives thrown so rapidly.

Jonathan asked for a hatch cover and paint. He dabbed tiny circles on the left, middle and right of the cover. Asking everyone to move to the sides of the deck, he placed the cover against the main mast and walked away 30 feet, his back to the target. Replacing the sheath on the belt against his back, he tucked his shirt over the top of it.

"Middle, right, and left, in that order" he said before whirling around in a slight crouch and throwing the knives so fast that the men watching his hand saw only a blur.

Those men focusing on the target saw the blades hit middle, right, and left just as he had called it. When they approached the hatch cover, the astounded sailors observed that the knives were buried dead center in each of the circles.

"If I hadn't seen it, I'd never have believed it," said Gael in an awestruck voice.

North Africa

1

"SMOKE ON THE BEACH!"

The cry came from the crows nest, 90 feet atop the main mast, as the ship approached within a mile of a large natural harbor almost entirely surrounded by grassy hills. Seamus' voice was changing and there was a bit of a crack as he shouted out the sighting.

"Aye," said Finn, standing with Cormac beside the helmsman, "My message from England got through."

"I see figures on the sand," called the boy a few minutes later.

"I wonder how many men Jugurtha brought," said the blond, "probably enough for ample protection on the way home."

"But they're all covered up," came the boy's cry a few minutes later.

Finn grinned at his brother and the helmsman.

"What do you mean 'all covered up?'" he shouted up to Seamus.

"They have long blue robes, their heads are covered with black things, and they have masks over their faces," called Seamus. "I can't see what they look like. Maybe they're enemies."

"No, they're our friends. Come on down here and I'll explain."

Sailors on the deck nodded in approval as the youth came down the rigging with the agility of a monkey. When he reached Finn, the blond explained that Tuareg men wore indigo blue robes and that the 'black things' were turbans.

"And those are not masks," he said. "They're veils. The men are superstitious about demons and always have their faces covered for protection. That's why you can't see what they look like, although you'll find that married women go without veils, just like Tiziri."

While they were talking, Gael had maneuvered the ship through a large gap between two fingers of land that protected the harbor from the open ocean and was preparing to drop anchor 200 yards from shore.

"If people are waving, I suspect we should get Tiziri over there straight away," said the blond, who had gone below and re-emerged clad in the blue robe and turban of a Tuareg warrior, but without the veil. "She hasn't seen her father for almost a year. I'll row the dory in with her and the ladies if you'll get the block and tackle ready for the horses."

Cormac nodded. "You take the family, Gael and I will be ready when you return."

Minutes later Finn was sending the dory swiftly toward the beach, where a group of blue-clad figures stood waiting. The boat hadn't even touched sand when Tiziri leaped from the bow, hiked her robe up and rushed through the shallow water.

"Father!" she called. "And Mother," as a black robed woman stepped forward. In a minute all three were embracing, casting the usual Tuareg formality to the wind.

Two veiled warriors grabbed the bow of the little boat and helped Fiona, Bran, and Abigail out, then one clasped Finn's right forearm in greeting.

"We wondered whether Jugurtha's son-in-law had reverted to Irish ways," said Gwasila, noting the robe and turban, a twinkle in his eye.

"When in Ireland, I can be Irish. When in Africa, I am Tuareg," said Finn. "Were we not willing to die together fighting the Pasha's men?"

"We were indeed close to death," said Tariq, extending his arm in greeting. "Your brother arrived just in time."

Suddenly two more black robed figures erupted from a nearby tent with cries of delight. "Trinitran and Tamenzut insisted on surprising their sister by coming with us," Gwasila explained.

"And I presume that Trinitran is now your wife?" asked Finn, noting the absence of veils on both of the young women.

"Yes, we were married not long after you sailed," said the warrior. "We celebrated our marriage along with Tariq and Tamenzut."

"Ahhh," said Finn, "the three of us are now family, like brothers. It's a good thing we didn't die in battle."

"A very good thing," said Jugurtha, striding forward with a right arm held out. He followed the formal greeting with an embrace. "I now have three sons to take care of me in my old age!"

"Hah," said the blond, stepping back to smile into the eyes behind the veil, clearly crinkled with a grin, "It's said that desert fighters never get old and I have brought you a new sword to prove it. As well as three excellent horses," he added.

Jugurtha's eyes gleamed. "When I got the message to meet you back here, I was hoping it was because you didn't want the Pasha or the Reis to know what you were bringing."

"Wait until you see them," said Finn. "I think you'll be pleased."

He went over to where the seven women were gathered, just in time to hear Tiziri say in English, "Mother, I want you to meet Fiona, Amnay's mother."

What happened next caused Finn's jaw to drop.

Kella said, "I am pleased to meet you," in clear English.

As he stood staring in shocked silence at his mother-in-law, a voice sounded from behind him.

"Remember, my son, she grew up in the Pasha's court. There were many English visitors," said Jugurtha, "and her father wanted his children to be gracious hosts."

"But, but, I never heard a word of English in all my years with you," stammered Finn.

"That's because you speak perfect Arabic," said the Tuareg in English. "However, in spite of you scaring us with the old Jamal at your wedding, we were both highly amused by your words to him. Something about not stampeding over the bride's parents on your wedding day?"

When the stunned Amnay spun around to stare at the Tuareg, he could clearly see the man's shoulders shaking under the robe.

"I ought to charge you twice for the horses!" was all he could say before grabbing the older man in a bear hug.

The language among the women had lapsed into rapidfire Arabic, with Bran and Abigail alternatively acting as interpreters. Tiziri was describing life at Baltimore with the O'Sheas and how Finn's mother had welcomed her and Abigail as her own children. Kella nodded and smiled.

"I've never had a sister," she said in English, "perhaps I've just found one." Whereupon Fiona walked to her and they embraced.

"I have only one sister," said Fiona, "and I need another."

Kella's eyes glistened with tears and her daughters beamed when Tiziri translated for them.

"I have some merchandise for my father-in-law," said Finn, tearing himself away from the happy gathering and turning back toward the water, "but it requires a little swim."

"When he came to the oasis, he would sit or swim for hours in the lake," said Kella, lapsing into Arabic and not comprehending what was going to happen. "After years of caravan slavery, he could never get enough of the water and I think the love of it will always be with him."

They watched as Finn rowed to the ship, turned his robe and the dory over to a sailor, jumped into the water and swam a little way off to the side. A large boom, with a horse suspended from it in a wide belly strap, swung slowly out over the water and a horse was gently lowered into the harbor. Finn loosed the strap, grabbed a handful of mane and began swimming with the animal to the beach.

"I had no idea that's what he meant," said Kella, hand to mouth, transfixed by the scene.

A striking gray mare, with black stockinged legs, lunged up on the sand. The Tuaregs stared in delight.

"She's beautiful," breathed Kella. Jugurtha nodded in agreement, unable to take his eyes off the horse. After parading the Lusitano before the entire group on the beach with only one hand on her neck, Amnay gave her an affectionate pat on the rump and the horse headed for the nearby grass.

"She'll join the camels on the hillside," he said as he turned back to the waiting dory. "She's been on board for a long time and will relish the grazing."

The operation was repeated and another beautiful mare emerged from the water. Jugurtha's eyes gleamed. These were magnificent animals. When the black appeared, he caught his breath. Here was a horse that he immediately knew would be fast indeed.

"Have you seen them run?" he asked Finn as they lounged on the sand around a crackling fire that night after he paid the brothers handsomely for the animals.

"Not in a race, but I've ridden all three and the two mares will be hard to beat. The stallion, however... his speed will allow you to plunder your brother-in-law and all his rich friends in Tunis *without* risking your life."

2

THE NEXT FEW DAYS WERE SPENT in leisurely fashion on the beach as Finn let the horses get 'land legs' back after the long ocean trip. Extra tents were set up for the O'Sheas, but most of them and the sailors preferred sleeping in the open under the brilliant desert sky. As he had done the previous summer, Jugurtha procured goats and sheep from a nearby village and each night the air was filled with delicious smells from a score of cooking fires spread along the sand.

Gael rotated a skeleton crew on the ship and the ex-slaves mingled easily with the Tuareg warriors. The entire crew spoke Arabic because of their years on the galley, so stories of the harem battle, Tuareg legends, and pirate ventures filled the air day and night. There was an affinity among all these men because the desert warriors knew many Tuareg raiders who had been captured and enslaved just like the Europeans.

The story of the attack in Marseille was told over and over, with Jonathan called on repeatedly to demonstrate his throwing skills on a plank brought in from the ship. Without fail, eyes widened and sharp intakes of breath sounded from behind veils as he unerringly hurled the blades into the smallest of targets. When the desert men heard that he was also a harpooner, lances were produced and he showed them his accuracy. This was unusual for Tuareg warriors who rarely threw a lance, preferring to thrust it into the enemy from a running camel so they wouldn't lose the weapon. When the harpooner produced the Toledo steel lance head, they promised to fit it with a shaft for him.

Seamus was fascinated by the camels. Once he realized they wouldn't hurt him, he loved to wander through the herd, often accompanied by Finn.

"This one is a 'naga' or female," the blond would explain. "And that's her wahr, or young one. They brought the juvenile to expose it to desert travel. It won't get too far from its mother. That really big one over there is a 'jamal' or male. A huge jamal saved my life when I escaped from the caravan and fled across the desert with me."

"Why do they growl?" the boy asked.

"That's not growling," said Finn, "they're talking to you. If you go up to them and rub their cheek or neck and talk back to them, in time they'll want to lean against you and follow you around."

The youth had observed that the camels did exactly that to the blond whenever he was among them.

"They know me from my years with them at the oasis," explained Finn. "Some of them were born while I was there and followed me around like children. They recognize my voice and smell."

Seamus noticed that Finn continuously talked to the camels when he was with them and as the days went by they began to associate the boy with Amnay and approach him as well. At first it was a bit intimidating to be surrounded by a dozen or more of the big animals thrusting their heads forward for attention, but he got used to it and started talking to them himself and rubbing their necks. To his amazement, when Finn wasn't there the camels began walking up to him for attention.

Finally the time came for the group to separate. Finn and Tiziri were taking the horses to the oasis with the Tuaregs. Seamus, wildly excited about the chance to ride a camel for several days, had begged to go along. After developing a deep friendship with Kella, and taking daily riding lessons from Finn, Fiona was accompanying them as well. The others were going back on the ship to deliver merchandise to Suleyman Reis in Tunis before journeying across the sands to the oasis.

Bran was looking forward to seeing Pinar, Kelebeck, and the First Wife. Abigail knew all of them as well, but her primary objective was to be near Cormac as much of the time as possible. When the redhead had recovered from the blow to his head, he had approached her one day as she stood with the other women watching dolphins playing in the bow wave. Ahead of them, the blue-green Mediterranean stretched away to the horizon.

"I don't remember anything after I was clubbed on the quai," he'd remarked, "But the men say you spit right in Drucker's face."

"Yes," she'd said, fingering the purple bruise still showing on her face, "It was such a cowardly thing for them to do to you, I couldn't help it."

"They also say that you had some words for him."

"I might have, I don't rightly remember, I was really angry." But deep red had flooded her face.

"Something about 'your man?'" he prompted.

Abigail had turned toward him with a defiant look, prepared to explain her outburst as mere rage, but what she saw in the deep blue eyes filled her with joy.

"I did call you 'my man,' but I had no right," she said softly. "We've never actually discussed anything about that."

"I should probably tell you that I wasn't actually asleep while you were bathing my head in Gael's cabin. You called me 'my love,'" he said, seeing her blush again at being discovered. "Perhaps it's time we do discuss these things...or maybe no discussion is needed..."

He caught her to him and they stood for a long while looking out at the ocean, her blond head against his shoulder, oblivious to the fact that the rest of the family had long since vacated the bow and that every nearby sailor was going about his business with a happy look on his face.

3

S AND-COVERED REEFS EXTENDED OUT in great half circles to enclose the vast harbor at Tunis, broken only by an opening roughly 200 yards wide through which ships could enter. As their vessel moved into the harbor, the O'Sheas stared somberly at the white city gleaming across the water in the afternoon sun.

"It's a much different feeling now than when we arrived here seven years ago," Cormac remarked to Abigail, Bran, and Jonathan standing beside him on the afterdeck.

"I was so scared," said his sister, "even though you and Finn were holding my hands and promising that we wouldn't be separated."

"I was still in shock over the death of my parents when I arrived. I really didn't care what they did," Abigail said. "Everything was a blur."

"Look at the men," said Cormac. Every sailor was either lining the railings or in the rigging, staring at the city. "All of them were brought here and put to work under brutal circumstances as galley slaves. They never left the benches, were fed starvation rations, and were expected to drive the boat at breakneck speeds. That combination was a death sentence. The crew entered this harbor countless times aboard the galley, broken with despair and often hanging on to life by a thread."

"Until this man arrived from the quarry and joined us," said Gael, from where he stood beside the helmsman. "He taught us the meaning of honor, in spite of our situation. He rescued our spirits while our bodies were still enslaved. As a result, in our final two years as thralls, we were well fed, strong, appreciated, and valued by the pirates we served."

"Appreciated and valued?" said Jonathan, struggling to understand.

"Yes. Your foster brother here, if I may call him that, saved the life of Suleyman Reis twice when he could easily have let him die; once in a terrible storm and once in battle.

"As a result, the Reis, and finally the pirates themselves, began to reward us with acts of kindness, including supplying us with quantities of good food and even clothing. Cormac was taken off the oars and made drummer. He taught us rowing cadences that made our galley second to none in the Mediterranean. When the Reis lost the use of his left arm, he elevated Cormac to second in command, in charge of galley tactics: from the oar to slave lieutenant, unheard of in pirate history.

"For the last two years, as you know, under Cormac's guidance we took no slaves and concentrated on plunder only. The Reis and his pirates prospered beyond their wildest expectations. When the time came and Cormac needed our help to rescue Bran, we were fit and strong; we would have followed him anywhere.

"You know the blue headbands that Fiona made for every man on the ship while we were crossing the Mediterranean? They match the headband he has always worn, even when it was but a scrap of cloth in the quarry. While we are in Tunis, the men will wear them ashore and everyone will know they are crew to MacLir Reis."

The two women and Jonathan stared at Gael. Even Bran and Abigail hadn't heard some of these details.

"Where did "Maclir" come from?" asked Bran.

"Just a name I chose," Cormac replied.

"MacLir Reis?" said the harpooner. "What is a Reis?"

"In the Ottoman Empire, the name is a rank, like 'Captain.'" said Gael.

"You mean Cormac is considered a pirate captain?" asked Jonathan.

"Not just a 'Captain,'" said Gael, "but one of the most respected pirate captains in all the Mediterranean. You see the flag we hoisted atop the mainmast this morning? Fiona also made that after I had a word with her."

"I was wondering about it," Jonathan said. "It has a blue circle beside links of a chain."

"It represents the headband he always wears," said Abigail, looking up. "But I'm not sure about the links..."

"That's easy," said the captain, "they represent Dumaka's deadly chains. Every pirate and sailor in Tunis, and throughout the Mediterranean, will know who owns this ship."

Jonathan started to ask who Dumaka was, but Gael had turned back to the helmsman to direct their approach to the vast wharf. Stretching far out into the harbor from the city walls, it was framed by a forest of masts rising from ships tied to it. Noting the many vessels anchored in the harbor, the sailor realized that Tunis was indeed a large commercial center.

"A famous pirate captain," murmured Abigail, staring up at Cormac with wide eyes. "Why, who would have ever known?"

This time it was the Irishman who blushed red.

"I still can't imagine what it was like to be so helpless," said Jonathan. "The city and harbor are beautiful, it just doesn't seem to match."

"The beauty is lost when you belong to others and your life could be forfeit at any minute," said Cormac, glad for the chance to change the subject. "When we were separated at the slave market, I told Bran and Finn that I would find them and we'd all escape, but I had no idea what I was saying. It was an impossible promise."

"But it happened," said the harpooner softly.

"Aye," said the redhead, his arm tight around the English girl and a distant look in his eye, "and I'm still trying to figure out why."

As the crew pulled the vessel against the wharf with great hausers, Jonathan moved to the port side, drawn by a cacophony of sight and sound. He had been in many ports during his years on the whaling ship but nothing came close to matching this.

The right side of the long stone dock was deep enough to accommodate ships, but the left side was too shallow. Consequently, along the left of the wide wharf, stretching all the way to the beach, was a solid line of small tents with awnings, each with different colors. This riot of hues was accompanied by a mass of humanity moving back and forth in front of the tents, emitting a deafening babble that drowned everything out.

As he watched, the sailor realized that each tent belonged to a merchant whose items for sale were displayed under the awning. The multitudes surging back and forth were shoppers: that whole side of the wharf was actually a gigantic market. Most large city docks have vendors nearby to attract people to their wares, but the sheer size of this market was compounded by a different style of shopping than in Europe.

Here, business was conducted at the top of one's voice and everyone seemed to be trying to outshout everyone else. Even though he didn't understand Arabic, the harpooner could see the merchants yelling almost non-stop and waving products in their hands at the people passing by. The customers, in turn, appeared to be negotiating in equally high volume, resulting in a din that was overpowering.

Countless seagulls were diving and swooping overhead. Jonathan was well familiar with these birds and knew they would pounce in on the smallest amount of food left unprotected even for an instant. He was certain the gulls would steal every scrap, because the food merchants were so tied up with haggling, until he noticed many small boys carrying long sticks, with palm leaves attached to one end, ducking and dodging among the crowds. Whenever a gull swooped in, a palm leaf on a stick would miraculously appear to drive it off.

On the right side of the wharf, thin, near-naked men in long lines were carrying goods either toward the city or toward the ships. The harpooner went pale when he realized that they were slaves, even before he saw overseers with whips. Every so often one of the whips would snake out and slash the back or legs of a slave, leaving a bloody mark. The man would struggle to remain upright and trudge on. The stark reality of what Cormac, Finn, and every sailor on the ship had endured was burned into Jonathan's mind.

4

Cormac explained that he needed to find a runner to let the Reis know they'd arrived. He descended the gangplank and started moving toward the shore, only to be stopped by a group of armed men who surrounded him to exchange greetings and hugs.

"Pirates," said Gael, as more men appeared from the crowds, "they're probably thinking he's come back to command the Reis' galley. Those who sailed with him were well rewarded."

Jonathan and the two girls could see that these were rough, hard men, but their affection for the redhead was evident. When a group of them came up the gangplank to greet Gael and the sailors, the three realized there was no exaggeration to what the captain had told them about the pirates' genuine appreciation for what Cormac and the oarsmen had done for them. Finally the men approached a startled Bran.

"Is it possible that you were the archer at the harem fight last year?" asked one with long black hair tied in a ponytail. "We heard that all the Tuareg fighters would have been killed, except for your arrows coming through the viewing port in the door. But you are so small and...ladylike!"

"My other brother and those men had their backs to the door," she said. "The eunuch guards wouldn't let me out, so I had to use the viewing port. One of the guards smashed out the grate, so I had room to shoot. I suppose it's not the size of the archer, but her accuracy that matters."

"The report is that you don't miss," said another who looked to be Jonathan's age.

"Not when my brother's life is at stake," she replied.

"We've heard of this other brother as well," said a tall pirate with a scar on his cheek. "They say he escaped from the caravans and made an impossible trip across the desert until he reached a Tuareg camp, where he was freed and became a great warrior. The story is that he killed many men in the harem fight."

"It's true," said Bran.

"Is it also true that you saved the First Wife and her daughters with your bow several years ago?" asked the first man. "Shooting four horsemen bent on kidnapping them within in a few seconds?"

"I was the guardian slave to Pinar, the Pasha's oldest daughter," Bran said, "and I was trained for years by Bako, one of the harem eunuchs who is a great archer. He would have had them down sooner."

There was silence for a moment as the pirates studied this diminutive girl with green eyes whose exploits were fast becoming legends.

"We salute you," said the first pirate at last. "Any of us would be proud to fight alongside you and your brothers."

To Bran's utter astonishment, the whole group bowed to her.

Jonathan, for whom Abigail had been translating in a whisper, watched in amazement as these hardened men trooped back to the wharf and disappeared into the crowds.

"The O'Sheas are famous here," he said, staring at Bran with unabashed admiration.

"Fighting men are valued in this society," said Gael, who had overheard the entire conversation. "For them to acknowledge a woman as a warrior was a compliment of the highest order. There is no greater honor they could have given her."

"To think that the ragged little girl from the garden crew that I trained to be a personal slave would come to be held in such regard by those men is overwhelming," said Abigail, giving her protege a big hug.

"Oh, that I could be worthy of such an embrace," said Cormac, who appeared at the top of the gangplank.

"Not this day," said Abigail with a laugh. "This day, your sister garners all the esteem. We wouldn't be surprised to see **her** in command of a pirate ship leaving the harbor."

When the tribute was described to the redhead, he nodded gravely. "Those men are no fools. Although we were long gone by the time they woke up the morning after the fight, they would have heard from the surviving soldiers what happened. One doesn't defeat the Pasha's forces, kill his most vicious henchman, take some of his finest horses, his daughter's personal slave, and the First Wife's personal slave, plus the harem's entire enslaved kitchen staff, without word getting around."

"You did all that?" exclaimed Jonathan with wide eyes.

"We did all that," said Cormac, sweeping an arm around to include his captain and crew. "Plus Jugurtha and his men, most of whom wouldn't have survived without Bran's arrows."

5

"I THINK THE REIS IS COMING," said a sailor about an hour later. He had found Cormac and the others on the starboard side of the poop deck, watching small sailboats and dorys ferry people to and from ships anchored in the harbor.

"Let's walk up the wharf to meet him," said the redhead, turning toward the gangplank. "The crowds are very large today and we're docked far out from the city."

"No need, he'll be alongside immediately," said the sailor.

Sure enough, when they reached the top of the ramp, they observed everyone on the right side of the wharf moving aside to open a wide lane through the crowds. Two men clad in gold shirts and loose black knee-length pants trotted along at the head of the opening.

"Make way, make way," they shouted over and over in deep voices, "make way for Suleyman Reis."

Behind them, on a magnificent gray Arabian stallion, rode a man dressed in a white silk shirt, purple silk pants tucked into high leather boots, black turban, and a long purple cape. His beard was black and his face as brown as any Arab, but if one looked closely, one would see that his eyes were gray. His immoble left arm was held securely at his waist by a black sash.

Behind him, on a striking white Arabian mare, rode a young man with sandy hair. He was dressed like the Reis in a white silk shirt and short purple pants; below bare lower legs his feet were clad in gold slippers. When they reached the ship, he jumped from the horse and handed his reins to one of the gold-shirted heralds. Hurrying forward, he took the reins of the stallion while the Reis dismounted. Giving the reins to the second herald, he followed the pirate captain to the bottom of the gangplank where Cormac, Bran, Abigail, and Jonathan waited.

Cormac stepped forward and gripped the Reis' forearm with his right hand.

"I trust you got the messages I sent from Europe," he said in Arabic. "The first, that the three of us decided to accept the offer of joining you in a venture. The second, that we proposed supplying fine merchandise from Europe for you to market in Tunis. Third, that we had filled the ship with goods in Marseille and were sailing for North Africa."

"I got all three messages, but before we go into that," the Reis growled in English, although Bran thought she detected a twinkle in his eyes. "I'm still angry about what you did to me."

"Oh?" said the redhead with feigned innocence. He had become almost like a son to this man after being given charge of the galley. He knew the Dutchman extremely well and wasn't fooled by the gruff remark.

"First, you absconded with the greatest group of galley oarsmen Tunis has ever seen. Then you commandeered one of my finest ocean-going ship, on which my eye detects some changes, by the way. If those two betrayals weren't enough, my profits have plummeted since you happily sailed off to Ireland. I ought to clap you and your sailors in shackles and put you back to work!"

Listening to the harsh tone, Jonathan's hand crept to his knife handles. He wasn't about to let this man make good on the threat. But Cormac wasn't through.

"My family and I almost lost our lives in Marseille because of the reputation we built for you throughout the Mediterranean. I was recognized by a pirate and they attacked us. Only through the deadly skills of the young man behind me and those of my sister, about which you already know, was the ship saved along with our lives and all of those on board, not to mention our highly valuable cargo!"

The redhead continued, "Over the months I've had time to calculate the exact amount of my percent of the plunder from those two years. The ship, the oarsmen, and the threat to our lives, comes to roughly 80% of my share. So, it's actually you who are indebted to me. If you don't have the gold on hand, we can make the adjustment through our business arrangement."

Silence dragged on as the two stared at each other. Gael, who had picked up most of the conversation from the top of the gangplank, turned his head and Bran didn't dare raise her eyes from the surface of the wharf. Abigail and Jonathan simply didn't know what to think.

"If you'd only asked, I'd have given you a second ship to take home, but you were in too much of a hurry to get away," said the Reis with a hearty laugh, finally stepping forward to put his good arm around Cormac's shoulders. "You'll just have to make do with what you took by leaving so quickly. Now, I'm a little older than when we raided your village and becoming weary of dangerous endeavors. Let's see how we can fare in respectable business.

"Francois will arrange for the goods to be moved to my warehouses. I've also directed him to make sure the ship and crew are supplied with the best food, just as we did in the galley days. You and your family are to be guests in my house; I promise the reception will be different than on your first visit."

"What just happened?" Jonathan whispered to Bran.

"You witnessed an exchange between the Reis and a man once considered such a troublemaker that he was condemned to death in the quarries," she murmured. "However, over time, by adhering to his honor Cormac became the greatest lieutenant, slave or free, the Reis has ever had. I would venture to say this is the beginning of a strong friendship and lucrative partnership!"

"Your own horse," said Cormac to Francoise, gripping his shoulder affectionately as they walked to the mare after the Reis had mounted the stallion.

"Things have changed even more since you left; I'll fill you in at the residence," replied the Frenchman, taking the reins from the herald and springing into the saddle. "In the meantime, I'll bring food and a crew to offload the goods."

With that, the little procession made its way back down the wharf with the two slaves in front clearing the way.

6

C ORMAC DIRECTED GAEL TO MOVE the ship out into the harbor after the merchandise was offloaded. He also arranged for three longboats to be available at all times to ferry sailors back and forth from the vessel and to take food out to it when Francois appeared.

"Be sure the men wear their headbands when in the city," he said, "it will avoid any possibility of trouble."

"Aye," said the captain. "But you are well known and word of your arrival will spread so fast there won't be any trouble."

"True, but take no chances," said the redhead.

The family's personal effects were assembled on deck for Francois to take back to the Reis' residence on the empty food wagon.

"We can ride with him on the wagon," said Cormac, "or walk through the city to the Reis' residence."

Bran and Abigail were interested to see how their European goods would compare with what local vendors were offering, and Jonathan was captivated by the raucous atmosphere, so they decided to walk.

As they made their way down the wharf, the cacophony of noise was astounding to the Englishman. Bran walked beside him to translate whenever he pointed out a confrontation that captured his eye.

"That man in the brown turban is shouting that the price of that fish the vendor is holding out is enough to buy three fish. The shopkeeper is yelling back that he should be charging twice the amount because they are so fresh," she explained as they paused to watch the dispute.

The turbaned man threw up his hands and started to walk away, pausing as the vendor shrieked something above all the noise.

"Now the seller is saying he'll chop another fish in half and include it in the price," she said.

The buyer waived both arms, and shook his head in the direction of the seller and turned to walk away. This time, the shopkeeper moved from behind the stall to the edge of the crowd and, holding up two fish, bellowed at the man as he started to disappear into the throng. The buyer stopped, then slowly turned around with hands on hips and stared at the shopkeeper.

"The fish monger just offered two fish for the price, saying his children would have to go hungry tonight," she said with a laugh. "See the buyer raise his hands and eyes to the sky as if he's been robbed? But notice that he's walking back, pulling some coins from his money bag. Both are satisfied with the transaction but each will complain that the other stole from him!"

"And it goes on everywhere," said Jonathan as his eye picked up similar situations at each tent along the wharf. He couldn't understand the language but the waving of hands, overacting, and visible disgust was plainly evident in both sellers and buyers.

"You're right," said Bran. "Bargaining is the way of life here. If the buyers don't feel they've taken advantage of the sellers they're not satisfied. Of course, the sellers accommodate the game by raising their prices accordingly," she added.

Jonathan noticed that shopkeepers with more than one customer had a decided advantage. If a buyer argued too hard, the vendor would simply shrug his or her shoulders and turn to another customer. This caused the first customer to raise both hands in the air and scream even louder.

"She's saying that she offered twice the price of what that small rug is worth," Bran translated as they watched a rug merchant turn away to another woman, "and that it's nothing more than an old rag from Europe, not really Persian."

When the rug dealer continued to ignore her, the woman pulled a sack from her robe and waved it in the air, shrieking at the top of her voice.

"She just increased the offer," said Bran, "but watch the seller offer it to the other buyer. See, the first woman shout and shake her purse in the air? She upped the offer again."

They watched as the rug merchant ever so slowly turned to the woman and gestured with his head at the carpet she was holding. The buyer screamed something and the merchant slowly nodded to her. Money and rug exchanged hands and the satisfied buyer disappeared into the crowd. Jonathan and Bran glimpsed the hint of a smile on the merchant's face before it was set in a serious expression as he turned back to the second customer.

Toward the end of the wharf they paused to watch a group of people descend the gangplank of a ship with cannon ports on its side. Armed men waited at the bottom of the ramp. Men and women, several carrying babies, slowly walked down, casting fearful looks. Bran felt sick as she watched them and remembered her own terror as clearly as if it was yesterday. Finn brushed hastily past Bran, striding to confront the slavers, but Cormac caught him by the arm and pulled him close. Reaching out gently with his other hand, he cupped Bran's cheek.

"Easy, brother, be still Bran, I know it is difficult, but this is not the time, nor do we have the numbers to make a difference here. Suleyman Reis was a slaver, but we have helped steer him on a new path, freeing many and gifting those on merchant ships that he might formerly have enslaved with continued freedom. We were saved through circumstances that we don't yet understand, but we can't stop this abhorrent practice today; we can only hope that these people receive the same guidance that we did." With his hand still on Finn's arm, he steered him down the wharf, but Bran could not tear her eyes away.

"Captives for the slave market," she said to Jonathan. "That's exactly how we looked when we arrived seven years ago."

"They don't look thin," said Jonathan, remembering the line of emaciated men he had seen earlier carrying loads down the dock.

"No, on the trip to Tunis the pirates feed the prisoners quite well. It means more money in the slave market if they're healthy," Bran said.

"Isn't there something we can do?" said the sailor, staring with horrified eyes as he began to understand the full extent of what was going to happen to these captives.

Suddenly a portly white-suited man in a straw hat emerged from the crowd and approached the captives. Wiping his face with a large linen handkerchief, he bowed and addressed the prisoners, who flocked around him with hopeful looks.

"Shrewsbury's still at it," said Bran dryly. "He's the English envoy assigned to Tunis. He greets every load of prisoners bound for the slave market and offers to try to get money from the King to free them. Little do they know that the Crown will advance no such funds and they are doomed to slavery. But it gives them false hope at the time of desperate need. We were no different," said she somberly. "I suppose he means well. I've heard he continues to beg for funds, although he knows his queries will go unanswered."

As the prisoners were herded down the dock they were passed by another long line of half naked men, many of whom looked like they couldn't possibly bear the weight of the loads on their shoulders. The contrast to the newly arrived prisoners was striking.

"Where are the newcomers going?" asked Jonathan.

"To the palace, where the Pasha will inspect them himself. He has the first choice of anyone the pirates bring in. He might pick one or two at the palace, but he doesn't want to offend the buccaneers, so his aides will bid later at the slave auction if others catch his eye. It's important for the pirates to make money so they will continue bringing human cargo to Tunis."

"When are the captives sold?" said the sailor.

"The auction is held on a large market street immediately after the trip to the palace," said Bran. "Buyers from every type of business will show up. At the market I was dragged away from Cormac and Finn and sold to a buyer for the Pasha's harem. Finn was sold to a caravan operator. When they grabbed me, Cormac tried to stop them and was badly beaten. After that no one would bid on a trouble maker so the Reis had to buy Cormac himself. He was sent to a quarry: actually a death sentence because no one survives the quarries."

7

L ED BY CORMAC, WHO WAS constantly greeted by robed Arabs and
pirates, the little group passed through massive wooden gates and
into the city.

"Everyone seems to know him," whispered Jonathan, as yet another
turbaned individual stopped the redhead and addressed him in Arabic.

"It's difficult to understand how a former slave could be held in
such high regard," Bran replied, "even I can hardly grasp it. But the two
years as right-hand-man to the Reis resulted in incredible prosperity for
the whole city. Suleyman's slave trade diminished, but the plundered
goods brought in and sold to the merchants vastly increased. Everyone
benefited and they all knew it was due to MacLir Reis and his pirat-
ing strategy. The fact is that Cormac's 5% share of the treasure vastly
exceeded the value of the ship we took."

"He's so gentle and fun loving with Abigail," murmured the sailor. "It's hard to imagine him as a fighting man."

"Don't be deceived," she whispered. "You know how strong he is. When those blue eyes turn gray in anger, he's more dangerous than any man in this city. I've only seen it once, and it was dark, but when he fought through the Pasha's soldiers to rescue us, he and Dumaka were like angels of death, one wielding a sword and the other whirling chains."

"Chains?" asked Jonathan.

"Eight foot lengths of iron chain in each hand," she said. "Dumaka's weapon of choice."

"In each hand?" he said incredulously. "That's impossible, chains like that are too heavy."

"Not for a man standing well over six feet tall, weighing at least 22 stone,* and strengthened by years of rowing," she said. "He was a great fighter from south of the desert who became like a brother to Cormac. Dumaka's uncle Bako is the archer who trained me."

The harpooner could only stare at her, trying to take it all in.

"And don't be fooled by Finn's slender build, he's a deadly swordsman," she added.

"Finn a swordsman?" The Englishman stared at her, "But, he's so easygoing and kind, like when he's with animals."

"True, but he was trained to fight by one of the great desert warriors: his father-in-law Jugurtha, whom you met on the beach. They were side by side at the harem door, holding off waves of attacking soldiers. The only thing that saved them from being completely overrun was the pile of bodies in front of them: men that had already fallen to their swords. If not for that barrier, and their swordsmanship, they would have been swarmed under."

"Plus a few arrows from behind the door," he said dryly, "I heard a wee bit about that earlier."

Bran dropped her eyes.

---

* One stone equals 14 lbs. 22 stone would be roughly 308 lbs.

"What was I going to do?" she said. "They'd come to rescue me. Just like you on the gangplank in Marseille. I had to do everything I could to help them."

8

A S THEY PROCEEDED INTO THE CITY, the haggling that took place
at the dock was repeated. On each side of the narrow streets were
colorful awnings over display tables in front of shops. Proprietors behind
or in front of the tables did their best to attract customers by shouting
that their goods were the very finest available in the city. If a passerby
stopped to look at merchandise, the merchant would begin waving his
or her arms over the assortment on the table and pointing to this or
that item with a questioning look. Once the customer indicated any
interest, a scenario similar to the one Jonathan had witnessed with the
fish vendor and the rug merchant would be repeated.

"It's actually a lot of fun if you have the right attitude," explained
Bran. "In the Arab world, a buyer can always determine what a fair
price is by bargaining. As I said, sellers raise their prices to allow the
buyer to beat them down and there's usually a price they won't go below.

When the buyer starts to walk away and the seller finally concedes, they have probably reached the proper price."

"But there's so much shouting and carrying on," said Jonathan.

"Behind all that is the satisfaction of playing a game. At the end, each side feels it has won."

"I don't know if I could do that," said the sailor.

"Oh, yes you can," said Bran with a laugh. "With a little training, you'll be a natural!"

As the little group continued through the crowded narrow streets they were assailed on all sides by an assortment of people in robes and turbans, often in bright hues. Occasionally someone, shouting to clear the way, would pass by leading a camel or donkey packed with bundles. Most of the buildings were two-stories high and whitewashed, contrasting sharply with the brilliant blue sky above. The general impression was that of a kaleidoscope of color accompanied by a constant thrum of voices.

All at once they emerged onto a much wider street on which all the shopping was confined to the right side. The middle of the thorofare was empty except for a long line of people facing a large crowd of Arab men on the left side. Spaced along the front of the line were men with swords: from all appearances, pirates.

As they watched, a robed and turbaned man with a black beard grabbed a teenage boy at one end of the line and marched him up to face the assemblage. The bearded man shouted a few words, some individuals came forward to feel the boy's arms and legs, and then hands were raised in the crowd as the bearded one shouted more words.

"What's going on?" asked the Englishman. Although he was certain that he already knew, he wanted the specifics of what was being said.

"It's the slave auction," Bran said through clenched teeth. "We were in that line seven years ago. It feels like yesterday."

All at once an Arab stepped from the crowd, handed coins to the auctioneer, grabbed the boy by the shoulder and marched him away.

"What will happen to him?" said the sailor.

"I don't know," said the girl. "It depends on what the buyer was looking for. He may have wanted someone to serve as a household slave, or to work in his stable or shop. I don't think he chose the boy for heavy labor, like the quarries or a galley, because he didn't look strong enough. The owner didn't appear to be a caravan operator; from what Finn has described, that boy wouldn't last a week in the desert. But slaves are used for everything you can imagine, even bookkeepers and scribes. There's no guessing where he'll wind up, let's hope it's not in a vicious situation."

While they watched, a girl in a pink dress was brought forward. Jonathan thought she looked about 10 years old. Only one hand was raised and the transaction was accomplished immediately. A small fat man with a pointed beard and an oily face stepped forward to pay the auctioneer. He was followed by a tall black man with graying hair who gently guided the crying youngster after the buyer.

"That's Fouad, buyer for the Pasha's harem," Bran said in a strained voice. "The very same man who bought me. The Pasha has first right at the palace to choose anyone for himself, but he buys almost every female at the auction to make sure the pirates have a good profit. Otherwise they will take the captives to Algiers or one of the other ports."

"What will happen to her?"

"If she's lucky, some day she'll become one of the Pasha's many wives and live a comfortable life until she becomes too old. With a little more luck, she'll end her days as a servant in a rich man's household."

"The black man appeared to be gentle with her," said Jonathan.

'Yes, that's Henry Blackstone, once a gunner in His Majesty's Navy, the same slave that led me away to the harem. He's a little stooped now and has some gray hair, but he probably saved my life."

"How did he do that?" Jonathan stared at her in astonishment.

"I was eight years old and absolutely terrified. My brothers were left behind at the auction and I had no idea what was going to happen to me. Henry spoke softly during the walk to the harem. 'Survive,' he said. 'Do what you're told and don't try to resist.' I never forgot it when I was treated so cruelly in the kitchen. If I had given in to my temper, it would have been tenfold worse. His advice kept me thinking up ways to outwit the overseers and finally led me to serve the Pasha's family, which ultimately led to freedom. I only regret that I never had the chance to thank Henry."

"You were treated badly in the kitchen?" said the harpooner.

"There were two women, sisters, who ruled the kitchen slaves," she said. "The thralls were either girls too young for wifely training, or women too old to become wives, but young enough for hard work. The sisters would beat us without mercy and for no reason. They weren't allowed to mark us, but years of practice had taught them how to hurt us without leaving evidence. Their methods ranged from standing us on the tips of our toes by grabbing a handful of hair, to throwing us into a cold, dark pool of water filled with garbage and leaving us there overnight. Those who resisted, which could have included me but for Henry's counsel, simply disappeared after screaming for hours in a locked room near the kitchen."

"They were killed?" Jonathan looked at her in disbelief.

"They were never seen again," she said grimly. "But I put an end to it before I left the harem last summer."

The sailor took one look at the smoldering rage in those green eyes and decided against asking any more questions.

9

GRADUALLY LEAVING THE CROWDED markets behind, the little group made its way up winding byways with ten-foot walls rising on either side, broken only by an occasional large wooden door. It grew quieter and quieter until their soft conversation and the sound of their footsteps on the street pavers were all that could be heard.

"This is a residential area," explained Cormac. "The higher we go on this hill, the more important the residents and the more luxurious the dwellings."

As they climbed, walls to either side prevented them from getting any perspective of height from the harbor. The brilliant blue sky overhead was the only indication that they were not in some sort of tunnel. Finally the redhead stopped in front of a large wood door in the wall to their right. He pounded on it twice with his fist and it was opened by a slave dressed in loose blue pants and shirt. He wore a white turban and looked European.

Walking through the door Jonathan didn't know what to expect, but the sight that met his eyes was astonishing. A large magnificent stone house, two stories high, faced them from across 30 yards of manicured lawns and gardens stretching wide to either side and criss-crossed with white stone walks. Across the second floor of the house, a series of glassed double doors opened onto individual stone balconies. Noting the position of the sun, the sailor guessed that the balconies faced the harbor.

"I'm not sure," said Bran when he asked her if he was right. "I've never been here before, but the Reis is wealthy enough to have one of the finest houses in Tunis. As a sailor, I've no doubt that he would like a view of the water."

They were interrupted by the figure of Francois hurrying toward them on the main walkway.

"I didn't expect you so soon," he said in Arabic, grasping Cormac's right forearm in greeting. "I was organizing wagons to transport the goods to a warehouse," he continued in accented English, after a glance at Jonathan.

"We strolled through the markets," said the redhead in English, "but we didn't take time to shop. That will wait for another day," he continued, winking at Abigail and Bran.

"I saw you at the wharf last year," said Francois with a little bow to Bran, "but it was dark, you had just been rescued, and I was concerned that you all escape safely. The darkness masked your beauty."

For perhaps the first time in her life, the Irish girl dropped her eyes from the direct stare of a man and blushed deeply. Abigail, who missed nothing, raised a hand to her mouth to cover her smile. Francois, with sandy colored hair and large brown eyes, was very handsome. He appeared to be a bit younger than Cormac and his English, with the slight accent, was captivating.

"I don't remember seeing you," the Frenchman said, turning toward Abigail. "Are you from Ireland?"

"No," she replied in Arabic. "I must have gone aboard while you were getting Tiziri and her sisters from hiding." She switched back to English for Jonathan's benefit, "I was a slave to the First Wife until your wonderful blue-eyed friend here and his men from the galley rescued us."

"I welcome you and Cormac's sister as honored guests to the residence of Suleyman Reis," he said, bowing again with a welcoming sweep of his arm. "MacLir Reis was locked up here twice as a thrall, but was a guest many times as the nearly free, 2nd in command of the Reis' galley." Francois noted that the redhead and blond were holding hands during the whole exchange, and reminded himself to ask his friend about it later.

As they followed Francois toward the house, Jonathan was aware of the soft sound of rippling water. Looking around, he saw that there were fountains scattered about which continually cascaded water down into tile channels cut through the lawns. Every so often the bottom of the channels were interrupted with a low obstruction of stones, causing the water to bubble and murmur as it passed over them. Birds sang from numerous flowering fruit trees and butterflies of all sizes and colors fluttered among the many flower beds artfully placed along the walks.

"There's nothing like this in England or Ireland," he whispered to Bran, "except perhaps at the King's palace."

"There's a vast desert surrounding the city," she said, "and desert people love water more than anything else in nature. The inside of the harem is the same; I worked for many months clipping grass and tending flowers."

"It's beautiful," he said, "and the smell of the blossoms is so fragrant."

"Yes it is," she said, "but when you're a slave working on your knees for endless days, it's harder to appreciate. Unless it took you out of the kitchen," she added wryly.

Entering the house, they turned to the right past a sweeping stairway and entered a large, high-ceilinged room with enormous windows looking out onto the gardens. Spectacular Persian rugs covered much of the granite floor, and comfortable furniture made from dark wood was arranged in convenient clusters. The walls were covered with tiles in soft hues of orange and red, creating a feeling of warmth despite the stone setting. A large floral tapestry, clearly Chinese, covered nearly all of one wall.

"The Reis is at the warehouse, ready to supervise the delivery of your goods," said Francois, "would you like me to show you to your rooms?"

"Not before I greet the cook," said Cormac. "She was an important part of the events that freed your guests."

"That she was," exclaimed the Frenchman, "and she's been asking for months about your return."

He led the way through a series of hallways, pausing to point down one darkened passage.

"Down there, on the left, is the empty storeroom where we kept your brother," he said to Bran. "First on his way to the quarry and later on his way to the galley."

"I'm sure the rats have never again seen the likes of the food Francois brought me," said the redhead. "But I ate so fast that all they got to do was run over my legs."

They entered a large room filled with the most delicious smells. There were several wood tables, a great stone hearth in one corner, and dried bundles of vegetables and herbs hanging from the ceiling beams. A stout older woman with gray hair was using a deep-bowled wooden spoon to sample something from the large pot on the hearth.

"That couldn't be the smell of Bread and Butter Pudding, could it?" asked Cormac.

The woman spun around.

"Oh laddie, you've come back!" she exclaimed in English, wiping a tear from her eye as she bustled across the kitchen to embrace him. "I wondered whether I'd ever see that red Irish hair again!" As she drew close, a few strands of reddish hair could be seen among the gray on her head.

"Someone has to keep up the tradition of fiery hair in the household, now that you only have a wee bit of it left," he laughed. "I've brought my sister and some friends to meet you."

"I heard she was coming and thought we should serve the pudding she never got to taste last year," the cook said, turning to the others. "Ahh, she's the one for certain! Black hair and green eyes."

She grabbed Bran and gave her a hug before stepping back to study the girl.

"I thought she was a bairn, but she's almost a woman!" exclaimed the cook.

"I'm about to be 17," said Bran, a bit defensively.

"And álainn*...that is to say, beautiful she is, don't you think Francois?" said Cook, noticing the direction of his stare.

This time it was the Frenchman who blushed deeply.

---

* Irish for beautiful

10

"THE MERCHANDISE YOU BROUGHT is excellent," said the Reis that night at supper, speaking English out of courtesy to Jonathan. They were all seated at a beautiful mahogany table beside large windows that looked out on the lovely gardens. "Some of the items have never been seen before in Tunis," he added. "We'll parcel them out slowly to the vendors to keep demand high."

"A great deal of credit for the purchasing goes to my sister and Abigail," said Cormac. "They have excellent taste for quality products from their years of service to the First Wife."

"I propose 35% of the sales proceeds for the three of you," said the Dutchman, plucking a fig from the platter before him.

"What do you think?" said the redhead, turning to Bran.

"50%," she said without hesitation.

"50%!" said the Reis, throwing up his arms. "Why, you were using my ship and my slaves to bring it here! 40% is more than fair."

"My ship and my men, bought and paid for with far less than you owed me for two years of dangerous work," replied the Irishman.

"Dangerous?" exclaimed the pirate in a harsh voice. "Hah, with that chain-swinging giant of yours, you never risked a hair on your head! I grudgingly concede 45%. That's my final offer."

Jonathan watched all this in awe. It appeared that Suleyman Reis was working himself into a rage, while Cormac remained calm as could be. Then he remembered Bran's explanation of how bartering worked in the marketplace. Glancing at her and Abigail, he thought he could detect the faintest twinkle in their eyes although their faces were fixed in serious expressions.

"Never risked a hair on either of our heads," Cormac corrected. "It was your ship and you were the captain. I was only a slave ordered to protect you."

"For 5% of the profits. And I would never have needed that help," roared the Reis," but for you jamming the ram into that cattle ship so the mercenaries could board us."

"The ramming was at your orders, of course, and the mercenaries almost killed you, but for the giant," countered the redhead. He turned toward Bran. "Thinking it over, and considering the portion of my 5% left in the Reis' treasury last summer, I think 55% is the right amount. What say you?"

"Absolutely," she replied instantly.

To Jonathan's complete surprise, the pirate leaned back in his chair and raised a cup of wine in salute.

"You know that I would have given you two ships in exchange if you would have joined me," he said with a laugh. "50% it is."

"I still think our share should be 55%." Bran couldn't resist the last word.

"Just like your brother," said the pirate, throwing both hands up. "It might have been four ships if all three of you had agreed to become pirates."

11

"GO TO THE HAREM AND TELL THE First Wife and my daughters that Hibah and Abraj are here," said the Pasha to a nearby slave.

"Hibah means 'gift' and is my Arabic name," Bran whispered to Jonathan, "Abraj is Abigail's name and it means 'beautiful eyes.'"

The Pasha of Tunis was seated at a long table covered with documents, surrounded by advisors. He had a closely cropped black beard and wide-set brown eyes which bespoke intelligence and command. A green turban with a large sparkling diamond pin on the front was matched by a green silk robe. The sailor estimated him to be in his 40's.

"Do you still carry a bow under your robe, Hibah?" he asked.

"Yes," she said with a nod of her head, shifting her shoulders slightly under the exquisite black garment trimmed in gold. She knew the Pasha's keen eyes would appreciate the elegant silk she had used to make the traditional outer covering, and wearing it to the palace had worked as an excellent marketing tool for the bolts they planned on selling.

"We'll never forget the demonstration you and Pinar put on with glasses along those windows," he said, gesturing toward a series of large windows facing the blue ocean. Many of the advisors murmured in agreement.

"It was our pleasure," she said. "Bako was a wonderful teacher."

"The First Wife was sorry to lose him at the harem," the Pasha said. He turned his eyes toward Cormac.

"You and Bako's nephew were like spirits of death coming toward us in the torchlight," he said. "It was a fearsome sight!"

"We were barely in time to rescue your brother-in-law from your own sword," said the redhead dryly.

"No, Pinar was responsible for that," corrected the Pasha, "she wasn't about to let me kill her uncle." He raised both hands and shrugged in a gesture of surrender. "The things our children do to save us from ourselves."

"One could speculate about all the training she and Hibah received from Bako, as you just mentioned," said Cormac. "Without it, you and your sister might never have been reconciled. Have you seen Kella lately?"

"Yes. She and Jugurtha brought two of their daughters and husbands to Tunis for a visit six weeks ago. We understand that my third niece was with your brother in Europe."

"Tiziri has had a taste of Ireland and France in the past year," said the redhead, "although she is happily at home in the desert right now with her parents. Was their stay in Tunis successful?"

"Quite," the Arab said with a smug expression. "Jugurtha brought a horse with him to race against my best animal. Even though he lured my beloved Stable Master back to the desert, we beat him handily."

"And received some payment in return?" asked Cormac innocently, although he already knew all about the race.

"Oh, yes. My brother-in-law was obliged to part with a large amount of gold," the Pasha said with great satisfaction.

Bran was softly translating this conversation to the sailor when they were interrupted by doors opening and three people entering the room. At the back was an extremely attractive woman in a purple silk robe. In front, leading the way at a run, was a girl about 12, dressed in scarlet silk. Behind her, trying but failing to maintain a walk was a young woman that could have been Bran's twin, except for brown skin and black eyes. She wore a striking yellow robe and Jonathan was transfixed at the sight of her.

"Hibah!" cried the younger girl and ran straight into Bran's arms. She was whirled around twice and set gently down before Bran stepped into the embrace of the other girl.

"Sister of my heart," said Pinar as they both burst into happy tears in spite of the men watching, "I never thought I'd ever see you again."

As they clung to one another, the First Wife turned to Abigail.

"Abraj, my daughters and I have missed you every day since you left. Your gentle manner and anticipation of our every need was irreplaceable."

"Thank you my lady," said Abigail. "I've found a wonderful new home in Ireland with the family of Hibah, MacLir Reis, and their brother Amnay."

"And perhaps more than a home," murmured the First Wife softly, noting how close Abraj stood to Cormac.

The Pasha suddenly stood up.

"We'll tend to all this business tomorrow," he said, dismissing the advisors with a sweep of his arm. When the room was clear, he turned to the others. "How about a cruise on the galley? I'll have lunch prepared and we can enjoy a celebration on the water."

Kelebek and Pinar loved the galley and he knew they would be delighted to have Bran to themselves all afternoon. He looked forward to discussing seagoing warfare with Cormac and the young sailor while he anticipated that the First Wife, who disliked boating, would want to take Abraj shopping.

And that's exactly how it happened.

12

Jonathan was dozing under his white cloak and hood, lulled by the heat of the sun and the rhythmic motion of his camel, when he heard Abigail's voice from the camel in front of him.

"There it is."

His eyes flew open. They were descending a long sand hill, which threw a great shadow from the lowering sun to their right. Below them was a scene of breathtaking beauty. A large blue lake covering several acres, bordered on the near side by extensive groves of palm trees, gave way to a vast area of grass edged by sand hills on the far side. A herd of camels and horses grazed peacefully in the open pasture, the black stallion and two Lusitanos clearly visible among them.

Scattered about under trees were the desert tents with which he had become familiar at the beach: a central peak tall enough to comfortably stand under, sloping gradually towards sides and back until it almost reached the ground. He had learned that the design was particularly effective against sand storms that frequently erupted across the desert.

"I think they've spotted us," said Jonathan as he picked out figures emerging from the trees to stand at the edge of the lake and stare in their direction.

The little caravan, guided by Gwasila, was three days out of Tunis. In addition to Cormac, Abigail, and Jonathan, three Tuareg warriors led five extra camels loaded with food and supplies. They had traveled no obvious route, seeming to proceed aimlessly through giant sand hills under the blazing sun each day, but by late afternoon each day they would arrive at a small oasis with water and a few trees. Skilled at deciphering direction from the position of sun and stars, the sailor knew they were generally headed west by southwest from the city, but he also realized that for periods of time Gwasila would travel toward other points of the compass.

"How does he do it?" Jonathan had asked Cormac. "We seem to be wandering around over and through these sand hills aimlessly, yet he always leads us to water for the night."

As for finding an oasis every night, Finn says that the Tuareg people have extraordinary knowledge of water sources in the trackless desert. Even if abandoned in the middle of nowhere, they would survive.

"He also told me that Jugurtha and Kella were hunted for years by her father's men," explained the redhead. "They had to stay far out in the desert at remote oases, prepared to move at a moment's notice if his lookouts reported patrols anywhere close. When her brother became Pasha, he was engaged in battles at sea and couldn't afford to have his soldiers constantly on patrol so they settled more permanently at this hitherto unknown sanctuary. Lemta had, and still has, an extensive network of informers throughout Tunis to provide reports of continuing patrol activity as well as news of rich caravans to her nephew. Spies were well rewarded with gold for accurate information."

The sailor pictured the spry old woman whom he had met during their stay in the city. Her front door opened off a narrow, dark alley well away from the hustle and bustle of the markets and her bright eyes and energetic manner were hidden in the guise of a shuffling old crone whenever she ventured into the city streets.

"Because of this arrangement, the Pasha's men never had a chance of surprising Jugurtha," said Cormac. "It also secured his position in the desert as one of the most successful caravan raiders of all time. The location of his camps has always been secret, with no direct route established to them."

"Wasn't the family reunited after the harem battle last year? Why would he bother to disguise his location now?" asked Jonathan.

"One can never be too careful," was the matter-of-fact reply.

By the time they entered the oasis, a group of people had assembled by the largest tent set along the lake's shoreline. Camels knelt at commands from their handlers and everyone slid to the ground. Trinitran ran forward to greet Gwasila, followed by her blue-robed and turbaned father, eyes crinkled at the edges behind his veil.

"Welcome to our home," he said, grasping Cormac's forearm and gesturing with his free hand at the surroundings. "It was into this very lake that Amnay stumbled with that troublesome jamal of his."

"Yours now, my father," said Finn, stepping forward to embrace his brother. "Don't forget that the jamal was my gift to you and Kella when Tiziri and I were married."

"If you can call him a gift," growled Jugurtha, "no one can get near that beast without risking attack." One couldn't be certain, but the sailor thought he saw a twinkle in the Tuareg's eyes with these words.

Cormac turned aside and coughed to hide his laugh. He and the others had heard all about the rogue camel that Finn had tamed and that later saved his life. The animal tolerated no human but the blond Irishmam, until he married Tiziri. After that the great jamal somehow knew that she was part of the family and extended his trust to her.

"How fare your new horses?" the redhead asked, to change the subject.

"Ahhh, now *those* are animals worth talking about," said the Tuareg leader. "The old Stable Master says there's not a horse in North Africa that can match the black. And the two mares are not far behind. I no longer need raids to acquire the Pasha's gold...the only danger with this plan is to take too much gold too soon and risk losing his desire to wager."

"Where's Bran?" asked Fiona suddenly.

She and Kella were standing together at the edge of the little crowd and Abigail, who had been softly translating for Jonathan, noted the obvious friendship between the two women. About the same height, both had black hair and wide-set eyes in beautiful faces, and there was something about the way they stood together that hinted at their bonding.

"She stayed in Tunis for an extra week," said the English girl. "She and Pinar have planned a variety of activities, including hunting rabbits in the hills from horseback and a trip to a small oasis outside of town with Pinar's friends. One of Lemta's spies will bring her here after that. However..."

"Yes?" said Fiona.

"Well, there may be another reason for her staying."

"And what would that be?" asked the Irish woman.

"I noticed that Francois secured permission from the Reis to escort the girls in the city each day, excepting into the harem, of course. As usual, the Pasha provided ample protection in the form of soldiers, and Bran herself was well armed, but she seemed to welcome the attention of the Frenchman. He is very handsome, you know."

The two older women turned to look at one another, eyebrows raised in speculation

At that moment, a smallish figure robed in blue, veiled, turbaned, and with a knife in his belt, approached Jonathan and held out his right arm.

"Welcome to the desert camp," he said in perfect Arabic.

Jonathan stared in confusion, not understanding the words until Abigail translated.

"Grasp his forearm in greeting," she instructed.

It was then that he noticed the figure's blue eyes, almost covered by the veil.

"Seamus," he cried and grasped the boy's arm in the Tuareg greeting. "How do you know Arabic?"

"I've been practicing for days with Finn's help," said the boy in English. "He's also taught me to ride a war camel and I'm learning to use a lance!"

"A lance?" asked the sailor.

"Well, so far it's a long stick, but when I'm ready they'll give me the real thing."

"How about your knife? Are you still practicing?"

"Every day," came the reply.

That night a million twinkling stars filled the sky as the two families sat outside around a large fire and shared their experiences since parting at the beach. Abigail described the welcome Cormac had received from everyone in Tunis. Jonathan, with her translating, explained the pirates' tribute to Bran. Finn and the Stable Master in turn talked about the training they were doing with the horses and about Seamus' natural riding ability on the camels.

"I would be progressing a lot faster if Amnay didn't keep running off to his tent all the time to check on his wife," grumbled the boy.

"What?" said Cormac with a concerned look toward the girl, "is something wrong with Tiziri?"

"Not really," said Finn, "But I worry nonetheless. It seems she's pregnant."

Cormac stared. Abigail gave what sounded like a little squeak and scrambled over to Finn's wife and hugged her.

Kella and Fiona tried to be matter of fact as they talked about it, but their joy was infectious. Kella spoke in English and Jonathan only needed translation when Trinitran or Tamenzut spoke. He learned that if it was a girl, she would be the most beautiful Tuareg child in the desert and if it was a boy, he'd grow into the greatest warrior in

North Africa. Fiona announced that she was going to be present for the birth, even if it meant not returning to Ireland for a year.

Later, drifting off to sleep with Cormac on one side and Seamus on the other, Jonathan reflected on the wonderous changes in his life that had surrounded him with a new family and friends since that fateful night on the whaling ship.

13

"WATCH THIS," MURMURED Seamus as he and Jonathan stopped. The menacing noise coming from the enormous camel a few yards in front of them sounded more like a lion than anything else. "No one in the camp dares get any closer to that animal than we are. Except him."

He pointed to Finn, who was walking up to the jamal, talking softly in English. It swung its great head gently toward him and gobbled the handful of figs he held out. As the Irishman stood beside it stroking its head and neck, the sailor swore to himself that the two were talking to each other. Finn would speak a few words, then great rumbling noises would come from the camel as though in reply.

"It was exactly the same when we arrived," said the boy. "The first thing Finn did was to walk right into the herd to find his old jamal. All the camels clustered around him, even though he's been gone for almost a year. He kept talking to them and made his way to this beast. At the sound of his voice, it actually ran up to him, scattering the other camels, and gently bumped him with its head. Then the conversation between them started, just like it is now."

"How can that be?" asked Jonathan.

"I don't understand it all, but Kella explained that a few of the caravan overseers once contrived a strategy to beat Finn severely, if not to death. They brought him this rogue camel, it attacked anyone who came near it, the night before the caravan was to leave Tunis. He was told to have it packed and ready by morning. He spent the whole night talking to it and at daybreak it kneeled quietly to be loaded. From then on it was his best animal, although no one else could approach it. Years later, Finn escaped with it although both of them nearly died in the desert before being led to this oasis."

"Being led?" asked the sailor.

"Yes, apparently a hawk led them for many days until the camel smelled the lake," said Seamus. "Jugurtha says that Finn was almost dead when he found him at the water's edge one morning."

"How could a bird lead them?" asked Jonathan.

"You'll have to ask Finn," said the boy. "Oops, what was that?" he said, stumbling forward.

14

JONATHAN REACHED OUT A HAND to keep the boy from falling and turned to see the cause of the problem. Half expecting to see a grinning Tuareg warrior having played a joke, he was startled by the sight of a camel standing there with an outstretched head. Used to the cargo camels he'd seen in Tunis, he noticed immediately that this animal was different. Although of similar size, it was far more slender and had slightly longer and thinner legs than he remembered.

"Akilah, what are you doing?" said Seamus, swinging around and scratching the ears of the head thrust toward him. "Do you want to go for a run?"

As the boy continued talking to the camel, the sailor realized he was copying exactly what Finn was doing with the huge jamal a few yards away. In a soft voice, Seamus inquired about how the animal had slept last night, whether it was hungry or thirsty, how its brothers and sisters were faring on this fine day, and on and on. As its ears and head were rubbed and scratched, the camel began to make sounds in its throat as though answering the youth.

"She's a young racing or fighting camel," said Seamus without changing his tone of voice or looking at Jonathan. "Finn has been teaching me to ride her. In the beginning it was hard because she's really fast, but over the past few days I've begun to get the hang of it. It's a different technique from just riding across the desert, like you did to get here, but very exciting."

"You'll have to show me," said the Englishman.

"We will, and I'm sure Finn will teach you himself if you want. Did you know that Finn's Tuareg name is Amnay? It means 'Rider.' The warriors say there's no one in the desert who can equal him on a camel. He doesn't need a rein or any kind of control when he rides; the camels seem to know just what he wants them to do."

Jonathan found this hard to believe until he saw a demonstration two days later. While it was still cool in the morning Finn, Seamus, and some Tuareg warriors brought several camels to the side of the lake near Jugurtha's tent, where the O'Sheas were gathered. From there level ground bordered the lake and the pasture beyond for at least 300 yards before sand hills rose up to block it.

Seamus mounted the kneeling Akilah and at his command she rose to face the far dunes. Jonathan was surprised to see the boy sitting behind the animal's hump on a small pad, his legs stretched forward along its sides. In one hand he held a rope attached to a leather halter on her head. With a cry the boy thumped her sides with his feet, leaned forward and shook the rope. The young naga took off at a run with speed that startled the family.

"I didn't know a camel could move that fast," Cormac said.

"The only ones I ever saw in all those years of slavery were heavily loaded and being led through the markets," said Abigail. "That animal can run!"

"I had the same reaction when we arrived here," said Fiona, "the camels we rode from the shore were the big ones, but Finn explained that the runners are bred for speed, important in both racing and fighting."

"The naga is faster than you see," said Finn quietly, "however, she recognizes Seamus is inexperienced and is careful not to unseat him."

They all stared at him.

"She's taking care of him?" asked Abigail incredulously.

"Yes, they spent every day together for at least a week getting to be friends before I decided both were ready for riding," said the blond Irishman.

Cormac, who had seen his brother in action with animals, nodded with understanding, "So how much more speed does she have?"

"A lot more," said Finn with a smile.

When Seamus returned and dismounted from the kneeling camel, everyone congratulated him. Behind the veil, which he insisted on wearing like the Tuareg men, his excitement was hidden, but his eyes gave it away.

"She won't go much faster for me yet," he said with surprising understanding, "but it's a lot better than when we started."

The naga wasn't breathing hard but Finn let her rest for a few minutes while he took off the halter and answered questions from the family.

"Ahh, Amnay are you going to show them how this girl can run?" asked Jugurtha, approaching from the tent, "Or are you going to keep it a secret from them as you usually do from me?"

"Why Father," said Finn, using the formal address which never failed to fill the Tuareg leader with joy. "How can you say such a thing? You always have the fastest mounts on the hunts."

"Hah," growled the Tuareg in a tone Jonathan now understood he used for effect only. "Hunting, yes. But when it's time for war, what happens? My son always claims that I have the fastest mount, but it turns out that his is just a bit faster. If I didn't know better, I'd think he was trying to protect me."

Finn's eyes widened in shock. "I am supposed to protect the greatest fighter in the desert? The man who taught me everything? The man whose sword skills are legendary? Impossible!"

The watching warriors nodded to themselves in agreement because they knew Jugurtha's statement was true. Freed from slavery by their leader, and married to his daughter, Finn's extraordinary skills with a camel would always be used to prevent any danger to Jugurtha in battle. In the fight at the harem they had known the blond warrior would have stepped in front of their leader to take a fatal sword thrust rather than see the Tuareg die first. It was a fierce loyalty which they all shared after spending their lives with the legendary Tuareg.

"Well, I think she's ready," said Finn to head off more discussion. He slipped on the animal and gave a soft command. In what seemed like one motion, the naga rose and set off running toward the hills, with no obvious guidance from the rider.

"See what I told you," said Seamus triumphantly.

Jonathan, Cormac, and Abigail could only stare in wonder. The animal's speed was much greater than with the boy aboard. Halfway to the hills, the naga swerved to the left and started back, weaving from one side to the other as though passing in and out of a line of stakes. Finn's hands remained on his knees and his body moved in perfect harmony with the camel's motion; there was no indication of guidance. When they reached the little group, the naga stopped and kneeled at a whispered word from her rider.

"It's like she reads his mind," said Abigail into the silence.

Finn dismounted and turned to face the group.

"Now, we'll show you…" he started to say, but stopped as his eyes suddenly caught movement in the distance.

15

Two camels had crested the top of the same sand dune east of the oasis which the group from Tunis had descended several days before.

"Were you expecting anyone to follow you?" Finn asked Gwasila.

"No," said the warrior. "When we left, Lemta had received no reports of upcoming caravans worth raiding. She told me that her spies had been advised to focus only on rich merchant caravans, since the Pasha and his family had been reunited. She suspects that the merchants' gold may now be carried by the Pasha's camels because the spies can find no report of gold on the regular caravans, but there's no proof. She said her nephew wouldn't attack the Pasha's camels anyway," he added.

Finn nodded absentmindedly, his eyes still focused on the riders now descending the hill.

"Something's wrong," he said.

Everyone swung around to stare. The two camels had started down, moving so rapidly they stirred a swirl of dust. One was slightly in front of the other, its rider clearly urging it on with occasional blows from his short crop, the second animal very close behind. Even though the distance was hundreds of yards, Finn could see that the second rider was swaying precariously from side to side, both hands on his riding pad.

"The first camel is leading the second," he said, "and something's wrong with the second rider. You and Jonathan lead these animals back to the herd," he said to Seamus before hiking up his robe and setting off at a dead run. Cormac, Jugurtha, and the others followed close behind.

"What do you suppose it's all about?" asked Jonathan as he and Seamus gathered the camels' lead ropes.

"I don't know, but it must be serious or they wouldn't be running like that. Let's get these animals back to the pasture and follow them," said the boy.

As they ran through the camp, Jugurtha shouted for his men to grab weapons and follow. Warriors bearing swords bolted from tents, joining them until there was a band of 20 racing toward the edge of the oasis. By the time they got there, the camels were almost down the dune.

The rider in front was clearly Tuareg although his robe was stained nearly black with sweat and his tagelmust disheveled. The rider behind wore what had been a white robe, now filthy with desert dust, and what had been a purple turban, also covered with dirt. A large brown stain covered the right side of his robe. He was barely able to keep his seat and when his mount reached level ground he slid off its back into the arms of two men who had anticipated his fall.

The Tuareg leaped from his camel, without commanding it to kneel, and ran to Jugurtha.

"Lemta sent me to bring you the news," he said. "We've been riding nonstop since night before last. I could have been faster, but he insisted on coming." He pointed at the figure lying on the ground, being attended by the two warriors. "He took a lance through his right side.

Lemta bandaged it and he made me swear I'd bring him to you. Since he's Suleyman Reis' right hand man, I had no choice."

"What happened?" asked the desert leader.

"Two huge warships arrived at Tunis from Constantinople five days ago. An Envoy came ashore and called on the Pasha. He said he was bringing greetings and gifts from the Sultan. The Pasha invited him to a feast the next day with all the leading citizens of the city. He had the plaza turned into a great outdoor banquet hall, but when the Envoy arrived that afternoon, his Janissaries fell on the Pasha's unsuspecting troops and made off with your brother-in-law and his family. They boarded a sloop and sailed out of the harbor. The janissaries were turned loose to plunder and loot the city. Part of it is in flames and no one is safe; the dead litter the streets."

"What about Suleyman Reis?" asked Cormac, who was standing beside Jugurtha. "Any news of him?"

"Ahhh, MacLir Reis," said the spy, recognizing the redhead, "I know nothing about the pirate, but the wounded man must have known that you were here and wanted to tell you what happened to Suleyman Reis."

With a sick sense of foreboding, Cormac ran to the fallen rider, whose head and shoulders were cradled by one Tuareg, while the other held a water skin to his mouth. It was indeed Francoise, his face very pale and eyes closed: water was dribbling unswallowed off his chin.

"Francoise," he said urgently, kneeling beside his friend. "It's Cormac. You found us. Don't give up now!"

"He's lost a lot of blood," said the warrior propping the slave up, "there's been no response since he fell from the camel."

"Francoise," repeated Cormac in a sharp voice, recognizing from years of battle that the man was beginning to slip away. "You must wake up and tell me what happened."

The man's eyes fluttered once, then twice, opened blankly and then widened with recognition at the great white scar, blue eyes, and shock of red hair. Closing briefly, the eyelids suddenly flew open again and Francoise stared with fierce intensity at Cormac.

"They double-crossed the Pasha," he said in a low whisper. "Promised gifts and greetings, then attacked."

"What of the Reis?" asked the Irishman.

"I was attending him in the plaza and tried to stop them from taking the Reis, but they lanced me and I fell under people trying to escape. When I woke, everyone was gone and I was barely able to drag myself to Lemta."

His eyes closed and his head started to slump to the side. Cormac grabbed Francoise' jaw and shook him gently.

"Not yet, Francoise," he said even more sharply than before, "Not yet. What happened to Bran?"

There was no response and Cormac repeated the question, now in a loud voice. With a supreme effort, the Frenchman forced his eyes open again and stared into the blue ones above him.

"They captured the Pasha, his entire family and the Reis" he whispered so softly that Cormac had to lean very close. "When Bran tried to fight, they took her also. I heard them say..."

His head slumped to the side and this time he couldn't be roused.

16

JUGURTHA DIRECTED HIS MEN to carry the Frenchman to his own tent, where Kella and several women skilled in dealing with battle wounds could tend to him. The spy was escorted to another tent for food and sleep, while Finn led the exhausted camels around the lake to pasture. When he returned, Cormac was standing outside Jugurtha's tent. His blue eyes had gone gray and his face was set like stone.

"He's near death," he said to his brother's unspoken query. "The lance went through his side and wouldn't normally be considered a fatal thrust. The Janissary must have been too occupied to finish him off. However, the exertion of getting all the way to Lemta and then the camel ride exacerbated the wound and took a great toll. The women are skilled healers, but he's lost so much blood that I doubt they can do anything to save him. I don't think he'll last the night."

Gripping his brother's shoulder in sympathy over the impending loss of a dear friend, Finn tried to give Cormac something to focus on. "We have to rescue Bran, if they haven't killed her already."

"Jugurtha has already directed riders to other camps," said Cormac, "but he said it will take some days to assemble a fighting force."

"I spoke with them as they headed for their camels," Finn replied. "When we planned the attack on the harem last year, the camps could only spare a handful of warriors each."

"I told your father-in-law I'm ready to go alone to gather pirate friends in Tunis," said his brother, "but he asked me to wait until we hold a counsel tonight. He thinks the spy Nasir will have more coherent information after he's rested a few hours. The man did not sleep for two days."

Finn nodded. "Abigail, Tiziri, Mother, and Seamus will be safe here," he said, "Jonathan will stay and Jugurtha will leave warriors to protect the camp; I think it unlikely that the Janissaries will venture into the desert anyway. In the meantime, I'm going to choose the camels we'll need and make sure Seamus will help the Stable Master care for the black and the mares. There's really not much question about it because the boy practically worships the ground the old man walks on. The two of them are already trying to convince me that Seamus should ride the stallion."

As the sun touched the western hilltops, Nasir appeared with Gwasila and joined Cormac, Finn, and Jugurtha in front of the leader's tent. More warriors appeared and they all sat on carpets laid over the ground as bowls of food were passed. Veils were lowered and the men ate with little conversation.

"It's practically the only time you can see their faces," whispered Seamus to Jonathan from their vantage point beside Finn.

Finally the bowls were put aside, veils raised, and a fire lit in the large pile of dried camel chips in the shallow pit before Jugurtha.

"Tell us again about the attack, everything you can remember," he said to Nasir.

"Two large warships, flying the flag of the Ottoman Empire, appeared five days ago outside the entrance to the harbor. They anchored on either side of the opening, so that any ship entering or leaving would have to pass between them."

"Cannons?" asked Cormac.

"It's hard to see, because the entrance is almost a mile from the wharf," said the spy, "but sailors from vessels in the harbor said that there are two decks of cannons on each."

MacLir Reis raised his eyebrows. "They must be ships of the line, the largest in the Empire. I imagine the captains were worried that the harbor's too shallow for their draft, but from that position they control traffic to and from the city. What happened next?"

"Longboats began bringing men ashore," said Nasir. "No one thought much about it because visiting ships, especially from far away, frequently bring their sailors to the city for food and drink. All the men wore the purple and gold of Empire Janissaries and all were armed, but they seemed to mingle well with the citizens. Merchants were pleased with the business. On the second day, an Envoy was rowed to the wharf and went directly to the Palace. It was widely reported that he brought greetings and gifts from the Sultan. The Pasha invited him to a great banquet on the following day.

"We heard that word went to all the leading citizens inviting them to the banquet. Pavilions were set up on the plaza between the palace and the harem, complete with tables, chairs, and countless slaves to serve. The next afternoon the Envoy appeared, accompanied by many men carrying what looked like gifts. He went straight to where the Pasha waited in a large tent with the First Wife and his daughters. Suddenly the Janissaries dropped their boxes, drew swords and surrounded the family. Several hundred Janissaries appeared from side streets and attacked the Pasha's soldiers while the Pasha, his family, and a few others were taken to the wharf. I was told that the scene was complete chaos: citizens trying to escape and palace soldiers being slaughtered."

"But why?" asked Cormac, to no one in particular. "I know that the Reis paid 20% of all his revenue to the Pasha as tribute. I presumed the

Pasha sent his tribute on to the Emperor. Tunis has to be an important source of income to the Ottoman Empire, why attack it?"

Jugurtha turned to the Stable Master, seated in a place of honor close to him, "Stable Master, in all your years at the palace, did you ever hear rumors of tribute withheld?"

The old Tuareg had been captured in his youth during a desert fight with soldiers defending a caravan. He was a skilled rider who had worked for decades training horses for the old Pasha and his son. Before eloping with Kella, Jugurtha had frequently raced the trainer during palace visits, never once beating him. Highly regarded by the palace soldiers, the Stable Master had taught Bran and Pinar to ride in recent years and considered the two girls the daughters he never had. Following the fight at the harem, Jugurtha offered him the chance to return to the desert and he had accepted immediately. The three new horses delivered to his care had filled him with so much energy and excitement that Kella swore he was 25 years younger.

"I never heard a whisper that the Pasha wasn't honoring his tribute," replied the old man. "It was said he grumbled about it, but always paid in full. I can think of no reason for such an attack. You say they took Hibah as well? Someone must have grabbed her quickly before she could free her bow, else she would have loosed death upon them and most likely been killed herself."

Jugurtha, Finn, and the warriors who had seen Bran in action all nodded. They knew the old Tuareg was right.

"How many men would be on those ships?" asked Jugurtha.

"I would guess 250 sailors on each," said Cormac, "and perhaps an additional 150 Janissaries on each, for a combined total of 300 fighting men."

"I can raise about 75 warriors," said the Tuareg.

It was quiet as everyone stared at the flames and considered the impossible odds. Sparks flickered up into a moonless night sky filled with stars. Suddenly, there was an audible gasp from Seamus.

17

TWO GIGANTIC MEN HAD SILENTLY materialized across the fire. Stepping from the dark desert night into the firelight, it looked as though they had appeared out of nowhere. They wore belted robes made of leopard skins, tied at one shoulder and stretching to their knees. Each held a lance in their left hand, the wicked looking blade nearly two feet long, a bow and quiver of arrows across their back, and a long machete thrust under their belts. Great black beards descended their chests, and in the firelight their skin was the color of ebony. As the Tuaregs stared in shocked silence, ten more men stepped into the firelight, similarly armed but more normal in size.

Only the hiss of the fire cut through the silence as the two groups stared at each other. All at once a Tuareg warrior pulled his knife and started to rise.

"No," roared Cormac simultaneously with so much volume that everyone jumped and people came from nearby tents to see what was happening. He had been studying the arrivals closely.

The startled warrior sank back to the ground, knife forgotten.

"We were told our friends needed help," rumbled a deep voice from the giant to the left. "We came as quickly as we could."

Cormac was now on his feet and circling the edge of the fire. He stopped in front of the behemoth who had spoken and, grabbing him by the arms, stared up into the bearded face.

"Dumaka? Can it be you?" he asked. "My old friend and brother, what are you doing here?"

"It is me," said the big man, handing his spear to the giant beside him and embracing the powerful Irishman with a hug that lifted his feet clear off the ground. "We were told to come because of danger to your family. And your family is our family."

Jonathan and Seamus gawked at the visitors.

"Did he say 'Dumaka?'" whispered Seamus. "I think that was the slave on the galley with him." Both had heard the stories about the two black slaves, but never comprehended in their wildest imaginations how big they actually were.

"If I'm not mistaken, that would be Bako the archer beside you," said Finn, now on his feet with Jugurtha. "The man who taught our sister to shoot."

"And the man who broke the grate in the harem door, allowing her to save our lives," said the desert leader.

"We would all have died in that fight but for Cormac and the two of you," said Gwasila, now on his feet also, along with the other warriors who had been at the harem that night.

"These are the sons I told you about on the beach before we parted last year." said Bako, gesturing proudly to the ten men beside them. "Each is worth two or more warriors in a fight. Six are my sons, whose families are grown. Dumaka's four are too young for families, but are highly skilled with weapons despite their age. The rest of our sons and their cousins we left behind to guard the village." The ten bowed their heads in greeting.

"Welcome to all. Make room around the fire and get food for these warriors. After they eat, we will hear the story of how they came to be here," said Jugurtha, rounding the blaze to grip each visitor on the forearm in greeting. Every Tuareg followed his lead, then space was cleared for the twelve visitors.

"Who told you to come and how in the world did you find the oasis?" asked Cormac when the last bowl of food was emptied.

"A great warrior appeared to us on the forest trail as we were returning from a hunt during the last moon," said Dumaka. "Half again our size, he wore a golden breastplate and held a huge shining sword in one hand. 'Your friends need help' he said in a voice like the sound of distant thunder. 'Take the camels you were given to return home last year and go to them. A hawk will guide you.' Then he vanished. The next morning a large hawk was circling the village. It returned every day while we made preparations. When we set out, it led us north and west until we arrived this evening and saw your fire."

"What of water?" asked Finn, remembering the terrible thirst he and the jamal had experienced as they followed their own hawk nearly five years earlier.

"We brought large water skins," said the ex-slave, "but there was water at least every second night. Sometimes a small oasis and more than once just a spring bubbling out of the sand. It took nearly a moon to reach you." Finn glanced at Jugurtha who shook his head and shrugged. In his lifetime of crossing the desert, he had no knowledge of the existence of such abundant water sources.

"My dearest friends, although the details of your appearance are hard to comprehend, you have indeed been led to us at a time of great need," said Cormac. "Just this morning..."

He went on to tell them the news from Tunis. When he got to the part about Pinar and Bran being taken, a low sound like a growl came from Bako's chest and he clenched his great hands in front of him.

"If the girls are harmed, those men will pay dearly," he muttered.

Kella, Fiona, and Abigail had been drawn to the edge of the circle by Cormac's shout. Seamus and Jonathan had slipped over to them for translation. Now Jugurtha and Cormac brought the two older women into the firelight and introduced them to the visitors.

"Thank you for saving my husband and our adopted son last year," Kella said, bowing to Dumaka and Bako. "My heart sang with joy when I learned they were alive."

"Her adopted son is my son," said Fiona through Cormac, "we are all one family. Thank you for coming."

"We will find and return our girls," rumbled Bako.

Aboard a Sloop in the Mediterranean

1

THE IRONY OF THE SITUATION was not lost on Bran as she held the terrified 12-year-old Kelebek close in the dark confines of the storeroom. Pinar was pressed against her on the other side, clutching her left hand, the First Wife beside her oldest daughter. Along with the very family she had once served as a slave, the Irish girl had been captured again and it seemed all of them were now destined for slavery, death, or worse in Constantinople.

It had happened so quickly. One minute they were standing beside tables loaded with delicacies, waiting for their guest from the Emperor's Court. The next minute they were grabbed by visiting soldiers and the one-handed Envoy was screaming epithets at the Pasha and the Reis, while Janissaries were killing the Pasha's men. She had thrown open her robe and reached for her bow, but one of the men had ripped it away and was about to slit her throat when the Envoy shouted at him to bring her along.

Rushed through the streets to the wharf, they were all forced onto a small ship and locked up below deck. The ship immediately began to move away from the dock, and memories of that hideous night in Baltimore, almost 8 years earlier, had flooded her mind. At the time she was almost nine, slightly younger than Kelebek, but there had been two older brothers to comfort her. Now, she was the one who needed to be strong for others. Her wits had saved her in the harem; perhaps they could do so again.

"This isn't so bad," she said. "When I was captured, there were 20 of us in a paint locker smaller than this."

"What's a 'paint locker?'" asked Kelebek in a quavering voice.

"Oh, a smelly place where they store paint for the ship," said the Irish girl. "You would have hated it."

"Will we starve to death Hibah?" asked the youngster.

"Why do you ask?" said Bran, stifling a slightly hysterical giggle brought on by the odd question.

"All the wonderful food on the table made me really hungry," said Kelebek, "but before I could touch any of it, the awful men grabbed me. I'm still hungry."

"Don't worry," came the First Wife's voice from the other side of Pinar, "I have a feeling that horrible man with one hand will feed us in spite of all his screaming at your father and the Reis. If they took us alive, they must want to keep us that way...at least for now."

Her words proved true. Two hours later the door was unlocked and they were directed to the deck by two stone-faced janissaries. Squinting against the bright sun, Bran could just see the coastline disappearing behind them. Bowls of watery soup and dried bread, along with a few bruised figs, awaited them. The three Arabs hesitated until Bran whispered to them.

"Eat everything, You will need all your strength in the days ahead."

"It's so unappetizing," whispered Pinar.

"I know, but prisoners have no choice in the matter." breathed the ex-slave, ducking her head as one of the soldiers shouted at them to be quiet.

The ship was much smaller than the one Cormac had 'bought' from Suleyman Reis the year before, with one tall mast and a long bowsprit stretching forward from the bow. The boom for the main mast reached almost to the stern and an enormous triangular sail stretched from the top of the mast to the end of the boom. From the bowsprit, three small separate triangular sails connected to the front of the mast. The way they were heeled over, slicing through the water, told Bran that the vessel had been chosen for speed. It seemed the captain wanted to get away quickly, although no chasing ship could pass unchallenged between the guns of the great battleships guarding the harbor entrance. Glancing at the sun, Bran estimated they were heading almost due east.

No sooner had they finished the soup than one of the mercenaries ordered them back to the storeroom. When they were out of sight, Cetin, the sloop's captain, approached Zehab. Cetin had been first mate on one of the warships and was chosen to command the sloop because he had previously captained a pirate ship of the same type. The sailors he brought with him, although somewhat inexperienced with the characteristics of the smaller vessel, were learning quickly.

"With all respect, sir," he said, bowing, "when I was a pirate we used to let captives have ample good food and full run of the deck during the day. In this way we delivered them in excellent condition to the slave markets, where they brought the highest value."

The leader grunted, but the message wasn't lost on him. Focused only on the kidnapping, he had left Tunis with such urgency that there had been no time to provision the vessel he'd commandeered. With at least three weeks of sailing to reach Constantinople, both crew and captives needed food. If one of the prisoners should die on board...he shuddered to think about the consequences.

"Make for Malta," he directed, "we'll provision at Valletta. Then Crete. And make sure the captives spend the day on deck in good weather."

Almost immediately the First Wife and the girls were returned topside and told they could move freely about on the front half of the ship, but under no circumstances could they cross to the rear half. The reason for this was soon evident as the Pasha and Suleyman Reis appeared on the stern.

"Father," shrieked Kelebek, and started toward them, only to be grabbed by Bran before she took three steps.

"We're not allowed to go to them," said the Irish girl just as one of the Janissaries shouted at them to be quiet and stay where they were.

"But why Hibah?" sniffled the girl.

"We're prisoners now, and these men don't want you near your father. You can't even talk to him. We have to be very careful, but maybe you can give him a little wave when they're not looking."

Bran made a game of it and for the rest of the trip she helped Kelebek sneak little waves to her father. Once he caught on to what they were doing, he joined in the game, happy to give some reassurance to his youngest daughter that he wasn't intimidated by this situation. Bran understood only too well the value of diversions like this: she had taught the harem slaves similar games to keep their spirits up. It became a great point of pride with Kelebek that during the rest of the trip they never once got caught.

One particularly beautiful afternoon as Bran, Pinar and Kelebek sat in the sun and, for a moment bathed in a warm ocean breeze forgot the peril of their situation, the Pasha's daughter casually mentioned that the English sailor who had arrived with the O'Sheas in Tunis seemed very nice.

"Yes," said Hibah, "he's become a great favorite with my family since we rescued him."

"His gray eyes and black hair go well together, don't you think?" Pinar asked.

"He's handsome indeed," Bran said, casting a quick glance at her friend.

"Very handsome," said Pinar without thinking, then blushed deeply as Bran turned to stare at her full on.

"Why, sister of my heart, I believe you're attracted to Jonathan," said Bran.

"No more than you are to Francoise," said Pinar defensively. "I've seen the way you looked at him on our trips around the city." Now it was Bran's turn to blush.

"Hibah and Pinar are in love, Hibah and Pinar are in love," shouted Kelebek, who had been hanging on every word.

"Hush," said Pinar, noticing that sailors were beginning to look their way, but that only caused her sister to shout all the louder.

The three of them erupted into a laughing whirl of arms and legs as the two teens rolled around on the deck with Kelebek trying to silence her shrieking. Watching them, the First Wife smiled for the first time since being captured in Tunis.

2

THE STOP IN VALLETTA TOOK almost three days because Zehab had to buy enough meat, bread, cheese, and fruit for the prisoners, plus a crew of 38. In addition to neglecting the proper provisioning of the vessel, he had failed to think of hiring a cook for the craft. There were no cooks for hire in port so he was forced to arrange for meat to be roasted, bread baked, and an adequate supply of fruit to be harvested.

"So close," thought Bran looking across the water of the little bay surrounding the village. From the anchorage, it would be an easy swim to freedom on the island. She knew Pinar could do it, although Kelebek and the First Wife were unknowns. However, the soldiers were well aware of the escape potential and watched them closely during daylight hours on deck. At night they were securely locked in the storeroom with a guard posted outside. The Pasha and Reis were shackled day and night for the same reason.

Zehab silently breathed a sigh of relief when at last they pulled anchor and set sail on the third afternoon. He had no idea what his own fate would be, but delivering these people in good condition to the Emperor was of the utmost importance. Under the leather wrapped around the stump of his left wrist he had phantom pain, but he knew that he was lucky to be alive and was determined to remain so. He had briefly lost control when confronting the Pasha and Reis at the banquet in Tunis, screaming that they were going to pay for what they had done to him although neither had the slightest idea of what he was talking about. Now he was focused on delivering them in good condition to the Emperor.

As the days progressed without incident, however, his desire for revenge grew and Zehab began to design ways to harass the prisoners without marking them physically. He paid no attention to the four women, not considering them instrumental in his own suffering, and focused on tormenting the two men. At mealtime, he would make them sit on the deck and watch him being served at a small table and chair. He took his time, lingering over one dish after another brought by a servant. The scrapings of his plate were dumped in a basin for the two men only after he was finished. They had to use their fingers to eat, while he lounged in the chair watching with a smug expression.

"Clean your bowl, dogs," he was fond of saying, "You need to have all your strength for what the Sultan has in store for you."

For a time the Pasha and the Reis conducted their own counter offensive. They made it a point not to look at Zehab during meals and would conduct meaningless conversations about the weather, past experiences and even horse racing, as though nothing was wrong in their world. It worked too well. The infuriated Zehab ordered Janissaries to stretch the men on their backs and force water into their open mouths until they choked and gasped for air.

"You will be silent and watch me while I am eating," he said, after they had recovered. "When it's your turn, there will be no talking; in fact, since your mouths are so busy talking, you will eat on your knees with your hands tied behind your back, like real dogs -- using only your mouths. Furthermore, you are not to talk while on deck."

As further persecution, he had the two men confined in separate storerooms below deck, although he didn't dare risk physical debility and continued to allow them hours of deck time every day. The two were resilient; however, and perfected talking with their mouths slightly open, using no lip movement. This was particularly effective on the windward side of the deck where sound didn't carry. The helmsman and sailors had other matters to occupy their attention and Zehab was frequently below, so the two could converse effectively without being detected. During one such conversation, the Pasha asked the Reis about the possibility of rescue.

"MacLir Reis will come after us," said the Dutchman without moving his mouth.

"How can you be sure?"

"As soon as they find out their sister is with us, the brothers will come," said the Reis.

"They will be stopped by the warships at the harbor entrance."

"The Captain can't leave the ships there indefinitely," said the Reis. "My suspicion is that they will stay until there is no chance of pursuit overtaking us, but MacLir Reis will come one way or another. He's the best captain I've ever sailed with. Though I was technically in charge, I left him alone in the years after I was wounded and the result was beyond my wildest imagination. The slaves idolized him and he knew how to get the most out of oars, sail, and weather to accomplish any objective. Later, I came to realize that in addition to his code of honor was the commitment to somehow reunite with his family. They are everything to him. He WILL come."

"Your tribute was extraordinary during those years," acknowledged the Pasha.

"Most of those same men now crew for him on his ship," said the pirate, "and out of loyalty to him, they'll do whatever it takes to recover his sister. If the Sultan doesn't kill all of us, you'll see what I mean."

3

"**T**HEY'RE REALLY SCARED."

Bran's eyes flew open at the sound of the voice. She was sitting on the hillside above Baltimore. The sun was high overhead and a soft breeze blew, stirring colorful flowers on every side. Beside her sat the little girl in the blue dress, curly blond hair moving with the breeze. Below them the waters of the harbor sparkled and danced. A ship, which looked strangely like Cormac's, was making its way out of the harbor toward the open sea.

"Yes," said Bran, knowing instinctively that she was talking about the First Wife and her daughters.

"Cormac and Finn know what happened," said the girl, plucking flowers and fashioning a bouquet.

"But even if they get past those warships, we have such a headstart they'll never catch up."

"The change of weather will help," said the little one holding out the bouquet to Bran. In the middle of it was a beautiful white gardenia. Then she was gone.

"What's that smell?" said Kelebek sleepily in the dark, cuddling closer to the Irish girl.

"Go back to sleep," whispered Bran, "it's the smell of flowers."

When she woke again, Bran felt the ship rising and falling in the grip of large waves hitting the bow. Timbers in the hull were creaking and she heard the faint shouts of men from above.

"What's going on?" said Kelebek in a frightened voice.

"Nothing to worry about," said Bran, "it seems we've encountered a storm. Cuddle with your sister and I'll go and see about it."

She felt her way to the door and peered into the passageway. No guard had been posted since they left Valletta and the way was clear to the stairs leading topside. The head of the steps was enclosed, but a low door opened onto the deck. A small pane of glass in the door allowed one to look forward towards the bowsprit. The little window was almost obscured by driving gusts of rain, but Bran felt waves now hitting the ship from the side instead of the front and the deck was strangely tipped to the left. Figures were unsteadily making their way to the rigging lines; two of them started climbing but the netting was almost flat and they looked like they were crawling on a floor. She realized the sailors must be trying to lower the sails. Relentlessly the tilt of the deck increased until Bran was sure they were going to capsize. For what seemed like an eternity the vessel lay on its side, the girl pressed flat against the bulkhead. Realizing that the steps were no longer up and down, but almost completely sideways, she was galvanized into action.

"I've got to get the others, or they'll be trapped and drown below deck," she thought, beginning to crawl backwards toward the passageway, the floor of which was now tipped up to almost 90 degrees. The sloop was so far heeled over that she wondered if she could get the family out before seawater started pouring in.

Suddenly there was a series of loud popping noises and immediately she felt the vessel start ever so slowly to come upright. When the hull was finally beneath her and the stairs were once again vertical, she rushed up them to the window. Men were running across the deck toward the port side.

"The sail," she thought, "perhaps it came loose, or they chopped the sheets to free it before the wind pushed the ship completely over."

The sloop had indeed stabilized and was again rising and falling with the oncoming waves. Bran knew that the helmsman had managed to swing the bow back into the wind to avoid getting sideways again and risk broaching. One of the sailors started for her door and she quickly slipped down the steps and back to the storeroom.

It was dark inside and she heard sobbing. Feeling about, she encountered the bodies of Pinar and Kelebek in the arms of the First Wife.

"I'm back," Bran said in the most cheerful voice she could muster. "We're in a big storm but everything's all right now."

"What just happened?"asked Pinar in a shaky voice. "We were rolled around all over the room."

"Yes, a big gust of wind came and knocked the ship on its side," said Bran, "but it came right side up again and the sailors have it under control."

"I'm glad of that," said the First Wife in a voice which indicated that she had an idea just how close they had been to tragedy.

As they sat in the dark against the bulkhead, the younger girl squirmed her way across Pinar and settled in between her and Bran. Gradually her sniffles ceased and silence descended.

"Kekebek, did I ever tell you the story about how my brother saved your uncle from a charging lion in the desert?" asked the Irish girl.

"Was it a big lion?" asked the girl.

4

WHILE THOSE BELOW SAT huddled in the dark, chaos characterized the deck above. The storm had come out of nowhere, with
no warning. The sloop had been cutting through the water at good
speed under clear skies, the helmsman nearly asleep at the wheel and
totally unprepared for the blast of wind that struck the starboard side
with terrific force. The wheel spun out of his hands and the bow swung
sharply to the left before he could recover. By then the power of the
wind was so strong that he couldn't turn the rudder. The sloop's large
mainsail was completely deployed, along with the three small triangular
topsails extending forward from mast to bowsprit: Zehab, concerned
about pursuit, had ordered the captain to maintain all possible speed
day and night. As the ship slewed to port, the mainsail became like a
wall the wind was going to knock over. If the mast hit the ocean, there
was a good chance the ship would start taking on water and sink.

The power of the wind was tremendous and the few men on duty were knocked to the deck before they could react. Sailors struggled to their feet on the tilting deck and rushed for the stern to loose the boom so it could swing downwind and release all pressure on the sail. At that moment a torrent of rain struck with such impact the men were knocked over again and driven against the port railing. By now sailors were pouring from their sleeping quarters, but the angle of the deck and force of the rain made it almost impossible to stay upright. Several of them fought their way to the rigging, now nearly horizontal, realizing that one way to release pressure would be to free the mainsail from the mast. Two men started scrambling along the rigging while others tried to make their way across the dangerously tipped deck to the sheets and release pressure on the sail. Unfortunately the deck was so slippery and tilted that most of them simply slid into the port railing.

At this point Captain Cetin, who was desperately trying to help the helmsman bring the ship back into the wind, realized they were about to go over. He grabbed an ax secured to the railing and somehow made his way to the now almost horizontal mast. Climbing on it like a man aboard a horse, with one blow he slashed apart the first rope connecting sail to mast. Hitching himself rapidly along, he cut the next, and the next. After the sixth loop split, the fury of the wind was such that the sail began to tear free with a loud popping noise, until it was no longer attached to the mast at all, swirling from the boom like a giant flag blowing across the surface of the sea. With a sound like the cracking of an enormous whip, it suddenly ripped completely off the boom and vanished into the stormy night.

Relieved of the pressure, the ship slowly began to right itself and the helmsman was able to start bringing the bow back into the wind. As the mast started to lift back toward vertical, the captain neatly jumped down onto the portside rigging rising below it and was on deck among the grateful sailors by the time the ship was fully upright. As the men congratulated him for his quick action, the wind suddenly died and the rain stopped. To their utter astonishment, within minutes, stars were shining overhead.

Zehab, ashen faced, appeared on deck.

"What happened?" he asked, obviously shaken but trying to maintain his composure.

"A sudden squall," said the captain.

"That was no sudden squall," the Envoy almost shouted. "I've been at sea. You nearly lost the ship!"

"Look around," said the captain calmly. "These conditions are exactly the same as they were before the squall hit. There's no other explanation. It was extremely violent, to be sure, and we had to cut loose the mainsail, but it's over."

"Do we have another mainsail?" said Zehab.

"I'll have one of the men check in the morning. Sloops usually carry a spare mainsail, and if it is damaged there should be a smaller backup; I didn't have the time to check when we commandeered the ship in Tunis. In the meantime, the foresails will give us some forward progress."

When dawn broke the spare mainsail was found and the captain set everyone to work making loops to attach it to the mast. By late morning they were ready to start hoisting the canvas. In the process, a crack was discovered in the mast.

"It's in the top third," said the sailor who spotted it. "The rigging may have prevented it from splitting."

"Lower the foresails," ordered the captain, grateful that the wind had been minimal since the storm. A strong wind could have caused the foresails to split the mast, requiring time-consuming repairs, and he knew Zehab was in no mood for further delays. He ordered the new mainsail to be reefed (rolled up), lowering the top of it to just below the start of the crack. The reduced spread of canvas would slow the sloop dramatically, but there was no other choice. The men were able to rig two foresails below the crack, adding a bit more speed.

When the prisoners were brought on deck in the early afternoon, Suleyman Reis instantly assessed the new sail configuration and knew what had happened. During the storm they had violently tumbled about as the ship nearly foundered and he had thought it was going to sink and take them with it.

"We missed the banquet only to drown at sea," he had remarked in a calm voice.

"All for nothing," the Pasha had replied in a quiet tone. "I just wish my children weren't involved."

"Maybe it's not our time," the Reis had said a moment later as the vessel slowly started to right itself.

Now, seeing the cuts on the mast from the captain's ax, he visualized exactly what had happened.

"Someone acted in the nick of time to free the mainsail," he breathed to the Pasha pointing at the gashes. "We're going to be much slower now, until they can replace the mast. It will help give our friends time to catch up."

5

"How long to Crete?" asked Zehab.

"About two days at this speed," said the captain.

"Where can we get a mast?"

"At Heraklion on the northern coast," said the ex-pirate, "I put in there many times for repairs."

"Very well. Make for it with all the speed you can get out of these sails," said the Envoy as he headed below once more.

The Reis and the Pasha had casually positioned themselves as close to the helmsman as they dared to overhear the conversation. After Zehab disappeared, on the pretext of watching a school of flying fish, they eased themselves as far away from the wheel as they could get.

"I think it's more like three days to Heraklion," murmured the Reis, "and then at least a week before we can get a mast fitted to the ship. Valuable time for MacLir Reis to catch up to us."

"And if he doesn't?" whispered the Pasha.

"He knows where we're going," Suleyman answered. "Constantinople. I'm not sure why but, in spite of his overconfident behavior, the Envoy seems anxious about pursuit. Also, he is treating us like chattel, but ones whom he wishes to deliver in the best possible condition. If it had only been a slave raid he would have taken a great many more than the six of us. So, we're not bound for the markets."

"Where then?" breathed the Pasha.

"My thought is that only the Sultan could have authorized two large warships for the Envoy's use. I think we are bound for Murad's Court."

"But why?" asked the Pasha, "I've not rebelled against him. What could possibly have caused him to incur the expense of sending two warships to Tunis?"

"I don't know," said the Dutchman, "Zehab's ranting at the banquet made no sense."

"Perhaps MacLir Reis can rescue us before we get there," said the Pasha.

"I'm not so sure that would save us," said the Reis. "From what I have heard about the Sultan, such an attempt could doom us all. Whatever the reason for our capture, Zehab will kill us and himself rather than allow us to be rescued. According to reports, a quick death is preferable to failing to perform a mission for Murad IV."

Three days later the sloop passed the massive fortress guarding the entrance to the port at Heraklion with its impressive array of cannons aimed across the water.

"Castello a Mare," explained the Reis as they glided slowly past. "It was built more than 100 years ago by the Republic of Venice. The cannons were put in place seven years ago."

"No ship could survive that battery," whispered the Pasha.

"That's why I never brought the galley here," said Suleyman dryly, "only entered peacefully with a sailing ship."

Despite all Zehab's attempts at persuasion and even bribery, the shipwrights moved at their own methodical pace and it took a full five days for the new mast to be installed. During this time all the prisoners, even Kelebek, were shackled and closely guarded because the sloop was tied to a dock; workers coming and going throughout the day. At night the prisoners' storerooms were securely locked, with two guards posted outside each.

Finally the project was complete and on the morning of the sixth day the captain eased the sloop out of the harbor. Raising all sails, he headed north into the Aegean Sea. The captives, free of shackles, clustered in their respective areas along the port rail enjoying the sun and breeze after the stifling heat at Heraklion. A number of ships were plying the waters that morning, bound for Greece, Cyprus, or perhaps Italy and Spain. Sails on all sides were filled with wind and the sight was stirring. Without a telescope, no one could see the ship far to the west, hull down on the horizon. It was flying a small flag from the top of the mast with a circular blue design.

Unlikely Army

1

"Cormac?" The whisper came from the far side of the tent where Francoise had been laid on soft blankets after his terrible wound was treated and rebandaged by Kella and Fiona.

The redhead's eyes flew open and his hand instinctively went to the sword close beside him, but all was peaceful in the dwelling. The partially open tent flap revealed the predawn gray. Conversation with Dumaka and Bako had gone late into the night and quiet breathing indicated the others, normally stirring at this time, were still sleeping.

"Cormac?" The whisper came again.

With one smooth movement the Irishman was on his feet and stepping over the bodies of Jonathan and Seamus. He knelt at the Frenchman's side, bracing himself for a painful farewell as his friend faded from life; none of them had expected Francoise to survive the night.

"I'm here," he whispered, reaching out his hand out in the dim light to let the dying man know he was close by. To his utter shock, Francoise caught it in a powerful grip.

"Where am I? I remember lying on the ground and seeing your face. During the night you were there again, but I thought it was a dream until I felt the blankets over me. I was so tired that I went back to sleep," the Reis' slave whispered. "When my eyes opened just now and I saw the tent above me, I knew that I'd found you. What happened?"

"You're in Jugurtha's tent in the desert. Lemta's spy brought you here yesterday," murmured Cormac. "Don't waste your strength. You were badly wounded, but you made Lemta and Nasir promise to bring you. When you arrived yesterday, you were near death, but you rallied enough to tell me what happened in Tunis. We didn't think you would live through the night."

"We've got to go after them!" said Francoise urgently, bolting upright on the bed.

"Yes, we will," Cormac softly assured him, "but you must lie back down. They ran a lance through you and you've lost a great amount of blood."

"I don't want to lie down," said the Frenchman, "there's no time to lose, they have Bran!"

"I know they do, but you won't believe what happened," said Cormac, trying to distract him. "We were sitting around the fire last night, talking about what to do, when a band of warriors appeared out of the dark. At first I didn't believe my eyes, but when he spoke I knew it had to be him."

"Had to be who?" In spite of his anxiety, something in the redhead's voice caused Francoise to pause.

"Dumaka. With him are Bako and ten of their sons, heavily armed for war."

"Dumaka?" asked the slave, now totally focused, "and Bako, who taught Pinar and your sister to shoot the bow?"

"Yes, their camp is on the other side of the lake."

"Why would they come back? This is the region where they were enslaved for years."

"They met a great warrior at home who told them we needed help," replied the redhead. "His hawk guided them here across the desert."

"His hawk?" Francoise's voice was dumbfounded.

"Yes, now lie down before you cause the wound to bleed again," this time Cormac's voice was firm. "Dumaka will come to see you before we leave."

"I'm going with you," said the Frenchman in a loud voice, rolling over and standing up. "We've got to get your sister back."

"You must lie back down," Cormac cautioned desperately, rising to his feet. "You're badly wounded and shouldn't be moving."

"What's going on?" Jugurtha's voice carried across the tent from where he and Kella slept.

"Francois won't listen to reason," said Cormac, "he thinks he needs to go with us to Tunis."

"Impossible," said the Tuareg, "He's delirious. Kella will know how to help him."

"*I'm* fine," said Francoise in a loud voice again, " but the Reis and your brother-in-law are in great danger. We must go after them!"

By now everyone was on their feet, the entrance flap had been thrown wide open, and the brazier lit, casting a soft glow throughout the tent. Kella hurried over to the patient, now standing beside the blankets.

"Let me look at your side," she said, handing a candle to Cormac.

Francoise pulled the robe away from his torso, revealing the great swath of cloth with which the women had wrapped him the afternoon before.

"Hold the candle closer," she directed Cormac.

"This should be soaked with blood," she gasped as the taper revealed completely unstained fabric

By now, everyone in the tent was gathered behind her, staring at the Frenchman. The Tuareg woman began unwrapping the cloth.

When she finished, there was dead silence in the tent. On the right side of Francoise's torso, just below his ribcage, was a large diagonal scar six inches long and an inch wide, running downward from the ribs toward the hip. The edges of the scar were perfectly sealed and the skin healthy. The Reis' slave looked down at it with interest.

"Someone did lance me when I tried to intervene at the plaza..." he said.

"Turn around," said Kella in an awed whisper.

The Frenchman pivoted to reveal his back. On the right side was a corresponding diagonal scar where the lance blade had entered, narrower and shorter than the one in front. It too was sealed and surrounded by healthy skin.

"Impossible," said Jugurtha for the second time, his voice tinged with awe. "I've seen battle wounds all my life. A lance thrust like that takes many weeks to heal, if it doesn't kill you outright. You were nearly dead when you arrived."

"I remember the pain as the blade went through my body," Francoise said, still peering at the scar, "but practically nothing else until I saw Cormac's face above me yesterday and again last night." He straightened up and stared at the shocked faces surrounding him. "Would it be possible to get some food? I'm quite hungry."

2

THE FRENCHMAN'S REQUEST FOR FOOD galvanized the stunned observers into action. Kella called for her servants to begin preparing dishes; Jonathan and Seamus went to get Finn, Tiziri, and Fiona; Cormac and Jugurtha left to summon Dumaka and Bako.

"I've never seen anything like that before," said the redhead as they walked around the edge of the lake. Even when the Reis survived a massive sword blow, it took him weeks to recover and he could never use his left arm again."

"I know," said the Tuareg. "Men are always wounded in fighting. Some die and some recover, but never overnight."

Cormac nodded, lost in thought as memories flooded his mind. They were only halfway around the lake when the two giant black men approached.

"We saw you coming and thought something must be important to rouse you so early," said Dumaka.

"Yes," said Cormac, "Francoise was at the plaza and can give us a first-hand account of what happened. We want both of you to hear it because of Bako's knowledge of the harem and your experience with me and the Reis."

"Francoise?" rumbled Dumaka, "You told me he was so badly wounded you didn't think he'd last the night."

"I didn't," said the Irishman, "Wait and see."

"It's impossible," muttered Jugurtha as Dumaka and Bako exchanged glances.

When they reached the tent, rugs had been spread about on the ground in front and Francoise was busily eating cheese, dates, and millet porridge from several bowls set before him, all the while commenting about how delicious everything tasted. Kella, Fiona, Tiziri, Jonathan, and Seamus stood to one side watching him with astonished expressions. Nasir was also there, his face registering shocked disbelief. Only Finn seemed unconcerned and sat beside the Frenchman talking and sharing food.

"Dumaka!" cried Francoise as the men approached. He jumped to his feet and ran to grab the great forearm in greeting. "I never thought to see you again! And Bako, well met! I only saw you through the grate at the harem."

"Bread and Butter Pudding," said the archer with a chuckle as they exchanged grips.

"How could we know the First Wife was away for the evening? We thought it was a good ploy," Francoise grimaced at the memory.

"You saved the lives of the slaves on the galley with the food you used to bring," said Dumaka, "but we never got this Pudding you two talk about. Perhaps it would have made us even stronger!"

"But you're not Irish!" countered the Frenchman.

The laughter of the two huge men was like distant thunder.

"Cormac said you were close to death last night," Dumaka said, "but you look very much alive this morning."

"All I know is that somebody visited me during the night and said not to be afraid, that everything would be all right. When I woke up, it was."

He got to his feet and opened his robe to show them the scars.

"Not a thrust that would kill instantly," observed Jugurtha, "but probably fatal if not treated immediately."

Both visitors nodded their heads in agreement.

"Who visited you in the night?" asked Finn.

"I thought it was Cormac because he was so gentle and concerned," said Francoise.

"Not unless I was sleepwalking," said the redhead. "I didn't get up during the night."

There was a long silence as everyone processed this information. "What did he look like?" asked Finn finally.

"It was dark and I couldn't see clearly, except for the eyes. They were so kind. So kind," he repeated, and then raised one hand to his mouth with a shocked expression. "But they were brown, not blue!"

Finn stared intently at Francoise for a long moment. "What happened next?" he asked.

"He touched my side, and then he was gone."

"Impossible," murmured Jugurtha for the fourth time that morning.

"No," said Seamus timidly, "I saw him too."

Everyone turned to stare at the boy.

"What did you see, Seamus?" asked Finn.

"I was sleeping beside Jonathan and Cormac," said the lad, "when something woke me in the middle of the night. I sat up thinking it was Jonathan whispering to me, but he was sound asleep. When I looked around the tent, I saw a man kneeling beside Francoise talking so softly that I couldn't hear what he said. He was wearing a light colored robe and was surrounded by faint light. After a moment he reached out and touched Francoise, then he disappeared."

After Finn translated the boy's words into Arabic there was another long silence. Among those listening, Finn nodded with understanding: he too had been visited by men who interacted with him and then disappeared. Oddly, Dumaka had a similar response: he simply smiled and squatted to receive a bowl of figs from the blond. Minutes passed before Jurgutha spread out both arms in front of him in a questioning gesture.

"MacLir Reis should have died in the quarry accident," he said, "Amnay should have died on his first caravan trip, and again during his escape across the desert; Hibah should have lived her life in the harem in servitude; their mother should have lived out her days alone; Dumaka and Bako should have died as slaves. Things happen to this family and friends which I do not understand. And since I have no answer as to why, it's time to eat and to plan an attack."

3

"Now, Francoise, tell us everything that happened from the time you arrived at the plaza," Cormac said after everyone had finished the meal. By now, Jugurtha's warriors and the ten sons of Dumaka and Bako had joined them in front of the leader's tent.

"The Reis' pirates reported the arrival of the two warships," the Frenchman began in Arabic. "They anchored just outside the harbor, to either side of the entrance. This immediately caught the attention of the Reis and his pirates because it meant that any ship entering or leaving would have to pass between their cannons. But they were flying the flag of the Ottoman Empire so they had to be friendly in spite of the threatening position, we thought. Boats began bringing men to the wharf, presumably for trading.

"The next day, when his telescope revealed a longboat entering the harbor carrying a man in splendid attire, Suleyman Reis sent me in a cart with gifts to meet him. Apparently a message had reached the Pasha because his personal carriage was already waiting at the wharf when I arrived.

"A man in purple and gold robes, wearing a magnificent turban of gold cloth, disembarked from the longboat and announced that he was an Envoy from the Sultan bringing greetings and a message to the Pasha of Tunis. I proffered the Reis' gifts to him and he ordered them loaded into the boat, then climbed into the carriage with two of his men and went to the palace."

"Can you describe the man?" asked the redhead.

"Average height, but slightly stooped. Closely trimmed beard of gray and black. He had no left hand; the stump of his wrist was capped in leather. Although he smiled frequently, I thought his gray eyes were cold."

"Is there a practice among the Ottomans of cutting off hands?" asked Cormac, staring around the circle.

"Yes," said Jugurtha. "It's common throughout the Empire for a thief to have one or both hands cut off. Normally the right hand if it's just one offense: makes it much more difficult for the thief to steal again or do simple tasks. Since this man has lost the left hand, the offense must have been different."

"What happened next?" asked Cormac, turning back to Francoise.

"I returned to the Reis and he questioned me about the incident, specifically concerning the oarsmen of the longboat. When I described them as clad in gold tunics and purple pants he became thoughtful.

"'Those are not sailors, Francoise,' he said, 'those are Janissaries: enslaved as children and incorporated into the Sultans army. I understand two of them accompanying the Envoy to the palace, but why were the rest acting as oarsmen?'

"Late that afternoon word came from the Pasha that my master was to join him in the plaza at a great banquet for the Envoy the following afternoon. The Reis looked thoughtful again and sent me with orders for his two pirate captains in port to move their ships away from the wharf, far out in the harbor, and to get word to your captain to do the same. I delivered the same instructions to the galley. In hindsight, I realize that he was uncomfortable about the circumstances, but didn't know why."

"It seems he was uncomfortable with good reason," said Jugurtha.

"The next day we went to the plaza in the early afternoon. The Reis gave me a short sword to hide on my back. It was fitted at an angle under a belt and covered with my robe so as to be invisible to the eye."

"A sword?" Cormac interrupted. "When did you learn to use a sword?"

"After he was injured, the Reis began giving me weekly lessons," said the Frenchman. "When you left last year, it became daily lessons. He had stopped going to sea, but on land I accompanied him everywhere, fully armed. I was to take your place at his left side if we were attacked."

"How have you progressed?" Cormac was astonished that his friend, enslaved at five years old and in charge of the Reis' household, was now also trained in the use of a weapon.

"The Reis is an excellent swordsman and a good teacher," said Francoise.

"I know what you mean," Finn grunted and looked at his father-in-law.

"Some sons almost exceed the skills of their fathers," said Jugurtha gruffly, but the eyes above the veil were laughing. "Almost…"

"My friend, I am so proud of you," said Cormac, staring at Francoise with affection. "What happened next?"

"We arrived at the plaza, along with all the leading families of Tunis. Colorful awnings had been set up over tables and chairs sitting on thick rugs. A great gold awning for the Pasha and his guests was in the very center, surrounded by a dozen of the elite Palace Guard. Slaves were everywhere, carrying platters of food to the tables.

"When we got to the Pasha's tent, he was already there with the First Wife, Kelebek, Pinar, and Bran, who had spent the night in the harem with them. All four were dressed in the most beautiful robes. Especially Bran," he added with an emphasis that caused Cormac and Finn to stare at him in wonderment. Fiona, for whom Abigail was translating, widened her eyes at the emotion accompanying the comment.

"All at once trumpets sounded and the Envoy appeared in the Pasha's carriage, drawn by two white Arabian horses. Following him was a double line of Janissaries carrying what we thought were boxes of gifts. Behind them marched more soldiers, all armed with swords and lances.

"'Too many Janissaries, I don't like this' the Reis said to me in a low voice. 'Stay close to me.' He was wearing what appeared to be a ceremonial sword at his side, but I knew that he had substituted his regular sword in the elaborate scabbard.

"The Envoy got out of the carriage and embraced the Pasha. 'Come and see your gifts,' he said, waving the soldiers forward. He lifted a beautiful gold vase out of the first box. 'For the first wife,' he said. She and the girls moved forward to admire it. Engrossed in the scene, I failed to see what was happening until the Reis jabbed me in the ribs. By then it was too late. Janissaries had quietly surrounded the tent while everyone was focused on the Envoy and his presentation.

"With no warning, they attacked. The closest Palace Guards were cut down and the soldiers were on us before we could draw swords. The Reis was grabbed by two men and rushed to the carriage, where the Pasha and his family were already being held. I saw Bran try for her bow, but she was immediately seized, bow and arrows ripped away and a knife held to her throat.

"'Bring her,' the Envoy commanded, 'that will make three pretty young ones we'll have to offer the Sultan.'

"People were screaming and fleeing. More Place Guards rushed into the plaza, only to be cut down by a flood of Janissaries that had been hidden in the streets.

"When the Reis was marched up to him, the Envoy stared for a moment, then his cheek started to twitch, his face flushed red, and he turned into a madman.

"'You,' he shrieked in an unhuman voice. 'You caused this,' waving the stump of his left wrist in my master's face. 'You ruined my life! You put me in the dungeon! You starved me to death! I hope the Sultan skins you alive and feeds you slowly to his dogs. And I want to see every minute of it!'

"'I've never seen you before in my life,' said the Reis in a calm voice. "I thought the Envoy was going to kill my master right then. Spit flew from his mouth, his wild eyes bulged and his voice became a high wavering scream. Even the Janissaries shrank back a step.

"'You and that demon of yours,' he screeched. 'Knocking men's heads off with his bare hands, roaring like a beast, ripping arms and legs off my men, drinking their blood and throwing their bodies to the sharks. You conjured him up to destroy me, but you failed. Now I'm going to destroy you!'

"Then the fit left him as quickly as it had started and he turned toward the carriage. "'Bring them all,' he said in a normal voice, 'and hurry.'

"When I saw them taking Bran and the girls, I reached for my sword but someone lanced me; I remember the sensation of great pain and then I collapsed to the pavers."

He paused and stared at them.

"I don't know how I got to Lemta, nor do I remember anything of the trip here."

Francoise stared at Cormac, his story ended.

"The cattle boat incident. You threw mercenaries off the galley to the sharks," said Cormac, looking at Dumaka as memories stirred. "He must have been in charge of the ambush."

4

"STABLE MASTER, I THINK THE Beach Gate is the answer," said Jugurtha to the old Tuareg. "You helped us to use it in the past to gain entry to the city. The Janissaries won't know anything about it and there are too many of them to take on in the open with our small force. We'll have to sneak in and strike small, isolated groups of them by surprise until we can get pirates in from the ships to help."

"You will have to figure out a way to get a man over the top of the wall to unlock the beach gate," said the Stable Master, "and of course there are horses in the stables right there, which might be used to advantage. I just hope the grooms have been taking care of them."

They had learned from Nasir that the Envoy had commandeered a sloop from the wharf and sailed across the harbor with his captives. Later the sloop was seen heading into the open ocean. The same evening swarms of longboats filled with Janissaries had arrived at the wharf.

The soldiers set about sinking every small boat they could find then began rampaging through the city, looting and burning.

"They weren't concerned about the big ships," said Cormac, "because none can escape without passing between the warships."

"Yes," said the spy, "and soldiers were left on the wharf to discourage men coming in from the pirate ships."

"What about the citizens?" asked Finn.

"People began to head for the desert when the looting started," Nasir said. "I was lucky to have my own camels since every available animal was being used to carry people and supplies out of the city. When we headed for your camp the following morning, a stream of men, women, and children of all ages and descriptions was headed for the western hills. It seems the Janissaries were letting them go because they wanted the desert to teach them a lesson they'd not forget."

"Teach a lesson?" asked Finn.

"Yes, their captains kept shouting at the crowds, 'Let this be a lesson to those who survive the desert: the Ottoman Empire is not to be trifled with. Never again cheat the Sultan on his tribute.'" said the spy.

Finn stared at the Stable Master. "Could you be mistaken about the Pasha's tribute?"

"No," interrupted Jugurtha firmly. "My wife's brother can be headstrong, but he's no fool. The Pasha of Tunis is a favoured position in the Ottoman Empire. He would never jeopardize it. The Stable Master is correct. Someone must have lied to the Sultan for there to be such destruction caused in the city."

"We have to act. How long before warriors from other camps arrive?" Cormac asked.

"Our message was urgent," said the Tuareg leader, "some should start to arrive tomorrow. By the following evening, we will be able to leave."

Cormac stared at Dumaka. Years of working together had created an uncanny ability in each to understand what the other was thinking. Nothing was said, but the slight nod of the head by the black man showed that a year had not changed that awareness.

"Dumaka and I will leave immediately for Tunis with Bako, their sons, Nasir and Francoise," the redhead said, "We will meet you five nights hence at the Beach Gate. It will be open."

Jugurtha nodded in agreement as the Stable Master raised one hand.

"There is a storeroom in the stables," said the old man. "It's full of bows and arrows for the Pasha's mounted troops. Perhaps it will be helpful."

Bako rumbled in agreement.

Gwasilia took Seamus and Jonathan to get fresh camels for the men that were leaving, while the others looked to their weapons and Kella arranged bundles of food. Jugurtha emerged from his tent with a sword and scabbard for the Frenchman.

"It served me well through many battles in my youth," he said, "including the fight to capture my wife."

Francoise, who knew the whole story, replied, "I will see that it helps rescue your family and friends."

A short time later, the small caravan was assembled outside the tents. The entire village gathered to see them off, Fiona and Abigail with arms around a tearful Tiziri. The reason for her sobs became clear as a fleet camel left the herd on the far side of the lake and raced along the shore and up to the kneeling animals waiting to be mounted. The young naga had no headstall and her rider was clad in the blue robe, veil, and turban of a Tuareg warrior.

"Did you think to leave without me?" asked Finn, looking down at his brother.

"I thought you would come with Jugurtha," Cormac said.

"I was going to, but Tiziri insisted that I come with you," said Finn. "She told me I would never forgive myself if something happened to you and I wasn't there."

"We're just going to open the Beach Gate. You could have had two more days with your pregnant wife," the redhead said.

"There are between 600 and 800 Janissaries in Tunis, based on what our friend here estimates. Anything can happen when you try to open that gate," said his brother. "And there are plenty of people here to look after my wife while we're gone."

"He's right," said the Tuareg chief. "If you are discovered, you will need every fighter you have to escape."

"Very well," Cormac said, grateful that his brother would be at his side from the beginning. He walked over to Abigail.

""Take care of Fiona and…," he started to say, but she threw both arms around him and buried her face in his neck.

"Come back to me my love," she murmured, "and bring your sister. She needs to be at our wedding."

The redhead pulled back and stared at her with a roguish smile. "That she does," he said, and kissed her full on the mouth.

5

CRESCENT MOON, SURROUNDED BY a million stars, shone down on the fire beside a small oasis lake hidden in the vast reaches of the great desert. Seated around the blaze was the group headed for Tunis.

"I think the Envoy put his captives on that sloop and headed for Constantinople. He left the warships behind to stop anyone from following," said Cormac. "We'll have to go after them as quickly as possible."

'But how?" asked Francoise. "How can you get past those warships?"

"Perhaps we create a diversion…" said Cormac as an idea began to grow in his mind. "But we need more men. Even with Jugurtha's fighters, we're no match for that many Janissaries."

"Our sons are excellent swimmers," said Dumaka, "a few of them might make their way to your ship and bring back men. Surely there are boats on board to use."

"Yes there are, but men posted on the wharf and beach will see them coming, even at night. With Janissaries looting the city, a force could be easily raised to stop them," Cormac replied. "And the same would go for any attempt to swim to the warships. Swimmers would be spotted either from the ships or the wharf."

They all fell silent and stared at the fire, realizing the odds against them were nearly insurmountable. Moments went by and no one stirred, each lost in his thoughts.

"Free the quarry slaves."

The voice was loud and commanding. Cormac involuntarily swung around to peer into the darkness, knowing in the same instant that no one was there. It had been more than three years since he had heard the voice but he recognized it immediately: the same voice that had spoken to him twice in the quarry and again on the galley. He pondered the words for a minute then turned to Francoise.

"How has production been from the quarry?"

The Frenchman looked startled for a moment at the odd question, but held both hands up with an expression of wonder on his face.

"No one can believe it. It's been more than five years since the Reis moved you to the galley, but production hasn't fallen off. The rock they produce brings the highest price in Tunis; every builder clamors for it."

"And the slaves, how are they treated?"

"Ahhh," said Francoise, beginning to see where the conversation was going. "The Reis commanded the same treatment for them as for the slaves on his galley. For as long as the production is maintained, we supply them with good bread, fruit, cheese, and plenty of fresh fish.

When you left, no one expected them to maintain their standards, but you taught them well and the Reis is shrewd: the cost of the food is dwarfed by his profit from the rock."

The next afternoon, the guard at the iron gate across the narrow canyon leading to the quarry was surprised to see men on camels approaching. He immediately noted that all were armed, but they seemed to pose no immediate threat. The two in the lead dismounted and walked to the gate. The one on the left looked vaguely familiar, although his head was hooded for sun protection. When he glanced at the man on the right, he gasped. The hood was thrown back to reveal a great mass of red hair secured with a blue headband. Deep blue eyes stared at him from beneath a wide white scar running across his forehead. The guard sucked in his breath in instant recognition. As a young overseer he had been present when a great scaffold had collapsed five years earlier. As the Arab stared, the man on the left spoke.

"Open the gate,"

"On whose orders?" asked the guard, regaining his composure. "It's only opened for wagons bringing food or taking rock slabs to the city."

"On the orders of Suleyman Reis. I am Francoise, Chief Aide to the Reis, and I command you to unlock the gate." said Francoise, throwing back his hood. "In case you don't recognize him, this is MacLir Reis, Pirate Captain for my master."

With the hood back, the guard immediately recognized Francoise, who had accompanied the Reis on every visit for at least three years.

"My sincere apologies, Chief Aide, you are dressed for travel and I didn't recognize you," he said, bowing low. "Welcome back MacLir Reis, I was here when the scaffolding fell."

Cormac nodded curtly as the man ran for a key and gestured for Finn to join them. When the guard rushed back to open the gate, the sight of a fully armed Tuareg warrior filled him with fear. These men of the desert were known to have no mercy and he, now completely rattled, didn't want to give further offense.

"Take us to the Head Overseer," commanded Francoise. A short walk past low dwellings built against the canyon walls brought them to an enormous open pit. It was over 300 yards square, enclosed by towering cliffs. Along the walls to the right and at the far end were several tall wooden scaffolds. Men were working everywhere: some high on the scaffolds chisling at the rock to break slabs away; others hauling great pieces of rough stone toward the entrance where teams of four men were working with chisels to smooth and form the slabs into building blocks. Except for the sound of tools on rock, the entire pit was shrouded in eerie silence.

Cormac stared at the scene as memories flooded through him. He had spent two years here, whipped, beaten, and filled with murderous rage until the strange voice had launched him on a strategy which ultimately led to his freedom. For years he had told these men in the long shallow cave where they sheltered at night that one day he would find his brother and sister and take them home. Most of the slaves had laughed because death was the only escape from the quarry. When the Reis took him away, many had wondered.

It was immediately evident to him that they had not abandoned his example of becoming the best quarry workers in North Africa. In time the strategy had resulted in more water, less beatings, and then good food to reward them for their effort. The men he now observed were fit and strong, bearing no resemblance to the defeated, skeletal slaves on site when he'd first arrived. They all walked upright with confident strides. He noticed with pride that every man's beard had been roughly trimmed below the chin; gone were the long scraggly masses of unkempt hair that used to hang below their waists.

A short, dark-skinned man approached. He wore a white robe and a long whip was wrapped around his waist. Finn noted this immediately. During his years with the caravans whips were always carried in one hand, ends dragging behind the overseer for instant use. He saw that every guard within sight mirrored this pattern.

"Chief Aide, it is my pleasure to welcome you," said the Overseer. "How can I be of service?"

"You may remember this man. He is now Maclir Reis, Pirate Captain for Suleyman Reis," said the Frenchman.

Cormac was amused by the shock that bloomed on the Overseer's face. The man looked at him twice, recovered himself, and gave a low bow.

"I am forever in your debt," he said with astounding honesty. "Your example elevated me, my men, and our quarry into favored status among all the quarries owned by the Reis. He has rewarded both us and the slaves generously. Without you, this never would have happened." He turned toward Francoise. "What is your pleasure?"

"The Reis desires to speak to the slaves. He will break the silence. Pass the word to your men to assemble them here."

As the Overseer hurried off, Cormac walked toward the stone-dressers working a short way to the left. He threaded his way through a number of slabs being shaped into blocks and squatted beside one on which four men were hammering chisels with wooden mallets.

"I'd recognize the strokes creating the perfect smoothness in that rock anywhere in the world," he said. "The other stone dressers are good, but their abilities will never surpass yours."

Their mallets actually paused in midair as three of the men turned to stare at him.

"Cormac," whispered one in a barely audible voice. "Cormac, is it really you? You've come back?"

"Yes, Angus, it's really me," said the redhead. "I've come back to offer you freedom. But there will be a price to pay before you fish off the London coast again. Cedric, you and Giovanni have more white hair now: it will shine beautifully in the sun over England and Italy. But who is this and where is Armando?"

Tears were streaming down Giovanni's face as he stared at the Irishman. "You said you would be free," he whispered, "but no one believed it, or dared to even hope it could come true until we saw you walk out of here on your own feet instead of being thrown in a grave. It's kept us going all these years. We work in honor of you and what you taught us. The new ones like Mateo here don't understand, but they will work for the food. He gestured toward a young man with long black hair working beside him. "He's Spanish and and a fitting replacement for Armando. The old Portuguese died last year, still believing you would find your brother and sister."

"And I did," said the redhead, getting to his feet. "Now the four of you come and stand beside me while I address the slaves."

6

Iᴛ ᴛᴏᴏᴋ ᴀ ᴡʜɪʟᴇ ᴛᴏ ɴᴏᴛɪғʏ all the workers, but before long more than 200 slaves were gathered in front of the visitors. Cormac paused until every eye was focused on him, then stepped up on a nearby block. He threw his hood and cloak back over his shoulders to reveal the loose white shirt, blue pants tucked into knee-high leather boots, and sword hanging from a wide leather belt. There was an audible gasp from his audience and a flurry of soft whispers as newcomers were told who it was. He waited for the whispers to stop, then began speaking in a loud voice.

"Yes, I am Cormac." he said, "I worked with you in this quarry for two years and together we made it the finest quarry in Suleyman Reis' possession. During those years I told you that I would find and free my brother and sister from slavery and return to Ireland. No one believed me; they all said that only death releases one from the quarry.

"But death did not come. Instead, the Reis heard about our work and rode out to witness it. He moved me from the quarry to his galley, where I rowed for two years. There, too, I was told death was the only escape. When I saved his life after a terrible storm, he made me cadence drummer, directing the 280 oarsmen. I saved his life again in a deadly battle where he was seriously wounded. You may have seen, during his recent visits, how his left arm now hangs useless."

At this many slaves nodded their heads in agreement.

"Because of these things he put me in charge of the galley with instructions to protect his left side in times of battle. The reward promised was a share in the profits and my freedom in two years if I survived. Last year I became a free man, found my brother and sister, and returned to Ireland...just as I told you I would."

As the men stared at him in disbelief, the redhead beckoned for Finn to join him on the block.

"This is my brother Finn, or Amnay, as he is called by the Tuareg people. He was a caravan slave who escaped across the desert to an oasis, only to be enslaved again by the Tuareg as a camel herder. Later he saved their leader from certain death and was granted his freedom. The man he saved, Jugurtha, is a famed raider and warrior who trained Finn to become a great swordsman. Now Amnay is son-in-law to Jugurtha.

"Our sister became the personal slave and protector of the Pasha's First Daughter. Bran, or Hibah, is a feared archer who killed four men trying to kidnap the First Wife and her two daughters in Tunis. She also saved my brother's life in our battle to free her last summer.

"How did all this happen? I continue to search for the complete answer. But, it started right here when I decided to become the best stone dresser in the quarry. They could enslave my body, but not my mind or spirit. Before long Cedric, Giovanni, Angus, and Armando chose to seek the same excellence rather than wait for death. In time others followed our example, until the builders in Tunis demanded the stone from this quarry above all others. Our overseers were praised, and rewarded us with more water. Suleyman Reis profited and ordered the quarry to be supplied with better food as long as the excellent work continued. It has, for five years now.

"Look at yourselves. You are fit and strong. Still slaves, but your heads are high and you bear no resemblance to the doomed men I saw when I first arrived; in fact, I'm sure you bear no resemblance to slaves in other quarries.

"In different ways, my brother and sister were guided to the same conclusion about honor, excellence of performance, and dependability, even while trapped in bondage. Finn earned his freedom. Bran earned the respect of the entire palace, although we did have to fight for her freedom."

Cormac paused. Every eye was focused intently on him; even the guards were transfixed, staring with something close to awe. For the slaves, he and Finn were the embodiment of impossible promises made and fulfilled. For the guards who had known him, he was like a figment of the imagination: someone bigger than life who could not possibly be real. But there was no denying the muscular man who stood before them was real, and they knew he was a leader favored by Suleyman Reis. Next to the Chief Aide, he was undoubtedly the most powerful individual in the Reis' forces.

"How many of you are sailors?" Cormac asked.

At least 60% of the slaves raised their hands. The Irishman nodded in satisfaction.

"How many were first mates or captains?"

More than 20 arms went up.

"Excellent, I thought as much," said Cormac. "The Chief Aide and I have a proposal for all of you." He went on to describe the events in Tunis.

"In order to rescue those stolen from us, we first need to rid Tunis of the Janissaries. When that's done, we have to get past the warships stationed at the entrance to the Tunis harbor. It could well cost the lives of everyone who sails with me; however, my crew and I faced death together many times as galley slaves and we will stand together in this as well."

A look passed among the slaves. Ex-galley slaves serving as free men under MacLir Reis was a powerful statement.

"The Janissaries holding Tunis are well armed, seasoned, soldiers. Driving them out will be extremely dangerous and lives will certainly be lost in the attempt, even if it succeeds. Dealing with the warships, rescuing our sister and the other captives will pose similar risks to anyone involved."

Cormac deliberately paused to let this information sink in.

"The Chief Aide and I are asking you to help us in this endeavor. If we fail, we will either be dead or enslaved in Constantinople; nothing new for any of us.. However, if we are successful, those who survive will be free men and given a ship to take them home. You have the pledge of Suleyman Reis through his Chief Aide and that of MacLir Reis who used to be one of you."

"I declare the silence of the quarry ENDED," Cormac shouted into the stillness, "who will join us?"

For a moment there was no sound as the stunned slaves considered these words. Then a roar went up which echoed back and forth between the quarry walls like thunder, as every man raised his arm and shouted his acceptance!

7

"**I**T'S A RAGTAG GROUP," said Finn quietly to his brother, as the slaves began assembling all the food they could carry for the afternoon's walk to Tunis. "All they have for weapons are chisels and mallets. They're going up against more than 600 professional soldiers, with years of combat training and experience."

"I know," said Cormac, "but our numbers have grown enormously and we'll have the element of surprise. And most importantly, never underestimate how hard men will fight for their freedom."

"Yes," the blond agreed, but in his heart he knew the odds were stacked against them.

When the Janissaries began looting Tunis, the caravan operators camped outside the southern wall had quickly moved their camel herds down the trail toward Bilma, settling in at oases along the route until things returned to normal. Word was sent to the salt-mine operators at Bilma that trade would be suspended until the Ottoman soldiers had gone home.

In the meantime, the vast staging ground outside the city, normally occupied by thousands of animals, along with hundreds of overseers and slaves, was left vacant. Dozens of wells were scattered through the area and many large overseer tents had been left standing in anticipation of a quick return to business. Finn knew the spot well from his caravan days and scouted it with two of Bako's sons as dusk fell the day they left the quarry.

Moving as shadows, the three quickly ascertained that the site was completely abandoned and led their large group in under cover of darkness. There were enough tents to accommodate the entire party. Since the men had been sleeping outside for years, the real value of the tents was to provide concealment during daylight hours. The slaves had brought all the food they could carry from the quarry. In addition, for a few days at least they were going to experience unheard of rest and an unlimited supply of water: conditions better than any they'd had since being captured.

Cormac had divided the men into groups of 50 before they left the pit, wisely putting Cedric, Angus, and Giovanni each in charge of a group. The three were widely respected because of their work and dedication to dignity and discipline; he knew the men would follow them. When Ibrahim, tears running down his face, stepped forward to welcome him, the redhead knew he had found his fourth leader.

"Old friend," said the desert raider, "you've now saved my life twice."

"And you undoubtedly saved mine with the excellent Arabic that you taught me," said Cormac, embracing him. "Are you still climbing the scaffolds like a monkey?"

"Of course," said Ibrahim, "but we check the lashings and supports every other day...there have been no more accidents."

"Would you take charge of 50 scaffold workers?" asked the Irishman, thinking of the city walls, "we may need some who are used to working at height."

"Yes, these men are agile, sure-footed and not afraid to fall," said the slave, "they can accomplish whatever task you set for them."

"Excellent," said Cormac.

"I have a question, though." said Ibrahim. "You mentioned that your brother is married to Jugurtha's daughter? THE Jugurtha, who dared to kidnap and marry the Pasha's daughter? Is he married to THAT Jugurtha's daughter?"

"One of his daughters," said Finn, who had just joined them.

"I was among those from our camp who answered Jurgutha's call for raiders to attack a caravan, more than 10 years ago," said the slave. "I was 18 at the time and during the attack my camel went down and mercenaries captured me and sold me to the quarry.

"One of my older sisters had left our oasis years before to marry a warrior in Jugurtha's camp. At the time of the raid she had a little boy 11 years old. His name was Gwasila. Would you know if he is still in that camp?"

"My friend," said Finn, grasping Ibrahim by the forearm. "Not only is he still in the camp, but he is married to my wife's sister. We are brothers-in-law. You will see Gwasila tomorrow night!"

"And his mother? Is she still alive?" said the stunned slave.

"Aaeedah is alive, well, and still beautiful," said Amnay, "she is one of the women who helped nurse me back to life after I arrived at the oasis nearly dead."

"You've not only saved my life," said Ibrahim, staring at the brothers with tear-filled eyes, "but you've also given me back my family, and opened the door to a new life with them."

Later, in the dark of night, Cormac assembled the four leaders with Finn, Francoise, Dumaka and Bako.

"I am going into the city with Dumaka, Bako, and three of their sons to look for weapons and assess the strength of the Janissary force," he said, "we will return before daylight. Finn and Francoise will stay behind and will take command if anything should happen to us.

"Find out whether there are any archers in your groups. We may be able to supply some of them with bows and arrows. Also inquire about swordsmen, there may still be swords in the Palace Barracks or the Armory. Ask everyone to have their chisels as sharp as they can make them and mallets firmly secured on their handles. Either tool can kill a man if applied with force."

Grunts from the leaders acknowledged this insight.

"Finally, Ibrahim, we will need you to select one skilled climber to scale the wall and open the Beach Gate," added the redhead

Ten minutes later seven indistinct shapes slipped across the sands toward Tunis.

8

B AKO LED THEM STRAIGHT TO the base of the south rampart, in the shadow of which it would be extremely difficult to be seen from above. From there a brisk ten minute walk brought them to the corner where the wall ran north for 200 yards along the beach at the edge of the harbor before connecting to the battlements of the palace itself. Halfway to the palace was the Beach Gate, primarily used for soldiers and caravan operators to exit without having to use the heavily trafficked West Gate on the opposite side of the city. The great wooden gate was slightly more than 12 feet high. Unlike the double West Gate, this one was single, opening on a massive set of hinges mounted inside the wall.

"How is it secured?" asked Cormac in a low voice to Bako.

"There are large iron bolts attached to the inside of the gate which slide into corresponding holes in the wall; one can easily slide them out," said the archer.

"Can you climb it?" the Irishman asked the scaffold slave Ibrahim had picked out for them.

"Of course," said the man.

"He won't have to," Dumaka said.

A minute later, one of Dumaka's sons was standing on the giant's shoulders, their combined height almost reaching the top of the gate. To the astonishment of those watching, the scaffold slave climbed up the two men like a great monkey, straddled the gate for a moment and disappeared down the other side. The men below gaped in wonderment.

"How did he get down?" one of the warriors asked.

" I don't know," murmured Cormac, "but I watched men like him scramble around the scaffolds for years with only the smallest hand and foot holds. Ibrahim's one of the very best at it, but I needed him to stay and command his group if we fail to return."

They waited. Overhead a sliver moon shone among a myriad of stars and behind them small waves from the harbor crossed the sand with a slight hissing sound.

"Chains. Sandbags, Climbers."

Cormac literally jumped at the sound of the loud voice, knowing simultaneously that no one had spoken. The others were lost in their thoughts, waiting for the slave to slide the bolts open. As he pondered the words, a daring and highly dangerous scheme began to take shape in his mind. Two minutes later, the large gate swung open just enough for the men to pass through.

"There's no sign of Janissaries," whispered the slave.

"They're probably in other parts of the city, looting…or worse," said Cormac grimly.

Once inside, Bako took charge. He slid the bolts in place and led them into the stables where the weapons were stored. Familiar with the layout from years of accompanying Pinar and Bran to their riding lessons, he quickly found the candles used to light the windowless rooms, but the weapons were gone.

"They're no fools," he said softly. "They can make good use of extra bows and arrows."

"What about the Armory?" said Cormac.

"Probably it and the barracks have been cleaned out," said Bako, "but we'll check."

Grabbing a handful of candles, the bowman led the way out of the stables and toward a low building some yards away. A door stood open and upon entering, the men were assailed by the smell of blood and death. The candle in Bako's fist revealed a scene of total devastation: smashed furniture, bloodstains everywhere, and bodies partially eaten by dogs scattered about where they had been slain.

"It looks like they were ordered to annihilate the Pasha's Guard," said Cormac as they stared. "There's nothing to be gained here, let's go to the palace.

A short walk brought them to the large marble edifice, its white walls seeming to glow faintly in the starlight. Inside the beautiful building, the candles revealed a different scene: very little had been disturbed. The beautiful dark wood tables, chairs, settees, and low benches stood in place. Thick persian rugs were scattered about the floors; doors were open but room after room was untouched.

"I think the Sultan must want to reward someone with this beautiful residence," said Cormac, "and I suspect the harem hasn't been disturbed either."

"I'll find out," said Bako and before anyone could stop him he was gone: a great black shadow darting down the grand hallway to the front doors. It was hard to believe that such a large man could move so quietly. In a few minutes he was back, materializing out of the night like a huge wraith.

"You're right," he said, "There's no one in the plaza and I spoke through the grate to the eunuchs inside the harem; we were guards for years together. They said the Janissaries have left them completely alone, even allowing food to be delivered on the normal schedule."

"Will they betray us?" Cormac asked.

"Absolutely not," said the bowman with a deep chuckle that sounded something like a lion purring, "it's the same as you going back to the quarry. They were overjoyed to see me. I told them to guard the women well; if we were successful in returning with the Pasha and his family, they would be freed."

"A bold promise," said the redhead.

"Not for one who spent years training the Pasha's daughter and her personal slave to defend themselves," Bako rumbled softly.

9

THE PALACE HAD BEEN CONSTRUCTED in such a way that the city wall was actually part of its foundation on the harbor side before extending on for more than a quarter mile to the gates at the great wharf. The result was a lower level to the palace, beneath the two stories of living area, containing the infamous dungeons, storerooms, and the Armory. It was accessed by a stairway behind an innocuous door in the entrance hall

In equipping Pinar and Bran with a series of increasingly powerful bows and finally deadly steel-tipped arrows, the former harem slave had been a frequent visitor to the Armorer. Now he led the little band down the stairs, another candle in his hand throwing soft light. At the bottom of the stairs, a hall extended to the right.

"Dungeon cells," whispered the bowman in explanation. To the left was a doorway. "The Armory," he said, pausing to listen. Nothing stirred and he stepped inside followed by Dumaka and Cormac, machete and sword at the ready.

The flickering light revealed a large room stretching away to darkness on either side. Before them was a small forge and several tables with implements for working steel scattered across them. Racks for holding weapons covered the walls...all empty.

"I thought as much," Bako said, "the Janissaries can always use more armament"

A quick trip down the hall revealed that all the dungeon doors were open.

"I doubt this was the work of Ottoman soldiers," said Cormac, "probably the family of some imprisoned citizen did this. What about the Pasha's galley? Do you know where it's docked?"

"Yes," said Bako," there's a small stone dock attached to the bottom of the wall. It's reached by an outside wooden stairway from the first floor. I was told the stairs are designed to collapse through an ingenious design of folding hinges if the city comes under attack."

He led them upstairs to the large room where the Pasha met with his counsellors and visitors. Large windows looked out toward starlight reflecting off the harbor's calm water.

"The two girls put on quite a demonstration of shooting in this very room," the archer said, pride in his voice. "It actually brought cheers from hardened advisors."

Behind heavy curtains, to the left of the big windows, there was a door leading to a small wooden platform and stairs descending to a dock. From the platform they could see that there was no galley moored there.

"That's odd," said Bako, "the Pasha's galley is always here because he frequently takes the afternoon to make a trip down the coast. As a young man he was involved in several naval engagements and never lost his love of the sea."

Cormac had been studying the dock, and gesturing for Dumaka to follow he quickly descended the stairs. The others saw the two of them bend over and appear to struggle for a minute before there was the sound of splintering wood. This action was repeated once more before they climbed back up the stairs. In each hand, the giant now carried an eight foot length of chain, the iron ring and plate for fastening them to the dock still attached.

"These were his weapons of choice on the galley," explained MacLir Reis, "they filled our enemies with fear and I have an idea that they will be helpful in dealing with the Janissaries. It will only take a moment in the Armory to cut the rings off with a steel chisel."

The task completed, they returned to the Beach Gate to wait for Nasir. He had left them on the way from the quarry to try and slip in the West Gate and find out if Lemta was safe, learn what was going on in the city, and meet them well after dark. No sooner had they arrived than a figure slipped from the end of the stable, slid between two rails of the horse pen and approached. The arrow notched in Bako's bowstring was lowered as he recognized the spy.

"How is Lemta?" asked Cormac. He had only met the old woman once, but he knew that she was greatly loved and respected by Jugurtha's entire family. Her house had also been the place of reunion between him and Finn after six years, a moment he would never forget.

"She's well," said Nasir. "The Janissaries weren't interested in the poor areas of the city where there's nothing to loot. They did make a quick pass through the alley, but she hid in a small chamber concealed under the floor of her sitting room. The trap door is covered by a thick rug; no one would think to look under it, but they didn't even enter her dwelling"

"Good," said the redhead with relief, "and what of the city?"

"After the initial days of looting, many of the soldiers have gone back to the warships, but both Janissary mobs and organized patrols continue to roam throughout the city attacking anyone appearing on the streets; the bodies of men, women, and children are scattered everywhere. The people who fled to the western hills don't dare to come back. Food is getting scarce. A few fishermen are allowed out daily, mainly to feed the intruders. They have to fish from the shore because their boats are gone. The sheepherders in the north are scared to enter the city. Those with gardens, like Lemta, are surviving, but others are nearing a state of desperation."

The thought of innocent lives lost filled the listeners with rage. Each knew, however, that the overwhelming Janissary forces could only be defeated if they remained disciplined and executed whatever plan the redhead was designing.

"Where do the patrols stay at night?" asked Cormac.

"I thought you might want to know," said Nasir. "One patrol has set up in the stores where the slave market is held; another stays on the wharf; and the third one camps just inside the West Gate. The off-duty mobs generally move to the beach for the night, build fires and carouse."

"Excellent," said MacLir Reis. "I have three favors to ask. First, see if you can locate a shop that sells cloth bags used to carry items purchased in the markets. Bring all that you find. Second, try to get into the Reis' house and see if his cook is safe. Third, and most important, see if the fishermen will loan us a small boat or two. It will be dangerous because you'll have to find your way up the beach to their village without being seen. We'll meet you here tomorrow night."

"There's one last thing you need to know," said the spy.

Cormac and the others paused to listen.

"On the second day of looting, the Janissaries made the slaves row the Pasha's galley out into the middle of the harbor." Nasir hesitated.

"Go on," said the redhead, but he had a terrible feeling that he knew what was coming.

"They set fire to it and watched all on board burn to death before it sank."

10

WITHIN HOURS, THE MEN FROM the quarry knew about the fate of 280 galley slaves. Their rage was tempered by Cormac visiting each group to assure them that they would have full opportunity for revenge. They were so infuriated that the sound of chisels being honed to razor sharpness lasted well into the night.

Cormac, Finn, and Francoise gathered some distance from their tent behind a small sand hillock to discuss strategy.

"The slaves are willing," said the Frenchman, "however they're no match for Janissaries in battle."

"Agreed," said Finn, "and I don't think Jugurtha will be able to bring enough men to change the odds. Even if we could defeat the soldiers in Tunis, those warships are waiting: no vessel can run that gauntlet and survive. ...Unless something changes dramatically," he added after a moment of quiet.

"Let me tell you what happened while I was waiting at the Beach Gate," said Cormac. He told them about the three words he'd heard. "'Chains' was easy," he went on, " because it instantly brought to mind Dumaka's method of fighting. 'Sand' and 'use climbers' were more difficult until I began to consider the problem as a whole." He then proceeded to outline a plan that was so bold that the others could only shake their heads in the dark.

"Madness," muttered Amnay, although the very daring of it captured his imagination.

11

THE NEXT DAY WAS SPENT sleeping and eating. The quarry slaves, unlike galley slaves who could sleep in port, never had a chance to rest during daylight and they slept for hours on end. Cormac placed observers hidden behind low sand ridges to watch the city, but no one was spotted on the walls.

When night fell, the redhead assembled Bako, Dumaka, their sons, and Finn to meet Jugurtha at the Beach gate. He also brought Angus and 20 of his men. The previous night Bako had slid his machete through the crack between the gate and the wall to ease the iron bolts slightly into the brackets. From inside the wall it would appear to the casual glance that the gate was secure, but opening it from the outside would be easy. Upon their arrival at the gate, shadowy figures rose from the base of the wall and greeted them. Cormac was startled to see Jonathan among Jugurtha's men.

"What are you doing here? I thought you were going to stay and guard the camp," he asked..

"Bran helped save all of our lives in Marseille," whispered the sailor. "I would never sit by and let you go after her...or her friend Pinar," he added obliquely. "Besides, Gwasila has been helping me with Arabic and I can now understand parts of the conversations, so I won't be a burden."

"One of his relatives taught me Arabic in the quarry," said Cormac, startled by the parallel. "You'll meet him soon. Now that you're here, there's no going back, but make sure you stay close to me when the action starts."

"Where are your camels?" asked Finn as he grasped his father-in-law's forearm in greeting.

"In a little valley about a mile down the beach," said Jugurtha. "I could only raise 45 warriors in such a short time, but all are excellent fighters. I have just 10 with me tonight because I didn't know what you've planned."

"We raised 200 men, not warriors, but highly motivated to fight," said Finn, who went on to explain their visit to the quarry.

"Such men can be dangerous," Jugurtha acknowledged.

"Your 10 men will be perfect, for Cormac's strategy requires a small force initially. I think you'll appreciate it after our experience at the harem last summer," said Finn. "By the way, one of the warriors you lost in a raid years ago is among the slaves with us: Ibrahim, uncle to Gwasila."

"He was hardly more than a boy when we went on that raid," said the Tuareg after a pause. "I've always regretted taking him with us."

"There's more to the story," said the blond, "Ibrahim taught Arabic to Cormac and Cormac saved Ibrahim's life in a terrible accident at the quarry which resulted in the white scar across his forehead."

"When this is over, we'll have much to catch up on," Jurgutha mused.

With bows and swords at the ready, the men waited while Bako used his machete to slide the bolts back and open the gate. Inside, all was still. Cormac led the way until everyone except Angus and his men were inside the walls. After a minute, a shadow detached itself from the stable and approached. It was Nasir, carrying a large sack on his back.

"The Reis' cook is safe," he murmured. " She has a hiding place, but I took her to Lemta; the two are better off together. And you were right about the fishing village. They left a few old boats on the beach to be destroyed by the Janissaries, but filled the the good ones with water and sank them in the shallows along the beach beyond the village to prevent them from being ruined as well. They said they would have a small one ready for you an hour after dark. And here are the sacks." He dropped the bundle on the ground.

"Where did you find them?" said Cormac.

"It was easy. Lemta told me to go to a small shop in another alley where the poor have been left alone, not having much worth looting." said Nasir. "But the poor need carrying bags like the rich. These are made from sturdy cloth, not silk. I collected all I could."

"Be sure to get word to the shop owner that the Reis will pay handsomely for the bags," said Cormac. "How many did you find?"

"I anticipated you would say that and reassured the woman who owns the shop that she would be rewarded, but there were only 25 bags." said the spy.

"That will have to do," said Cormac carrying the bundle through the gate to Angus.

"Take these back to the tents and fill each one with sand, to the size of a small melon," he said to his old friend, making a circle with his hands, "and tie them off. " Angus whispered his understanding and set off with his men.

12

CORMAC REJOINED THE OTHERS and spent some time explaining his plan and the importance of executing it to maximum effect. After answering a few questions, he led the way across the plaza and into the narrow twisting city streets: behind him came silent phantoms hugging the darkness that clung to the edge of the buildings. Before long they were poised on the outskirts of the wide market thorofare where slave auctions were held. Across the street, several shops were lit from within; raucous laughter and shouting pierced the night.

Dumaka advanced to within a few yards of the lighted windows, his great outline just visible at the edge of darkness. Beside him stood Cormac, red hair highlighted in the glow. Behind them, to either side, and completely hidden in darkness, were positioned Bako and the black warriors, bows at the ready. Flanking them were Finn, Jugurtha, and the Tuareg warriors, swords out. When everyone was in place,

Dumaka thundered a war cry which echoed off the buildings with an ear-shattering din.

The shouting stopped as though cut with a knife. For a moment it was deathly quiet. Then 20 men burst from the doors to learn what had caused the awful roar. What they saw was a giant that looked part animal, part man, advancing on them with great whirling, snaking arms. The Janissaries were professional soldiers and well acquainted with battle; however, they had heard the story of the demon that the Grand Vizier had described to Murad, which was later confirmed by Zehab. Although the Janissaries were brave men, superstition was part of their lives and this fearsome sight, half hidden in the dark, froze them in their tracks.

"Attack!" The patrol captain shouted and rushed at Dumaka with his sword drawn. Before he could close, however, a chain snaked out and crushed the side of his head, dropping him instantly. The few men that followed him were quickly cut down by Cormac's sword or the chains. The rest fled back into the shops.

"Return to your ships and go home," this time it was Cormac who roared, "lest I loose the demon to kill you all!"

There were scrambling noises from within the shops as men fought to escape to back alleys. In a few moments all was still. Cormac and Dumaka had retreated immediately to the dark on the far side of the market, to make it seem like they had disappeared. The rest of the men had remained concealed in the dark since the patrol had given up so quickly.

"Well done," said Bako, "we didn't have to fire a single arrow."

"When I heard Francoise describe the Envoy screaming about a demon, I realized the men probably embellished the cattle-boat defeat to save themselves from punishment," said the redhead. "During the years after the cattle-boat fight, Dumaka's reputation became known throughout the Mediterranean, although most viewed him as a warrior not a demon."

"Those men certainly feared more than a warrior," said Jugurtha, "did you hear them fighting with each other to get out the back?"

277

"Let's not celebrate too soon, we're not done yet," said Cormac.

Three fires flickered just inside the open West Gate. The Janissaries had decided to leave the massive barrier open in the hopes of capturing people attempting to enter or leave the city and forcing them to disclose the locations of any remaining goods to loot. Since nighttime was ideal for slipping in or out of the city, the patrol camped on the street just inside the gate.

Concealed in a side alley, Cormac counted ten men around each fire. After the bowmen and Tuaregs were in place on either side of the street, hidden in the shadows, he and Dumaka walked to the middle of the thoroughfare and advanced until they were just outside the light from the first fire. When Dumaka's war cry pierced the quiet, some of the men at the fires actually jumped. All of them whirled to stare down the street. In the broken light, the leopard skin robe, whirling chains, and massive size of the man coalesced in their minds as something from the underworld. The bellows of the man standing beside the apparition about loosing his demon on them had their desired effect. As one, the 30-man patrol fled through the open gate and into the desert.

The detachment camped on the beach at the wharf was on edge. An hour before, a group of terrified soldiers had appeared, babbling that demons were loose in the city and that they were heading for the safety of the warships. The captain in charge had tried to stop them, but some had held him at bay with swords while others untied longboats. In minutes they had disappeared into the dark of the harbor. More torches were lit until the camp was ablaze with light. The normally hardened Janissaries gazed into the surrounding darkness nervously.

The roar came from the city gate a few yards away. Standing there, just at the edge of the torchlight, was one of the demons the fleeing men had described! It had the legs and head of a man, the body of a leopard, and whirling snake-arms impossibly long for any earthly creature. Beside it was a man shouting at them to leave the city or be killed. Within a minute, their courage gone, the men had piled into the remaining longboats and vanished.

While the rest of the force silently exited the city through the Beach Gate and returned to the caravan staging area, Cormac headed up the beach with Dumaka to find the boat which the fishermen had readied for him.

Escape

....

1

"DEMONS? DEMONS?" the Commander shrieked at the patrol members assembled before him on the warship early the next morning, "Only one or two men died! Elite soldiers of the Empire don't FLEE from ANYONE!" His emphasis on the last words wasn't lost on the men: cowardice among Janissaries resulted in gruesome torture and death.

Placed in charge of the two great vessels by the Grand Vizier, Commander Mahfuz was a seasoned naval officer and veteran of numerous sea battles. He was an imposing figure, just over six feet tall and powerfully muscled. A jet-black beard cascaded down his chest and thick black eyebrows overshadowed piercing brown eyes. He had heard the story of the demon that terrorized mercenaries aboard the cattle-ship, but shrewdly ascribed it to men seeking to justify their defeat. To see his own men so cowed, however, told him that something had indeed happened in Tunis during the night; something so intimidating that three seasoned patrols had fled to the ship's safety. 'Retreat' was not a word in his vocabulary and he had scores of men at his disposal on whom he enforced the same principle.

"I'm sending you another 100 Janissaries. Increase the patrols to 50 men," he ordered, "and sweep the city. It shouldn't be hard to find and kill one demon."

Within minutes a stream of longboats carrying heavily armed men headed for the wharf. At first, the additional soldiers scoffed at the stories of demons from their comrades, but as they saw the obvious fear in the eyes of men they had fought shoulder-to-shoulder with in the past, doubt began to creep in. The West Gate patrol had returned late in the night from their flight to the desert, reporting that at least three demons had attacked them. When that group refused to change the story in the light of day, even the most hardened Janissaries found themselves holding weapons at ready as they approached the wharf.

For the rest of the day they combed Tunis, but found nothing. The citizens acted cowed and compliant because Nasir, after bolting the Beach Gate behind the raiders, had spent the night spreading the word not to resist the search that would be coming. As night fell, the Janissaries split into four groups of 50, adding the harem plaza to the previous outposts. Unspoken was the idea that the plaza would be the safest location because its size and openness would protect the soldiers from an ambush. Large fires were lit at each location and guards placed around the perimeter of light.

Cormac, who had returned with Dumaka just before dawn that morning, waited until well after midnight before leading the fighters to the Beach Gate. Clouds had begun to move in from the ocean, blocking out stars, and visibility was poor. Jugurtha brought his full force of warriors and Giovanni added his entire 50 man command. Armed with chisels and mallets, they were also carrying pieces of brush and canvas scrounged from the staging area. Dispersed along the base of the wall, the entire group stood in total silence until the soft sound of bolts opening indicated Nasir had arrived. He slipped outside and described the Janissary outposts.

"Are your fighters as accurate as you with the bow?" Cormac whispered to Bako, once he understood the outpost configuration in the plaza.

"Maybe not quite as fast, but just as accurate," said the eunuch.

"Good, they'll need to be."

A quiet strategy session was held and everyone agreed that Cormac's idea was sound but would need to be perfectly executed. Bako and Dumaka led the way, followed by their sons and Jugurtha's men. Giovanni's team brought up the rear. They eased past the stables and barracks until they could see the plaza. Three large fires had been built in the very middle. About half the soldiers appeared to be sleeping; the other half was either standing or sitting around the fires. Eight guards surrounded the patrol, standing just at the edge of the firelight and facing out into the plaza.

Giovanni and his men remained concealed against the walls of the palace while the others moved silently onto the plaza, normally lit by starlight but now quite dark because of a heavy cloud cover. They formed two concentric circles: Bako and his 10 warriors comprised the inner circle, positioned in darkness about 25 yards beyond the guards; Jugurtha's men 10 yards behind them as the outer circle. Dumaka, Cormac, Finn, and Jugurtha positioned themselves at the openings of the two major streets entering the plaza.

The Janissaries at the fires could easily make out the shapes of the guards surrounding the fires since the sentry's backs were highlighted against the flames. Sitting nervously around the fires, the soldiers heard the sound of a soft thud. As they peered about, anxious to identify the source, they heard another. Finally, squinting into the night, several of the soldiers realized that the sound of each thud was accompanied by the disappearance of one of the silhouetted shapes of the guards. They immediately shouted a warning and the rest of the Janissaries exploded into action to create a perimeter around the fires; however, backlit by the flames they fell victim to a deadly barrage of arrows coming out of the dark. Men began to collapse right and left. The Janissaries that had been sleeping fared no better, picked off as they jumped to their feet in confusion. The patrol leader realized they were going to be overrun: men were falling all around him with arrows through their throats or chests.

"The market," he shouted, "head for the market!"

He took off running, followed by a dozen remaining soldiers. The archers slid into the night and let them pass, to be cut down by Tuareg swords. The leader managed to break through the desert fighters and head for the street leading to the next outpost. The last thing he saw was a huge form looming out of the dark. He barely had time to scream, "Demon!" before his skull was split by one of Dumaka's chains.

It was over in three minutes. Bako was so fast with the bow that he alone accounted for a third of the soldiers killed by the archers, all of whom agreed that the Janissaries were easy targets, silhouetted as they were by the fires.

Cormac had kept Jonathan by his side during the attack and now sent him for Giovanni and his men. Working quickly and quietly, Giovanni's contingent carried the dead bodies out the Beach Gate and far away down the beach dunes so that the inevitable sound of hyenas finding the corpses wouldn't be heard in the city. They then returned and set about cleaning all bloodstains from the pavers with the canvas they had brought, then using the brush they had brought with them, carefully swept the area clear of sand and dirt. When they were done, the fires were extinguished but the ashes were left. In less than two hours, those ashes were the only sign that a patrol had occupied the plaza.

Before leaving, Bako went to the harem door. The speaking grate was open and he could dimly make out the face of one of his old friends.

"You were sleeping and saw or heard nothing," he said.

2

Telescope to eye, Gael watched the next morning as a second fleet of longboats, loaded with soldiers, headed to the wharf from the warships.

"Looks like he was successful last night," the captain remarked to the first mate.

"They're sending another 100 men. Will the two pirate captains loan us their large dories?"

"Yes," said the mate, "when MacLir Reis explained his strategy, both captains thought he was crazy, but their respect for him and Dumaka is such that they agreed, particularly since there's no direct risk to them. They'll have boats ready when we signal."

Gael had been stunned when, roused from sleep two nights before, he was told that Cormac and Dumaka were waiting for him on the deck. For one thing, he had never expected to see the black giant again, and for another he'd thought MacLir Reis was out in the desert. By the time he got topside, the few ex-slave crew members on duty had already gathered to greet Dumaka, with whom they'd shared years as galley oarsmen. A short time later, in his blacked-out cabin, Gael learned about the Envoy's abduction of Bran and the others.

"We saw the sloop leave the wharf," he said. "When it headed straight for the harbor entrance we thought it would be blown to bits by the warships. Instead, it stopped at one of them for a short time before heading to the open sea. We assumed it was carrying a message for the Sultan because at the time we hadn't heard about the attack in the plaza. That night a fisherman slipped out in a small boat and told us some of what happened, but we still didn't know anybody was taken."

"How are you provisioned?" asked Cormac, concerned about the welfare of his men.

"We have plenty of food and water on board. When the warships positioned themselves outside the harbor, we and the two ships owned by the Reis immediately stocked up and headed away from the wharf to anchor out here. We're no match for warships, but in the harbor longboats are no match for us."

"Aye, well done," said the Irishman, and proceeded to lay out his plan.

When he had finished, Gael stared at Cormac for a moment, awe in his eyes. "If you succeed," he said, "the story will go down in history. If you fail, we'll all be dead."

3

When one of the Janissary soldiers reported that an entire patrol had disappeared from the plaza, Captain Mahfuz stared at him in disbelief.

"What do you mean 'disappeared?'" he asked.

"Vanished without a trace," replied the man shakily. "The only thing left is the ashes from their fires."

Mahfuz could see the fear in the soldier's eyes and knew that he expected to be killed for making this report. Not one patrol leader had volunteered to bring the news, for the same reason. He wisely knew that unchecked anger at this time would only make the men more guarded. Despite the faint tendrils of uneasiness working their way into his own mind, the Captain knew it was the time for reassurance.

"The plaza you say? Isn't that between the palace and the harem?" he asked, remembering the Envoy's plan for capturing the Pasha. "What about the harem guards? Did anyone speak to them?"

"Yes," said the soldier, "the other patrol leaders questioned them at length through the speaking grate. The eunuchs said they heard nothing during the night and were startled to see that the patrol was gone at daybreak."

"Very well," said Mahfuz, "I'll send the remainder of our Janissaries with you. Tell the leaders I want five patrols of 50 to search every foot of the city. Make sure the city gates are locked so that no one can escape."

The man hurried off, thanking the gods that his life had been spared. A short time later he was leading the last 100 janissaries to the wharf. The 25 men added to his longboat brazenly snorted and rolled their eyes when he told them about the vanished patrol, but when they stepped onto the deserted wharf, every one of them had drawn his sword.

Little did they know that their trip had been observed by a telescope hidden in the dunes south of the city.

4

ONCE AGAIN, ALTHOUGH THEY searched every alley, house, and shop, the patrols found nothing in the city. One group even searched every room in the palace, careful not to disturb anything for its future occupant, but were unsuccessful. Toward evening, the leaders decided to position their camps close to one another for mutual support, unwilling to admit the superstitions now manipulating their thoughts. The initial report of demons had caused some jesting for those still aboard the warships, but it was unnerving as night approached to be in the same area where 50 experienced comrades had vanished.

The leader of the West Gate camp pulled his men back from the gate until he could see the fires of the next camp, which in turn was positioned to see the men camped at the slave market street that Dumaka had terrorized on the initial raid. The fourth group placed itself where it could see both the slave market fires and those of the men camped on the sand just outside the Wharf Gate. Even though the streets twisted and turned, the Janissaries, in their fear, had managed to create a more-or-less straight line of camps from the West Gate to the wharf...all of which was discreetly observed by Nasir.

In the late afternoon clouds began sweeping in from the east and by nightfall the stars were again obscured by a low overcast highlighted in red by the immense fires lit at each patrol camp.

As soon as it was completely dark, two camels, each led by a Tuareg warrior, appeared in the caravan staging area where the slaves had been hiding. The animals were loaded with the sacks of sand Angus' men had made, long coils of rope obtained from the stables, and several bladeless lance shafts wrapped in cloth. The Tuaregs and their camels, plus Jonathan, Ibrahim, and three scaffold climbers, then set off to circle the city. An hour later they reached the fishing village and loaded the gear into two small boats arranged for them by the fishermen. As the desert warriors headed back around the city, Jonathan set out in one boat with two of the climbers. Emile, former sailor turned scaffold-climbing slave, followed behind with Ibrahim. The two craft slid quietly through the water toward Cormac's ship--identified by a flicker of light from a partially covered lantern.

Whenthey reached the ship, Gael greeted them on deck and briefly raised the cover on the lantern to send a shaft of light toward the two pirate ships. While they waited, the quarry slaves were warmly welcomed by crew members and taken below for food. Jonathan stayed on deck to share with the captain his version of the events that had transpired in the desert. About 20 minutes later three large pirate dories pulled alongside. Jonathan slipped down the ladder and helped transfer the gear from the fishing boats onto two of the dories. The loaded dories were secured to the ladder and the pirates disappeared into the night on the third dory. A short time later Jonathan and Emile headed back to shore in the fishing boats.

When Ibrahim and the other two quarry slaves returned to the deck, Gael took them aside.

"By now, you've undoubtedly heard," he said, "that all of us aboard this ship spent years rowing with Cormac and Dumaka on a galley. When he freed us last year, he made good on his promise to deliver everyone to their homes. But some of the men had lost their families when they were captured and others no longer had families to go home to, so many of us chose to stay on as crew for this ship. We all believe that, with his record, whatever new ventures he's planned will be worthwhile and rewarding."

"It was the same at the quarry," said Ibrahim. "He actually saved our lives when he taught us to take pride in our work. Half of the men camped on the other side of the city would be dead by now were it not for Cormac. I'm one of them. The scar on his forehead came from saving my life in a scaffold accident."

"Suleyman Reis is a smart man. When we heard that he actually offered the three siblings a chance to join him in the merchant business, we were astounded. When they decided to accept his proposal, we were flabbergasted! But when they explained that profits will be shared with the crew, we began to realize the opportunities that might open for all of us and our futures. Everyone on this ship is committed to see them succeed."

Ibrahim was silent, contemplating this novel and unexpected concept.

"I could never have imagined such an idea," he finally said. "The men and I are focused only on gaining our freedom."

"Perhaps this will help clarify our feelings. My ship has only one small dory." said Gael. "You will see that each of the dories left by the pirates has two sets of oars, requiring a total of four oarsmen. Each has more carrying capacity, speed, and stability than mine. Later tonight, you and your men will put yourselves in extreme danger with Cormac and Dumaka. When the Irishman explained what he has in mind, every man on this crew volunteered to row, although there's a high probability every one of you will be killed. We actually had to draw straws to pick the four oarsmen. That's an indication of the regard the crew has for these two men."

"We don't know Dumaka," said the Tuareg, "but we do know that Cormac accomplished the impossible in finding his brother and sister and returning them home. There is something about the man that inspires others to do what they never thought possible. I promise you that my men and I will accomplish our task tonight. We are used to working at height in the worst imaginable conditions."

"That's good," said Gael with a nod, "because all of our lives will depend on it tomorrow."

5

NASIR EASED OPEN THE BOLTS of the Beach Gate and slipped outside. In a few minutes he had explained the day's events to the men waiting for him, including the linear positioning of the patrol camps.

"It's fascinating to see these seasoned fighters glance behind them throughout the day as though expecting to be attacked," he said in a low voice. "There's no doubt that you've sown fear in their minds and it's obvious they don't want to be isolated. Have you seen the reflection of the fires? They're enormous!"

"What of Lemta and the cook?" asked Jugurtha, "Did they survive the search?"

"Yes, I spoke to them just at dark. The Janissaries came into the house and did a quick search. Lemta shuffled about crying and wailing that she was out of food and I don't think they imagined an old whining woman could be hiding anything. The cook was in the space below the floor, but they never lifted the rug."

"The camps are almost in a line from the West Gate to the beach?" Cormac asked, as an idea began to take shape, "Can you guide us through the city to the West Gate without being seen? We're a big group, almost 250 men."

"Yes," said the spy, "but we will be quite close to the camps a few times so everyone will have to be absolutely quiet."

Cormac quickly outlined his idea to the others.

"It might work," said Jugurtha, "but, as before, we'll have to stay beyond the edge of the firelight and draw them out. If they see just ordinary men, the odds are in their favor and we'll be overwhelmed."

"There's a high degree of risk," Cormac acknowledged. "Does anyone think we should wait? Bako, Dumaka, Finn?"

"We love your sister and Pinar," said the bowman without further comment.

"We've definitely set the Janissary nerves on edge, " said Finn, "and if we execute the plan properly they could panic. Every day puts the sloop farther ahead. I say we attack."

"I agree," said Jugurtha, "Kella would want us to take risks to save her brother, nieces, and Bran."

"Angus, Cedric, Giovanni?" asked the redhead.

"Our men have been given a taste of freedom," said Angus, "we will do whatever it takes."

"Very well, lead on Nasir," said Cormac.

Shutting the gate behind them, lest the Janissaries be somehow alerted, the unlikely little army slipped into Tunis with Cormac, Finn, Dumaka, and Bako at its head and Jugurtha's warriors bringing up the rear. In between, the well rested and fed quarry slaves padded along on bare feet, gripping mallets and chisels, hungering for a fight.

Once out of the plaza, Nasir kept to quiet streets well away from the market thoroughfares. An occasional barking dog was the only sign that a large group of men was passing through the night. Peering out of a narrow alley 30 minutes later, the leaders saw the massive West

Gate a few yards to their left. Well over 100 yards to the right, flames from a great fire rose nearly eight feet in the air. The wide street in front of them, far from the flames, was completely dark and the men moved forward until the entire force was gathered staring toward the fire.

Cormac was about to review the strategy when he was interrupted. *"Not yet. Wait."*

In spite of himself, the redhead swung around to see who had spoken. Even as he tried to make out faces in the dark, he knew that no one had opened their mouths.

"We will wait for a while and let them settle down," he said.

The word was passed and the men sat on the pavers to wait.

"Look," Finn whispered 30 minutes later.

The cloud ceiling had lowered and wisps of fog were beginning to float across the street. Suddenly there was a clap of thunder and it began to rain, softly at first, then growing to a downpour. As the street filled with fog, Cormac heard the voice again.

"Now."

It was time to move.

"Let's go," he said above the storm. "Archers to the side of the street, quarry slaves, follow Dumaka and me, Tuaregs at the rear."

Down the street, the Janissaries were desperately trying to keep the fires going, but it was hopeless in the deluge. Soon, only embers were hissing and sputtering despite the soldiers' best attempts to rekindle the flames. A thick fog settled in, obscuring everything: men had to be within three or feet of one another to discern any features.

Toward this scene Cormac's men crept silently.

6

SERKAN WAS 13 WHEN CAPTURED in Egypt by an Ottoman expedition sent to teach the Mamluks a lesson. The Ottomans had never been able to control this fierce warrior class and long before had resigned themselves to let the Mamluks govern the territory on their behalf. Every so often, however, the nominal rulers would get out of hand and the reigning Sultan would send a small army to bring them back in line. Success never lasted for long because the Mamluks were themselves rebellious slave-soldiers, like the Janissaries, and prone to defy the distant Sultan.

Such expeditions did yield a supply of young captives brought back to Constantinople as slaves, and subsequently trained as fighters. Serkan had excelled at the training and was given his Turkish name, which meant 'leader.' He was skilled with the mace and battle ax, although he preferred the latter in war. Now 35 years old, he had served in many conflicts, most recently the successful campaign against Baghdad, and had volunteered for the raid on Tunis.

He was a smallish man, just over five feet five inches, but equipped with the massive shoulders and arms necessary to wield his weapons. Similar to Janissaries from throughout the Empire, he had retained the ideology he'd been taught as a child and Seth, the Egyptian god of warfare, storms, and disorder, was his favorite deity. As the fog thickened, he grabbed his battle ax and offered a quick prayer to his animal-headed god.

"Circle up," shouted the patrol leader, his voice muffled by the heavy mist.

The janissaries formed a large circle around the remains of the fires, standing shoulder to shoulder peering into the thick gray. The tempest had stopped as suddenly as it started and it was deathly still. The silence dragged on for minutes.

"Did you see that?" cried the man on Serkan's left.

"No, what?" asked the Egyptian.

"A figure in the mist, I thought I saw a figure in the mist," said the Janissary. "There it was again," he almost yelled, his voice rising.

"I saw nothing," said Serkan, but the word 'demon' whispered in his thoughts.

"Agggh," came a strangled cry from the left and Serkin no longer felt a shoulder touching his. He slid his left foot out and felt a body. The man had suddenly fallen for no apparent reason, but the seasoned Janissary recognized the death rattle emanating from the fog at his feet.

He began to hear the muted shrieks of other soldiers, but he could see nothing. Then he glimpsed movement in the mist and a horde of near-naked shadowy figures rushed silently at him, brandishing peculiar instruments in their hands. Serkan was no coward, but these silhouettes looked unearthly, and when he saw the gigantic shape materialize in the mist behind them his courage failed. It had a dark human head, animal-looking body, and impossibly long, swinging arms. He knew that the body of Seth was composed of both man and beast and the thought immediately flashed through his mind that Seth had turned against him. For the first time in his life he dropped his battle ax and fled from a fight. When he felt the talons of the demons tearing at his back through the tunic, he screamed at the top of his lungs and ran like he had never run before. So great was his speed that he passed many of his comrades who had left at the first sign of figures in the mist.

The rout was complete. The Janissaries who survived the attack raced down the dark street through the heavy and dank fog into the next patrol camp. A couple of them were almost cut down by their fellow soldiers as they suddenly appeared out of the gray cloud that had settled over the area.

"The demons are coming!" they shrieked, not pausing in their headlong flight.

Only Serkan had the presence to stop in front of the patrol leader, blood streaming down his arms and off both hands from deep chisel cuts in his shoulders.

"Run," he said, trying unsuccessfully to keep his voice under control. "Run, they're right behind us." Without waiting for an answer he sped away into the fog.

The leader had fought alongside Serkan and knew him well. Never had he seen the man so shaken. Whatever had happened, it was time to leave.

"Prepare to march," he shouted, but it was too late.

His men started falling right and left as arrows, shot at point blank range from the mist, pierced throats and chests. Then the horde of brown bodies swept through the camp bludgeoning soldiers to the ground with mallets and finishing them off with razor sharp chisels. The leader's last impression was of a bright blade coming at him from a demon with a great white mark on its face. Then all went black.

Serkan and the few survivors from the first patrol swept through the third camp with the same warning cries, but the Janissary in charge was a tough old campaigner who had repeatedly seen men lose their courage in battle. He correctly assumed that the weather conditions were contributing to such behavior and was unmoved by the panic.

When no one followed the fleeing soldiers, he decided to investigate. He ordered torches lit from the last embers in the ashes of the fires.

"Form up by twos and follow me," he roared, "unsheath your weapons and be alert."

He proceeded slowly and cautiously up the street, barely able to make out anything in front of him. His tidy column of men had no chance, lit up as it was by their own torches. Bako and his sons heard them coming and simply stood to one side until the men had nearly passed before unleashing their deadly arrows from the fog. Muffled screams alerted the leader that an attack had ensued behind him, but he had no time to react before he and those still standing were overwhelmed by the slaves. In minutes every soldier was dead.

The superstitious leader at camp four wasted no time in following Serkan and the few other survivors. Throwing all caution to the wind, he and his men chased after them as fast as they could through the mist and burst into the beach camp, echoing the warning. The fifth patrol, already edgy because their fires had been doused by the rain, needed no urging. They dropped everything and ran for the longboats. By the time Cormac and his little army arrived, the beach and wharf were empty. Only 90 minutes had elapsed since they left the West Gate.

7

A̲FTER ROWING THE LITTLE fishing boats back to the beach, Jonathan and Emile sat on the sand at the edge of the water, staring at the low bank of fog covering the city under brilliant starlight overhead. The Frenchman spoke a little English and Jonathan knew a smattering of French so they were gradually able to share their backgrounds as the evening wore on. Jonathan was just describing the fire on the whaling ship when two figures loomed out of the dark. As they approached, the enormous size of the one on the right reassured the watchers that these were friends.

"Right where we expected to find you," said Cormac in greeting, "although I didn't think we'd be here so soon. Are the others aboard the ship?"

"Yes, and the pirates delivered the large dories. All the gear has been loaded onto them," Jonathan said. "Did you fall into the ocean?"

He had noticed the Irishman's clothing sticking to his muscular frame like a second skin.

"No," said the redhead with a low chuckle, "we were in a bit of a downpour back there."

"What about the others?" asked Emile.

"I asked Francoise to take them to the warehouses and make food and clothing available," Cormac said, "they'll be well taken care of until we return."

Leaving one boat pulled up on the sand, they all climbed into the second one and with Dumaka at the oars, headed swiftly for Cormac's vessel. On the way Cormac explained what had happened in the city.

"It appears that our first two raids had the desired effect," he said, switching back and forth between English and Arabic so all of them could understand. "We were able to get so close in the fog and rain that the archers couldn't miss. Then, when the soldiers caught a glimpse of my large brother here," he grinned at Dumaka, "they panicked. Your comrades from the quarry were the final straw: they were totally noiseless as they attacked with their strange weapons, turning the silence that had long been enforced on them into a weapon of terror. Their sun-browned bodies were indistinguishable from the rags they wore. In the minds of the Janissaries it must have seemed like a horde of demons conjured up from the underworld and they ran for their lives. By the time we reached the wharf, the few survivors and the entire fifth patrol had fled to the warships."

"Now comes the dangerous part," rumbled the black man in his deep voice.

The four were silent as they contemplated his words for the rest of the trip. When they reached the ship, Cormac checked the gear in the dories then followed the others up to the deck.

"I didn't expect you for a couple of hours," said Gael, "although we heard quite a racket a while ago. It appeared that a number of longboats were headed across the harbor. The oarlocks were clattering and men were yelling at the oarsmen to go faster."

"I'm not surprised," Cormac said, and proceeded to fill his captain in on what had happened. "Let's go below and get some food; it's not time to leave just yet."

Once again, Dumaka was enthusiastically greeted by his former comrades in the lighted crewroom. The cook had been alerted earlier in the evening and produced fresh bread and a thick stew. When he had finished eating, Cormac stood and addressed the crew.

"If we make it back to the ship tonight, the job will only be half complete. Tomorrow you will have the chance to finish it. It will be extremely dangerous and some, or all, may lose their lives. You have been free men for a year, able to make your own decisions about the future. There's a fishing boat attached to the ladder and more available on the beach. Gael and I've agreed that any man is free to go ashore. If we're successful, you can rejoin the crew if you want when we sail for Constantinople."

He waited, but not one man moved. Then Patrick stood and cleared his throat. He was the fiery Scotsman who had taken the redhead's place on the oar when Cormac was made drummer.

"Michty Me! And turn our back on all the practicing Gael has put us through since you were here two days ago? It would be a bloody waste!"

The room dissolved into cheers and laughter.

Two hours later, ten men descended the rope ladder into the dories. Two oarsmen, Dumaka, Emile, and a climber named Jacques were in one; two oarsmen, Cormac, Ibrahim and Andras, the other climber, in the second. The oarsmen had brought cloth to muffle the oarlocks and the two boats were soon underway across the harbor in complete silence. Half an hour later they drew near the break in the reefs. Beyond, on either side of the opening, with bows pointed toward the open ocean, loomed the vast bulks of the anchored warships, decks ablaze with light from many lanterns. Although the ships were more than 600 yards apart, any craft that tried to pass between them would be highlighted against the glow from the opposing warship; lookouts, positioned in crows nests atop the three masts, would immediately see them.

Seated at the rudder, Cormac whispered to the men to stop rowing and raised a hand signalling the trailing boat to do likewise while he studied the situation. The lanterns were effective against a large vessel but the dories were small enough to stay in shadow and approach the warships unseen from the rear. He gestured for the second boat to approach, grabbed its bow and passed his strategy to Emile, who transmitted it to Dumaka in the stern. Waiting for his friend's acknowledgement, he felt a subtle change in the air.

"The wind's shifted," he murmured to himself.

Indeed, the constant breeze off the ocean all afternoon, which had brought the overcast to Tunis, had changed and was now out of the west at their backs. Cormac turned and glanced behind him. He was astounded to see tendrils of fog beginning to stream from the shrouded city in their direction.

"Tell Dumaka we'll wait," he murmured to Emile, "The fog's coming."

All four rowers dropped the blades of their oars into the water and steadied their craft in the little swell coming in from the ocean. In 30 minutes the fog had increased enough to dim the lanterns strung along the rigging of the great ships; 15 minutes later, the watchers could barely make out any light at all.

"Good luck," said Cormac to Emile as he pushed away and directed his oarsmen through the break toward the warship on the left. Dumaka followed, steering for the ship to the right.

8

THE DAY AFTER CORMAC HAD come to the ship and shared his plan, Gael had spent hours studying the Ottoman vessels with his most powerful telescope. He had then drawn a side-view of the hull from waterline to railing as accurately as he could for Ibrahim and his climbers. The four had finalized strategy with Cormac and Gael before boarding the dories.

As they silently approached the ships, the value of Gael's work became evident. There was no guessing about how to proceed: everything was exactly as the captain had shown them. Below the main deck there were two decks displaying 12 cannon-ports each. The cannons on the higher deck were offset from those below: placed above the space between guns on the lower deck. This arrangement allowed for a deadly field of fire if the cannons were properly shot in sequence.

The stern of each ship was quite high, providing spacious living quarters for commanders and captains, but it was the outer construction of the hull that had caught Gael's attention. First, the hull was not constructed vertically: it had a slight slope, like the outside of a bowl, as it rose from waterline to railing. Second, the hull wasn't smooth. Four partially-exposed lateral ribs ran along the side, from stern to bow. Three of them were between waterline and the lower cannon deck; one between it and the upper cannon deck. Gael had surmised that the ribs were for added strength against the tremendous sideways pressure as cannons were fired, but they were an ideal climbing feature for the scaffold slaves.

In spite of the dense fog, there was danger of the sailors above hearing the dory hit the side of the ship, since the slight swell caused the little boat to rock unevenly. But Cormac and Gael had thought of this and the rowers pulled their port-side oars across the boat, letting them rest on the gunwales, then stood up and steadied the craft by grabbing the edge of the lowest rib. Ibrahim and Andras, a Greek who had partnered with him for years, each had a coil of rope over one shoulder, a sack of sand lashed to their belts, lance shafts slung around their necks and a razor-sharp machete at their waists. As the swell lifted the little boat a bit higher, both men stepped on to the top of the rib and scampered up the hull like two great monkeys. Anyone with less experience might have struggled with the fingertip hand holds between the ribs, but these men went up like they were climbing a ladder.

When they reached the lower cannon deck, Ibrahim and Andras stopped to either side of the first gunport. The muzzle of the 12-pounder poked out under the raised cover, ready for firing. Used to working in total silence at the quarry, the Tuareg gave a simple hand signal to the Greek and climbed up to the next gun deck. Andras chanced a quick look past the cannon into the ship, but the faint light from a hanging lantern showed nothing. Standing on the rib and steadying himself with one hand on the gunport, he quickly untied the sack of sand from his waist and slid it into the mouth of the cannon. A quick flip of the loop around his neck loosened the cloth-wrapped lance shaft, which he used to push the sack down the barrel and tamp it securely around the cannon ball. Replacing the shaft around his neck, the Greek tied one end of the rope around his waist and let the rest fall into the dark below.

The next part of the strategy was both difficult and highly dangerous because the men would be exposed to anyone inside the ship. Since there were only enough sandbags to spike roughly half the cannons, Maclir Reis had come up with a plan to disable the other half. Each cannon carriage was attached to the bulkhead by a length of thick hauser called a 'breech rope,' which stopped the cannon carriage as it recoiled from the shot backward on its wheels across the deck. Moving to the next gunport, Andras loosed his razor-sharp machete. After peering carefully into the gundeck to make sure no sailors were present, he reached down through the gunport and quickly sawed the breech rope halfway through.

As he moved to the next opening, a tug on the rope indicated that Cormac had tied on another sack of sand. He pulled the sack up and tamped it into the cannon barrel. The skill and agility of the scaffold workers was such that it only took less than 10 minutes to finish two gunports.

In the meanwhile, Ibrahim was doing the same thing on the deck above, although he started by cutting the rope on the first cannon and plugging the second, thus alternating the pattern from what Andras was doing below. All went well until they reached the last four cannons. The crew quarters and storerooms were forward of amidships on the third deck down, accessed by steep sets of stairs descending from deck to deck, well lit by lanterns.

Ibrahim was cutting the breech rope on the next-to-last cannon when his machete, dulled by all the sawing, skidded on the hawser and fell from his hand. It clattered to the deck, striking the iron ring which held the rope to the bulwark. At that very moment, two crew members were descending the stairs to get a sack of flour for the galley from one of the storage rooms.

"What was that?" said the stocky Armenian with a knit cap who was leading the way. Both sailors paused and peered about. "Did it come from port or starboard?"

Ibrahim had pulled back and was watching them from the lower edge of the gunport. The cannon was in shadows, but if the sailors investigated and found the machete all would be lost. As the men swung toward the left side of the ship, he put head and shoulders through the opening, spotted the machete and reached down to grab it; there were only seconds before the men swung back to look in his direction. As he withdrew the blade, it clinked ever so softly against the iron ring holding the rope.

"Starboard," said the Armenian and, jumping to the deck, rushed over to the gunport and peered about. Seeing nothing, he leaned out the opening and looked around in the fog. Minutes dragged by as he studied the situation. The fog was so dense that he could barely make out the gunports below, but he kept staring about, determined to find the source of the sound they'd heard.

Clinging to the hull directly above the raised cover of the gunport and invisible to the sailor, crouched Ibrahim. He was now just inches below the top deck railing and could plainly hear the muffled voices of sailors on the main deck. Below, Andras had finished plugging the cannon just behind the gunport from which the Armenian was peering and was preparing to move forward. Ibrahim risked a glance down and saw the Greek's arm move from under the gunport cover along the edge of the wood brace. In another moment the man's head and body would be fully exposed to the sailor.

Suddenly the vessel was rocked by a large swell rolling in from the ocean. There was a rattle and a clink from one of the lanterns swinging on its hanger above the starboard cannons.

"Oh, here's the culprit," called the sailor standing at the bottom of the steps. "It's the bracket for this lantern. It failed."

The Armenian pulled his head back as his companion grabbed the lantern and pulled. The light hung by a chain from a bracket screwed into the side of an exposed beam. A crack was visible in the bracket and when the sailor pulled, the metal screeched as it was forced wider apart. When he released it, the lantern swung gently and the chain attached to the bracket clinked softly against the underside of the beam.

"Better get a carpenter to fix that," growled the Armenian, coming to study the problem, "could burn the whole ship down. Let's get that sack for Cookie." They headed down to the storeroom two decks below.

As soon as they disappeared, Ibrahim climbed back down and advanced to the next gunport, but was stopped by two hard pulls on the rope: Cormac's signal to come down. In seconds he joined Andras aboard the dory.

"Time to go," said Cormac, in response to their whispered explanation that there was one cannon on each deck that remained untouched. "Fog's beginning to lift and I don't dare risk being seen."

The oarsmen gently pushed the craft away from the warship and with powerful strokes sent it swiftly toward the harbor opening.

9

ONCE INSIDE THE HARBOR they encountered Dumaka's dory, waiting in the dispersing mist. It seemed that discipline on the right-hand vessel was quite relaxed: despite the lanterns prominently displayed, the climbers had encountered no sailors. The reason for this had they known, was that Captain Umar, unlike the stern Mahfuz, was fond of wine. Alcohol was banned throughout the Empire by the Sultan, but at sea such rules were hard to enforce and captains desiring drink retired early to their luxurious quarters to imbibe. In this case, the junior officers were also fond of alcohol; in the absence of authority, most of the crew had retired to their quarters to gamble, drink, or sleep. Emile and Jacques, a fellow Frenchman, able to move quickly through the cannons, had finished well before Ibrahim and Andras.

After a brief greeting, the two boats headed for Cormac's ship as the fog continued to dissipate. By the time they were on deck, the night was clear and millions of stars twinkled on the water. After thanking the scaffold slaves for their work, Cormac beckoned Jonathan.

"Please row Ibrahim and his team to shore in one of the fishing boats and take them to Francoise at the warehouses," he said, adding instructions on where to find the buildings.

"Let one of the men take them, I'm staying with you," said the Englishman.

"Jonathan," the redhead began, but he was cut off.

"No," said the harpooner stubbornly. "You saved my life and I'm not letting you do this alone."

Waving the others away, Cormac put both hands on Jonathan's shoulders.

"You returned the favor in Marseille," he said gently. "We've already talked about this. Dumaka and I spent years with these men facing danger and death. We've all agreed to make this run together, for better or worse. Even if we fail, we will probably cause enough damage for you and the others to take a ship and go after the sloop.

"Should you be unable to rescue them, I still need you to take care of Abigail, Fiona, and Seamus. Finn will have Tiziri and the baby to look after; he may even have to stand with his father-in-law if a new Pasha tries to hunt him down. My mother and the others will want to return to Ireland and I only have you to take them."

"Abigail will die of a broken heart if you don't come back. Take heed of that! And if you make it through this gauntlet, swear we will all go on together! I was alone and you gave me a family. Family stands as one!" With a muffled sob Jonathan hugged the redhead, turned and made his way down the rope ladder.

"He's a good lad," said Gael. "Saved all of us in Marseille he did. Now get below and rest. You and your friend have had quite a night."

A few hours later Cormac woke to the light touch of a crew member. "The sun's coming up and Gael said to tell you that the wind's still out of the west," he said.

When the Irishman reached the deck, the great orb of the sun was just clearing the eastern horizon, sending bright rays onto the white walls and buildings of Tunis. The sky was cloudless; a brisk breeze from the west ruffled the harbor waters. It promised to be a beautiful day.

"Assemble the men," said Cormac, "I think we should leave while the wind favors us."

In a short time the whole crew was gathered at the main mast facing Cormac and Gael on the afterdeck.

"Time for it," said Cormac. "The breeze should carry us steadily between the warships; however, if it dies and leaves us adrift, we will be lost in spite of our work last night. One last chance for anyone to go ashore." No one moved. "Very well. The ships are about 600 yards apart. Going between them places us in the maximum killing zone of each, but the opposite is also true: it's hard for us to miss at that distance. We have 12 cannons to a side; they have 24. I know that Gael has had the gun crews practicing almost non-stop since I was here two nights ago and he tells me that you have the reload time to just under five minutes. Well done, it may give us two volleys from each side.

"Before we set sail, angle the carriages so the cannons are aimed as far ahead as possible; I think you might gain 10 degrees. Crew chiefs, depress the barrels. We want to hit the warships at the waterline, or just above, starting about 100 feet behind the bow. Continue with as many shots as you can reload and fire until your cannons are past the ships. The target is that last 100-foot section of the bow, just at the waterline. Gunners, do you understand?" Following the affirmative nods, he continued, "Our front cannons will certainly be off, but runners will carry the angle information to the crews behind. We will fire in volleys of four cannons at once. With luck, each group of four can run the carriages back and reload for a second shot to the same area. I will direct fire for the cannons, alternating four on the port side with four on the starboard.

"Some of their shot will hit us in spite of the work we did last night, but we will be moving and they are stationary. Their surviving gunners will have to compensate for our speed. Any questions?"

"What about Dumaka? We can't keep the wee fellow out of all this fun can we?" said Patrick, bringing guffaws from the men and a grin from the black giant.

"He has a task on deck," said Cormac. "Once we get out of the harbor he'll move below and help roll the gun carriages back in place. He'll probably do it one handed."

This drew a cheer, since the cannon and carriage of a 12-pounder weighed around 1500 pounds and rolling it back up to the gunport after firing was back-breaking and exhausting work for everyone on the five-man crew. The Irishman studied their faces for a moment, searching for any hint of fear or hesitancy, then turned to Gael.

"Take her out Captain," he said.

10

Captain Mahfuz was enjoying a second cup of strong Turkish coffee when he was disturbed by a knock on the door of his luxurious cabin.

"Enter," he said irritably.

"Sir, the watch sent me to tell you that one of the ships in the harbor is making its way toward the break," said a boyish ensign upon entering. He stopped just inside the doorway and bowed low.

"What?" growled Mahfuz, jumping to his feet. "Out of my way." He shoved the hapless sailor aside as he hurried to the companionway.

Once topside, the Captain strode to the starboard railing on the high afterdeck and accepted the proffered telescope from his first mate. Even without the instrument he could see the taut white sails and open gunports of a ship heading toward them.

"Pirate ship," he muttered to the mate, "one deck of 12 cannons."

"Yes sir," said the man, "it appears they are going to make a run for the open ocean."

"They're committing suicide," said Mahfuz, "rouse the gun crews and signal Captain Umar."

"Yes, sir," said the mate, turning to shout orders to a nearby petty officer.

Below decks, gun crews raced to their positions and Janissaries, alerted by the commotion, poured onto the main deck to watch the action. Flags were run up to alert Umar's vessel to prepare a barrage against the approaching ship and affirming emblems quickly appeared on the other ship.

"Guns rolled out and loaded?" asked the Captain, the telescope still held to his eye.

"They've been loaded and ready since we anchored here, sir," said the mate. "Crews checked them two days ago. We're ready."

But Mahfuz didn't respond. Something on the approaching vessel had caught his attention; flying at the top of the main mast was a small flag. Still almost a quarter mile away, it was hard to see, but showed a blue and black circular design against a white background. No nationality flew such a flag. Then something clicked in the Captain's brain and he lowered the instrument to focus on the rear deck of the approaching vessel. Several men were gathered near the helmsman, but his eye was drawn to two standing slightly apart from the others, facing forward. As he stared, a great rage began to build and his face became flushed. One of the men, dressed in a white blouse, blue pants and boots, had long red hair secured by a blue headband. The other was an enormous black man clad in a great robe of leopard skin. Near him on the deck were coiled two lengths of chain.

"Demons? demons?" bellowed Mahfuz, as understanding flooded his brain. He ran to the railing that overlooked the Janissaries gathered on the main deck. "They fooled you! There were no demons, just men like yourselves. Cowards! You're all cowards and the Sultan will deal with you when we return to Constantinople! COWARDS," he roared once more before returning to the side railing to stare again through the telescope. As they drew closer, he could clearly see that both of the men were smiling in his direction.

"As soon as that ship clears the harbor and enters the water between us and Captain Umar, I want to deliver a full broadside from every cannon. Signal Umar to do the same. I want that ship obliterated," he shouted in an enraged voice.

The mate, a seasoned naval veteran, knew that many of the gunners would miscalculate distance, as well as the speed of the target, and would need at least a second firing to compensate for their mistakes. Normally, some of the crews held their fire for this very reason: watching where the first balls hit, they would adjust the elevation of their cannons to counter early mistakes. He was about to make such a suggestion, but one look at the Captain's red face with a muscle pulsing along his jaw convinced him to remain silent.

The pirate ship tacked once in the harbor and then headed straight for the break. It was a magnificent sight: square white sails unfurled from the foremast and main mast, a large triangular sail aft from the mizzenmast, all taut from the wind behind. It was moving at close to eight knots, a somewhat difficult target for cannons fired from a stationary position. Normally, an attacking ship would be moving also and the gunners had an easier time of estimating the trajectory of their cannon balls.

First to emerge into the open ocean was the bowsprit, then bow, midship, stern. Mahfuz watched with undisguised glee as the vessel gradually moved completely broadside to his warship. In his excitement he failed to notice that the black man had disappeared from the deck. Only two others remained beside the helmsman. One was facing Umar's ship; the redhead had turned and was looking directly at him.

"FIRE!" screamed Mahfuz.

11

FINN, JUGURTHA, AND BAKO, telescopes focused from their vantage point on top of Suleyman Reis' house, saw an enormous belch of white smoke emerge from the far warship as it fired all cannons along its length. It was followed by a similar cloud from the near Ottoman vessel. The boom of the cannons reached them an instant later.

"What's he waiting for?" muttered Finn, just as a small white cloud rolled out from the port bow of Cormac's ship, matched seconds later by a puff from the starboard bow.

By now, the far warship was completely obscured by smoke, and the stern of the near one seemed to have slewed at an angle from its earlier position pointing straight out to sea.

"He's been damaged," said Bako, focusing on the masts of the Irishman's craft. "The second mast is crooked and some of the lower spars broken; sails hanging useless. Somehow a few of the small topsails are still holding the wind."

"The main mast itself looks intact," Jugurtha observed, "and most of the spars are still in place, although some sails are shredded, but she's still making headway."

Indeed, the vessel was still moving ahead, but slowly. After the first volley, the warship to the left had gone completely quiet; the ship to their right was still firing cannons occasionally, but the rear anchor chain seemed to have broken, causing the stern to swing sideways in the wind, and the shots were either short or wide, as the Ottoman gunners tried to adjust for the movement of the target and the new angle of their hull.

The situation on the main deck of Cormac's ship was chaotic; wreckage from the masts was strewn about, along with bodies crushed under the debris. A cannonball had partially struck the rear mast, sending a shower of deadly splinters, one of which pierced the helmsman's chest and emerged from his back. When the man fell, the first mate grabbed the wheel and kept the ship on course until another crewman could replace him. Many cannon balls had splashed harmlessly in the water as Ottoman gunners underestimated the distance, but a few had blasted through the hull just above the waterline, shuddering the vessel with each hit.

The salvo from Mahfuz' ship had been fired before Cormac's front cannons were in line with the Ottoman bow. Standing beside an open hatch, with debris raining down on him, the redhead waited for what seemed an eternity to the anxious gun crews on the deck below.

"Fire one through four!" he finally roared in a voice that could be heard throughout the entire gundeck, "Port side first."

The crews had already lined up their cannons to the best of their ability for range and elevation. When the port gunnery chief dropped his raised arm the first four cannons were fired. The sound was deafening and the ship rolled slightly to starboard from the force exerted against the hull. The starboard chief waited until he estimated the ship had rolled back level before dropping his arm to fire his four guns.

The process of firing a cannon and reloading took five men. They had to wait until the breech rope stopped the carriage before they could begin the process of swabbing out the barrel to eliminate burning embers, and jamming in a sack of gunpowder, the cannonball, and wadding. Each step required tamping with a stout shaft. The team then hauled on block and tackle to roll the carriage back up to the gunport for firing. A taper was inserted in a hole at the back of the barrel. When the taper was lit by the gunner it quickly burned down and ignited the gunpowder, firing the ball.

Dumaka positioned himself just aft of the first four starboard cannons. When the men had reloaded, he leaped forward and lent his great strength to moving the first carriage back up to the gunport. The second crew had reloaded their cannon just in time for him to help roll it forward. Repeating the effort for number three and four cut precious seconds off the firing time, allowing a second round to be fired by all of the first four starboard cannons. The importance of this was evident when all four cannonballs of the second firing hit the warship. The extra time created by Dumaka allowed the crews to make the elevation adjustment shouted by the gunnery chief after seeing the first round hit the water harmlessly.

"Fire four through eight!" shouted the chief, after relaying the elevation settings to the crews. Smoke belched as the cannons fired.

By now both of the Ottoman vessels were silent, completely obscured by smoke pouring from the gunports

Cormac's cannons roared again, first one side then the other. Because their forward speed had been slowed by damage to the sails, the second group of four guns were also able to get off two rounds to either side. Then guns nine to twelve fired.

"Did we damage them?" yelled Gael to Cormac on the main deck.

"I can't see through the smoke," Cormac shouted, "but we must have because I haven't seen any splashes since our first round."

At last they were in the open ocean and past the warships, although heavy damage to the sails kept their progress sluggish. Gael immediately called for an injury report and directed the crew to begin clearing the decks, an almost unnecessary command because most of the men had survived battles on the galley and understood the need for immediate damage control.

"We have five dead and 27 injured, including Dumaka." Patrick reported within minutes. "Several with broken arms or legs, and one man lost an eye. All should fully recover. Uhh, make that 28 injured," he added as he noticed Cormac's blood soaked left sleeve. "Let me look at that, friend."

A few deft slices with his knife cut the sleeve away to reveal an eight inch wooden sliver through the underside of the redhead's upper arm. "This'll smart, but I'm going to pull it through in the same direction that it entered," said the sailor, "don't want splinters in the wound from pulling it out backwards." He pushed the end of the splinter with his palm to expose more of the tip protruding from the wound. While Cormac watched impassively, Patrick smoothly pulled the sliver out of the arm, immediately wrapping it with a sleeve cut off his own shirt to stem the flow of blood.

"Thank you," said the Irishman. "Dumaka?"

"Took a metal shard across the top of his right shoulder, close to his neck, as he bent to move a carriage back into position. If he'd been standing upright, it would have killed him. As it is, just a nasty wound."

"Five men, and nearly six, gave their lives for my sister and friends," muttered Cormac, his eyes turning gray.

A few hundred yards out, Gael ordered an anchor lowered to stabilize the ship while they waited to see what would happen. Men on the anchor windlass were told to stay in place in case it appeared they would be pursued and needed to head out to sea. Gradually the western wind began to clear smoke from the warships.

Standing at the stern and peering through their telescopes, Gael and Cormac could see gaping holes along the gundecks of both ships and figures running about the main decks. But it was the damage to the bows that held their attention. At, or just above, the waterlines of each vessel were multiple holes, sometimes overlapping to form jagged rips in the hull. All of the openings were beginning to emit streams of black smoke.

12

AN INSTANT AFTER MAHFUZ gave the order to fire, a giant convulsion of the ship threw him through the railing of the afterdeck and down onto the main deck. He had expected the craft to rock mightily as all 24 starboard cannons were fired simultaneously, but this was different: the vessel had seemed to hurl itself up in the air and crash down on its port side before righting. Smoke from the cannons blanketed everything, but he was aware of men staggering around dazeed and bodies underfoot as he scrambled upright. One of the ensigns appeared in front of him, blood pouring from a gash in the side of his head.

"What happened?" shouted the Captain, through the deafening ringing in his ears.

"I don't know, sir," yelled the man, "but the first mate is dead. He was thrown into the side railing and it snapped his neck."

Although he could hardly hear the man, Mahfuz signaled him to follow and led the way to the stairs leading down to the first cannon deck. Halfway down, a scene of incredible carnage met his eyes. Massive holes had been blown open in the line of gunports by the exploding cannons that Cormac's men had sabotaged: strewn everywhere with great splits were the barrels, carriages twisted and broken apart. Other carriages holding discharged cannons were lodged against the port bulkhead, their breech ropes snapped and bodies of gun-crew members crushed beneath them. The acrid smell of gunpowder, and swirling smoke, permeated the entire scene.

"The guns must have been plugged, sir, and breech ropes cut," screamed a gunnery officer at the top of his voice when Mahfuz signaled that he couldn't hear. The man's clothes had been almost completely blown away and powder burns covered his body.

"The second deck?" yelled the Captain.

"I think it's the same Captain, but I haven't been below," bellowed the man.

"Let's go," Mahfuz shouted, and they made their way to the next set of stairs.

The scene of destruction was the same on the lower gundeck: wreckage and bodies strewn everywhere, survivors staggering about with terrible wounds or simply sitting with their heads in their hands. The Captain, pointing upward, led the way back to the main deck. Just as they reached it, the ship shuddered.

"We're taking fire, sir," shouted the officer directly into the Captain's ear, but when both looked up, the furled sails, spars, and masts were untouched. They realized that the shots were striking the hull.

"See what you can find out," Mahfuz cried, "I'm going to see if Umar damaged him."

Feeling his ship shudder again, the Captain climbed up to the high afterdeck and retrieved a spare telescope from its case on the railing. He focused it on the pirate ship, which was still moving ahead and almost clear of the Ottoman vessels. It was obvious that some of their shots had struck it: the rear mast was in shambles and the hull had been penetrated in several spots, but it was still under sail, moving slowly. Across from him, Umar's vessel was oddly angled, anchored only at the bow.

"They must have severed the stern anchor chain somehow," he thought, scanning the rest of the hull. To his horror, gaping holes appeared across both cannon levels. "They sabotaged her also," he mumbled to himself.

Then he saw white smoke burst from the aft guns of the pirate ship and an instant later felt his ship shudder. He and the others on deck had instinctively flinched and ducked, but when he saw no resulting damage, he wondered why they still weren't firing at his masts or the main deck. If they wanted to escape, he reasoned, they should be trying to disable his masts and sails to prevent pursuit. Despite the damage to his cannon decks, he could still give chase and make repairs while doing so. His port cannons were all intact and it would be easy to clean up the decks and move some of them to the starboard side. The actions of the pirates made no sense, even less so when a short time later they seemed to have anchored a quarter of a mile away. Mahfuz was mulling this over when the gunnery officer approached at a run.

"Captain, you've got to come!" he shouted at the top of his lungs to compensate for the ringing in both of their ears.

"What?"

"We're on fire!" bellowed the officer, "at the bow."

Both of them leaped down to the main deck and set off rapidly toward the front of the ship. The officer ran to the starboard railing some 20 feet short of the bow and pointed down. Joining him, the Captain leaned over the rail and stared, blood draining from his face. A thick column of oily black smoke was rising from below.

"I think it's in the magazine..." the officer started to say.

He never finished, as the tons of gunpowder and shot stored in the forward compartments erupted in a series of massive explosions that were heard for miles. Out of the black smoke that enveloped the ship, an enormous sheet of flame rose hundreds of feet into the air. Seconds later a matching blast and sheet of flame enveloped Umar's vessel. When the smoke finally cleared, both warships were gone.

Constantinople

1

Standing beside Cormac on the afterdeck a few days later, Finn was lost in thought as the ship cut cleanly through the blue Mediterranean under a cloudless sky. The great white sails above them were filled with a quartering wind from the west and below them on the main deck men were busy polishing away the last vestiges of evidence from the battle. Dumaka and Bako were on the foredeck, introducing their sons to the wonderful sight of dolphins riding the bow waves. Jonathan was trying to coax Francoise to climb the rigging and experience the view from the crows nest.

"Where did the idea come from?" he asked Cormac.

"What idea," asked his brother absently, his mind taken up with thoughts of Abigail.

"The idea to fire on the magazines of those ships. Even though we were far away, when the noise reached us on the roof of the Reis' house it was like claps of thunder! And the fireball..." he mused. "Not once but twice. Jugurtha and I both lowered our telescopes at the first blast to stare at each other, hardly able to believe that you'd done it. When the second blast came, Bako, still glued to his telescope, simply said 'they're *gone*.' We didn't know what he meant until we looked. Only one ship was left on the ocean; yours. The strategy was brilliant."

Cormac was silent for minutes, staring off into the horizon. Finally, he turned to look Finn in the eye.

"The idea came to me the first night we were outside the Beach Gate waiting for it to be opened. I heard the words 'chains, sandbags, climbers,' from the same voice that has spoken to me through the years. The word 'chains' was obvious because of Dumaka, but 'sandbags and climbers' made no sense until a picture flashed in my mind of Ibrahim climbing up the side of a ship, hauling bags of sand. Right after that I saw the image of a magazine hold filled with powder. Magazine holds are always low in the bow of a ship, to be as far away as possible from the captain and crew. Within a very short time I knew what we had to do.

"We've talked many times about what Mrs. Doyle said to the other women on the ship to Tunis,

'*He will give his angels charge over you to guard you in all your ways...*'

"The three of us were protected and guided throughout our years of slavery. Jonathan was protected in the shipwreck; we survived in Marseille when Bran's knots were untied; Francoise should have died from his wound. Consider the fog coming over Tunis for our 'demon' attack and then blowing out to cover us at the warships..."

He paused to stare at the blue expanse of ocean sparkling in front of them.

"I don't believe it's been random, but the priests never taught us that God does things for us personally. Yet things have happened time after time. How can it be, and why us? Some day when this is all over we need to find the answers."

"Yes," said Finn, "I've never forgotten the man who saved my life the first week on the caravans; led us to water when the jamal and I were dying after our escape; then guided us with his hawk to the oasis."

The two were quiet for a while with their thoughts, then Finn put his arm around Cormac's shoulders. "In light of all this, I have a feeling that we will be successful in recovering Bran and our friends despite the odds against us. When that is accomplished there will be a wedding to celebrate." he said.

"I'm sure Mother, Kella, and the girls will have made plans," his brother replied, a faint blush coloring his face. "Abigail was already inquiring about hiring Shrewsbury for the ceremony. He's certainly no priest, but he does represent the Crown and that's good enough for her. I have no idea what to expect, but I'm sure they'll have it all worked out."

"After the recent events, I think the people of Tunis will want a reason to celebrate," Finn said, thinking back to the moment days before, when Gael eased the damaged ship alongside the wharf.

2

THE CAPTAIN AND CORMAC HAD given the crew time to clean up debris before conducting a funeral for the five dead men and committing their bodies to the sea. By the time the ship limped back to Tunis, hundreds of people had crowded onto the great dock and beach to greet them. Everyone had heard the explosions and it didn't take a telescope to see that the Ottoman ships were gone: the Janissary reign of terror was over and life would return to normal. Vendors, pirates, quarry slaves, and citizens great and small, cheered unabashedly when Cormac, Dumaka, and Gael appeared at the railing.

The injured were the first to leave the ship. They were loaded into carts supplied by the merchants and taken to various doctors for treatment, amid rousing shouts of encouragement and thanks by the crowds. Jugurtha, Finn, Bako, and Jonathan waited at the foot of the gangplank to offer their congratulations and to satisfy themselves that their friends weren't seriously wounded.

Both Cormac and Dumaka shrugged off their concern, but the Irishman had a request for Jugurtha and Finn.

"We have at least four days of repairs before sailing," he'd said, "is there enough time to get our family here to say goodbye before we leave?"

"Excellent idea," Finn had replied. "I want to see how Tiziri is doing anyway. I'll get Gwasila and we'll leave immediately on the fastest camels we have."

"Why don't you bring her, Kella, and the whole family," Jugurtha had suggested with sudden inspiration.

In the days that followed, every local shipwright sent their best crews to swarm over the O'Shea vessel. They installed a new rear mast, replaced torn rigging and sails, repaired hull damage, scrubbed cannons, cleaned decks and replaced powder and shot.

Virtually every quarry slave, led by Angus, Cedric, and Giovanni. volunteered to replace the 31 sailors injured or killed in the battle.

"I'm sorry, my dear friends, but I need you for other tasks," said Cormac when the three approached him the day following his return. "Your leadership is important for Jugurtha as he conducts the affairs of Tunis while we're gone. But most importantly, if we fail to return from Constantinople, I need your word that you will see to it that my mother and Seamus return to Ireland if that is their wish."

"Brother, it is our pledge," said Angus, as the others nodded their heads.

"Good. I've asked Gael to choose the 31, since he is Captain of the ship. The only addition I will make is to add Ibrahim and a few scaffold climbers. Somehow I have a feeling we may need their skills again."

In addition to the ship repairs, a great deal was also accomplished in the city itself. The quarry slaves, guided by their four leaders, joined with the citizens to remove dead bodies for burial, clean up debris, and make repairs to damaged buildings. The people of Tunis marveled at the speed and skill of these men in restoring broken stonework.

Jugurtha's motivation in directing these efforts concerned rebuilding confidence within the city in the absence of the Pasha. Kella was the Pasha's sister and the family reconciliation the previous year was well known to the population. She and Jugurtha would move into the palace to perpetuate the Pasha's presence and authority until he was rescued. The former quarry slaves, headed by Cedric, Angus, and Giovanni, would supply the necessary manpower for conducting municipal affairs. Their efficiency, dignity and compassion as they went about their tasks smoothed the way for the populace to accept the change in station from recent slaves to administrators.

The Tuareg fighters summoned from different camps had been sent home with gifts of appreciation. Both Jonathan and Francoise had announced that they were sailing with Cormac and Finn. The brothers speculated privately about whether there might be extra motivation for the two joining the rescue party: after all Francoise had insisted on being a guide for Bran and Pinar, even though they knew the city as well as he did, while Jonathan had made more than one reference to the First Daughter's beauty.

On the afternoon of the fourth day of repairs, Francoise had appeared at the wharf with a carriage. He brought news that Finn, Gwasila and all members of both families had arrived and were waiting at the Reis' house. Only Seamus was missing: he'd chosen to stay and help the old Stable Master with the horses. When a servant opened the gate a short time later, Abigail didn't wait for Cormac to approach but raced headlong down the path, blond hair flying, into his arms. In the excitement she never noticed the slight wince as his wound was jarred.

Supper that night concluded with the delicious Bread and Butter Pudding for which the Reis' cook was famous. At the end of the meal, she appeared in the dining room.

"The two of you are a credit to Ireland for saving the city," she said to Cormac and Finn, speaking in Arabic for everyone's benefit, and fixing the brothers with a steady gaze, "but I don't consider the job done until you bring back the lasses."

The next morning they had set sail.

3

"I'VE ONLY BEEN HERE ONCE," Gael announced as they glided past the cannon emplacements of Castello A Mare and into the port of Heraklion. "We were on the way to Rhodes to trade for wine and developed a cracked rudder to the west. Stopped here to get it replaced."

"That's a formidable set of cannons," said Finn. "I'd hate to be an invader."

"We'll provision here and head straight for the Dardanelles," Gael continued, "there are lots of islands in between, but it would take more time to get what we need in the smaller ports. Besides, I want to look for an extra top spar for the main mast. The one the shipwrights put on in Tunis is a little undersized. We should be able to leave with the tide in the morning."

While the others set out to explore the town, and the 1st mate began to order supplies, Cormac and Gael went in search of a shipwright.

The first one didn't have a ready spar, but referred them to another shop along the harbor where they found exactly what they needed.

"Will you be wanting us to install it?" asked the owner in English, an older man with a limp and a slight Scottish burr.

"No, thank you. It's strange to find a Scotsman, if I'm not mistaken, so far from home," said Cormac. "Where are you from?"

"Aye, Scots it is. Aberdeen, laddie, on the east coast. Grew up fish'n with my Daddy and couldn't leave the sea when he died. A shipwreck stranded me on Crete with a broken leg and I've been here ever since."

"Aberdeen. I was just there last winter," Gael said, "delivering the sweetest little lassie you ever saw back to her grandparents. She lost her mother and father in North Africa."

The shipwright hesitated and gave him an inquisitive look, but didn't pursue the topic.

"We don't need you to install the spar, but if you could deliver it to us up the quay, we'd be in your debt," Cormac said, "We acquired a replacement in Tunis, but it's a bit short.

"Tunis, you say? I just repaired a sloop out of there. Broken mast. Captain said they almost capsized in a terrible storm, and took significant damage. Did you encounter the tempest also?"

"No," said Cormac with a puzzled look. "We've had clear sailing, with the wind at our back the whole way."

4

"THAT'S THE YEDIKULE," said Andras, joining Cormac and Gael on the afterdeck as they sailed past a massive fortress with great towers on the portside shore a few days later. "It was built 200 years ago to protect the entrance to the city after Constantinople became part of the Ottoman Empire. Initially it housed treasures of the Empire, but for a long time now it's served as a prison."

They had sailed up the Dardanelle Strait linking the Aegean Sea to the Sea of Marmara, which bordered the legendary city, and were approaching the harbor.

"You've been here before," said Gael.

"Yes, for a while I served on a ship out of Thessaloniki carrying trade goods between here and there, principally coffee beans from Constantinople. You're in for a treat with Turkish coffee," he added with a smile, "I can almost taste it now."

"I'm looking forward to it. Ahhh, there's the entrance to the harbor," said Gael as an opening appeared to the left. "Just as the maps show."

"'The harbor and the river that flows into it at the far end is called 'The Golden Horn,'" Andras said. "It has a long history of naval battles against enemies attacking the city. For centuries a great chain was strung across the entrance to prevent ships from entering. Several wars involved invaders actually hauling their ships on rollers over land to launch them behind the chain, from the shore facing the city. On at least one occasion, the defenders destroyed those vessels with fire ships loaded with a substance that burned so hot that it ignited anything the ship came close to. The entire attacking army, vessels and men, burned up on the harbor."

Cormac and the Captain stared at him in horror. Shipboard fire was a dreaded danger.

"Just like the janissaries did to the Pasha's galley," said the Greek slave, "only vastly more men died."

As soon as the ship was anchored among the many vessels in the harbor, Francoise, Jonathan, and Bako went ashore in the dory to find what news they could about the sloop. All were dressed in nondescript white robes and turbans. In addition to information gathering, the three were charged with bringing back some of the 'legendary' Turkish coffee.

Gael had anchored at some distance from the nearest ship in order to escape prying eyes, so the entire contingent on board was able to lounge about the decks on a warm summer afternoon, sharing stories and experiences. More than one man questioned Andras about the so-called 'greatest coffee you've ever had.'

"Just wait and see," he said. But when the scouts returned, they had an interesting report. "The Sultan has banned the drinking of coffee in public," Francoise said, "it's now an offense punishable by death! Apparently he's scared it will somehow stir the Janissaries up so much that they'll think about revolt. Since he came into power when they revolted against his uncle, his fear is understandable. However, the wholesale selling of beans is still allowed, probably because it's a source of revenue for the Empire, so we procured a sack and a grinder." Andras' praise of the product was proved correct as every man voiced his approval of the brew that night. "Far better than anything I've tasted in Tunis," was heard over and over.

The conversation grew sober as Francoise reported that the sloop had arrived two days earlier and the prisoners were locked up in the Yedikule prison towers until the Sultan returned from a hunting trip. "No one knows precisely when, but he's expected back within the week," said the Frenchman. "He'll attend to the affairs of the Empire as soon as he returns, although it seems his Grand Vizier handles routine matters when he's away."

"Perhaps we should appear before the Vizier right away to set the stage," said Finn. He, along with Bako and Dumaka, had come up with a daring plan during the trip to Constantinople but it required some creative embellishment.

The following morning Cormac and Bako, clad in plain robes and armed with some of the Reis' gold brought along by Francoise, entered the cities' shopping district. They returned in the afternoon with several large bundles and disappeared below. A short time later Bako and Francoise appeared at Gael's cabin, completely transformed. Bako wore a magnificent yellow and brown silk robe with matching turban. Large gold bracelets adorned both wrists and several gold rings, inset with diamonds, flashed from his fingers. A great gold pendant hung from his neck, with a matching pendant encircling the turban. Rich leather sandals completed his attire.

Francoise wore a loose white silk blouse and matching turban. His red silk pants ended just below the knees and he wore red slippers with upturned toes, trimmed in gold. In one hand he gently waved a four foot staff with a hoop of white silk on the end.

"To cool my master," he said with a small bow before adding, "The jewelry and clothing cost the Reis a significant amount."

"I don't think he'll complain if we succeed," said Cormac. "If we fail, it won't make any difference. But I have one more suggestion."

A few minutes later, Jonathan appeared, clad in a simple white cotton shirt, matching white turban and knee length pants. He carried a broom with long straw fibers on the end.

"His Arabic isn't good enough for speech yet," said the redhead, "but he understands most of what is said. A simple slave brushing the street ahead of his Master doesn't need to speak, but he'll have the knives with him just in case."

5

THE TWO GUARDS OUTSIDE the street entrance to the Sultan's Court were stunned at the entourage approaching them through the crowded street. People melted to either side as an enormous black man clad in a magnificent robe and turban, bedecked with gold jewelry, strode purposefully forward. At his side a slave waved the air above his head with a silk fan; in front of him scurried another slave sweeping the street ahead of his steps. Behind him in two columns strode ten heavily-armed, fierce-looking, black warriors. The man halted in front of the great oval doorway, both slaves on their knees to either side.

"I wish to see the Sultan," he growled in a low voice.

"He's not here, what's your business?" asked the senior guard in a cold tone.

"I am the Grand Al-Mahdi, a supplier to the Empire and I've been robbed by his Janissaries. I've come a long way to demand satisfaction," said Bako in an irritated voice.

"Robbed by Janissaries?" said the man, in a more obsequious voice. He himself was a Janissary and subject to the consequences of actions by his fellow soldiers.

"Yes, they took 300 slaves I was delivering to Tunis for the Pasha and shipped them off to Algiers for their own profit without paying me. The Pasha told me the captives were to be sent to Constantinople as a gift. Thus they robbed the Sultan of a gift, as well as tribute because I doubt the Janissaries will forward a portion of the Algiers profits to Constantinople."

"I think this is a matter for the Grand Vizier," said the guard, now thoroughly accommodating. "Let me see if I can find him." He disappeared through the doors, to return a few minutes later. "Please follow me, the Grand Vizier will see you now."

With Jonathan bent over furiously sweeping the tile before him and Francoise gently waving the silk hoop over his head, Bako strode regally into the court followed by his sons and nephews. He stopped before the long table at the bottom of the dias, briefly eying the eight purple-robed, white-turbaned men sitting just above him before raising his gaze to the two Viziers sitting one level above them. He deliberately paid no attention to the magnificent throne on top of the dias.

"The Grand Al-Mahdi from Tunis," announced a page slave, refraining from mentioning the business at hand.

"Timbuktu," roared Bako in a voice that startled everyone. "I just came from Tunis to seek redress for crimes committed against me by Empire Janissaries."

Every single man on the dias was an ex-Janissary of one rank or another and a criminal matter against the corps was serious business because they could be held accountable. Kemankes Mustafa, Grand Vizier, seated just below the throne, was wearing a white silk robe and turban. He was startled by the black man's boldness, and decided to be cautious. Captain Mahfuz, whom he'd picked to command the warships carrying Zehab, had a long record of naval service to the Ottomans, but one never knew what a man might do far from the eyes of Constantinople.

"Crimes by the Sultan's soldiers?" asked the Grand Vizier in what he hoped sounded like a shocked voice. "In Tunis? We just had an Envoy return from that city and he mentioned no crimes. How have you been damaged and what is the nature of your business?"

"I am the Grand Al-Mahdi, Overlord of Caravans in Timbuktu," said Bako in a loud voice. "No trading to the east or west is done without my blessing. No caravan departs or enters the city without paying for my protection."

"And how might that concern us in Constantinople?" asked Kemankes in a placating voice, still uncertain about what might be coming. "Timbuktu is not part of the Ottoman Empire."

"But it does business with the Ottomans," said Bako, "in Algiers, Tunis, and Egypt." He paused for effect. "A great deal of business."

"And the Sultan appreciates your business," said the Grand Vizier, knowing well the shortage of revenue to operate the far-flung Empire and not wanting to jeopardize any source of funds. "Please describe the circumstances of what happened to you."

"Many months ago I received a message from the Pasha of Tunis," Bako said in a more normal voice, appearing to have calmed down. "He requested 300 elite slaves delivered to him directly. He did not want to trade for them but instead promised to pay in gold when they were delivered. Quality was important, the message said, because the slaves would be sent on to the Sultan in Constantinople as a gift.

"I immediately began to purchase the choicest prisoners delivered to Timbuktu from the south, but it took some time to assemble the required number. When I had more than enough to compensate for deaths on the way, I personally led the caravan to Tunis. I made sure we had more water and food than normal so the slaves would arrive in good health. This required extra expense, I might add," he said pointedly. Kemankes nodded sympathetically.

"North of Ghadames, we began to encounter camel herds at the oases with no loads. We were told that Ottoman Janissaries had taken over the city of Tunis and all trading had been stopped. I was encouraged because if Ottoman ships were there I might command a higher price from the Pasha, since transport was readily available to take the slaves to Constantinople.

"However, when we arrived at the staging area outside the city, a large group of Janissaries appeared, announcing that they were now in charge of the city. They said that the Pasha was gone and they were taking the slaves to the Algerian market. When I demanded payment, they said I was lucky to escape with my life, and ordered me to leave. I didn't have enough men to resist and was forced to flee. Three days later I sneaked into Tunis with a small group of handpicked fighters, commandeered a vessel and sailed for Constantinople."

There was silence in the Court as the assembled men contemplated this story. Kemankes started to sweat. If the story was true, he had been a fool to hint that the Pasha of Tunis might have been shorting the Sultan's tribute. This generous gesture would contradict the image he had created of a duplicitous leader in Tunis. Furthermore, if the forces under Mahfuz had committed a serious crime, the Sultan would hold him personally responsible.

"You were right to come all this way and report these things to us," he said in the most appreciative tone he could muster. "Come back tomorrow and we'll render our decision."

The Grand Al-Mahdi stood for a minute staring first at the Viziers and then pointedly at the Janissary Captains before spinning on his heel and exiting the court. Jonathan led the way sweeping the immaculate tile with a vengeance.

6

When Bako appeared at the doors of the Court the following morning, the guards crossed their lances in front of him.

"The Sultan returned unexpectedly yesterday and is conducting the affairs of the Empire," said the leader.

"What affairs of the Empire are more important than a Janissary betrayal?" roared Bako.

"The betrayal of one of his Pashas," said the guard, unmoved by the outburst. "The Pasha of Tunis, his family, and a pirate were just brought from the prison to be sentenced. You are to be allowed in after he has dealt with them."

For the next hour Bako and his entourage waited silently, the only movement being the fan waved by Francoise. Finally, the door opened and guards escorted the Pasha, Suliman Reis, the First Wife, and girls from the Court. All of them looked stunned and stared at the ground, except Bran. Holding Kelebek by the hand, she strode with head held high and defiance in her eyes. She glanced at Bako briefly and then her gaze snapped back in recognition. The slightest tilt of his head acknowledged her before she passed.

Bran was dumbfounded. Without question, it was Bako waiting outside the Sultan's Court, although clothed in glorious attire. What was he doing in Constantinople dressed in all that finery? She had said goodbye to him on the beach south of Tunis a year ago, never expecting to see him again. Yet he was staring right at her when they came out of the Court and gave her a subtle sign to confirm his identity. Her brain was whirling as she walked away, head held high.

"The Grand Al-Mahdi from Timbuktu and the matter of slaves in Tunis," announced the page as Bako strode up to the mahogany table in front of the dias. On the throne lounged a giant young man dressed in a shimmering gold-embroidered purple shirt, matching turban and pants, gold slippers on his feet. He was cradling an enormous mace and had a quizzical look on his face as he stared at the man below who was surprisingly a bit larger than he was. A quick glance by the archer revealed a smug expression from the Grand Vizier and confusion on the faces of the Janissary Captains. Something had changed.

"State your case," said Kemankes in a commanding and arrogant voice.

"Excellency," began Bako with a bow, "I am here to seek redress from the Empire." He then described the same story he'd presented the day before, noting that Kemankes was openly smiling in disdain. When he was finished, Bako bowed again.

"But the Pasha of Tunis was in this very room a few moments ago and told us that he never ordered prime slaves as a gift to the Empire," said Murad, slapping the mace gently against one hand.

"Eminence, this man is clearly lying," said the Grand Vizier.

"I want to hear what he has to say," said the Sultan in a tone that brooked no argument. "Al-Mahdi?"

"Excellency, are not your slightest wishes carried out by this Court as well as by all your advisors and servants?" asked Bako, thinking quickly and knowing from his years of experience as a slave how the Pasha's affairs were handled at the palace. "I suspect that it's possible one such as the Pasha, or even yourself, might forget a casual remark made to someone in his entourage during the heat of other, more important affairs?"

The Sultan just barely nodded his head in acknowledgement but said nothing.

"The original message to me was a note from the Minister of Commerce for Tunis. It arrived by caravan in Timbuktu almost a year ago." Bako said "It had the Pasha's seal, so I knew it was authentic; however, there was no direct communication from the Pasha himself.

"The caravan operator also reported that there had been a serious battle in Tunis between desert renegades and the Pasha's soldiers just before he left the city. The Pasha himself was involved in the front lines of the fighting and nearly lost his life. My guess is that he had mentioned the idea of the gift to an aide immediately before that battle. Based on his injuries, I'm not surprised that he doesn't remember it."

Bako was taking liberties with his description of the harem battle, but he was counting on the fact that no one in Constantinople could challenge his story.

"You say the Pasha was on the front lines?" asked Murad, himself proud of leading his own men in battle.

"Excellency," interrupted the Grand Vizier, "there is no way this man could have known that."

"Be quiet Kemankes," said the Sultan in a dangerously soft voice that caused sweat to turn cold in the Grand Vizier's armpits.

"Eminence, the Pasha is well regarded in Tunis and the story was confirmed by numerous caravan operators in the weeks that followed," said Bako. "If I may be so bold, Sire, surely the Janissary soldiers would not be allowed to benefit personally from the sale of my slaves in Algiers. Their leader and those who organized the expedition to Tunis would certainly pay tribute to the Empire before sharing the profits."

There was dead silence in the Court and Bako saw the Grand Vizier go white. He'd taken a chance with the remark and now realized that

Kemankes had indeed been charged with carrying out the Tunis expedition. From the man's reaction, Bako knew that he'd been successful in sowing doubt. He could see that Murad was undecided about whether he'd been double-crossed or not. From the look on the Sultan's face, the archer knew he was capable of torturing or killing anyone in the room to get the information he wanted. At last the young man spoke..

"You've done well to come to Constantinople and advise us of these things," he said, "but I will pay you nothing for the loss of the slaves. If your story is true, they were to be a gift to the Empire anyway. As for the conduct of the Janissaries, that is for me and my advisors to decide."

"Please forgive me for taking another minute of your time, Eminence, but I'm told the Ottomans struggle with disloyal subjects," said Bako, "Your long war with the Safavids is well known, but equally well known is your personal courage in leading your men. The Pasha's bravery in leading his men during the battle against rebels last summer mirrors your own. My caravans have delivered goods to the Pasha for years and never once have I been treated unfairly in payment. In my experience, the combination of courage and character in men is rare indeed. If I may be so bold, perhaps the record of the Pasha might be examined more closely." Bako knew that he was risking the anger of the Sultan by continuing, but he wanted to insert one more thought into the minds of those watching. "Furthermore, reports have come to me that one of the Pasha's subjects has the ability to conjure up demons. Forgive me again, Eminence, but the underworld can be very dangerous."

There was silence as the Sultan contemplated these observations, gently slapping the mace into his left palm.

"Perhaps," he finally said. "I had ordered him and a pirate to be executed in front of my soldiers tomorrow morning as the penalty for disobedience to the Empire, but I think I will save the Pasha for a few days while I decide on this matter. I invite you to join us tomorrow, I think you will find it amusing. I don't tolerate disloyalty and have devised ways to prolong the victim's agony to make an impression on my soldiers."

"It would please me to attend," said the Grand Al-Mahdi.

7

THAT AFTERNOON TWO MEN dressed in simple but expensive blue robes approached the guards on duty at the gate of the Yedikule Fortress. One was clearly European, with long blond hair and brown eyes flecked with gold. The other was a dark-eyed Arab, veil across his face. The European addressed the guards in flawless Arabic.

"Is this the famous Fortress of the Seven Towers, or Dungeons of the Seven Towers?" He asked with an inquiring look. "I just arrived with merchandise from Europe and was told I must see one of the great structures in the Ottoman Empire."

"Yes, it was built nearly 200 years ago using part of the city's protective walls and two towers originally constructed by the Romans," said the guard, flattered by the inquiry from a wealthy foreigner.

"Why was it built?" asked the European.

"Partially for added defense, but also to house the city's treasure," said the guard, warming to his role as historian. "The treasure was moved to a different location and now the fortress is used to hold valuable prisoners for the Sultan."

"Oh," said the visitor, suitably impressed. "Are there any important personages currently held here?"

"Yes there are," said the guard with pride. "None other than the Pasha of Tunis and a famous pirate. They and the Pasha's family were brought in last week and locked up in Tower Two." He pointed at a tower built as a part of the city's outer wall.

"Do the towers have actual dungeons as one name suggests?" asked the merchant.

"Oh no," the Janissary said, almost visibly swelling with importance as he warmed to the subject, "there never were actual dungeons. All the cells are within the walls you see, with the highest ones reserved for the most important prisoners."

"Why is that?"

"Well," he turned and pointed to a tower, "see Tower Two? It's built right into the wall protecting the city along the sea. Notice the barred windows at the very top: those are the cells to house important prisoners. They can look at the sea, which represents freedom, but even if someone could squeeze through the bars, the 35 meter (100 feet) walls are so sheer they would fall to their death on the rocks below. So it's a form of torture while they await their fate at the hands of the Sultan: freedom so close and yet so far."

"It looks in such excellent condition for being built two centuries ago," said the Arab, "may I examine it?"

"By all means, have a look," the guard waved a hand at the nearby wall. "You'll see that it's in nearly perfect condition."

"Do you suppose the Pasha of Tunis would warrant a cell on top?" inquired the European as the other man strode a few away and began to look at the walls.

"Oh yes." The guard was now thoroughly and egotistically immersed in the role of an expert on the Fortress. "He and that famous pirate have cells side by side looking right out at the ocean."

"Surely the family wouldn't warrant such a location?" asked the merchant.

"No, they were in windowless cells lower down while they were here."

"They were freed?" asked the European casually.

"No, they were taken to the harbor yesterday afternoon. We heard that the Sultan has sent them as a gift to the ruling Mamluk in Egypt who appreciates beautiful women, although I hear they do *not* return the sentiment." The guard sneered conspiratorially.

"The rock work is amazing," said the Arab as he joined them. "I can see why it's held up all these years. It is a tribute to the Empire."

With profuse thanks to the guard, who was so puffed with pride at the attention that he could hardly contain himself, the two strode away toward the city.

"Rotten," said Ibrahim when they were far enough away not to be heard, "the rock in the tower is solid, but the mortar is rotten. No problem to climb it."

8

"A DIPLOMATIC GESTURE," said Dumaka by way of explanation to the brothers and Gael later that afternoon when Finn reported that the women had been sent to Egypt. "Our villages are in the hill country east of the Second Cataract on the great Nile River. We're not part of Egypt, but travelers bound for the western desert pass through and keep us advised about its affairs. As soon as I reached home last year I learned about developments in Cairo during the time I was gone. The present Governor is Sultanzad Mehmed Pasha, but the real power rests with Ridwan Bey, a Mamluk Emir in charge of the army.

"The Mamluks are a society of slave warriors, not unlike the Janissaries, that have always exercised great power in Egypt because, unlike the civil authorities, they control the soldiers. They are continually prone to rebel against the Ottomans. With the difficulty of controlling them from Constantinople, all the Sultans resort to bribery to keep them peaceful.

"Sending the Pasha's wife and daughters to the Emir for his harem is clearly such an attempt to keep Ridwan Bey happy and loyal."

"Now that you mention it, I did notice a sloop weigh anchor and move out of the harbor yesterday," said Gael, "but I gave it no thought. It was probably the same ship that brought them here: it's faster and easier to provision than a full gunship."

"We don't have much time if we're to catch them," said Cormac. "We need to talk with Ibrahim."

An hour later a plan had been developed and crew members set to work with saws and adzes. Another team assembled 50-foot coils of rope. An extra dory was acquired at the harbor wharf and a few hours later, as evening fell, the new craft slipped away down the harbor carrying Finn, Ibrahim, Jacques, and Andras. Each oar was manned by one of the crew and, once clear of the anchored ships, powerful strokes sent them out of the harbor and east along the shore of the Marmara Sea. To their right along the shore rose the formidable walls that protected the city. Staying 100 yards off shore, they could easily have been taken for night fishermen by anyone observing from the walls. Since it was a peaceful time for the Ottomans, Finn hoped that any such watchmen were more concerned with dinner and drink than studying the small boats of fishermen.

As they approached Yedikule Fortress, he pointed out Tower Two in the growing dark. As the guard had described, it rose right from the rocky beach as part of the protective wall. Just below its top, two barred openings were dimly visible. The oarsmen held the dory offshore until it was fully night, then eased it into the beach and secured it to a boulder. Several big bundles, plus three rope coils were carried to the base of the wall.

"Same condition as you examined at the gate?" murmured Finn as Ibrahim and the others ran hands over the blocks that formed the tower's walls.

"Exactly" breathed the Tuareg after a few minutes.

"Good," Finn replied.

"We'll get to work," said Ibrahim after a whispered conference with the other two climbers.

The night was clear and a half moon rising in the east gave faint light to the scene. Ibrahim pulled a chisel and mallet from one of the bundles and began tapping softly on the wall at a seam between two pieces of rock. The Irishman could hear little pieces of mortar dropping to the ground. He had a moment of panic as he worried whether the sound would carry to the top of the walls adjoining the tower, but a cool breeze suddenly caused three foot swells to begin crashing on the shore, totally obscuring the sound of the tapping and scraping. After a few minutes, Ibrahim reached into his sack and withdrew a narrow piece of wood about 18" long with a sharpened end. He inserted the wood into the seam and tapped it with the mallet until half of it had disappeared between the two rocks.

"Just as I said, the mortar is rotten," he murmured to Finn. "and the seams between rocks are wide enough to make it possible for us to insert these stakes."

The Arab reached up and inserted another wood shaft into a seam about two feet higher. Stepping on the first shaft, he pressed down with his foot to test its strength.

"Maybe a few more centimeters," he said, dropping to the ground and tapping it and the shaft above a few more times. When he put weight on the wood again, he gave a satisfied grunt. Hooking his right knee around the higher shaft, he reached up with both arms and inserted, what Finn observed to be, a third step. The whole process took about six minutes. A few taps of the mallet against a chisel, some scraping of debris and rotten mortar, and a piece of wood was inserted into the wall. Moving up a step, Ibrahim repeated the process. Although they had explained it, Finn was amazed to see the scaffold worker easily building a rudimentary ladder up the face of the tower. He was astounded at how fast the man worked and how easily he could balance with one foot and a knee in order to free both hands to work. When the Tuareg was 25 feet up the wall, Jacques climbed up to deliver another sack of stakes. The higher the men went the more obvious it became to Finn that if his foot slipped while Ibrahim was using both hands to insert a stake he would plummet straight down onto the rocks.

"Don't forget the Reis has one useless arm," Finn whispered to Jacques when he descended.

"We've got enough rope for each to get down to the beach," the climber said. "All three of us will help them, especially the Reis."

Finn shook his head in the dark. To him it seemed impossible, but these men had been operating at height on flimsy scaffolds for years and he was reminded of Cormac's description of them as big monkeys on the sides of the warships. He sat against the wall and put all thoughts out of his mind about one of them plunging to his death, concentrating instead on how they were going to recover Bran and the others. The night was only disturbed by Jacques reappearing from time to time for more stakes and the blond found himself dozing.

9

Suleyman Reis stared out the barred window at the Sea of Marmara. A fishing boat just offshore bobbed on orange waves set aglow by the setting sun. Despite his confident assurances to the Pasha, Cormac had not appeared. Now they had less than 24 hours before suffering a horrible death. The Sultan had stared down at them with cold eyes, playing with his enormous mace while describing their fate.

"The pack of wild dogs in my pit is kept near starvation," Murad said. "They're ready to attack any food offered, willing to kill one another if necessary to fill their bellies. One of you will have the pleasure of watching the other hung by the arms from a windlass and lowered until his feet and calves are barely within reach of a jumping dog. When the flesh is gone, the body will be lowered further. Bets will be taken on which of you will stay alive the longest.

"Your end will be described in all the principal cities of the Empire to insure that no one else tries to cheat the Sultan." And with that he had ordered them returned to the prison.

Darkness closed in as the Reis thought about the years that had passed since he left Holland to seek his fortune with the pirates of North Africa. His success was legendary in Tunis and through it he had developed a close relationship with the man in the next cell: the most powerful figure in that region.

His mind drifted to his other relationships and settled on Cormac and his extraordinary code of honor. He knew he should have been dead twice-over but for the redhead with the great white scar on his forehead. He smiled as he pictured the ship the Irishman had appropriated in lieu of five percent of two years' profits. The Dutchman hadn't lied when he told Cormac he could have taken two of his ships to Ireland: profits had been staggering during the time the Irishman commanded the galley.

Now Francoise would be left to deal with Suleyman's fortune. Though he had not formally freed the French slave, the Reis knew that everyone understood Francoise was in charge of his affairs. The Frenchman could sail to Europe as a free man with no opposition, and the Reis found himself sentimentally wishing success and happiness for the man who had served him since age five.

Consumed with this musing, the Reis realized with a start that it had grown completely dark outside. The only light in the cell came beneath the door from the torches outside, so he groped his way to the straw pallet covered by a thin blanket and lay down, not expecting to sleep.

Sometime later, a soft 'clink' woke the Dutchman. It was pitch black in the cell; the torches in the stairwell had burned out. He thought he was dreaming until there was another 'clink' and a soft voice.

"Pasha or Reis?" It came from the window.

Fearful that the Sultan might be playing a cruel trick, Suleyman froze in place.

"Who's in here? The Pasha or the Reis? Cormac sent me."

"It's the Reis," whispered Suleyman, scrambling to his feet, "who's out there?"

There was a soft chuckle. "The only person it could possibly be: one of your quarry scaffold slaves."

Several clinks were followed by the sound of something falling to the floor with a thud. More clinks and a second thud. The opening darkened as a man crawled through, then lightened as he dropped to the floor.

"We've come to rescue you and the Pasha," whispered Ibrahim, reaching out to touch the Reis. "I'm going to tie a rope around your waist and we're going to help you down the wall."

"Impossible," replied the Reis. "One of my arms is useless, I can't go down."

"Yes you can," said Ibrahim in a low voice that brooked no argument. "We've made a ladder for you and the Pasha to descend. There are two of us. One will be below you to guide your feet and I will keep you secure with the rope from above. Now we have to hurry, there's no time to lose."

The Reis found himself picked up by strong arms, as though he were a child, and directed feet-first toward the window. As his legs passed where two of the bars had been removed, two hands grabbed his ankles and guided his body through the opening until he was sitting on the window ledge outside. Below him the tower disappeared into darkness while faint light from the sliver moon and stars reflected on the water off shore.

The Reis feared no man, but the sheer height of the tower filled him with dread. There was no time to dwell on it, however, because instructions immediately came from below his dangling feet.

"Ibrahim will keep you secure with the rope. Slide forward and I will guide your right foot to the first step. Directly below it is the second step. They form a ladder we have set into the wall. Use your good arm to grasp each step and keep you secure as you go down."

A hand grabbed his right ankle and pulled him forward, stretching the leg downward. Only the rope, tight around his waist, prevented

Suleyman from succumbing to pure terror. Suddenly he felt secure support under his foot; almost immediately his left leg was pulled down until its foot rested on another narrow surface.

"Now, reach down with your right hand and grab the first step," came the instructions, "and lower your right foot to the step below the left."

Secured by the rope, the Reis did as he was told and felt his hand grasp a piece of wood protruding from the tower. Squeezing the right leg past the left was tricky but the guiding hand from below helped him.

"Good. Now that you understand the ladder, we have to move as quickly as possible," said the voice, "We still have to get the Pasha down."

Emboldened by his success, and reassured by the rope, Suleyman began to move down the wall as fast as he could.

"My scaffold workers are all free men after this," he thought to himself, exhilarated by his success. He hardly noticed that the pressure on the rope had disappeared. Halfway down, he was congratulating himself on his speed, when his right leg pushed the left off its perch on the way to the step below. With no foothold, his right hand was pulled from its support and he plummeted into the night.

10

A SCRAPING NOISE AND A muffled cry from above roused Amnay. Expecting the sickening thud of a body hitting the ground, he moved under the line of stakes and looked up but couldn't see anything at first. Then movement about 40 feet above caught his eye. A dark shape was swinging across the face of the tower accompanied by scrabbling sounds and more muffled cries. Two objects were sticking out above the shape, moving rapidly back and forth. Concentrating on the form against the faintest gray beginning to show in the sky above, Finn realized with a shock that the objects above the shape were legs kicking wildly about in the air: a man was hanging upside down, banging and swinging across the face of the tower at the bottom of a rope!

All at once, another shape appeared to one side and the swinging body was arrested. A soft murmur carried down to Finn and he saw the legs swing around to a normal position below the body. Nothing moved for a minute or two, but the Irishman could hear the faint whisper of talking from above. Finally the two shapes began slowly descending the wall together.

Minutes passed before the figures arrived just above Finn.

"Grab one of his feet and guide it to a stake," came Jacque's low voice. "Then the other one to the bottom stake."

"Good, you're down," said the scaffold climber as Suleyman Reis collapsed into Finn's arms.

"If I could have seen what they had in mind, I might have stayed in the cell," muttered the Reis. "Without the two of them, I'd be dead. Although it would have been quicker than what the Sultan has in mind for us tomorrow."

"These men are from your own quarry," murmured Finn. "Cormac brought them with us because of their unique skills. In fact, we would not be here right now except for what they did to disable the warships outside the Tunis harbor."

"We've got to get the Pasha," said Jacques untying the rope from the Reis' waist and scrambling up the stakes into the dark.

Finn guided Suleyman to one side and sat with him against the wall. The man was breathing hard and rubbing his head.

"I think I cut my face and head when I fell," he said. "My left arm is completely useless and it was awkward in the extreme to grab stakes with my right hand. How those two managed to get me down is beyond my understanding."

"Their ability was gained as your slaves," said Finn. "More than that, if Cormac hadn't taught the quarry thralls how to take pride in their work, you wouldn't have provided proper food for them and these men wouldn't have had the strength to rescue you."

There was a long period of silence as the Reis digested this statement. He could feel blood running down into his right eye and held his good arm against the side of his face to stem the flow with the sleeve of his shirt. Sometime later faint noises from above alerted them that the Pasha was on his way down. By now a thin band of red on the eastern horizon made it light enough to barely make out the four figures slowly descending the wall.

"With two arms, he's a lot quicker than I was," observed the Reis.

And it was so. The Pasha was also secured with a rope, but had quickly adapted to using both hands and feet to descend. Below him, Jacques hardly had to guide his feet to the stakes because there was now enough light for the Pasha to see them. Above them a fourth man, whom Finn knew to be Andras, was steadily descending, pulling stakes free from the rock and placing them in the bags suspended from his neck. The Pasha was able to jump down from the last stake, but Finn had to grab his arm for support as he staggered and nearly fell.

"Impossible," said the Arab. "It was impossible for these men to accomplish such a thing. Getting up to the cells and then getting two of us to the ground. No one would believe it."

"And they won't," said the Irishman, picturing the disbelief at court when the jailers reported that the prisoners had vanished. "The bars?" he asked Ibrahim when he joined them on the ground..

"They came out easily," said the slave, "no one had bothered to secure them after all this time, probably because of the sheer drop to the ground. I reset them and packed loose mortar into the holes. Unless someone digs around, they look completely secure. And unless someone actually climbs down the wall, they'll never see the holes in the mortar where we placed the stakes." He chuckled, " I also smoothed out the pallets and emptied the refuse buckets onto the roof just above. It will look as though no one has even been there.

"We had a bit of excitement when the Reis fell, though," he added. "I'd stayed in the cell to feed the rope: sitting with both feet against the wall to provide a secure brace. They went down so smoothly that I finally stood up and leaned out to check their progress, creating slack in the rope. That's when the Reis decided to fall! The rope started sliding through my hands so fast that I had to throw myself backward to the floor to stop it. Nearly knocked myself out on the stone…"

The sun was just beginning to show above the eastern horizon when a ship appeared, heading southeast on the Sea of Marmara, and a line was thrown to the dory bobbing in the swells offshore.

11

THE GRAND VIZIER WAS ENJOYING his second cup of Turkish coffee in the immaculately landscaped garden behind his residence, secure in the knowledge that the brew was allowed in the privacy of a household. The quiet of the walled area was broken only by the gentle stream of water splashing from the mouth of a marble dolphin set in a small pond and the occasional chirps of birds flitting among the flowering bushes. A large butterfly with gold and blue wings wavered its unsteady path across his view towards a patch of flowers.

A slave silently approached on the tiled walk, a large orange gerbera flower in hand. "The flower vendor is at the front door with a selection for your consideration," murmured the man, bowing low.

"I'll see her," said Kemankes, rising, "find a vase and bring more coffee when I return."

The man bowed again and stood aside as the Vizier strode toward the house. The flower woman was in fact one of his spies and wouldn't have come this early in the morning if it wasn't important. Another slave opened the door and Kemankes stepped out onto the street, gesturing for the door to be shut behind him. Waiting a few steps away was the slightly hunched figure of a woman in a plain brown robe, face hidden under an extended hood.

"Flowers, sir?" came a slightly cackling voice from within the cowl.

"What do you have today worth buying?" asked the Vizier, marveling as always at the disguise. Without the attire, one would have seen an attractive woman about 30 years old, with long black hair and matching eyes. Expert in disguises, she frequented the city listening and watching for anything that might be of value to Kemankes.

"The gerberas are especially beautiful right now," she cackled.

When he drew close to examine the bouquet, she murmured, "There were two men looking for shops and housing inquiring about expensive clothing and jewelry at the taverns the other day."

"Yes," he muttered, tamping down his impatience. The woman's information was always reliable if somewhat slowly given

"One was an enormous black man, the other a European."

"What were they wearing?"

"Simple white robes and turbans. But that wasn't all. When I offered them flowers, the European politely refused in perfect Arabic. That's unusual for all but a few of them."

"Yes?" Kemankes was longing for the third cup of coffee waiting for him in the garden.

"As he spoke, the European casually tucked back some hair that had escaped his turban."

"And?" Now the Vizier displayed impatience.

"The hair was bright red. And his eyes were strikingly blue. Wasn't there a rumor about a blue-eyed pirate with red hair who conjured up a large black demon to fight his enemies?"

Kemankes went cold. The name 'Maclir Reis' flooded his mind: the pirate who had for years protected the left side of the very man they now had in prison at Yedikule. The man who had a black ally that Kemankes had characterized as a demon to the Sultan in order to keep attention away from himself. A huge black man who called himself the Grand Al-Mahdi had stood in the Court yesterday and glared at him. Could it be true? Was Al-Mahdi really a demon, or had the redhead simply brought a human companion to rescue Suleyman?

"Thank you, I'll take the whole bouquet," he said in a loud voice for the benefit of passersby. He handed her a heavy gold coin worth ten times the flowers, grabbed the bundle and turned toward his door.

"You're too kind!" screeched the figure and shuffled away.

Back at his table, the vizier mulled things over as he sipped his coffee. The few renegades they had recaptured from the cattle boat disaster had described a demon, but he had written it off as an attempt to save their lives. However, it had been a convenient way to distract Murad from looking closely at Kemankes' own responsibility in the affair.

"Well, there's one way to find out," he told himself, despite flickers of uncertainty about the supernatural creeping into his mind. "The Grand Al-Mahdi is coming to witness the execution of Suleyman Reis this very morning. I'm sure a little persuasion from the Sultan's torturers will bring out the truth. We'll just add him and his men to the ceremony. That will please the Sultan to no end and insure my continued good standing.

Taking a deep swallow of coffee, Kemankes congratulated himself on his success. He had assured Murad that all entrances to the prison tower would be heavily guarded during the night to secure delivery of the Pasha and the pirate for the festivities. It was indeed going to be a great day.

Egypt

. . . .

1

"I still can't believe you climbed that wall in the dark and set those stakes," the Pasha said to Ibrahim as the ship left the Sea of Marmara.

"I still can't believe that you got me down," echoed the Reis, shaking his heavily bandaged head. "If I could have seen what you planned, I would have stayed in the cell...or at least thought about it despite what the Sultan was going to do to us."

"I'm surprised you didn't scramble down those stakes with no help at all since you knew what was in store for you if you stayed," rumbled Bako, the late caravan operator Al-Mahdi. "After all, I was invited to be the guest of honor at the occasion, and I'm quite certain I would not have enjoyed how THAT turned out...one way or another."

In spite of the wry statement, all fell silent as they contemplated the horror of what Murad had planned.

"You're right," said the Reis, "better to fall to my death than suffer such a fate."

It was a beautiful morning on the eastern Mediterranean as they sailed from Rhodes toward Egypt after a brief stop to reprovision. The Pasha and the Reis were sitting toward the bow of the ship, surrounded by the scaffold climbers and a group of ex-slaves, including Dumaka and Bako.

A strange transformation had come over the two men after their rescue. All pretense gone, once on board the ship, the two men had engaged with Ibrahim, Andras, and Jacques about their incredible escape: describing their surprise when the Tuareg appeared like an apparition outside the barred opening, their amazement as he quickly loosed the bars, and their fear at the prospect of descending the sheer wall in the dark. This had led to conversations about the dangers of scaffold work at the quarry, including Cormac's rescue of Ibrahim when one collapsed. As the days passed, off-duty crew members would join the discussions, adding harrowing stories of their times at the galleys to the mix, until virtually every member of the crew participated when they had the time.

Cormac, Finn, Gael and the others stayed on the perimeter observing the daily group, all sipping coffee and exchanging stories of the past with the Pasha and the Reis. One day, a roar of laughter erupted from the group as the Pasha described Jugurtha "sneakily" kidnapping his sister and fleeing to the desert despite all efforts to stop them.

"After that, the rascal eluded us by sending anonymous messengers to the palace that they were hiding at this or that oasis. I'd assemble a detachment of soldiers and we'd race to the spot, only to find it empty, with no signs that anyone had been there. On more than one occasion, we found a robe or sandal belonging to my sister fastened to the trunk of a palm tree."

This drew another big laugh and Finn, walking past, made a note to ask his father-in-law about his habit of "stirring the pot" with his enemies.

"It's amazing," Finn said to Cormac. "Here are two of the most powerful men in Tunis drinking coffee and exchanging stories with former slaves."

"Perspective changes when those slaves save your life at great risk to themselves," said his brother. "You could have let the lion kill Jugurtha, or I could have let the Reis die in the cattle-boat fight. But it wasn't the right thing to do."

"What do you think will happen when we get back to Tunis?"

"*If* we get back," corrected Cormac. "The Reis has already told Ibrahim and the others they are free men, and he will do the same with the rest in Tunis, as well as supplying a ship to take them home. The Pasha is talking about offering paid employment to his servant slaves who agree to stay on because of long tenure. Not all of them have been treated badly and some have served for many years."

"Before we look to the future, we have to rescue Pinar and the others," said Jonathan, who had come down from the crows nest where he spent most of the day.

"They better not hurt those girls," growled Francoise, standing nearby.

"They'll pay with their lives if they do. They'll pay dearly for having laid a hand on them in the first place," said Cormac grimly.

Two days later Jonathan cried from atop the main mast, "Harbor to port on the horizon."

2

The entrance to the harbor at Alexandria passed between a peninsula to port and an island to starboard. Between the island and the mainland was a long causeway that appeared to have been created by great rocks piled on the harbor floor.

"That's the Heptastadion," explained Gael, "built 1,900 years ago by Alexander the Great. He wanted his engineers to connect the mainland to Pharos Island. Later a famous lighthouse was built on the island to guide ships into the harbor."

Questioning eyes turned toward the Captain from those gathered nearby,

"I came here several times as a sailor before being given a command," he said, anticipating the questions, "the locals love to talk about Alexandria's history."

"I too was here with a Dutch ship, years before moving to Tunis," said Suleyman Reis. "Alexandria was one of the great cities in the ancient world. There was the Mouseion, translated from Greek meaning 'Seat of the Muses,' that brought scholars from all over the Mediterranean to study. It had many buildings, lecture halls, and beautiful gardens. Part of it was an enormous library which held writings from some of the greatest authors in the world. Citizens say the number of books in the library exceeded 100,000."

"What happened to it?" asked Jonathan after a moment of shocked silence.

"About 500 years after the library was built, there was a war with the Romans and it was destroyed."

"Destroyed?" echoed Jonathan incredulously. "What happened to the books?"

"Lost," said the Reis, a sad tone in his voice. "It was the greatest collection of mankind's thoughts and imagination. A most terrible tragedy for the world. Priceless information lost forever."

Everyone looked at the Reis with new-found respect. None of them would have guessed that the renowned pirate had such an appreciation for history.

The rattling of the anchor chain interrupted them. Gael had positioned the ship apart from a number of others anchored in the harbor, but still within an easy row to the docks. Against them were tied a number of large boats with odd-looking bent masts angled toward the stern. The Captain pointed at them.

"Those are called 'Dahabeeyah,'" he said, "they're flat-bottomed boats used for traveling up and down the Nile: the river is too shallow for any craft with much draft."

"And I believe that's our quarry," said Cormac, pointing to an anchored sloop on the far side of the harbor, "it's the only one of its kind here."

It was decided that Francoise and Finn should go ashore to make inquiry about the captives and seek transportation to Cairo. Minutes later the dory set out for shore with the two dressed in simple robes.

The men on deck watched Finn disappear into the city while Francoise ambled down the dock, casually stopping to talk with the usual vendors and shoppers congregated there. When he reached a point nearly even with the sloop, Francoise engaged in a long conversation with a man who was clearly a sailor, turning several times to point back at the ship, then waving his hands animatedly.

"He's negotiating something," said the Reis. "I've seen him do that many times in the markets. Ahh, he's even starting to walk away. Now the other man is throwing up his hands and gesturing him back. They've made the deal, whatever it is."

As they stood watching Francoise, a wink of light from across the harbor caught Cormac's eye. Grabbing a nearby telescope, he crouched behind the railing and focused it on the sloop.

"There's a man watching us from aboard that vessel," he announced, "probably the Captain. If he studies us closely, he'll see the disguised gunports and realize that we're not a simple merchant ship. My guess is that we've arrived close enough behind him that he's wondering who we are."

"We've no nationality markings or flags," said Gael, "so he should have no reason to be suspicious."

"I don't think it's a coincidence," Cormac replied. "He's definitely interested in us."

On the sloop, Cetin lowered his telescope. He had in fact noted the arrival of the merchant vessel, but gave no thought to it until he saw the dory set out for the dock. Normally it took time for the captain of a merchant ship to organize his bills of lading in preparation for delivering goods, but this dory had departed almost immediately after the anchor was dropped. As he watched, something about the ship's lines gave him pause and he picked up a telescope to study it. Just as Cormac had feared, he recognized the disguised gunports and knew that this was no ordinary commercial vessel. When he focused on the men clustered on the afterdeck, he immediately spotted bright red hair and blue headband.

"MacLir Reis," he muttered to himself, "what's he doing here?"

Stories of the famous galley-slave-turned-pirate abounded in the Mediterranean and many of them had reached his ears even after he had gone to work on the Ottoman warship. He knew about the cattle-boat incident, but he vaguely recollected something more. Searching his memory, he remembered a rumor about the redhead being captured in an Irish fishing village and winding up as an oarsman on a galley operated by Suleyman Reis, the very man they had delivered to the Sultan. Snatches of conversations niggled away at his consciousness and then he had it! There had been a brother…and a younger sister. She had been taken into the Pasha's harem, but that's all he could recall. Suddenly he was thunderstruck. One of the young women they had taken to Constantinople and then to Alexandria had black hair, green eyes, and a fair complexion. She was constantly comforting the youngest daughter of the Pasha's First Wife. Could she be MacLir Reis' younger sister, harem slave to the Pasha's family!

Breaking into a cold sweat, Cetin deduced that the feared redhead had followed them to rescue his sister. But how had he known they were coming to Egypt unless he'd been to Constantinople? What had happened there? He picked up the telescope and studied the other ship more closely. His eyes widened and he gasped as he recognized the Pasha of Tunis and Suleyman Reis among the gathered men. How was this possible? Zehab was on his way to Cairo with the hostage women and must be warned of the pursuit. But how?

All at once he knew what he had to do.

3

"I THOUGHT YOU SAID BAKO WOULD rescue us!" whimpered Kelebeck for the 100th time since they'd left Constantinople. The girl whispered softly, glancing fearfully at the men nearby. She was huddled between Pinar and Bran on the deck of a dahabeeyah making its way up the Nile. Across from them, ten janissaries sat with their backs against the gunwale, most dozing in the warm sun.

"He didn't have time," murmured Bran, repeating the explanation as she had so often since she had recognized the disguised former slave. "He was going into the Court when we were coming out. We went straight to the ship. He couldn't have known that we were coming here, but I know he saw me and will do everything he can to free us. I can't imagine why he was there in the first place, but he won't stop until he finds us. That much I know!"

She looked over the girl's head to Pinar. Her former owner and best friend had held up well since their capture, but the strain was beginning to tell. Bran could see fear in her eyes that hadn't been there on the trip to Constantinople. An incident shortly after they left Alexandria had undoubtedly contributed. Zehab had started to have them roped together but the boat operator stopped him.

"No need," the man said. "See those bumps in the water?"

All of them looked over the side: two pairs of raised eyes stared at them from 20 yards away.

"What are they?" asked the Envoy.

"Crocodiles," replied the operator. "There's two more over on the bank."

On a sandy strip at the edge of the water lay two 15-foot crocodiles basking in the sun. Even from a distance, the beasts had a deadly appearance. Suddenly one of them raised itself on stubby legs and with amazing speed ran down the bank and into the water with a big splash, followed immediately by the other. The carcass of a pig was floating down the river toward them; in seconds it was enveloped in an explosion of frothing water as the beasts attacked. 30 seconds later the surface of the water was calm again.

"Same for anyone who goes overboard," the man said with a harsh laugh. "Better than any ropes."

On the other side of Pinar sat the First Wife. With smudges of dirt on her face, a ragged robe, and dishevelled hair, she was a far cry from the elegant woman who had received Bran as her daughter's personal slave. So far she had maintained her composure in the face of all that had beset them, constantly comforting Kelebek and telling her how proud she was of her, but the Irish girl knew it was difficult. Although they lived in the harem by tradition, the First Wife and her children had experienced a life of luxury and privilege because of her marriage to the Pasha. All three enjoyed frequent visits with him at the palace, and unlimited shopping excursions under the protection of his soldiers.

Zehab had treated them relatively well on the voyage to Constantinople because he sought the Sultan's favor for a successful mission, but the trip to Egypt had been a different matter. They had been ordered to clean the galley every day, and sometimes twice a day when the cook picked up in Constantinople deliberately dumped all the utensils on the deck and poured hot grease over them. The lye soap chaffed their bare hands, and their knees bruised from crawling on the planks. If everything was not perfectly clean and in its proper place, they had to start all over again. Sometimes they were told to scrub the deck while the sailors, normally charged with the work, sat around and made fun of their efforts.

In the beginning, the First Wife had voiced a complaint about this treatment to Zehab, only to see Kelebek tied up and carried screaming on the shoulder of a sailor up the rigging to a tiny spar which served as a crows nest for the sloop. The sailor untied her hands and left her there for two hours, clinging to the mast in abject terror.

Although she had been conditioned years before not to react to any indignity, Bran burned with cold anger at the psychological torture inflicted on Kelebek. A few days later, when Zehab was passing the galley while they were cleaning, Hibah pretended to lose her grip on a heavy iron pan so that it struck him full on the stump of his left arm. He screamed in pain and staggered backward to the amusement of some nearby Janissaries. Hardened soldiers, they appreciated the spirit of the Irish girl. Zehab would have killed her on the spot except for the wise intervention of Cetin.

"If you fail to deliver all the prisoners, your life will ultimately be forfeit," he counseled the enraged Envoy. "Let me administer the punishment."

Bran's wrists were tied to a long rope attached to the mast and she was thrown overboard to be dragged behind the ship. By desperate effort she was able to keep her head high enough to catch a breath every so often. Only when Cetin saw that she was losing strength and in danger of drowning did he order her pulled aboard. For many minutes she lay on the deck, sputtering and coughing up seawater before being dragged below to the stiflingly hot storeroom where the others waited.

"Hibah, why did you do that?" cried Pinar, wrapping arms around her soaked and shivering friend.

"I...I..."started Bran, but passed out in the grasp of her best friend.

For the rest of the trip the four of them were careful not to arouse anyone's anger. They went about their tasks quietly, although perhaps more slowly than necessary to stay out of the storeroom. Their diet of dried bread and watery soup with oily bits of fish caused all of them to lose weight, but Zehab paid no attention. He knew that a gift to an important Mamluk was not to be treated lightly, but Ridwan Bey held no power over him and all the Sultan needed ever to know, or care about, was that the gift had been delivered.

Now, as they moved up the Nile, Bran studied the Janissaries. All were armed with swords, but two carried bows and arrows. If she could get her hands on one of the bows and a quiver she could do a lot of damage, even at close quarters. Most of the soldiers were older men that looked battle-hardened, but one of the bowmen appeared to be no more than 20. If she could somehow get his weapon during the night...

Her plans were dashed when evening fell. The boat was made fast to shore. After tying the family tightly to each other and then to the gunwale, Zehab, the crew, and all the Janissaries went to stretch out and sleep on the bank, surrounded by well-maintained fires, and a rotation of guards throughout the night. Splashes and grunts in the river, plus an occasional jarring bump against the bottom of the dahabeeyah, kept the prisoners wide awake for hours.

4

"THEY LEFT FOR CAIRO yesterday morning on a riverboat," said Francoise. "The Envoy, ten soldiers, and four women. I've secured a dahabeeyah for us to follow them."

"How long does it take to get there?" asked Cormac.

"A little over four days if the winds are favorable," replied the Frenchman. "The boats tie up to shore every night to avoid hitting an obstacle and capsizing in the dark. The river is full of crocodiles."

When Finn returned two hours later and heard the news, he smiled grimly.

"I found a camel herder on the far side of the city," he said. "All his animals were hired for carrying trade goods upriver, except for a particularly unruly young jamal. I secured the use of the animal to take me to Cairo. I can be there before the riverboat."

It had taken a while, but eventually the blond Irishman had located the herder at the eastern edge of the city. The old man dealt primarily in cargo camels for merchants who had heavy loads for Cairo.

"All I have at the moment is that half-wild jamal over there glaring at us like we're going to roast him for supper," laughed the herder. "I'm the only one that can get close to him, and that's only because I bring him food."

Finn nodded and walked slowly toward the animal speaking slowly in a language the herder couldn't understand. An hour later the Irishman returned to the herder with the jamal following placidly so close that it occasionally bumped him in the back with its head.

"You certainly know camels," said the old herder insightfully, "you must have spent a lot of time with them. Unusual for a European."

"Many years as a camel tender on the Sahara caravans," Finn said obliquely.

The old man nodded but refrained from further questions. Camel tenders on the Sahara were slaves. It was hard to picture this handsome man with the slightly hawkish nose as a caravan slave, but his gift with the camel was unmistakable. Amnay agreed to pay him in the morning and either return the animal to Alexandria or to the herder's son in Cairo.

Back on board, when Cormac told him about the sloop captain, Finn nodded. "I'll leave the ship in the dark. By daylight I'll be well on the way and he'll never know anyone has gone."

Cormac and the others would follow by river boat. At the last minute the redhead picked Ibrahim to join them. "I don't know if your climbing skills will be needed," said Cormac, "but a mallet and chisel might come in handy, and a friend is always welcome."

Actually, during a meeting below decks that night, the entire crew had volunteered to come along to support Cormac. When the voices quieted, he expressed his appreciation for everything they had already done and explained why they needed to stay on board.

"I don't know what's going to happen," he said, "but Mamluks are fighting slaves just like Janissaries and they control this country. If we're successful, we'll have to return down the river. If they chase us, there may be a fight to board this ship. I suspect they would use those riverboats and the sloop to block us.

"I've asked Gael to anchor the ship broadside to the docks, but with enough angle to fire at the sloop. Since we'll have only one bank of cannons, he's going to have the starboard gun crews assist the port teams to reload and fire with all possible speed. Gunners, if they do attack, you will want to hit both soldiers on the dock and boats coming at you. If they close, the rest of you will have to repel boarders."

He paused. "Our lives may well depend on all of you."

The men were silent as they considered this possibility. Heads began to nod as they grasped the truth of what he was saying. Finally, Patrick leaped to his feet.

"For the family of MacLir Reis," he shouted. A roar of approval from the rest of the crew accompanied his words.

5

THE BLUE-CLAD AND VEILED Tuareg browsed casually through the Cairo street vendor's collection of knives while the proprietor engaged in a heated negotiation with a buyer. When the customer had departed with his purchase, satisfied that he had outwitted the seller, the vendor approached his next patron.

"These appear to be fine knives," said the Tuareg.

"Made from the purest Damascus steel," said the proprietor, surprised that the customer had begun with a positive remark. "I'm the only one in Cairo who can provide them," he lied with enthusiasm.

The client carefully ran a finger along the edge of a dagger long enough to be considered a short sword, remarking "excellent edge," in a complimentary tone.

"I hone every one to a sharpness fit for shaving," the man said proudly.

Sighting down the length of the blade while turning it from side to side, the Tuareg casually inquired about the massive walled complex rising on the hilltop above them, explaining that he had just come across the desert and was new to the city.

"Oh, that's the 'Qala'at Salah ad-Din'" said the vendor, anxious to please his prospect and proud to show off his knowledge. "It's a fortress that was originally built 500 years ago by Salah ad-Din to defend Cairo from the Crusaders. In the centuries that followed many rulers have added to it, creating a great complex within the walls. We now call it The Citadel. "

"500 years ago, that's impressive," said the buyer, picking up an elegant knife with an ivory handle, "how is it used today?"

"The northern section has barracks for the Mamluk soldiers and palaces for their commander." Saying anything to please a buyer holding the most expensive knife on the table, he continued. "The southern section is the seat of government and has the harem, and palaces for the governor. There are great halls for meetings and extensive gardens throughout. On the extreme southwestern end is the Maydan."

"What's that?"

"It's a large field of trimmed grass on which parades are sometimes held, but it's primarily used for training horses. The stable complex is right beside it."

The Tuareg turned to a shopper who had paused to look over the table and handed him the ivory handled knife.

"This would be perfect for you," he said, turning on his heel and disappearing into the crowd, a gleam of satisfaction in the gold-flecked eyes.

Later that afternoon, Finn strolled through one of the enormous gates in the Citadel's walls, blending with the crowds coming and going on assorted errands. The complex was vast and its somewhat haphazard layout coincided with the vendor's description of multiple rulers adding on to it. Extensive buildings in the northern area included barracks for soldiers along with numerous large and beautiful buildings for use by their commanders, including what he guessed was a structure housing the Bey's harem. He casually asked a man cutting grass with a scythe about the building with a gold dome and four ornate columns rising high into the air from the four corners.

"That's the residence of Ridwan Bey, Mamluk Commander," said the gardener.

In the southern sections, even more ornate structures of all sizes and designs were interspersed with extensive lawns and gardens. He figured that the somewhat blocky, two story edifice with enormous guards at the door was the Governor's harem.

Moving steadily, to maintain the impression of being on important business, Finn arrived at a gate opening to the Maydan. A gentle slope ran for a few yards downhill from the gate and ended at the edge of a flat field of cut grass. It was 300 yards square and to either side a string of low stone buildings with outside paddocks were obviously stables. More than 50 riders were scattered across the field, some executing agility maneuvers with their animals, others attacking targets with swords or lances.

Finn walked through the gate and casually strolled down to the stables. A slave was grooming a horse at the edge of the field.

"Beautiful animal." said the Tuareg admiringly, "not many like it in the desert."

The groom straightened and rested one hand on the animal's back: a light gray Arabian stallion with black mane and tail.

"A compliment from one who would certainly know horses," said the man, noting the blue robe, veil, and tagelmust. "These are the most well trained horses in the world."

"I'm sure their speed and stamina is excellent," said Finn, ignoring the obvious embellishment.

"Unparalleled," said the groom proudly. "They can alternate between trotting and cantering for hours on end and cover a lot of ground."

"Does each soldier work with the same horse?" asked the Tuareg to keep the man talking while he studied the stables with quick glances.

"Each rider has three horses to work with," the slave said, "and works with at least one of them every afternoon."

" Do they ride only in the afternoon?"

"Yes, they train on foot near their barracks in the morning. The Bey rides with them in the afternoon because his mornings are occupied with business affairs. He must have important matters to deal with today, otherwise he'd be here right now."

"Three horses each," said Finn in an impressed tone. "Surely they're not all housed in these stables?"

"Oh, no," said the man, pointing across the field, "Down the hill below the edge of the field are stables for twice as many horses."

Finn gave a low whistle, "These Mamluks are very lucky."

"They are indeed; however, I suggest you get back up through the gate. Citizens are not allowed near the stables, but I voiced no alarm because I know you are a man who appreciates horses."

The Irishman thanked the groom and returned to the gate, pausing to look at the field once more. Just off the field's far edge he saw the roofs of what undoubtedly was the lower stable complex. Beyond it open country stretched away for miles, a line of green marking the border of the Nile. As he turned to go back into the Citadel, his eye caught sight of three triangular shapes rising from the desert far to the west. He made a note to ask Bako or Dumaka about them.

6

THE TWO ODD LOOKING SAILS of the dahabeeyah filled out as the boat cleared the harbor in Alexandria and started up the Nile. Cormac, noting that the craft was handled entirely by the operator and two crewmen, asked about the long poles lashed to the gunwales.

"Those are for sandbars," said the captain. "The river bottom changes constantly with the current and we frequently get stuck on a sandbar that's developed since we passed the last time. The poles are for pushing us off."

"I don't suppose anyone wants to jump into the water," said the redhead, "I've heard about the crocodiles."

"That's why we keep a good supply of poles on hand," laughed the operator.

The day passed uneventfully as the boat progressed upriver. Gael had supplied them with ample provisions and the men sat quietly talking, dozing, or watching the amazing array of birds flying about in the palm trees and undergrowth that lined the shores. Knowing that Finn would reach Cairo quickly, Cormac curbed his impatience and studied the surroundings. There was a surprising amount of traffic on the river, including wide-bodied barges loaded with grain bound for merchant ships at Alexandria, although by late afternoon most of the boats had tied up for the night and the river was almost clear. It seemed that no one wanted to risk travel in the dark, but their captain was holding steady, bound for one of his favorite overnight spots.

"Just another 30 minutes," he announced. "Our destination has a grassy bank under the trees that's perfect for sleeping, and well established fire pits to keep the crocs away."

Cormac had been vaguely aware of another dahabeeyah behind them for most of the afternoon and now noticed that it had not pulled off for the night either, but had closed to within 100 yards. He wondered whether they were heading for the same camping spot and if there was enough room for both vessels. He got up and moved to the stern, where the captain was holding the rudder.

"Do you suppose that boat wants to beat us to your favorite spot?" he asked.

"I don't know," the operator replied, glancing back. "It's one of the Alexandria boats, but I don't recognize anyone aboard. They're carrying a little more sail than I am and may be heading for the same spot, but there's plenty of room for both of us."

Cormac returned to his place beside Jonathan, planning to ask his opinion about the odd sail configuration of the dahabeeyah, but his attention was drawn to Dumaka sitting across from them, chin on his chest, gently snoring.

"It's a habit from the old days on the galley," said Cormac nodding at his friend with a smile, "we were instantly asleep when rowing was over."

Dumaka was dreaming about a lion hunt when a hand shook his shoulder. His eyes flew open and he saw a familiar figure in a white robe bending over him.

"Beware, there's danger in the approaching boat," said the man and disappeared.

The ex-slave was on his feet in an instant, staring at the other riverboat, now even with them and only three feet from the port gunwale. "Can you tell us where to stop for the night?" a man in the bow called, just as the boats touched. Suddenly, hooks were slammed across the gunwales locking the boats to each other and 25 heavily-armed men rose from where they had been crouched low on the second vessel and started to jump into the dahabeeyah with swinging swords.

Taken completely by surprise, Cormac and the others would have been killed had it not been for Dumaka. With a roar like the lion he had been dreaming about, the black giant snatched a machete from his belt and partially severed the head from the torso of the first Janissary to enter the boat. He then grabbed the slumping body and threw it full into the face of the four soldiers following him. They all collapsed back into their boat, slipping and sliding to keep their footing in the blood from the dead man.

Another roar echoed as Bako jumped up and the attackers hesitated for an instant at the fearsome sight of the two enormous men clad in leopard skins facing them with deadly blades. That was all it took for Cormac and Francoise to spring to their feet, swords flashing.

"Protect the Reis," bellowed Cormac as he was attacked from both sides by Janissaries leaping into the boat.

The Pasha had leaped up, but Suleyman was slow to rise because of the useless left arm and only the expert swordsmanship of the Pasha prevented him from being cut down. When he finally gained his feet, the two of them were facing four attackers and the Reis had to desperately parry blows aimed at his left side. One of the Janissaries moved in behind the Reis and raised his weapon to deliver a killing blow to Suleyman's unprotected neck, but Francoise, appearing out of nowhere, cleaved the man's arm from his elbow with a tremendous blow of his sword. As the soldier staggered away with a shriek of pain, he was grabbed by Bako, lifted high in the air and thrown completely over the attacking boat and into the water. Two sets of eyes in the middle of the river sank below the ripples and in seconds the man's screams were cut short as he disappeared in a cloud of boiling crimson spray.

When Francoise left his side to assist the Reis, Cormac was immediately attacked by a third Janissary. It took every bit of the redhead's strength and skill to keep the swords away from his body. The soldiers sneered and spread out around him; unable to counter all of them, he realized that he was doomed. The man to his left was swinging at Cormac's torso when a heavy hardwood mallet struck him full in the forehead, dropping like a rock. Suddenly a wiry figure was on top of him driving a razor-edged chisel deep into his chest.

"You'll not take that one's life," said Ibrahim as he pulled the chisel from the dying man.

By now the sons of Bako and Dumaka had joined the fight with their machetes and the struggle started to even. Two of them made their way to the front of the boat on Bako's shouted instructions and strung their bows. The resulting hail of deadly arrows striking Janissaries turned the tide.

Cormac, still dealing with two attackers, slipped on a pool of blood and went down, sword knocked from his hand. One of the Janissaries gave a triumphant shout and raised his weapon high, prepared to split the Irishman's head. Ibrahim threw himself towards the soldier, chisel in one hand, but the distance was too great. He watched in astonishment as the sword suddenly dropped harmlessly to the deck and the soldier stumbled backward with the handle of a knife protruding from his throat. An instant later the second Janissary suffered the same fate. The Tuareg swung around to see Jonathan crouched on the deck, a third knife in his hand.

And then it was over.

Cetin was no coward, but he had counted on the element of surprise to overwhelm the other boat and planned to follow the lead man across the gunwale. When the giant warrior had suddenly appeared and killed his first in command, the ex-pirate stopped short, staring directly into the machete. As momentum shifted and his men began to be decimated by swords and arrows, he screamed for them to retreat and began to cast off the hooks holding the boats together. The last man slipped as he tried to leap the widening gap between boats and fell into the water, to disappear in a churning swirl of red froth and spray.

Cetin stood up to assess the situation and was struck in the shoulder by an arrow fired at point-blank range. He stumbled back and tripped over the dead body of the very first attacker. Struggling to keep his balance, the captain's feet slid in a slick pool of blood and he fell backward over the far gunwale. Before he could open his mouth, great reptilian jaws dragged him below the surface, and his last view was of a dizzying swirl of bubbles and blood as his body was hopelessly contorted by the death-roll of the gigantic beast.

The dahabeeyah drifted slowly downstream on the sluggish current, the groans of its wounded and dying men gradually growing fainter and fainter. Four days later, alerted by three survivors about what had happened, the remaining crew decided that they owed loyalty to no one. They eased the sloop out of the harbor at first light and made their bid for freedom.

7

SITTING BESIDE DUMAKA that night at the campsite, Cormac stared into the flames, lost in thought. It had been close: but for the black man's warning they might all have been killed in the attack. As it was, three of the African warriors had suffered serious slashes from swords; the Pasha had been stabbed in the right side when reaching across the Reis to parry a blow; and Jonathan, desperately deflecting a sword with a cushion he'd been sitting on, had suffered a deep cut to his left arm, although the blinding cloud of feathers had given him time to stab the Janissary with one of his knives.

It turned out that Dumaka's son, Torg, was an expert in dealing with wounds. The Pasha's injury was the most serious, and upon inspecting it the warrior asked the boat operator to head for shore immediately. He and one of his brothers disappeared along the bank while others quickly made a fire. When the two returned, they were carrying an assortment of little plants and several large green leaves. The plants were boiled in a small iron pot while Torg produced from his kit a wickedly sharp thorn, pierced on one end, and thin strands of animal gut. Making the Pasha lie down, he cleaned the wound, softened the strands in the liquid solution, and deftly sewed the gash in his side closed then applied a poultice from the boiled plants over it. Next, a couple of the large leaves were cut to size, laid over the plaster, and the whole dressing bound with strips of cloth cut from a robe. The process took less than 20 minutes.

"The little plants will stop the bleeding, and prevent infection," he explained to the Pasha, "and the larger ones will accelerate healing. You will be sore for a few days, but otherwise unaffected. Because you stretched over to block the sword aimed at the Reis, the stab only hit the fleshy part of your side. A handbreadth to the left, and the wound would have been very serious."

In like manner Torg moved among the others, stitching and bandaging wounds where necessary and simply cleansing and bandaging others. A short time later, they reached the campsite.

Now, with the flames rising into the night sky, everyone was asleep on soft grass well away from the river. Only the two old friends were still awake.

"How did you know we were going to be attacked?" Cormac finally asked. "If you hadn't jumped up and stopped that first man we might all be dead."

"I didn't know," said Dumaka, "I was sleeping when he shook me awake and told me there was danger in that boat."

"Who shook you?"

"The messenger."

"What messenger?" asked Cormac, although he sensed he wasn't going to be surprised at what was coming.

"The same one who appeared to us in the desert while we were on the way to meet you."

"Where is he now?"

"I don't know. He vanished as soon as he warned me, just as he vanished that night in the desert after talking to us."

"He talked to all of you?"

"Yes. We sat around the fire and he told us about a great and wonderful King who wants all of us to be part of his kingdom. The things the messenger described were…" Dumaka paused, looking for the right word. "Beyond compare." he finally said.

"Where is this kingdom?" asked Cormac, as a wonderful feeling suddenly washed over him.

"You have to ask…" Dumaka started to raise one hand toward the sky, but he was interrupted by a loud snort. Into the firelight strode a massive animal with piglike eyes. It stopped and stared at the two men, then opened an enormous mouth showing four large tusks.

"Hippo!! It's going to charge," bellowed the black giant, galvanizing into action.

He leapt to his feet and grabbed the end of a large branch burning in the fire. With amazing speed, the ex-slave ran straight at the animal with a bellow and shoved the blazing log straight into its open mouth. The hippo snapped its great jaws shut, severing the branch but Cormac, following Dumaka's lead, was in its face waving another burning branch. The fire in its eyes and burning its throat was too much for the animal and it turned and rushed toward the river 50 yards away. A heavy splash marked its retreat.

By now, others were up, weapons at the ready. Even the Pasha, holding his wound with his left hand, was on his feet with his sword drawn.

"What was that thing?" asked Jonathan, "I've never seen such a mouth!"

"Hippopotamus." said Bako. "One of the most dangerous animals in Africa, although it doesn't usually get this far from the water at night. It has a bad temper and frequently attacks and kills people going for water in the morning or afternoon. Fortunately, it seems the fire stopped this one from immediately charging, or the ending of our encounter might have been different."

"Never had that happen before," said the boat operator, "although we do make sure a fire is burning all night."

Later, when the fire had been built up to a roaring blaze and everyone had settled back down, Cormac turned to the giant lying beside him, "We need to talk again, I want to learn more of what the messenger said about this kingdom."

8

As soon as the dahabeeyah touched the dock at Cairo, on the east bank of the Nile, Zehab ordered the Janissaries to tie his prisoners' wrists in front of them. Mindful not to cause visible blemishes, he had a rope loosely fashioned around their necks connecting them together: the First Wife in front and Kelebek at the back. Only then did he lead them onto the dock, cursing the boat operator under his breath for arriving in the late afternoon despite the Envoy continually urging him to go faster.

Cognizant that the Mamluks took a dim view of Ottoman Janissaries, he took only two men with him and left the rest on the river boat. With luck they could all return to Alexandria in a day or two. An inquiry with the dockmaster about the residence of Ridwan Bey resulted in directions through the city to the northern gate of the great Citadel towering above.

"You may be too late," warned the man, leering at the four prisoners, "the Bey usually does business in the morning and rides with his men in the afternoon. There are prison cells just inside the gate where your captives can spend the night."

With one soldier leading the woman and the other bringing up the rear, Zehab strode through the crowded streets, fuming at the delay. If the operator had put on more sail they could have arrived hours ago and have been on their way back downriver by now. He resigned himself to spending time fawning over the troublesome Mamluks whom no Sultan had ever been able to control.

Reaching the massive North Gate, they encountered a squad of heavily armed soldiers. Despite a stream of people coming and going through the gate, many of them sellers with carts of merchandise, the sight of roped captives caused the squad captain to stop and question Zehab.

"What do you have here?" he said, eyeing the women.

"A gift from the Sultan in Constantinople to Ridwan Bey," said the Envoy in the most courteous tone he could muster through his irritation.

"Pretty sorry looking lot for a gift from the Ottomans," said the captain dubiously, running his eyes over the disheveled hair, dirty skin and torn attire of the prisoners.

"Oh, they'll clean up nicely," replied Zehab firmly.

"Maybe so, but you can't deliver them now. The Bey is training horses on the Maydan right now and hosts a banquet tonight. He only does business in the morning."

"What am I to do with these prisoners until then?" The Envoy struggled to keep his tone civil.

"Just inside the gate, the building on the left has a series of cells and a jailer. You can leave them there overnight. I suggest you meet with the Commander first and ask him for the opportunity to clean them up before delivery...lest this "gift" of yours insults him. Most gifts sent...for his amusement...don't survive very long, but it would be best not to take a chance."

"Thank you," said Zehab, acknowledging to himself that this was sound counsel and deciding to untie his charges to prevent any more marks on their skin.

In short order the jailer was consulted, the women were untied and shoved into a dank cell with filthy straw, and Zehab was on his way back to the dock. Neither he nor the Janissaries paid any attention to the blue-clad Tuareg lingering nearby among the crowds.

Deliverance

....

1

COLD, HUNGRY, AND MISERABLE, the women huddled together on soiled straw in the stone cell. A small shaft of light coming through the grate in the door illuminated bowls of rancid soup and crusts of bread the jailer had left, but no one felt like eating. Kelebek was pressed tightly between her mother and Pinar, terrified and sobbing softly despite the First Wife's words of encouragement.

"So this is what it's like to be a slave. Our lives, suffering, and maybe our deaths are at the whim of a stranger," said Pinar.

"Yes, but take courage, things could be worse. I suffered more harshly than this at the hands of the sisters in your kitchen," said Bran. "And the overseers in charge of my brothers, given the opportunity, would have killed them at a moment's notice, yet we all survived."

"Life in the harem was so comfortable that we never considered the workers as slaves."

"You never even noticed the garden or kitchen slaves until you saw my little dolls," said Hibah.

"If I hadn't been so bored, I might never have seen them," said Pinar "The dolls were so small and the women were so careful to keep them hidden that it was only by chance I noticed them. I watched you collecting grass and flowers and when I saw the doll with the bow on my bed, I knew who had made it."

"Remember all that happened after that," said Bran. "We both became archers and riders, able to hit speedy rabbits from our running horses. Good things happened to both of us, but I never could have imagined it the first time I was thrown into the rubbish pool in the kitchens."

"That's what I want to do," interrupted Kelebek, memories distracting her. "Be just like the two of you, riding and shooting."

"It takes a lot of practice, little one," said Hibah, trying to keep up the positive train of thought.

"I'm almost 13," said the girl defensively. "Just about the age you both were when Bako started training you. Pinar told me when you first tried to shoot, the arrows went everywhere; the first thing you ever hit was the foot of the target!" In spite of their circumstances, the three others gave way to quiet giggles at the description.

"Well, when we're free again, Hibah and I will start teaching you, but it's hard and she's right, it takes a lot of practice. A lot." emphasized her sister.

"And you'll probably fall off the horse a few times," said Bran, "and that hurts."

"I can do it, I know I can," said Kelebek firmly, all thoughts of their situation gone as she imagined herself racing on a white Arabian, shooting at impossibly fast rabbits.

Gradually the light coming through the iron grate in the door faded as evening gave way to night. Distracted by these memories of a happier time, and exhausted from their ordeal, the four fell asleep. Sometime in the night Bran woke to a rustle in the straw, but her eyelids were heavy and she fell back asleep to experience the most wonderful dream.

She was sitting on the hillside above Baltimore with the little blond girl in the blue dress. Once again it was a beautiful sunny day and ripples in the harbor below were sending out flashes of sunlight. The girl was fashioning a bouquet.

"Why don't you go outside?" she asked, staring at Bran. Somehow the Irish girl knew she was talking about the prison cell.

"Because the door's locked," said Bran.

"Have you pushed on it?"

"No."

"I think you should," said the little one innocently, winding two daisies together.

"All right," said Bran and in the dream she got up and pushed on the cell door. It swung open.

"I told you," said the girl, adding a flower to the bouquet and holding it up for examination. "Why don't you get the others and leave?"

"Good idea," said Bran and saw herself rousing the others and leading them out into the street.

"Now, go down the way you came up," said the girl.

"What about the guards?" asked Bran.

"Don't worry, they're sleeping."

Bran saw herself leading the others past the guards, all slumped inside the gate fast asleep. The great gate doors were open just wide enough for them to slip through.

"I think we need these blue ones," said the girl, adding two more blossoms to the bouquet. "Oh, go down the street to the Inn at the bottom of the hill."

Bran saw the four of them walking down the deserted street in the dark. At the bottom of the hill on the right side was a building with a sign in Arabic that somehow she could read perfectly: 'Tavern and Rooms.'

"Go in and up the stairs to the last door at the back of the hall on the left. Knock softly," said the girl, studying her handful of flowers.

Bran watched herself walk up to the tavern just as the door swung open. She saw them all climb the stairs and go down the hall to the last door on the left. When she knocked, nothing happened for a moment, then the door opened and a half dressed Finn, sword raised, stared at her.

"Bran?" he asked, frozen in disbelief.

Then, dropping the sword, he grabbed her so hard it squeezed the air out of her. She gasped for breath and opened her eyes. She was no longer lying on straw; her fingers felt real skin and muscle on his back and she could make out her brother's great mane of golden hair. Turning, she saw bewildered faces behind her dimly lit by a candle in the sconce down the hall. She reached out and touched Pinar's cheek, feeling the wetness of tears. Kelebek was gripping her other hand so hard it hurt, staring at her with wide eyes. Their mother had a look of complete shock and befuddlement.

Only when Finn gripped her by the arm and ushered them all into the room did Bran begin to think that this was no dream. She could feel his hand squeezing her arm, the wood floor under her feet, and the tightening at her waist when Kelebek threw both arms around her. She raised a hand to her ear and pinched it hard: the pain was real.

As Finn closed the door, a scent of gardenias filled the air.

2

"Sir, I have brought you a gift from the Sultan, Murad IV," said Zehab, with a bow. He handed Murad's letter to a slave who passed it to Ridwan Bey, seated behind a huge mahogany table.

The Mamluk Commander was of medium size and dressed in matching yellow turban and robe. His full gray beard covered a battle-scared face and the robe hid a fit, muscular body; piercing black eyes left no misunderstanding about his strong personality. He scanned the letter and raised his head to stare at the Envoy with a faint grin.

"It would seem our ruler would like to favor his unruly subjects in Egypt." His tone was amused but the eyes were cold.

"I'm sure you will find the gift pleasing," said Zehab, "although some soap and water would help remove the effects of our journey."

"See to it," said the Bey, waving his hand at an assistant. "I'll receive them in the morning."

"Thank you," said the Envoy, bowing and turning to follow the assistant; the Bey already turning his attention to another document.

"I'll take them to the harem," said the assistant when Zehab explained the gift, "they'll be cleaned and dressed in colorful robes when they appear before the Commander tomorrow."

"Excellent," replied Zehab, relieved that his mission was over and he could return to Constantinople with a favorable report for the Sultan.

Reaching the gate, they found the jailer and followed him to the cell. He turned a heavy iron key in the lock and swung the door open. The Envoy stepped inside.

"Time to go," he said cheerfully, waiting for his eyes to adjust to the gloom and glad to be rid of his charges after so long. "You're due for a nice bath, so the Bey can see you in all your beauty and decide how best to deliver his...intentions. I hear he is a violent man," he added with a smirk.

An empty chamber met his gaze.

"You opened the wrong cell," he growled to the jailer, who stepped in and looked around.

"I know I put them in here," said the man. "Look, there's the four bowls of soup and the bread I gave them."

Zehab stared at the food and turned on the jailer with a roar that carried into the street.

"You let them out! You did it. Someone bribed you!" he shouted.

"No, I was sleeping in my cot at the guardpost all night and the keys never left my belt," argued the man, "I don't know how they got out!"

"Don't tell me that," shouted the Envoy, grabbing the jailer's robe, "I know it was you and you'll pay for it!"

"What's going on here?" asked the captain of the guard, hearing the commotion and entering the cell.

"He let my prisoners go!" Zehab's voice approached a scream. "They're gone and he's the only one who could have done it!"

"Ahmed, didn't you share cheese with us and settle down with the off duty guards to sleep last night?" asked the captain.

"Yes," said the jailer. "I didn't go home because I wanted to be here when this man came for his prisoners."

"Was the cell locked?"

"Yes, I locked it after bringing them soup and bread, and I used the key to unlock it just now," the jailer held up the heavy key. "When I opened the door the prisoners were gone."

The Envoy started to speak but the captain held up his hand for silence and led the way across the street to the one-room structure that served as the guardhouse. Four men lounged at a table drinking coffee; another four were stationed at the open gate just outside.

"Were you the night-duty guard?" The captain addressed the senior Mamluk soldier at the table.

"Yes sir, the four of us were relieved at dawn."

"The gates were closed?"

"Yes sir, shut and barred after the last merchant left at dusk. I personally attended to it."

"Did you see anyone come from the prison cells and try to leave the Citadel?"

"No sir, we were awake all night," lied the guard, "and saw no one move on the street." His three companions nodded their heads vigorously in agreement.

"There you have it," said the captain, turning to Zehab. "None of my men are responsible."

Zehab could only stare at him with incredulity.

"I don't know what happened," said the Bey's assistant, turning to leave with a wicked gleam in his eyes, "but you'd better locate your prisoners before the Commander hears of this."

3

WHEN BRAN OPENED HER EYES, sunlight was slanting into the room through the open window. Kelebek was snuggled in between her and Pinar, the three were on the floor under a blanket and the First wife was on the bed beside them. She gently lifted her head to look for her brother, who had been lying nearby, but he was gone. She shut her eyes and opened them, but the sunlit room was still there and the soft breathing of the others continued to resonate in her ears. With mixed hesitancy and wonder, she tried again, this time rubbing her eyes when they were closed, but the result was the same: she was not on filthy straw, surrounded by rock walls. She was on a wood floor beside a bed, with the clucking of chickens audible from somewhere below.

"We're free," she dared to tell herself. Except for the visible evidence she was almost immediately ready to deny it.

She went back over the night's events. Refusing to touch the disgusting soup, the four had settled on the smelly straw as best as they could. She vaguely remembered waking once, then falling asleep to the most wonderful dream, in which the little girl had directed them out of their cell, through the great gate, and right to Finn's room. When he opened the door and threw his arms around her in astonishment, she had lost her breath and opened her eyes, gasping. But that didn't end the dream as it should have: the others were actually there with her and they all were shepherded into Finn's room, where they settled down for the rest of the night.

Now she was wide awake, but the dream wouldn't subside; indeed everything around her was real. She shut her eyes once more, but nothing had changed when she opened them. All at once the door opened and Finn appeared carrying a sack and accompanied by the most delicious smells.

She raised her head and he gave her a smile. Pulling a piece of fresh-baked bread and hunk of cheese from the sack, he placed them in her outstretched hand. The first bite of the simple yet delicious food finally convinced her that this was no dream.

Kelebek rolled over and said sleepily, "I want some too."

In minutes all were sitting up and munching on the bread, cheese, and figs that Amnay had brought.

"The markets open early," he said, "and I thought you all might like some good food."

With their mouths full, all the rest of them could do was nod vigorously in appreciation.

"There's a public bathhouse nearby," he said, producing another bundle from the sack, "it would be best to go there early before they find you missing. It's a risk, but it's important to wash away the stink of imprisonment as quickly as possible."

He pulled out four black robes and tagelmusts

"I know the tagelmusts are for men," he said, "but maybe you can fashion them in such a way as to appear to be unmarried women with veils."

Not long after, a fully veiled Tuareg warrior, followed by a single line of black-clad and veiled women, left the tavern and made his way the short distance to the bathhouse. He briefly entered the men's side, then waited outside for more than an hour before the women reappeared.

"I tried to get them out of the warm water sooner," the First Wife murmured, "but they just wouldn't leave and since there was nobody else in there I felt it was safe."

"We had quite a lot of soaping and rinsing to do," said Kelebek, "particularly my sister and Hibah, just in case Jonathan and Francoise show up." The two girls lunged for her, but she ducked behind her mother.

"Let's not do anything to draw attention to us," advised Amnay, his amusement hidden by the veil.

Later that morning a Tuareg caravan operator arranged for spacious accommodations at an establishment near the docks catering to merchants. The proprietor paid absolutely no attention to the four women accompanying him.

4

"If I didn't know the Mamluk guards and jailor so well, I might think you were trying to keep the Sultan's gift for yourself," said Ridwan Bey in a frigid tone from across the great table. "You boasted that the mother and the two young women are particularly attractive…"

"Sir," Zehap spoke in a steady voice that masked the terror almost choking him, "If I had wanted to steal the Sultan's gift, I would never have come to Cairo."

"Unless you planned to give the gift to the Governor in return for certain…commercial privileges."

"I swear to you that I had no such intention. The Governor doesn't know I arrived from Constantinople."

"On the contrary," said the Bey, "one of my spies reported that he learned of your arrival within hours of you reaching the dock."

"Surely your spy reported that I brought the prisoners directly to your gate," said the Envoy.

"You have two days to produce these women," said the Commander, ignoring the statement. "Fail and my men will use you as a target for saber practice on the Maydan."

The Envoy could barely keep his composure as he left the room, fully aware that the Bey would do exactly as he said if the women weren't found. The exchange had sparked a desperate idea, however, and once outside he asked for directions to the Governor's palace. A short walk through the Citadel brought him to the magnificent building which housed the seat of government for Egypt.

Representing himself as having an urgent matter for the Governor to consider, Zehab was told that he would be given an audience when the morning's matters were concluded. Three hours later he was shown into the enormous Hall of State where Egyptian affairs were conducted. In the middle of the room, behind a desk larger than the Bey's and surrounded by a crowd of advisors, sat Sultanzad Mehmed Pasha. He was a thin man with a narrow face and a beard trimmed to a point below his chin, certainly not a soldier but ruthlessly greedy, and given to appropriating wealth from affluent Egyptian families.

"You have an urgent matter for me?" asked Mehmed in a bored voice.

"Yes, Eminence," said Zehab, "I arrived recently from Constantinople."

"I know."

"I brought three beautiful women and a girl from the Sultan as a gift for the Emir Bey. They are the family of the Pasha of Tunis."

"I was told they looked like ordinary slaves from a captured ship."

"Ahhh, that's because they've been prisoners for many weeks. They are truly beautiful when cleaned up."

"I heard they escaped last night," said the Governor.

"Yes," said Zehab, covering his surprise. Mehmed must have an extensive network of spies. "I'm sure the jailor let them out and the Mamluk guards are covering for him."

"What's that to me?" asked the Governor.

"Perhaps we could work out an arrangement that would benefit both of us," said the Envoy. "I have a fast sloop in Alexandria captained by an ex-pirate. Help me recover the women and I'll assign the ship to you. You can use your own men as crew; I'm told the eastern Mediterranean is an excellent source for plunder and slaves. We can split profits, say 75% to you and 25% for me."

"90% for me and 10% for you," said Mehmed without hesitation. "Knowing the Bey, I suspect you don't have much time."

"Agreed," said Zehab, more quickly than he wanted to, but deviously anticipating he would somehow manage to escape with the ship.

"I'll put my men to work on it," said the Governor. "Come back in the morning."

Once outside, the Envoy headed straight for the docks. He cursed himself for conceding so quickly to the Governor's split of profits. He didn't trust the man, but he had no choice: there were only two days to find the prisoners before he faced death at the hands of the Bey. He also knew he wouldn't be allowed to leave Cairo unless this matter was resolved. The Governor had spies and he himself had almost 20 Janissaries at the dahabeeyah that he could put on the streets to find the women. Someone must have seen them hustled away by the jailor or the Mamluks on guard at the gate.

After Zehab had left, Mehmed turned to his assistants.

"Have our spies locate those women, but leave them alone. We'll let the Bey deal with this man; then I'll take the women and the sloop for myself."

5

AFTER THE ESCAPEES WERE SETTLED in their new accommodations, Finn took to the streets to find out what he could about the reaction to their absence from the cell. Once again, he strolled among the market stalls near the North Gate appearing to study merchandise, but keeping his ears open to conversations. Almost immediately he learned that the word was out among the citizenry and that, despite being out of the immediate clutches of their captors, the women were still in a dangerous situation.

"Did you hear about the escape?" one shopper said to her companion. "Prisoners in a cell at the Citadel Gate vanished overnight."

"What do you mean 'vanished,'?" asked the other. "People don't just vanish."

"One of the vendors said that when the jailor unlocked the cell this morning, no one was there."

"He simply forgot to lock the door," said the companion with a shrug.

"No, he said the door was locked, just as he left it last night."

"Well, then he unlocked it during the night and let the prisoners go."

"The guards at the gate say he spent the night with them and never moved."

"They must have done it then."

"Do you know the punishment for guards who help a prisoner escape? First, 40 lashes, then left far out in the desert with no food or water. A certain death sentence."

"Well, there's got to be *some* explanation. Do you think these pomegranates are ripe?"

And so it went as Finn moved about. The escape was so bizarre that it seemed most of the population had heard about it. What caught his attention, however, was a comment from the leather dealer operating near the Citadel's South Gate.

"I heard that the prisoners were to be a gift to Ridwan Bey. He has so many spies throughout the city that he'll find them quickly."

"He has operatives in Cairo?" asked the Tuareg.

"Oh, yes. He and the Governor both have countless agents, primarily to keep each advised on what the other is doing. The Mamluks and the Ottomans have an uneasy relationship in Egypt, although the Emir makes a pretense of allegiance to the Sultan's governing appointee."

"You would think each would limit visitors to prevent the other one's spies from learning about their affairs," said Finn.

"In times of peace all the gates are open from sunrise to dark because both men, particularly the Governor, have a constant stream of merchants and vendors seeking favor for various enterprises. These business arrangements are so lucrative that trying to keep spies out isn't worth the effort," said the merchant.

"This must be a good location for you then," said the Tuareg admiringly.

"The best," said the man enthusiastically, "I get sales from merchants coming and going. Especially 'going' if they've been successful in promoting their businesses!"

The information about spies caused Finn to re-examine his plans. He expected Cormac to appear the following day and had initially planned to intercept him at the dock, get the women aboard, and head back down the river. He realized now that this strategy would never work if both the Governor and the Bey were monitoring river traffic. He also had to rule out camels because the herds would undoubtedly be under observation as well

Staring up at the South Gate, and thinking about his visit to the Maydan the day before, he was suddenly struck with a thought. No spies would have reason to watch the Maydan stables and every morning the riders were up at their barracks for drills. He began to devise an audacious plan to steal horses from the Mamluks and ride to Alexandria.

6

It was just past mid-day when Finn spotted Cormac's riverboat approaching the dock. He immediately left the vendor display he'd been browsing and strode to the dahabeeyah, grabbing one of the ropes thrown by a crew member. Kneeling to tie it to a cleat, he spoke rapidly but softly to the men on board.

"Make sure your hoods are up and covering your faces. There are spies everywhere."

The startled passengers turned their backs to the dock and quickly did as he advised. When they turned back, Finn extended his right arm in greeting and approached Bako.

"Al-Mahdi! I brought some fine desert horses as you requested," he said in a loud voice for the benefit of anyone nearby. "Are these the men who want to buy your ivory and my animals for the European trade?"

"The very ones," said Bako, without missing a beat. "They're still eager, although we had an encounter with pirates a day out of Alexandria and suffered some minor wounds. It slowed our progress, but not their enthusiasm for our goods."

"Welcome," said the Tuareg, turning toward Cormac and the others with a bow. "Please follow me, I've arranged accommodations where we can negotiate our business arrangements over the next few days."

Finn led the way through the streets, loudly discussing the exchange of ivory and horses for silk and jade to throw off any spies among the crowds. Upon reaching the large hostelry catering to business visitors, he suggested a meeting with Bako, Dumaka, Cormac, and the Reis in the spacious gardens out back after they had settled in.

A short time later, a soft knock summoned Bran to the door of the rooms her brother had secured for them. Expecting Finn, she was stunned to see the Pasha, Jonathan, and Francoise standing outside.

"How did…" she gasped, unable to believe her eyes. Recovering quickly, she blurted, "They're in the next room," and pointed to a doorway.

"May we come in?" asked the Pasha in a formal tone.

"Of course, of course," Bran stammered, swinging the door wide, still not believing what she was seeing.

"Cormac's in the garden planning our escape, he will be up shortly," said Jonathan, giving her a hug before following the Pasha across the room and through the next doorway. A little squeal told Bran that Kelebek had spotted her father. She heard him tell the girl to be gentle with him because he had a small wound. In the meantime, Francoise was still standing in the hallway staring unabashedly at her.

"Are you going to come in as well?" asked Bran, lifting her eyes to his and blushing at what she saw.

"Only if you ask me," said Francoise.

"Then I'll ask you," said Hibah, desperately composing herself. She looked him directly in the eye and gave a slight bow and said, "please come in."

They walked into the other room, where Kelebek was holding both her father's hands and jumping lightly up and down while the Pasha stared, transfixed, at his wife. Jonathan and Pinar stood a few feet apart, speaking softly in Arabic with eyes only for each other.

"Jonathan," asked Bran in English, to distract herself from the feelings she was experiencing with Francoise so close, "when did you learn to speak Arabic?"

"Ibrahim has been giving me lessons all the way from Tunis," he replied in flawless Arabic, never taking his gaze from Pinar, "just as he taught your brother at the quarry."

"Oh, oh," Kelebek started to say as she saw Bran and Pinar obviously taken with the two men, but she was interrupted by her mother before she could pester any more.

"Not a word," said the First Wife in a low firm voice. "Now," she continued more loudly, taking control of the situation, "We have the most amazing story to tell you of how we escaped."

"I might be able to match it," said the Pasha, "but tell us your tale first."

In a secluded part of the garden, Finn and the others sat in the shade sipping strong coffee while the blond described the women's miraculous escape from the prison and the subsequent uproar it caused in the city. Cormac, Ibrahim, and the Reis stared at him in utter amazement, but Dumaka and Bako simply nodded their heads appreciatively.

"Both Ridwan Bey and the Governor have intricate spy networks and my guess is that they're scouring the city to find the women. I brought them here disguised as my Tuareg wives, but I can't be sure any group of four women will escape notice," said Finn. "While I was waiting for you, I saw soldiers checking every riverboat departing downstream and I suspect the camel herders are being watched for the same reason."

"What are the chances of outwaiting them?" asked Cormac.

"Not good," said Bako. "Even up-river we know about these spy networks: they've been around since our ancestors' time. Gold is promised for information, making every citizen a potential informer."

"Yes, I use the same technique in ports around the Mediterranean," said the Reis.

"I do have a plan," Finn said.

They spent the next hour discussing his daring idea about the Maydan stables.

"It will take some additional shopping," said Bako, "but Dumaka and I were here last year after we got home and I know of three establishments that have what we need and can be trusted to remain silent."

After he and his nephew left to go shopping, the other three joined the happy gathering upstairs.

7

THE NEXT MORNING, the usual crowds gathered at the Citadel's South Gate to present the Governor with a variety of proposals and petitions for business affairs. As always, it was a mixed group. There were Europeans, Arabs, Turks, and even a small group of Chinese traders in distinctive black slippers. The sound of different languages blended together to make a low hum as the assemblage waited for the gates to open.

Among them was a contingent of colorfully robed African men and eleven Tuareg warriors dressed in blue, tagelmusts and veils revealing only their eyes. These two groups were engaged in a heated debate centered on the matter of hunting elephants and whether desert horses were agile enough to be used for such a dangerous activity. The black men argued that horses would be frightened by the huge quarry and the Tuaregs argued that their horses could be trained for anything.

Just before the gates swung open, Zehab hurried up to the back of the crowd. It was the last day of the Bey's order and, despite their intense efforts, neither he nor his men had been able to learn anything about the escaped prisoners. After considering all escape options, he knew he would never get out of Cairo alive and fervently hoped the Governor's spies had found the women and were holding them in the harem. He tried to push his way toward the front of the crowd, but was skillfully blocked by others more experienced in this daily ritual. Grinding his teeth in rage, the Envoy was forced to wait his turn.

The crowd surged forward as a gong signaled the soldiers to swing open the great twin doors. Each contingent declared the purpose of its visit to Mehmed's principal assistant, positioned on the left-hand side, who prioritized their appearance before the court in order of which venture promised to bring the greatest tax revenue to Egypt (a large portion of which would go to the Governor's personal account).

"A matter concerning trade with England for cannons," announced a white haired gentleman through an interpreter.

"To bring silk and jade to Cairo from the Orient," declared another interpreter for the Chinese group.

"The latest fashions from Marseille to benefit Cairo's merchants," said an elegantly dressed woman in perfect Arabic. She twirled a small parasol as she spoke.

And so it went.

Not far ahead of Zehab, a large black man with a gold turban announced, "The proposed trade of ivory and horses for European art and antiquities." The assistant couldn't help but give a small nod: there was a great demand for art in Cairo; taxing the outgoing ivory and horses, plus the incoming merchandise would be profitable indeed.

When it was Zehab's turn, he simply said, "The matter of the escaped prisoners." The assistant made a note putting him at the bottom of the list and waved him along.

Inside the gates the walkway to the Governor's palace passed beneath beautiful shade trees and was bordered on either side by exquisitely manicured lawns and gardens. Occasional broad paths to either side led to park-like areas and other facilities.

Halfway to the palace, Zehab noticed the group of ivory hunters and Tuareg warriors take one such path to the right. In itself this wasn't unusual because he had seen other contingents waiting outside the palace in the gardens until their audience with the Governor. But something odd about these men caught his attention and he paused to watch. The warriors and most of the Tuaregs were of average size, except for the two massive leaders and four small Tuaregs in the middle of the group. Alone, the diminutive or large figures would not have been too noteworthy, but in combination the contrast in their sizes was highlighted. They were strolling leisurely along when the smallest Tuareg stumbled on his robe and fell to his knees. The two men to either side quickly reached down and pulled him upright but in that instant Zehab clearly saw two small bare legs exposed before the robe covered them again.

In a sudden flash of insight, it all became clear to the Envoy. The smallest Tuareg was a girl and the other three small ones were women. They must be his prisoners! But what were they doing with these men in the middle of the Citadel? It seemed that the group was going to appear before the Governor...to what end? Was someone double-crossing him? Keeping a discreet distance, Zehab followed; when all of them turned right and headed for the Southwest Gate, he knew they had no intention of meeting with the Governor.

8

The gate above the Maydan was open but, unlike the afternoon when dozens of riders just below provided security, in the morning only two guards were on duty. Having anticipated this, Finn and Bako strode up to them and announced that they were there to bring desert horses up from the city to demonstrate equestrian elephant hunting tactics for the Bey that afternoon.

"We weren't told about any such thing," said the Mamluk in charge, "and you aren't allowed on the Maydan anyway."

"You know how busy the Emir is," said Finn, "and I thought he might forget about this event, so I asked him for written permission."

He handed over a paper written in Arabic with official-looking lettering, and what appeared to be an authentic seal, but in reality was a patch of candle wax pressed onto the paper and decorated with the tip of a knife. As they had hoped, the effort wasn't necessary because neither soldier could read; however, both inspected it with the appearance of intense study. Others had crowded in behind Finn and Bako and the distracted guards were felled with quick blows from sword butts by Cormac and Francoise before they realized anything was amiss. The Mamluks, securely tied and gagged, were deposited under a shrub against the battlement wall many yards away.

"We're going to need a lot of horses for Dumaka and Bako to get up-river and for the rest of us to reach Alexandria," said Finn as they approached the line of stables on the right. "Everyone get inside while I pick them out. If you find slaves, give them the option of freedom and escape into the city or to be left tied up for the soldiers to find."

"I'd choose freedom every time," said Ibrahim, "though it cost my life."

The stables had a central aisle, with stalls to either side, and a wide door at each end. In short order everyone was inside and the doors shut. Finn moved quickly to each stall and with uncanny perception picked out mounts for each person; choosing the strongest stallions in the building for Dumaka and Bako. The horses were being saddled when Torg, watching at the door, hissed a warning.

"Soldiers coming."

Cormac and Dumaka rushed to the entrance and peeked out. Down the hill from the gate came a stream of armed Mamluks led by a robed and turbaned man who could be heard screaming, "They're here, I know they're here."

"Who is that?" asked Cormac.

"It's the Envoy," said the Reis, joining them to look out. "The one who captured us in Tunis."

"We can't let them trap us in here," said Cormac, "we've got to go out. Bako, get your archers and come with us. The rest of you stay inside until we have cleared the way."

"Never," said Bran forcefully, throwing back her robe to reveal the bow and quiver Bako had obtained the day before. "You're not going out there without me."

"Hibah AND me," said Pinar, grabbing her identical bow and stepping forward.

Scowling, but knowing he had no time to argue, Cormac threw off tagelmust and robe, pushed the door wide open and strode out, his sword in hand, with Finn and Dumaka to either side. Bako followed and veered right, Bran to his left and Pinar to his right, bows notched and extra arrows clustered in their bow hands. The black warriors formed a line to Cormac's left, arrows at the ready on their bows.

When they came to a halt facing the soldiers, Bran and Pinar realized that Francoise and Jonathan had taken position at their sides, shining blades bright in the morning sun.

"Eyes and throats are your targets," murmured Bako to the girls.

"I suggest you stop," said Cormac to Zehab in a calm voice when the Envoy had approached within 15 yards. "Another step and my friend will put the first arrow right through your eye."

Bako raised his great bow and drew the notched arrow back. It was aimed directly at Zehab's face. The Envoy felt cold fear wash over him and stopped in his tracks.

"Stop," he screeched to the soldiers.

Normally the soldiers wouldn't have responded to a command from an outsider, but every one of them recognized the steady positioning of the drawn bows and the extra arrows held by each archer. If they attacked, all of them in the front line would die before getting close enough to use swords or lances.

"Those two girls are the least experienced of us and can also put an arrow through your eye from twice this distance," added Cormac to reinforce what the soldiers were thinking and discourage a rash charge.

Mamluk weapons were lowered and the officer beside Zehab said, "Why don't we call for the Bey? This matter is really his affair."

"Excellent idea," said Cormac, pointing his sword at the ground. The others loosed tension on their bowstrings and aimed arrows at the ground, but kept them knocked and ready.

The officer spoke to a Mamluk beside him and the man set off at a run for the gate. By now more than 300 men occupied the little hillside and 50 mounted soldiers had arrived from the stables below the Maydan and were lined up at the edge of the field 20 yards away, lances at the ready. All was quiet as the little group outside the stable faced this formidable array.

9

"MAKE WAY FOR THE EMIR, make way" came a shout from beyond the soldiers, now backed up all the way through the Southwest Gate. The crowd parted to either side as Ridwan Bey rode down the slope on a magnificent black Arabian stallion. He started to come forward past Zehab, but reined in as Bako's now fully-drawn bow was directed straight at his face. The Emir was a brave man, but no fool.

"What have we here?" he blazed.

"Treachery," said the Pasha in a loud voice, emerging from the stable. "Treachery, plain and simple."

"And who might you be?" asked the Bey.

"I am the Pasha of Tunis. In the stable behind me are my wife and youngest daughter. My older daughter no doubt has her bow trained on you or one of your men. Anyone who underestimates her or the other girl, will forfeit his life. They were trained by the giant aiming at you.

He is the greatest archer south of the desert, known far and wide. If his men and the girls loose their deadly arrows among you, your men will die without knowing what struck them.

"The vermin standing to your left came to Tunis under the pretext of bringing gifts from the Sultan, but when I welcomed him with a great feast his Janissaries attacked us and he and took me and my family to Constantinople where I was falsely accused of shorting my tribute to the Empire."

"You say 'falsely,' did you never short your tribute?" interjected the Bey.

"Never," said the Reis, coming through the door to stand beside the Pasha, "Neither he nor his father before him."

"Who are you?" asked the startled Emir.

"I am Suleyman Reis, friend of the Pasha and his family. I operate ships in the Atlantic and Mediterranean. The man standing beside you tried to destroy me and my galley several years ago through treacherous means. He is a scoundrel and not to be trusted.

"I pay enough yearly tribute to the Pasha that neither he nor his father have ever needed to short the Empire."

"Suleyman Reis and MacLir Reis. Even we in Cairo have heard those names," said the Bey. "But you are at a disadvantage now. Why should I do anything on your behalf?"

"Because I suspect the archer will not let you leave here alive, otherwise," said the Pasha.

"Perhaps I could trade your young daughter's life for my own," said the Bey, as a scream erupted from the stable and two soldiers walked out the door holding knives to the throats of the struggling First Wife and Kelebek.

Everyone except Bako swung around to face the Mamluks coming up behind them.

"You see, the stables have a back door," said the Emir.

"Kill either of them and you die," rumbled the giant archer, never taking eyes off the horseman.

"As you wish," said the Bey, "I'll just take them to the harem, since they were promised to me." He gestured at the two men to bring their captives forward. "If a bow is fired, cut their throats."

Suddenly Jonathan dropped his sword and ran in front of the Mamluks who were pushing the screaming Kelebek and her mother forward. He fell on his knees before them, hands stretched forward.

"Please don't take the girl," he cried, "I've known her since she was a baby. Take the mother but not the little one, she's like a sister to me."

"Out of the way," sneered one of the men, lifting a foot to kick the sailor in the chest. It was the last action of his life as the handle of a knife appeared as if by magic in his throat right below the jawbone. His companion just had time to look at him in shock before a second blade caught him under the chin. It happened so fast that most of the watching soldiers didn't realize what had caused the two men to fall. Quick as a cat Jonathan was on his feet and thrust the two women into the hands of the Pasha and the Reis.

Bran, who had turned her head slightly at Jonathan's cries, swung back with her bow raised as a slight sound alerted her. It was too late. Literally frothing at the mouth, eyes glazed with insanity, Zehab had grabbed a lance from the soldier beside him and was racing across the grass, the deadly blade a few feet from Cormac, who was still looking back at Jonathan.

"Watch out," she screamed, loosing an arrow at the Envoy's right arm with which he held the lance. But, alarmed for her brother, she hurried the shot and the arrow flew through the fleshy part of Zehab's forearm, enough to make a formidable wound, but not enough to cause the crazed man to drop the weapon.

At this instant the Bey threw himself off the far side of his stallion as he saw Bako's eyes flick to Cormac and the approaching madman. Fast as he moved, an arrow from the archer's bow still sliced across the top of the Mamluk leader's shoulders, opening a deep wound that pained him for the rest of his life.

10

IF HE HAD THROWN THE LANCE, Zehab would have killed the Irishman, but in his crazed state he was obsessed with feeling it penetrate Cormac's body. The fraction of extra time to cover the distance, plus Bran's warning scream, gave Dumaka time to act. With lightning quickness, he stepped in front of his friend and took the full thrust of the blade into his own body, simultaneously unleashing a mighty backhand swing with his machete that completely severed the Envoy's head from his shoulders.

Cormac, turning at Bran's warning, heard a grunt and was knocked down by a great body. Twisting sideways, he saw to his horror Dumaka on the ground beside him, the blade of a lance buried beneath his rib cage. Leaping to his feet, Cormac gently removed the lance then fell to his knees beside his friend, tears pouring down his face.

"NO!! Not you, my friend, my brother! Why? Why did you do it?" he implored. "Your sons need you. It was me he wanted."

Dumaka coughed and blood ran from his mouth. "You saved my life and gave me time they would have stolen from me," he said. "They tried to kill my will and would have killed my body, but you showed me the way to freedom. You saved my spirit and my life.

"I have spent a year with the sons I thought I would never see again. They are fine men and will do well.

"You have a family and a beautiful woman to marry. Your sons are yet to be born.

Besides, I am going to join the King in a wonderful place."

"What King? What place?" asked Cormac, hardly able to see through his tears.

"Remember, I described messengers who told us to return to you, who visited us in the desert, and who warned me about the attack on the river?"

"Yes."

"That night in the desert, one sat with us around the fire and told us about the King who wanted us to join Him in His Kingdom and be a part of His family. We all accepted the invitation that night. That's why I wasn't surprised about Francoise's healing, or the womens' escape. I knew it was the work of the messengers, on behalf of their King." Dumaka's voice was growing fainter and Cormac bent close to hear. "He said others like them had spoken to you, your brother, and your sister in the past. Seek information about the King; ask for one of His messengers to come to you. I want you to be with me in the Kingdom."

Cormac, stricken with grief, stared into the dark eyes. He knew his friend was close to death and there was nothing he could do.

"Kill them all!" Ridwan Bey, his breath momentarily taken away by the searing pain of the arrow, stood back up, his shoulder pouring blood, and roared in a voice that carried clearly to Cormac and to every Mamluk in the crowd, now well over 500 men.

The redhead was aware of his friends and family closing around him. Glancing up he saw Finn on the other side of Dumaka and felt

Bran's presence above him. He knew he needed to rise and fight, but instead of the expected onslaught of shouts and war cries, utter silence had suddenly fallen over the scene. Dumaka reached up a hand and grabbed him by the arm.

"Ahh, there's a messenger now," he said with surprising strength, pointing straight up with the other hand.

MacLir Reis raised his eyes.

Standing to either side of the little band were two men towering 30 feet tall. Each carried an enormous shining sword in his right hand. Each wore a white tunic, belted at the waist, reaching to his knees. On their chests were gold breastplates and their forearms were encased in gold vambraces. Sandals with straps criss crossing their legs completed their attire.

They were clean shaven, with shoulder-length hair, and the grim expression on their noble faces left no doubt that they were capable of fierce anger. Slowly, the one to Cormac's right pointed his sword directly at the Bey. The one on the left pointed his sword straight at the Governor, standing in the gate, having been summoned to observe the capture. Not a word was said, but each official was seized by such an overwhelming terror that they actually flinched away from the gaze directed at him. In all his years as a soldier, the Emir had never turned his back on a threat, but his knees were so weak he thought he might fall. The Governor felt like he was going to faint.

The redhead rose to his feet and turned toward the stables. Surrounding them and filling every part of the Maydan, stood a vast army of giant warriors clad exactly like the two in front. The silence dragged on. Then the sound of weapons falling to the ground filled the air as the Mamluks, mounted or on foot, stared in abject fear at the assemblage facing them. At last, both the Bey and the Governor turned slowly, as though scared to expose their backs to the great warriors, and made their way unsteadily into the Citadel. They were followed in total silence by the terrified Mamluks. In minutes not a soldier was left.

Cormac looked down at Dumaka. "They'll take me with them, just as the messenger promised," said the black giant as he took his last breath.

Tears streaming down his face, the Irishman raised his eyes. The huge men were gone.

11

THEY BURIED DUMAKA on a rocky bluff above the west side of the Nile, a few miles upstream from Cairo. On top of the massive cairn of boulders marking the spot was a smooth block inscribed by Ibrahim in Arabic:

'Here Lies Dumaka
Father, Warrior, Friend, Brother to MacLir Reis'

To the others, Bako and the ten warriors appeared strangely uplifted during the whole process, but when asked why, the archer would only say that Cormac would explain everything.

Their camp at the river was luxurious, with tents, numerous servants, abundant food and animals: camels for Bako and the warriors to get home; fine Arabian horses for the rest to get back to Alexandria.

After the happenings at the Maydan the giant guardians had seemed to disappear, but everyone in Cairo could see faint images of them out of the corners of their eyes when the visitors were nearby. Not even the bravest Mamluk was prepared to threaten Cormac's group, who had boldly returned to their quarters in the merchant's hostelry.

When the first reports of these images came in, both the Governor and the Bey decided to see for themselves. The morning after the confrontation at the stables, each ventured into the city and experienced the sight, only for them the effect was accompanied by numbing fear. Retreating to the Citadel, they exchanged messages and met that very afternoon. Despite all past differences, the two immediately came into agreement. They would combine resources and treat the visitors as highly honored guests, catering to their slightest needs in the desperate hope that these people and their fearsome guards would leave Cairo as soon as possible. Assistants were sent to convey the best wishes of both men and to fulfill every request the group might have, all of which resulted in the extravagant burial camp, abundance of animals, and countless gifts.

The morning after the burial, camels were loaded and horses saddled as the friends prepared to go their separate ways. Bako had declined the offer of servants to accompany him home, so Cormac and his friends had the benefit of a large support staff for the ride down the river. When the time arrived to leave, the archer's camel was the last one kneeling.

He approached the Pasha and Suleyman Reis and solemnly gripped each one's forearm with his massive hand.

"But for the honor and bravery of that family," he said, with a nod toward the O'Sheas standing nearby, "it's certain that the three of us wouldn't be standing here as free men…and there's a high probability we'd all be dead."

Both men bowed their heads in recognition of the truth.

After staring at them intently Bako said, "It took the actions of three slaves to show us a better way to live. When you return home, I hope you will take that into consideration with your future dealings."

Walking over to Cormac and Finn, the great archer embraced each one. "I don't know you as well as Dumaka did," he said to the redhead. "And neither of us knew your brother, except for Dumaka's brief conversations with him during water breaks on the caravan to Tunis, but your sister is like a daughter to me. On our recent trip across the desert we agreed many times that all of you should learn about the King that we pledged our lives to. His messengers have guided and directed the three of you ever since you were enslaved. Seek them out on this matter."

When he walked up to Pinar and Bran, Bako bent down and gathered both of them to him, hugging them with his huge arms.

"If the Mamluks had attacked, I know each of you would have put down at least eight before we were overrun," he said. "I'm so proud of the fine young women you've become. Continue to set an example for others by treating everybody with the kindness and compassion I can see is so deep in your hearts; however, don't forget regular practice with your bows. It may come in handy when you least expect it."

"Since we began shooting, you've looked after us like we were your own children," sobbed Bran, "thank you Baba*."

"I'll never forget the demonstrations for Father and his men," said Pinar, tears running down her cheeks, "you helped us show them that we weren't just silly girls."

"I don't think those two see you as silly girls," Bako said with a nod towards Jonathan and Francoise standing nearby. "They are good men, treat them as such."

With that, the archer walked to his camel, swung aboard and gave it the command to rise. Not wanting the young women to see the tears now streaming down his own face, he led the way up-river without a backward glance.

Three days later, a sailor drew Gael's attention to a flurry of activity on the docks. Horses, camels, boxes, and people were swarming

---

* 'Father' in Arabic

about. Even at a distance he could see the familiar red hair of MacLir Reis. Raising a telescope he began counting.

"They did it," he finally announced to the gathering group of sailors, "The prisoners are all accounted for!"

A great cheer arose and men sprinted for the dory to be the first to welcome them back.

Epilogue

....

The arrival of the ship *Dumaka* was announced by a thunderous volley from its cannons just before entering the harbor. Telescopes quickly spotted the now familiar blue-circle flag flying atop the mast and word spread like wildfire.

Jugurtha's family, Fiona, and Abigail were at the front of the crowd assembled on the great wharf as hawsers drew the vessel in and the gangplank was run out. First down was Finn, to be embraced by a quite pregnant Tiziri. Cormac followed and Abigail hurled herself into the redhead's arms to the sound of deafening cheers.

Over the days that followed, Seamus was sent for and arrived with the Stable Master--both aboard fleet racing camels. The youth was now fully conversant in Arabic and fast becoming a skilled rider. With them came Ibrahim's sister Aaeedah, mother to Gwasila, for a joyous reunion with her brother. Suleyman Reis immediately designated one of his ships to take all the freed quarry slaves to their homes in Europe, but deferred to their unanimous request to delay departure until after Cormac's marriage. Both harem guards were freed by the Pasha for their role in helping rid the city of Janissaries.

It was a magnificent wedding. The Pasha and the Reis spared no expense in providing for the celebration designed by the First Wife, Fiona, and Kella. The entire city of Tunis had been invited and the population turned out in force to honor MacLir Reis and his bride.

The plaza was filled with canopies covering countless tables and chairs; dozens upon dozens of stewards stood ready to serve a continuous flow of food from the palace kitchens. Shrewsbury, in perhaps his finest hour as representative of the Crown, conducted a brief, but surprisingly eloquent ceremony hastily put together from notes he found in an old Bible.

After a delicious Bread and Butter Pudding prepared by the Reis' Irish cook, the bride, groom, and the rest of the family moved out from the great central pavilion to mingle with friends and citizens, leaving Jugurtha, the Pasha, and Suleyman Reis drinking the excellent Turkish coffee Gael had brought from Constantinople.

"Romance blossoms," said the Pasha. "Did you see Pinar and Hibah actually walking hand-in-hand with those boys? Such a thing would never have been remotely possible for the Pasha's daughter before the lessons Hibah and her Irish family taught us. The sailor's actions in saving Kelebek and the First Wife speak volumes about his character and suitability as a new member of that family."

"We'll probably see more hand-holding now that the Reis has made available his complete house and staff to the newlyweds and we're all moving into the palace with you." laughed Jugurtha. "By the way," he continued after a moment, "I visited the stables while you were gone. You have many excellent horses."

"Best in North Africa," said the Pasha. "The old Stable Master frequently told me that he'd never seen better. I can't understand why he gave up my stables for your oasis. Camels aren't really his thing."

"Hard to say," said Jugurtha, pausing for emphasis. "But I do have a couple of new fast horses out there in the desert. Might give your animals a run for their money."

"Care to put some gold behind that statement?" asked the Pasha, remembering his success the last time the Tuareg had brought horses to Tunis.

"I believe I would, but I doubt the two of you could put up enough to tempt me," said Jugurtha.

"Whatever you ask," said the Pasha as he and the Reis nodded at one another.

The Tuareg blessed the veil that hid his smile.

Request For Reviews

....

I hope you enjoyed this book. Would you do me a favor?

Like all authors, I rely on online reviews to encourage future sales.

Your opinion is invaluable. Would you take a few moments to share your assessment of the book wherever you purchased it, or on your favorite online review site? Your opinion will help the book marketplace become more transparent and useful to all.

Thank you!
David Sage